LOVE REALIZED

By Melanie Codina

Terri,

Real love should
always be realized!

♡

Much love
Codina
xoxo

LOVE REALIZED

Cover design/art done by the awesome Regina Wamba over at Mae I Design and Photography. For more information visit her website at: http://www.maeidesign.com/

Or find her on Facebook at
https://www.facebook.com/MaeIDesignandPhotography?fref=ts

Editing done by the fabulous Madison Seidler.

Published by Melanie Codina, San Diego, California.

ACKNOWLEDGEMENTS

It's hard to know where to start here since there are so many people to thank, so I'm just gonna start throwing it out there.

To Regina Wamba at Mae I Design and Photography, thank you for having the ability to take one sentence, and turning it into my cover. Your talent is unmatched and I am so looking forward to working with you again.

To one of my oldest friends, Sonya, thank you for being the first person to read my work all those months ago, and then texting me in the middle of the night saying, "OMG, I want more!" It was one of the coolest text messages ever!

To my group of friends who really know how to "Keep It Real". Angie, Kristy, Jen, Denise, Brenda, Jennifer, Marivett, and Miriam, thank you so much for listening to me and talking me down off the ledge. You have made doing this less stressful and I value your advice more than you could possibly know. A2 here we come!

To Madison Seidler, editor extraordinaire, thank you so much for not only editing my work, but for loving it too. I found that I looked forward to your comments in the margins more than I care to admit. Your ability to clean up my overabundance of words is truly valued.

To my two boys, thank you for letting Mommy ignore you while obsessing over her laptop. Thank you for enjoying cereal for dinner and being able to find your socks in a basket of unfolded clothes. Your ability to melt me with a hug is cherished and I love you more than words can say.

To my two girls, I am so happy to call you mine. You are beautiful and perfect and I love you so much. Thank you for pretending that I wasn't crazy when I started to talk about fictional characters as if they were real. Thank you for inspiring my sarcasm and humor and always making me laugh. There is a little bit of each of you in this book, both good and bad, and I look forward to all the things you will do in the future to inspire me more.

To two authors who I follow shamelessly, the awesome Liz Crowe, and the amazing Laura Kaye, your books have guided me and provided me with a goal for achievement. I appreciate the times you took to chat with your fans and show me what kind of author I would like to be. I am forever your fan and look forward to the day I get to shake your hands.

To the Facebook pages and blogs that supported an unknown author, I appreciate you taking a chance on me. Twinsie Talk Book Reviews, First Class Books, One More Chapter, Romantic Reading Escapes, Shh Mom's Reading, Island Lovelies Book Club, Angie's Dreamy Reads, Literati Literature Lovers, Great Books and Author Elizabeth James; your support and promotion have been appreciated and I hope you and your followers enjoy my work.

And last but not least, to my husband Daniel. You are my biggest supporter and I love that you no longer question the weird things I get excited over, you just strive to make them happen for me. You had me at hello and are the only exception. Thank you for being proud of me, tolerating the lack of attention, and the sink of dishes that I promise to get to soon. Thank you for listening to my storyline and plots, and giving me direction, I value your opinion and hope you continue to do this with me again in the future. It wouldn't be the same without you.

Table of Contents

LOVE REALIZED   1

ACKNOWLEDGEMENTS   3

Table of Contents   6

CHAPTER ONE   8

CHAPTER TWO   24

CHAPTER THREE   35

CHAPTER FOUR   51

CHAPTER FIVE   66

CHAPTER SIX   76

CHAPTER SEVEN   96

CHAPTER EIGHT   117

CHAPTER NINE   131

CHAPTER TEN   140

CHAPTER ELEVEN   146

CHAPTER TWELVE   157

CHAPTER THIRTEEN   167

CHAPTER FOURTEEN   183

CHAPTER FIFTEEN   200

CHAPTER SIXTEEN   211

CHAPTER SEVENTEEN   227

CHAPTER EIGHTEEN   244

CHAPTER NINETEEN   257

CHAPTER TWENTY   271

CHAPTER TWENTY-ONE   284

CHAPTER TWENTY-TWO   296

CHAPTER TWENTY-THREE   310

CHAPTER TWENTY-FOUR   326

CHAPTER TWENTY-FIVE   341

CHAPTER TWENTY-SIX   356

CHAPTER TWENTY-SEVEN   368

CHAPTER TWENTY-EIGHT   383

EPILOGUE   390

About the Author   396

CHAPTER ONE

Gillian heard the words "cannon ball" screamed about two seconds before the giant splash of water hit her back, startling her and refreshing her all at the same time. "You're *so* lucky my hands are full," she yelled over her shoulder toward the pool, "or I'd be coming in after you."

Standing in the midst of chaos, a smile spread across her face. What person wouldn't enjoy spending time outside today? The clear blue Southern California sky stretched above, with the only disturbance to the horizon being the periodic wisp of a cloud. The sunny eighty degrees made it hot enough to take a dip in the pool, but not so hot that you couldn't stand in the sun without melting. This was the weather San Diego was known for. It was the perfect type of day to spend in the yard, she thought, around the pool, surrounded by most of her favorite people, celebrating the birth of her youngest son, Dylan.

Of course the turnout was just as she expected, almost everyone was present and accounted for. But then, that was never a doubt because their friends were just like that; they would always come. Those who couldn't make it for the whole gathering would come as soon as they were available, because with this crowd of people, the parties were never over quickly. And let's not forget that everyone loved her kids—let's face it—they were great kids. *Duh!*

Okay, okay, so maybe she was a little biased on that subject matter, she laughed inwardly. But standing there in the midst of friends and family, she couldn't help but feel a slight lump form in her throat when taking in her surroundings. The lump got bigger when she caught sight of her youngest playing with the other kids in the pool. As sappy or cheesy as it sounded, her children were her biggest accomplishments in life. They always found new ways to shock her, infuriate her, overwhelm her, and make her smile. All in equal parts too. Jonathan, Madison, and Dylan ... they were her world.

Some people may not feel that way about their own lives, especially if they had started parenting at an early age like her. But Gillian had no regrets. Sure, things could've been easier for them, but she had seen plenty of people who followed the stereotypical timetable for having a family, and of course they didn't all have success stories. All of that aside, when Gillian did start her family, at the ripe old age of seventeen, her life was no longer hers. It belonged to the little baby she had brought into the world, and she had absolutely no problem with that.

When the shocking announcement was made to family and friends that Gillian was "in that way," it was as if there was some type of time warp to the 1950s when everyone would look at her with some kind of pitiful look and shake their heads as if she was the only teenager who had ever had sex with her teenage boyfriend. Some even felt it necessary to point accusatory fingers at her boyfriend, Logan, since he was older than her. Not older by much, but he got the bad rap because he was a year ahead of Gillian and had already graduated when she had Jonathan.

It was comical to think about how that really used to get a rise out of Logan, like he was the evil villain who stole her virtue. Well he didn't steal it per se; he did take it, but that was because she presented it on a silver platter to him, complete with an invitation to return anytime he wanted. Yep, mutually beneficial was a good description of what happened. You know that saying—her parents liked to use it—"it takes two to tango"... well, of course it does; it wouldn't be fun, otherwise. Regardless, the results of all that "tangoing" had a prolonged effect on their lives, but Gillian wouldn't change that for the world. She and Logan became a statistic the minute that pregnancy test showed its double blue bars to them. And the result of those little blue bars was a bouncing baby boy, Jonathan.

Some people attempted to call her Jonathan a mistake, or an accident, simply because she had gone and gotten "knocked up" in high school and had him before she graduated. Gillian's defense to this point of view was, well at least she could hug her *mistake,* and he hugged her back. And what nice hugs they were! Jonathan loved his mom and never hesitated to show her that with hugs— not those stupid one-armed hugs kids give when they're too cool to show affection—real, full two-armed hugs, daily, and kisses to the cheeks whenever he came or went. Those one-armed hugs seemed to come exclusively from Madison. That is, if she was even blessed with the opportunity of getting that close to her daughter.

Yes, Jonathan was a momma's boy, and Gillian loved every minute of it. He was the outgoing, Varsity soccer-playing, polite, good-grade-getting, seventeen year-old boy, who was about to be a senior in high school. His rapid growth spurt over this summer had brought him only one inch shy of his father's six-foot two-inch height. With his thick, wavy brown hair, bluish-grey eyes and a smile that was electric, she knew he was going to be a heartbreaker. Probably already was, if he was anything like his father. Jonathan had the looks, the personality, the brains, and the athletic talent; he was the total package. And as his mother, she couldn't be more proud. However, being the oldest of three, he certainly provided a misconception for Gillian that all children listened to their mother and were never difficult.

Yes, her oldest son was an anomaly. Needless to say, other mothers were jealous. His good behavior, coupled with Gillian's age difference from other mothers, never made her very popular on the sideline of the soccer field, or the playground for that matter. Especially since it seemed that everyone expected her son to be an out of control child with the social skills of a common street thug, or have shitty grades simply because his mother was a teenager when she had him. God, how she hated stereotypes and statistics, even more so when they affected other's opinions of her kids. But the upside to being grouped in a crappy statistic was proving said stereotype wrong … and oh how she loved doing that!

Those stupid stereotypes were the very reason she made Logan wait to marry her. Of course, he proposed when she was pregnant with Jonathan, but she turned him down and told him that having a child was no reason to get married. Waiting to get married 'til Jonathan turned one was the smartest thing they could've done. Logan understood her reason for wanting to wait, but she was certain that it must've been a blow to his ego for her to say no that first time. Gillian wanted to marry for love, regardless of the fact that she and Logan couldn't seem to keep their hands, and other body parts, to themselves.

Once she accepted his marriage proposal, and they got married, the second addition to their new family came just shy of ten months later when Madison was born. Madison quickly changed all of Gillian's expectations she may have developed from Jonathan.

Madison was the highly emotional, soon-to-be sophomore, fifteen year old girl that was always demanding attention. She was the typical "Daddy's Little Girl," who recently decided that they were no longer allowed to call her Maddie. Somehow, the nickname they had called her for years suddenly sounded "immature." Gillian snorted to herself, thinking that the only immature thing about using the nickname was how Madison acted. She would ignore you if you called her Maddie and would just wait until she heard her full name, except if Logan called her that, of course. Daddy's Little Girl and all; it was adorable and annoying as hell!

So, to put it simply, it was only immature when her mom called her that. Well, she had always heard that mothers of teenage daughters were expected to battle with them over the littlest things. True to form, they battled just yesterday over the way Gillian yelled too much at Madison's soccer games. She played soccer for a competitive club team, and there was certainly no way that Gillian could contain her enthusiasm when the team was doing so well. Besides, she knew for a fact that she wasn't one of those crazy-screaming-for-no-reason-soccer moms that she couldn't tolerate. She knew this because she had verified this with anyone that she could ask. Talk about being paranoid that your daughter might get upset.

Many other parents, as well as other players, had reassured her that she was not the crazy soccer mom. This was only the case if you asked her daughter. *God, she hoped she wasn't like that with her mom.* There really wasn't anything wrong with her cheering from the sidelines, other than it was just Maddie being a moody teenage girl. Besides, she didn't think she was doing anything different than when she cheered on the boys' team, and Jonathan had no problem with that. Just another thing to add to the list she liked to call The-Teenage-Daughter-Hates-Everything-Her-Mother-Does-List.

Unfortunately, Madison recently made the decision to give up her high school soccer career and tried out for cheer instead. Of course, she made the team; she had been doing dance competitions since she was five years old. And while it bummed Gillian out that Madison wasn't going to be playing soccer at the high school, she quietly did a fist pump, since she was a cheerleader in high school, too. But of course, she kept that bit of information to herself and avoided pointing this out to Maddie. Because it's a known fact that the moody teenage girl would definitely change her mind, simply because of that. It was exhausting to step over all the proverbial land mines that her second child placed in front of her. The other battle with her daughter being a cheerleader was Logan acting like the stereotypical father and not wanting his daughter parading around in those short skirts and jumping up and down.

Recalling her conversation with him about Madison making the team made her giggle a bit. Gillian's reply to his blatant "Hell no" didn't help her cause at all. Considering her defense was, "Well I was cheerleader," in which his reply was, "Exactly my point Gillian; I know exactly what I was thinking when I saw you in your cheer uniform each and every time. You think I want all those pimple-faced high school boys thinking that about my daughter … hell no!" And really, her only way to diffuse the situation was to distract him. Okay, so seduce him was the more appropriate term for it.

She lowered her voice to a seductive whisper and leaned her body against his. She looked up at him through hooded eyelids while her hands rested on his chest and said, "And what exactly was it that you were thinking about when you saw me in my cheer skirt? Did you like what you saw?" Logan's low growl, as his lips crashed down on hers, was a firm answer that he liked the thought of her in her cheer skirt. Then she softly whispered in his ear and asked him if he would like to see her in her cheer skirt again sometime; he lifted her up and carried her to the bed. All thoughts of his daughter were surely gone as he proceeded to show Gillian exactly how much he liked the thought of her in her cheer skirt again.

Once that was taken care of, she was able to focus on other cool aspects of her daughter being on Varsity cheer—first and foremost, when attending the Varsity football games, her daughter would be none-the-wiser that her mom was yelling her support for the school from the stands with all the other parents. The crowds allowed that, and it was another private little victory for Gillian. Small pat on the back for that, considering those are quite rare wherever Madison was concerned.

Rounding out the family, last but not least, the role of little big man belonged to Dylan, who turned eight years old today. She felt her smile get bigger as she watched Dylan playing in the pool with his too long, dark brown hair, which he wanted to grow out. He really needed a haircut, but she felt she could indulge him a little while longer. Dylan was a lot like his older brother, Jonathan, and certainly idolized everything his brother did. She could only be thankful that he was a great role model; otherwise they would surely have problems.

Dylan also played soccer and had to make sure he wore the same jersey number as Jonathan did or else he wouldn't play. What else could she say about Dylan other than he loved his Legos, was usually found attached at the hip to his best friend, Ryan, and possessed actual magical powers. That's right, her son could literally melt his mother's heart with a smile. He was definitely the perfect conclusion to the family they started so many years ago.

Speaking of good role models ... She caught sight of her oldest as he emerged from the house. "Hey Mom!" Jonathan called toward her as he made his way into the backyard, followed by two of his friends, all wearing their soccer uniforms, having just come from a game. She felt a little guilty for not being able to go to his game, but she knew he understood. She smiled back at him as they made their way over to where she was standing. Jonathan leaned over and kissed her on the cheek, thankfully avoiding hugging her since he definitely smelled like he just came from a game. His friends, Nick and Robby, also leaned in and kissed her, simultaneously, on both cheeks while carefully avoiding the tray she was carrying. They had all been friends since elementary school and had spent plenty of time in her house.

She accepted the kisses and smiled at them. "Hi boys, how was the game? I'm sorry I couldn't make it."

"Don't worry about it, Mom; I know it's a rare occurrence for you to miss a game—you're allowed a free pass every now and then. But you did miss my goal." Jonathan feigned like he was hurt, but she could see the smile he struggled to hide. "Oh and we won 2-1;

it was a tough game." She congratulated him on the win and ignored his horrible attempt at giving her a hard time and looked to his friends.

"Why don't you all go in and change out of your gear so you can come and eat. We're about to put the meat on the grill. But do me a favor, don't leave all that sweaty gear lying around, we have guests. Last time I couldn't figure out where the smell was coming from 'til I found a set of shin guards under the couch."

"Thanks Mrs. B!" they said in unison as they followed Jonathan into the house to change.

Yes, lucky just wasn't a strong enough word to describe how fortunate she was to have what she had. Well, maybe she felt that way because she was always the type of person who saw the glass as half full.

Logan, however, her husband of sixteen years, never sees things the same as her. To him, the glass was always half empty. She liked to think that that was what made them so compatible. She was the positive to his negative. Her optimism was the direct contrast to his "worst case scenario" attitude, and in lots of situations, she could apply just a little direction to his overwhelming thoughts and bring him back to level ground. Heck, in some cases, his attitude, coupled with his ability to speak his mind freely, had her diffusing situations in his wake. For instance, when they were out to dinner and the poor waitress got a full dose of Logan-the-ass because he had a bad day. Of course, this always prompted Gillian to give an apologetic look and place a few extra bucks on the table. While she understood and accepted his surly attitude at times because she loved him, she also knew that the girl behind the counter at a coffee shop didn't have to, and why should she?

No, Logan Baxter had never been accused of being anything less than intense, and with great intensity such as his, he often left her in awe. Unfortunately, Gillian was not the only one Logan had in awe over him. He was definitely attractive with his light brown hair, eyes that reminded her of blue jeans and nicely tanned skin from all the Southern California activities they took part in. Sadly, and as could be expected, combine his good looks with his inability to realize he had all he needed, there were definitely skeletons in the closet of their marriage. Fortunately, though, they had moved past it, locked up those skeletons, and things were good between them. Oh sure, from time to time those skeletons tried to fight their way out of said closet, but Gillian had made sure it stayed locked up good and tight.

Gillian caught sight of Logan standing by the new backyard bar situated by the pool, which he proudly built with Jonathan, just for this party. "What better event could there be to finish a bar for than an eight year old's birthday party," was Logan's argument when she questioned why he was doing that instead of what she directly needed accomplished. Statements like that only had her rolling her eyes and walking away, but she was still smiling, though.

She recalled the look on his face when Logan fed her that line of crap, which was promptly followed by Jonathan rolling his eyes and shaking his head. He stood behind his father, where only Gillian could see him, and directly acknowledged to his mother that he knew his father was a total smartass and completely full of shit. The replay of the memory just made the smile spread across her face again.

As if he heard her thoughts, Logan looked up at her, and one side of his mouth quirked up into a devilish half smile, while he arched an eyebrow giving her that "how you doing" flirtatious look she loved. And yes, it made her blush and giggle slightly. *That's right, she's a giggler.* It always amazed her how he could do that to her. She loved it and got equally irritated by it because she knew there were times he got away with far more than he should have.

There she was standing amongst her party guests, blushing and smiling like a fool when she had things to be doing. Attempting to focus on her role of hostess, she turned toward the house when a voice rumbled in her ear.

"What's that smile for, sexy?" Her smile got even bigger. Now the day was perfect; Jake was here. Always falling into the playful banter with one of her oldest and dearest friends was second nature for Gillian. Jake Michaels was always a flirt with her; it stretched all the way back to high school, and it was just part of their relationship. Of course, it was also easy to do since he was as sweet and sexy as they come.

Tall, dark, and handsome was certainly a phrase that could easily be used to describe Jake, with his chocolate brown hair and light brown eyes that resembled topaz. And let's not forget the broad shoulders and chest that sported the perfect proportions for his six-foot two-inch frame. Seriously, she had no idea how she ended up with all these good-looking men in her life? Hell, when they all were indulging in pool time, it looked like freaking spring break, with *real* adult males instead of those still trying to grow chest hair.

Jake leaned in to kiss her on the cheek, which she offered up gladly because he was easily one of her favorite people. "Just relishing in the joy of all these handsome men in my life," she said with a wink.

"Well then it's a good thing I got here, so you really have something to smile about." Both of them laughed as Jake winked back. Gillian loved that she still had Jake in her life, even after all these years; they always had a good time together.

"Hey, I found some party guests at the front door, and I brought them in for you since they said they rang the doorbell. Hope that's okay; he says he works with you."

"Oh, thanks, I didn't even think about people who aren't used to just walking into my house like the rest of you guys do," she said as she nudged him with her hip.

"Well if I announced myself, then you may not let me come over, and then how will I get to have dinner with one of the hottest moms I know."

Gillian couldn't contain her giggle. "Damn Jake, you sure know how to make a girl's day. Now go check in with the birthday boy, he was looking for his "favorite uncle" earlier. Of course, that always gets under my brother's skin when he hears Dylan say that."

Jake laughed out loud at that. "Which is exactly why I have trained Dylan to call me that, just to get under Sean's skin … it's so much fun. How about Ryan, has he been good?"

"He is always good for his favorite aunt. Both boys have been in the pool for hours … the two of them should be sprouting gills any minute now."

Ryan was Jake's son, from a brief marriage to a woman who couldn't be bothered with settling down with just one man. They divorced when Ryan was only one, after Jake walked in on her with another man. She then followed this man to Florida and didn't have any problems with granting Jake full custody of Ryan. Jake loved his son and didn't want him to be subjected to a woman who couldn't seem to focus on anyone but herself.

"Hey, we have matching titles: you, the favorite aunt, and me, the favorite uncle. It's a wonder the rest of these yahoos ever get paid any attention at all." Jake smacked her on the ass and walked away to search for Dylan and Ryan while yelling toward the pool, "Has anyone seen the birthday boy? His favorite uncle is here!" Gillian just laughed as she turned around to look where her brother, Sean, was sitting with his wife, knowing that Jake only did that to rile him up. Boys will be boys, regardless of their age.

Turning toward the house, she spotted Adam, her co-worker, standing by the gated entryway to the pool area with who she assumed was his wife, bent forward talking to their daughter. Gillian quickly tried to recall what her name was, but failed, and hoped he would introduce her. When Adam spotted her, he smiled and waved. He looked a little too excited to be there, but she knew that since they had moved to the area recently, they were probably short on friends. Gillian smiled back at him and started to head in his direction, wanting to say hello and welcome them before bringing the burgers and dogs she was carrying over to the grill.

As she got closer, the woman standing next to Adam stood up and turned around to resume her position next to him. All of the oxygen suddenly vacated Gillian's lungs, and apparently the need to bring in more seemed to escape her mind. Forgetting to breathe, forgetting everyone around her, she stood there staring into the eyes of this woman. A woman whose eyes and face had already been etched into her mind. A woman branded into Gillian's memory. A woman who has, until now, only existed in Gillian's mind or in secret pictures she had come across in the past. A woman who was not supposed to be here, in her yard, at her son's birthday party … or even in this damn state for that matter! A woman who sure as hell should not be within an arm's reach of Gillian. A woman who possessed the power to bring Gillian to her knees from heartache.

This was not just any woman; this was *the* woman! The Other Woman! She could just hear the hinges of her marital closet creaking open with a deafening metal on metal sound. *Exit skeletons!* Jody Spencer was the other woman who Logan loved. *Loves*? Now would be a very good time for the ground to open up and swallow her whole. Because, as unbelievable as it should be, Logan's mistress was standing there in front of her, staring back at her.

Gillian just stood there and stared at the woman. She saw the realization cross the woman's face when she figured out who she was looking at and where she was. She hadn't figured it out as quickly as Gillian did, but then again, it was doubtful that she gave much thought to Gillian, other than maybe to laugh at her while wrapped in Logan's arms. Dammit! *This cannot be happening*, she silently begged, the desire to have someone knock her out and put her out of her misery was climbing by the second.

Gillian's concentration was broken when she heard a loud clattering sound causing her to jump. With a sudden intake of air, she realized that the sound was her dropping the large metal tray carrying all the meat for the grill, which now resided in a pile surrounding her feet. Damn! She didn't have to look around to know that everyone was looking in her direction. *Good job, Gillian! Way to draw attention to the mistress.* Adam bent over to help pick up the mess, as did someone else, but Gillian couldn't take the time to look because she couldn't break her eye contact with Jody. Wouldn't that show weakness? She was sure there was some animal kingdom show that said the predator never takes his or her eyes off the prey … yeah, don't break eye contact; show her who has the power here … or some shit like that.

Jody looked wide-eyed and even a little scared. She should; she essentially just walked into the lion's den. At that realization, a tiny bit of sympathy passed through Gillian, but was quickly squashed down. Jody then flickered her gaze to Adam and then back to Gillian, before slightly glancing around the crowd of people. *Good, she broke eye contact first. I win.* Maybe she watched one too many shows on Animal Planet. Maybe she was looking for help or even an escape route. Maybe she was looking for Logan to confirm that she was, in fact, standing face-to-face with Gillian Baxter.

She couldn't believe this was happening here. This was sacred ground to Gillian; the mistress had no business being on her turf. She was a threat, and Gillian needed to protect her family from this evil woman. She needed to protect herself from the embarrassment that was going to follow when everyone found out who this was standing in front of her.

The rambling going on in Gillian's head was interrupted when Adam stood up with the tray, and Logan suddenly appeared in front of her. Looking at Gillian, he asked, "Babe, what happened?" She wanted to look at Logan, but she couldn't take her eyes off of *her*—the threat—the one person who could provide her with the ultimate of embarrassing situations. This woman almost destroyed her world, and possibly still possessed the power to successfully destroy her world for good this time.

When Gillian didn't turn to look at Logan, he must have turned to see what, or rather who, she was looking at. She realized that this interaction between them was obscured from where Logan was sitting. The arm that Logan had placed on Gillian's back stiffened, and that was when she knew he had realized that the shit was about to hit the fan.

CHAPTER TWO

Damage control needed to be done, and fast, before everyone in her life figured out what was going on! *Think Gillian think! Come up with something!* She didn't go through all the horror of his affair alone, never confiding in anyone; just to have it all erupt here and now. *Hell no!*

When an idea sprung into her head, she hoped that she was going to be able to actually speak, since her throat felt like she had swallowed sand, and her tongue felt like it was ten times bigger than it was. She turned to Logan, made eye contact with him, and saw the pleading look he was giving her. She knew that he was begging her not to say anything and cause a scene.

She also knew that look he gave her was him begging her to hear him out. Yes, she had seen that look before. *Yeah right!* Like anything Gillian did at this moment was to make things easier for him, no way! In fact, the desire to swiftly knee him in his manhood was pretty hard to control right now. This was not about him. This cover up was about protecting her and their kids from his screw up, and the complete and total shame she felt because of it.

"A bee," she managed to get out of her drier than dry mouth. Clearing her throat she continued, "I think I was stung by a bee … on my hand. It caused me to drop the tray." She then looked back to Adam and his family, and for the first time, noticed the little girl standing next to Jody. She looked like she was shy and probably frightened by the bit of commotion caused by the clattering tray.

Gillian bent down and smiled at the little girl. "I'm sorry, sweetie, if I frightened you. I didn't mean to, but we will just blame it all on the bee." After a pause, the little girl was still looking a little uncomfortable, so she continued, "My name is Gillian, what's your name?"

Paying attention to the child helped distract her from what was actually happening. The shy little girl with dirty blonde hair and big brown eyes gazed at Gillian and then smiled, suddenly relaxing and said, "Rachel." Gillian smiled back; she was a cute kid, probably close to five or six, and it certainly was not her fault that her mother was a slimy whore. That could not be held against her. Thankfully, the kid was a spitting image of Adam so there was no concern whose kid it was. *Dodged that bullet Logan! Gotta look for the silver lining here, people.* "Well Rachel, I sure hope you brought your bathing suit because all the kids are in the pool. Can you swim?" The little one nodded to Gillian and then begged her mom to allow her to get in the pool.

And that is when Gillian heard, in person for the first time, the voice of "the other woman." Gillian had heard it once before, over a year ago when listening to the voicemail she had left for Logan. It sounded different in person. It was painful to hear and sliced right through Gillian. *Like nails down a chalkboard.* That was the voice that Logan listened to, the voice that left him messages, the voice that whispered in his ears when Gillian had no idea it was even happening. This was the voice that Gillian always feared he would want to hear instead of her own.

Suddenly, shame and humiliation enveloped Gillian, filling her with the need to run, curl up in a ball, and pray for this to not be happening. *NO! No, dammit! How dare she have that kind of power?* She could not let this happen again. Feeling the sudden burst of energy course through her body, she squared her shoulders and turned to Logan, glared at him and said, "Logan, baby," in a sickly sweet voice that he would know was her I'm-pissed-and-putting-on-an-act-voice, "this is Adam. He recently started in the radiology department at the medical center, and this is his family. I'm sorry, what was your name again?" she said as she looked to Jody. And since she had to put on a show, she put out her hand in an offer to shake. Jody responded with a timid handshake and said, "Jody. Thank you for inviting us; you have a lovely home."

Gillian had a quick image flash through her mind of using Jody's hand, which she currently held, to hold her in place while simultaneously pounding on her with the other. Of course, she also managed to visualize her girlfriends jumping in the mix, too. She knew they would have her back, if only they knew what the hell was going on. The image in her mind of beating the crap out of this woman made her feel a little bit better and brought a smile to her face. An evil smile, but it was a smile nonetheless, which was appropriate, considering she was supposed to be smiling. Remembering she needed to respond to Jody, "Why thank you Jody. This is my husband, Logan; he and his partner remodeled it and can take credit for it." Gillian watched as Logan appropriately extended his hand out to shake Adam's, and then Jody's, hand. She was once again filled with anger at the site of the brief contact of Logan's skin against Jody's, causing her to stiffen. Logan picked up on it, and immediately pulled Gillian into his side, with his arm securely holding her in place against him.

The front she was trying to put on was beginning to collapse, though. The contact with Logan made it weaker as she thought about the enormity of this situation. She could hear the muffled rumbling of Logan's voice as if it were coming from somewhere in the distance. "Welcome to our home, please come on in, relax. It already appears that your daughter is comfortable with her surroundings since she's already in the pool. Beer is at the bar, soda and juice is in the cooler. Please, help yourself." As soon as he rushed to expel all of that, he turned his attention toward her and said, "Where did the bee sting you? Was it on the hand? Let's go check it out, and put some ice on it." Then turning back to Adam and Jody, he said, "Please excuse us." Logan then quickly took the tray from Adam with his free arm and handed it to someone. He ushered Gillian into the house and away from everyone else—away from Jody. Smart man; it would certainly benefit him to get her away from Jody.

White noise and numbness started to overwhelm her. She could hear buzzing sounds that must belong to the people around her. *Why does it sound like I'm in a tunnel? Or maybe even underwater?* Yes, white noise is the best way to describe it. Gillian numbly walked inside the house, escorted by Logan. He held her hand positioned in front of her like there was something wrong with it. *Oh wait, there was supposed to be something wrong with it. A bee sting.* Clever thinking on her part. She would definitely pat herself on the back for coming up with that one, but she couldn't right now because she was faking a Goddamn bee sting! Ugh! Gillian's thoughts were drowning her, so she just allowed Logan to lead her through the house.

Holy shit! Did that really just happen? Was Jody really here? How long has she been here, in town? Oh God! Did Logan know she was here in town? God dammit! Think Gillian! Try and remember... what did Adam say? That he had been here for six months before transferring to the medical center where they worked ... and that was over four months ago! Ohmygod! She has been here, in this city, the same area code, for at least the last ten months. Ten! Fucking! Months!

Her silent freak-out didn't faze Logan, who continued to escort her through the house, most likely taking her to the bedroom where he could talk to her. *This should be good.* You could almost hear the wheels turning in his head, trying to think of what he was going to say. A small giggle escaped her mouth. *Yep, definitely losing it! Wonder what he is going to say to handle this. What could he do but deny it? Did he know she was in town? I have to ask him ... Oh god ... what do I do if he did know ... and has been with her the whole time?*

Logan's hands were anchored on Gillian in a very possessive way; maybe he thought she was going to bolt. That didn't sound so bad to Gillian, actually. *But wait, this was Gillian Baxter's life and this place, these people, were Gillian's! No way was that ... that person ... that bitch out there gonna get them, too!*

Another giggle threatened to escape her as she realized she was referring to herself in the third person. *Keep it together Baxter!* She chastised herself for even the possibility of falling apart. They finally made it to their bedroom where Logan urged her to sit on the bed. Feeling almost zombie-like, she complied. He then knelt down in front her and clasped her hands in his. She was looking directly at him and could see his lips moving, but couldn't hear a

28

thing. *Could someone turn up the volume please? Snap out of it, this is something you wanna hear. It's time to climb out of the well of humiliation you were flung down and see what's going on.*

Still staring at his lips moving, no sound was registering in her numb mind. Concentrating, she felt the numbness begin to subside. At that, the enormity of what just happened washed over her. Tears began to form and roll down her face unbeknownst to her. *Never show weakness dammit!* But her traitorous tears continued to fall. Then a sob escaped, and she gave in to it. The skeletons that had escaped the closet were now dancing in circles around the bedroom. Seriously, she knew they were there, why did they have to be so rude? She needed to pull it together and focus. The mistress was not brand new information to her, just her location was. Her world may have been tilted on its side, but this was also her son's birthday party, a celebration is going on outside, and she refused to allow this to ruin it.

Focusing, she looked Logan in the eye and the sound of his voice began to slowly register through the fog. *Getting clearer. Come on, just a little more.* "Gilly, baby, talk to me ..." *There!* She was back. Logan continued, "Gilly, baby, you're scaring me. Please talk to me. Are you okay?"

"Did you know?" was all Gillian could get out. Logan's eyes went wide, but he remained silent. She repeated herself, this time through gritted teeth as her body began to respond to the adrenaline that it was producing. "Did. You. Know?" she implored again, emphasizing every word. The deer in the headlights look remained, and she knew the answer ... he did know she was in town. The mistress now lived in close proximity to her husband, and he was fully aware of it. Rage and fury started to churn in her stomach, causing bile to rise. Fortunately, she hadn't eaten yet, so there was nothing to bring up. But rage and fury were good; she could handle them, it was far better than humiliation and shame she felt three minutes ago, that's for sure.

"Are you still seeing her?" she snarled at him. But her question was once again met by silence. *Okay, take a deep breath—in through the nose, out the mouth. Just breathe.* The skeletons must have picked up on her fury because they decided to stop dancing and just stood in the corner quietly.

"Are you going to respond to any of my questions? Don't you have the balls to answer my questions Logan? Or should I go ask her?" Once again, it came out through gritted teeth. Her jaw was beginning to hurt, but that got his attention.

"Yes, I did know she was living here now, baby. I'm sorry I didn't tell you."

"That's one way to avoid the other question. Your evasion of it, though, can only lead me to assume that you are, still in fact, *involved* with her!"

"Gillian, please, let's not get all worked up over this. We have guests here, and this is something we can talk about later."

He really had some nerve! Where did he get off counseling her on how to act? She was about to pounce on him, to take out her rage on his clueless expression, when Jason rushed into the room.

Jason Michaels was Jake's slightly older brother, but more importantly, Logan's business partner and best friend. A tall, broad-shouldered, brooding, Alpha male, he could command the attention of everyone when walking into a room, simply with his size. Brooding aside, he was certainly a good-looking male specimen. In fact, the brooding might even enhance his attractiveness. He looked intimidating, and could probably glare a weaker man into submission, but to those of us who knew him, he was a total marshmallow on the inside. Especially when it came to anybody important in his life needing his support or attention, it was clearly a family trait.

"Logan what the hell is going on?" Jason growled at Logan as he proceeded to sit next to Gillian and put his arm around her. He was glaring at Logan expectantly, while awaiting an answer, but he remained silent. Well, at least Logan was being consistent with his lack of answers. The shocked look on his face was priceless as he stared back at Jason. Jason then turned and looked at Gillian, his face softened and asked, "Are you okay, Gilly? What do you need me to do for you? Should I ask her to leave the party?"

That was when she realized that Jason knew who Jody was. Of course he did! Why wouldn't he, he was Logan's best friend? But for some reason, just knowing that Jason knew what was happening, and that he was supporting her in the matter, brought more tears to her eyes. She turned and quickly threw her arms around his neck, taking in the comfort of a friend's support. Jason, of course, hugged her back affirming that she could lean on him if she needed. She could hear the muffled sound of Logan grumbling at Jason over the big shoulder and chest muscles that seemed to be drowning him out. "Jason what the hell are doing? I'm trying to talk to my wife here. Get the fuck out!"

"I don't think so, man! What the hell is that woman doing here?"

"I didn't invite her here! Gillian works with her husband, apparently, and *she* invited *him*!"

"That's not what I mean, and you know it! What the hell is she doing in California?" Jason growled at Logan while still holding firmly onto Gillian. She just smiled inwardly as she let Jason do all of the questioning. Unfortunately, Jason's questions were once again met by silence.

Gillian pulled her head back and looked up at Jason, who relaxed his hold, but still held onto her. "Thanks Jason, I appreciate you asking. Obviously you know exactly who Jody is, but does anyone else know?"

Jason smiled down at her. "No Gilly-girl, I don't think anyone else knows who she is. Your secret is safe with me. What do you want me to do?"

"Could you please knee your best friend and business partner in the nuts?"

Jason flinched. "Ouch! I am sure that shit-head you're married to deserves that, but it's against the guy code to do that unless under the most dire of circumstances, sweetheart. But I could deliver a right hook to the jaw, if it would make you feel better."

"Thanks, but no, that would just earn him sympathy. It's his boy-parts that keep causing me pain."

"How about a direct blow to the gut, would that help a little bit?" he asked with a teasing tone, but Gillian knew that Jason would do it for her.

Logan decided to chime in with a disgruntled bark. "What the hell man, I'm sitting right here! Quit talking shit!"

Jason turned his mean glare on his best friend once again and growled at him. "Can it Logan! It's complete bullshit that your goddamn mistress is crashing your son's Eighth birthday party and that your wife has to deal with this. This is not about you, so I suggest you shut the hell up!"

Even though it was nice to have someone else in the know, it still didn't change the fact that there needed to be some form of action here. Glancing between the two of them, she knew it appeared that things could definitely escalate from verbal to physical quickly. "Stop, please, both of you." Gillian turned toward Jason. "Thank you for your offers, but you really have no idea how much of a help you have been just by knowing." She hugged him again.

"I'm sorry, Gillian. I didn't realize what was going on 'til it was too late." When she pulled back to look at him, the look in his eyes was pained and sympathetic. He knew everything. He was confessing that he knew what Logan had done and was silently begging her to accept his apology. It surprised her how strangely comforting it was that he knew. She didn't have to explain anything to him.

Logan interrupted her thoughts and was obviously trying to take her attention off Jason and what he was saying. "Gilly, baby, we need to talk." She turned to face her husband of sixteen years and was slightly startled at how panicked he looked. This was not the usual Logan Baxter. He was always so put together. This realization just further confirmed the fact that he knew he was caught, and that he had, in fact, still been involved with another woman. She shook her head at him. Jason still had his arm around her, and it made her stronger. "No Logan, now is not the time. Clearly, you have some explaining to do … but as you already pointed out to me, we are supposed to be celebrating our son's birthday. And that is exactly what I plan to do. I strongly suggest you suck it up and put on a happy face, for his sake. You will not mar his birthday with your inability to control yourself." With that, she stood up to leave the room.

CHAPTER THREE

"Dad, are you gonna come in the pool with us?" Ryan yelled to Jake from the water. "Yeah buddy, I will in just a little while. I haven't had anything to eat since breakfast, so I want to grab some food first."

"Okay, Dad." Ryan proceeded to duck under the water and swim away. Well, Jake assumed he was dismissed to get some food. He strolled over to the new bar Logan had built to see what he could find. The bar looked good; Logan always had the ability to craft up crap like that. It was almost like the guy had everything. *Talent, skills, the girl of his dreams. Oh wait; he did have everything!* Damn, where the hell did that bitterness come from? Okay, so he knew exactly where it came from, but he just wasn't prepared for it. It had been a while since he felt that jealousy toward Logan, but when he came out the back door and saw Gillian standing there, just smiling at the kids, she was as beautiful as ever, and it kind of took his breath away.

Gillian was the kind of person people gravitated toward. She cared about everyone around her, always put herself last, and never hesitated when she felt someone needed her. He supposed that these were all traits that made her such a good nurse. But those were just her inner beauties. She was both attractive on the inside and the outside. They had been friends since junior year in high school, and she has only become more beautiful over time.

She was of average height and build for a woman, coming in somewhere around five-foot five-inches, with bright green eyes and long, golden brown hair. There was a slight wave to her hair, and some women would probably use an iron to straighten it, which Jake didn't understand, but hey he had a penis, what did he know? He did know that he loved her hair and the way she let hang over her shoulders and down her back. And even though there was a lot of hair, she didn't hide her face behind it.

Gillian exuded confidence with her body and her looks, and she could make sweats look attractive, mainly because she really didn't care what people thought about how she looked. She possessed a woman's body and wasn't rail thin like culture implied men desired, rather, she was curvy in all the right spots, and flat in all the others. She was beautiful and perfect in every way. *Wow! Way to sound creepy, man. Damn, I must really need to get laid.*

Sometimes he couldn't stand the fact that Logan had a treasure like Gillian. He loved Logan like a brother, and had seen him just that way, but that didn't mean he didn't want to kick his ass sometimes. And it definitely didn't mean that he didn't covet what Logan had. But he conceded to Logan back in high school when he had clearly won Gillian's heart before Jake even had a chance at trying.

God, he really sounded like a love sick stalker today. It's not like he'd been pining over her for the past eighteen years. He just always had a soft spot in his heart for her. Gillian was one of his best friends. He only wanted her to be happy … and Logan made her happy. *Now ain't that just fucking fantastic!*

Jake thought he had found his "Gillian" quite a few years back, even married her and had Ryan. But Wendy was nothing like

Gillian. He found that out the hard way when he came home early to his ten-month old son crying in his crib while his wife entertained her boyfriend in their bedroom. Now that was a great day! Thankfully, Wendy packed up and followed what's-his-name to Florida, and Jake was happy to see her go—thankful that she signed over full custody of Ryan to him. There was no way he was going to let a woman, who apparently cared more about her next orgasm than her baby in the next room, be able to claim any rights to his boy.

Well fuck! Was it take-a-trip-down-shitty-memory-lane-day? He needed a beer. He made it to the bar and saw that there was a keg … cool! Jake guessed when Logan did it, he did it right. As he reached behind the bar to get a cup, he saw his brother Jason get up and grumpily make his way into the house. *Wonder what's wrong with him?* Shrugging, he filled his cup and took up the seat across from Sean, Gillian's brother.

"Hey Sean, got the whole day off?" Sean glared at Jake, and he knew it was because of the favorite uncle comment. Jake couldn't help but smile back; it was so easy to get under Sean's skin. He was like a grumpy bear: fun to poke a stick at, but once you got him riled up you better haul ass before he got his hands on you. Although Sean was technically Dylan's only uncle by blood, the Baxter kids had plenty of men they called uncle in their lives. There was not a lacking of male role models for them, that's for sure.

Once he was done glaring, Sean replied, "Yeah, my schedule just changed. I'm working ten-hour shifts for four days then have three days off. I finished my first week on it yesterday so I have the next three days off. I can definitely go for that." He reached over and squeezed his wife, Morgan's, hand as she rubbed her very swollen belly. "Morgan needs me around more and more lately to take care of her."

Morgan then smiled indulgently at her husband and said, "Don't you think you've done enough? I already feel 'taken care of,'" she said, making air quotes and gesturing to her belly. They all laughed at that. Jake leaned over and kissed Morgan on the cheek, and she was all smiles.

"Hey, go get your own girl, that one's mine," Sean growled at Jake. This, of course, made Jake and Morgan laugh more.

"Well, duh, everyone knows she's yours. You keep knocking her up! Give the poor girl a rest." Jake sat back down, but didn't miss how Sean scooted his chair closer to Morgan. "How are you feeling, Morgan?"

"Oh, I'm great, just busy gestating these days. Got six weeks left to go, and I'm counting the days."

"I bet. I don't know how you women can do that. There is clearly a reason why women were chosen to have the babies. If it were up to us men, the race would have died out long ago."

"Isn't that the truth?" Morgan agreed.

"Where did my brother stomp off to? He looked angry or something."

Morgan gave him a quizzical look and replied, "I'm not sure, but I didn't think he stormed off. I guess there did appear to be a purpose in his stride." She pondered silently for a moment before continuing, "Maybe he followed Logan and Gillian inside ... I think she got stung by a bee or something. I saw Logan hustle her inside after she dropped the tray of food."

"Maybe he was just mad because Gilly dropped the tray of meat on the ground … he's a big guy and needs his meat," Sean added in a sarcastic tone.

Morgan gave her husband an I-can't-believe-you-said-that look before saying, "Oh yeah, like you aren't a big guy who needs his meat. Gimme a break, Sean, you are probably considering the discarded stuff that hit the ground right about now."

"I'm not worried about it; I know my sister would never let me go hungry," he replied with a smug smile. Morgan rolled her eyes at her husband then turned to Jake and said, "Like she would let any of you guys go hungry—you're all quite spoiled."

Jake smiled at that; there was no argument there. He was always being fed in the Baxter household. Gillian always made sure there was enough for everyone in her house and any extra mouths that always seemed to drop in. Present company included. He couldn't help it. Ryan always wanted to hang out with Dylan, and who was he to disappoint his son. *Man, he really was full of shit.*

Morgan interrupted his thoughts. "Hey Jake, why don't you go check on Gillian, you being a paramedic and all. It's not like her to not be out here taking care of her guests, and now I'm worried. Do you know if she is allergic to bee stings?"

Hmm, that's a good question. And now, of course, she had him worried. "Good idea. I'm not sure if she has ever been stung before. But I've got my kit in the truck." He stood up to head inside and asked Sean to keep an eye on the pool. It wasn't like

39

any of the adults still outside weren't already keeping an eye on the kids in the pool, but since he had just gotten there, he had no idea who was sober or not. Sean's nod of compliance was good enough for Jake.

While making his way into the house, he debated on whether or not he should get his kit from the car. He always kept it there for emergencies and knew it contained an EpiPen for situations of severe allergic reactions. Since he had just checked its contents last week, he knew it was in there. After thinking about it, he figured he should just go check on Gillian and then get it if needed.

Someone was trying to talk to him as he made his way toward the house, but he just inclined his head and gave a simple wave to acknowledge to them that he heard them, but was busy at the moment. He was a little distracted with tunnel vision now, looking for Gillian.

He had just made it in the back door when Jonathan, Gillian and Logan's oldest, stormed past him, bumping into his shoulder. "Hey Jonathan, where's the fire? Is there a problem or something?" Jake could tell something was wrong with Jonathan just by the look on his face.

"Sorry, Uncle Jake," was all Jake got as Jonathan continued his little war path out of the house and proceeded to the side gate, exiting the yard and the party. Well, one thing at a time, Jake thought. Let the kid burn off some steam.

Nobody was in the family room or even the kitchen, so he made his way toward the front of the house. He found Madison in there talking on her cell phone and looking completely animated in the process. Man, was he glad he had a son. He didn't think he could handle all that fire, energy, and attitude that came with a daughter like Madison.

"Seen your mom?" he asked her and was blessed with a pointed finger in the direction of the hallway that led to the stairs and the master bedroom. He assumed they were that direction, but was hoping for a little more info from the teenager. Maybe if he texted Madison he could get more details ... isn't that how to best communicate with the teenage race? That made him laugh a little and shake his head as he made his way toward the stairs. Who was he to talk? He spent plenty of time with his phone.

He had made it to the first step when he heard voices coming from the master bedroom. Glancing toward the door, he saw that it was closed most of the way leaving only a crack of it open. He moved to knock when he heard Logan talking, "Baby, please, let's just take a minute to figure this out."

Then he heard Jason grumble at Logan, "Back off man, you heard what your wife said. And honestly, you're lucky I'm listening to her because I would really love to thump you right now. You have always been one to do stupid selfish shit, but this ... you went too far this time!"

What the hell was going on in there? Deciding against knocking, Jake opened the door to see Logan on his knees, holding Gillian's hands in his and Jason standing next to Gillian with his arm around her shoulders. *Seriously, what the hell was going on in here?* Let's just set aside the fact that Jason had his arm around Gillian, which admittedly, made Jake a bit jealous. But why was

41

Logan on his knees? The only conclusion Jake could come up with, without assuming the worst, was that it wasn't good.

All three of them looked to Jake as he made his way into the room.

~*~*~*~*~*~*~*~*~*~*~*~*~*~

"Hey guys, what's going on?" Jake asked, looking between the three of them. When nobody answered, he looked to Gillian and continued, "Gillian, I heard you got stung by a bee; are you allergic and I didn't know?" Jake asked, his eyes full of concern. Of course, being a paramedic, Jake would slip into that mode. Not to mention he was extremely protective of his loved ones. He started to advance on her, reaching for her hand when she stopped him.

"I'm not allergic, Jake, it was just slightly painful, but I'm okay. I need to get some ice on it. Would you mind getting me an ice pack from the kitchen?"

She knew that the pleading look in her eyes would have him off and retrieving the ice pack promptly. As Jake left the room, she turned to both Jason and Logan. "You both know Jake would not be happy with the events that have led to this current problem. You know how he feels about cheaters," she said, giving Logan a pointed look. He actually looked down when she did, which of course, once again proved how guilty he was. She continued, "So I beg you both, don't say anything to anyone, at all, about who that woman is and what role she plays in my marriage."

Jason still had his arm around her shoulders and squeezed her to him in a one-armed hug. "You know I wouldn't do that to you

Gillian." He kissed her on top of her head in the age-old way he did like she was his little sister. "You go get the ice pack on your hand to keep the charade up ... I want to have a word with Logan."

"I have seen your definition of 'talking' before Jason. So please, no split lips and no black eyes when you leave this room. That would destroy the charade, too, you know."

Jason just smiled at her indulgently and said, "It takes a good twenty-four hours before the black eye would show." And then he scooted her out of her own bedroom. As she made her way down the hallway, she heard the door shut behind her and thought that whatever was going to happen behind that door was most likely going to result in the need of another ice pack. Taking a deep breath to gather her strength, she made her way toward the kitchen and Jake. She prepared herself with a big ass fake smile on her face.

~*~*~*~*~*~*~*~*~*~*~*~

Something was wrong. He could tell. He wasn't sure who the hell she thought she was trying to fool with that smile on her face as she came around the corner into the kitchen. The fact that Logan was on his knees didn't bode well for him, so one could only assume that he was the cause of whatever emotions she was trying to hide. Oh, she was good at hiding it, but Jake knew her, and he knew that face. She was trying to be strong for some reason. He realized then that he needed her to know that he was there for her, regardless of what was going on, she had his support.

"Let me see that hand, girl." Gillian stood there looking at him with a blankness coating her features, but he saw it when she schooled her emotions and blinked at him. "My hand is fine Jake—nothing to worry about."

She attempted to reach for the ice pack he had in his hand, but he was quick and grabbed her other hand in his to have a look for himself. She tensed for a minute and tried to pull her hand back, but must have realized it was useless to try. He gave her a smug smile and proceeded to check her hand. There was nothing on it. No red mark, no induration, no sign of any bee sting. *What the hell. That didn't make any sense.* He rotated her hand and wrist around, checking all surfaces, and found nothing indicating anything had happened.

He looked up at her face, about to question her, when he saw the pleading look in her tear filled eyes. "Please Jake, I'm fine. I promise." She placed her other hand on his cheek and gave him a slight nod of the head with a weak smile that clearly didn't reach any other part of her face.

"Gillian, what's going on? 'Cause you sure as hell don't look fine!" He realized it came out a little harsh, and she didn't need that from him. He dropped her hand and placed both of his on her shoulders. "Gillian, what's wrong?"

Gillian closed her eyes, and the tears that had been pooling in her eyes slowly found their escape down her cheeks. She took in a deep breath, in what Jake could only assume was her way of trying to reign in some deeper emotions. He gently rubbed his hands up and down her upper arms from shoulder to elbow, letting her know that she could tell him anything. When she finally opened her eyes, he saw that pleading look again. "Why is it that whenever someone asks you 'what's wrong' it just makes you want to cry more?" Gillian asked with a weak tear-choked voice. *Fuck! What the hell's going on!* He screamed internally because he knew she didn't need the overprotective ogre in him coming to the forefront. Oh, he knew she would take him to task if he said or did something to piss her off, but she looked so fragile and vulnerable right now. His internal warning lights went off just in time for him to avoid that mistake. Gillian needed something from him, and it certainly wasn't for him to act like an ass.

~*~*~*~*~*~*~*~*~*~*~*~*~*~

I can't do this right now! Of course Jake would see right through her. But she knew that she couldn't tell him right now. If she did, he would probably go ape-shit on Logan. Not that the bastard didn't deserve an ass-whoopin' from the Michael brothers, but there was still a party going on outside. She knew she was going to have to let him in a little, though, or else he would cause a scene—something she was desperately trying to avoid.

"Jake, I can't do this right now. I beg you to understand that I can't explain at the moment, but I do need your help." That's right, it was low of her, but she wasn't above playing on his Neanderthal-I-need-to-be-the-hero ways by reaching out to him as if he could save her day. *Desperate times call for desperate measures, my friends.*

"I ruined the meat when I dropped the tray. Do you have anything to grill at your house maybe? Or would you be willing to run to the store for me?"

Jake stared at her for a few moments, while he continued to rub his hands up and down her arms, trying to comfort her. Then he nodded and said, "I have some burgers and dogs in my fridge. How about I run and get those, drop them by here and then go get more from the store. That way you can get started with feeding some while I get the rest."

She felt the tension in her shoulders subside slightly. Jake was giving her a pass. She knew it was only temporary. When he wanted to know something, he was like a dog with a bone. Not much got in his way. What the hell was it with all these pain-in-the-ass-Alpha-males in her life anyway? Seriously! Who was she kidding, they might be a pain in the ass when you wanted to keep them in the dark about something, but in most other situations, they came in real handy. That made her smile a little.

"That would be perfect. Let me just grab my purse to get you some cash." As she went to leave the confines of his grip and stare, he squeezed his hands a little tighter and said, "Gilly, I'm not sure what's going on, but you *will* tell me later. I understand and see that you are trying to hold everything together right now." He then pulled her into a big, comforting hug—the kind that just made you feel better. She sighed and melted into him while trying to hold the tears back again. *Dammit!* She hated feeling this pathetic!

"I don't need any money, sweetie; you feed Ryan and me so much that I'm sure my tab is in the six figure range. So I got this." He pulled back as she did and gave her a reassuring smile. "Do you need me to get someone for you? To help you?"

She shook her head silently, while continuing to control the tears that threatened to take over. "I'll be fine." He leaned in, kissed her forehead, and said, "I'll be right back." Then he turned to leave the room just as Jason and Logan entered the kitchen on their way back toward the back of the house. *Oh crap*! Please don't let this fall apart now, she thought to herself as she braced for Jake to question them.

~*~*~*~*~*~*~*~*~*~*~*~*~

When Jake saw Jason and Logan, he knew for certain that whatever was wrong, it was big. Gillian's tear filled eyes already told him that, but the confirmation that clearly Logan was at fault was evident. Jake looked at Logan, but the man avoided eye contact with him. Further proof. Jake then made eye contact with his brother. Jason was only two or three inches taller than Jake, but they were close enough in height to where one wasn't looking down at the other by much. He raised his eyebrow at Jason in silent question as to what was going on. The slight shake of Jason's head was heard loud and clear. It was a silent message that he knew what the problem was, but this wasn't the time or place for it to come out. Jake nodded at his brother so he knew the message was received.

"I'm heading over to my place to get some meat out of the freezer to throw on the grill before heading to the store for some more. Will one of you be handling the grill for Gillian?" he asked with a tone to imply that one of them better be doing it.

Logan actually spoke up and said, "Thanks for doing that, Jake. I appreciate it. I got the grill covered." He then made his way past Jake and patted him on the shoulder as he did. Logan looked like a

47

beaten dog. His eyes were sad and contrite, and his face belied that whatever had happened, he knew he had some serious ass kissing to do as he made his way toward his wife, who had her back to them and was staring intently out the window at something.

Jake turned back to his brother as he was making his exit. "Not sure what the fuck is going on here, man, but I'm going to assume you will make sure Gillian is okay?" he said in deliberately low tones so that neither Gillian nor Logan could hear him.

"I got it, man. Just get the meat; Gillian doesn't want anyone else to know something is wrong. So the sooner you get back, the sooner the party can continue." Jake heard the anger and irritation in Jason's voice. *What the hell did Logan do?* he thought to himself as he left the kitchen and made his way out the front door.

Jake made it out to the driveway and was about to get into his jeep when he noticed someone sitting on the ground on the other side, leaning against the wheel. He made his way around the front of the jeep and found Jonathan sitting there with his knees bent, elbows resting on top of them with his hands firmly cradling his forehead.

"Hey, Jonathan, you okay?"

Jonathan looked up, startled for a moment, before recovering. "Um … yeah, Uncle Jake, I'm fine," he declared with a tone that clearly expressed he was suppressing some kind of emotion. *Like mother, like son.* Not believing the kid, Jake asked, "Headache or something? You want me to get your mom for you?" He motioned over his shoulder in the direction of the house.

"No!" Jonathan declared, almost too quickly. "Really, Uncle Jake, I'm good … I promise."

Jake was still not convinced, but knew it was stupid to push the topic. Seventeen year old boys didn't respond too well to that, if Jake remembered anything about his teenage years. As he made his way back toward the driver's side of his jeep, Jake responded. "Well, okay. I'm heading to get some meat for the grill since your mom accidentally dropped it all. You wanna go for the ride?"

"No … thanks. I'm going back inside. Nick and Robby are here. I just came out here to make a call," he said as he raised his hand and gestured to his cell phone. Then he slowly unfolded his long body to stand up. As Jake watched him get up, he couldn't help but notice how tall the young man had gotten.

"Okay, man, but if you need anything, just let me know." Jake wasn't sure why he said that to Jonathan. He was sure the kid knew that, but something about the look in his eyes made him feel like it was necessary. Maybe it was girl troubles. Jake remembered what it was like at that age when you didn't get the girl you thought you were destined to be with. Ironically enough, Gillian was that girl.

So, yes, he remembered what that was like and hoped that poor Jonathan wasn't going through that, too. Jonathan nodded at Jake's statement and made his way into the house as Jake climbed in the jeep. It didn't take him long to get the meat from his house back over to the party, and then he made his way over to the grocery store. He felt an urgent need to get back to the party; maybe he should bring some chocolate or maybe some ice cream back for Gillian. Better yet, he'd bring some chocolate ice cream. Kill two birds with one stone—the chocolate and the ice cream together—two comfort foods at the same time. Seeing a container of Rocky Road ice cream, and knowing it was her favorite, he picked it up and put it in the basket. Hopefully this could put a small smile on her face.

CHAPTER FOUR

Gillian couldn't tell if everyone was just hanging out longer at the party for no apparent reason, or if this was the norm, and she was just so ready for this day to be over that it seemed to be dragging on. This thought made her feel bad, of course, because this was for her son, and he deserved to have all this attention. It was his birthday after all. That made her realize that she still needed to do the cake. No wonder everyone was still here. She really needed to pull her head out of her ass.

She had managed to keep her distance from the whore. *Or was slut a better title? Hmmm, how about Slutty McWhore?* That made her giggle a little, even though she was disappointed she couldn't share the name with anyone else. Well, in any case, she noticed that the woman was also keeping to herself and staying close to her husband, who seemed to be enjoying her attentions. It was almost as if it wasn't the norm for the two of them.

This made Gillian wonder if her clinging to her husband was unusual or if maybe *Slutty McWhore* was doing it to get Logan's attention. *That bitch! Whoa ... hold on there, girl! You really need to get a hold of yourself.* She was going to lose her mind with all this inner bickering. Funny part about the inner bickering was that it was keeping her distracted from what was going to happen after everyone left. Yes, she really didn't want to entertain people, but she really didn't want to have the conversation that she was going to have to have when the final person left. Maybe she could just sneak out the back while Logan was distracted. *No it's not running away, it's called distancing myself to gain some perspective on the situation.* Yeah, that's a strong argument.

The truth of the matter was that whenever she looked up, Logan was looking at her. She was sure he knew what she was thinking, but she managed to avoid him most of the afternoon. It was a dance—he moved, she moved. Her escape plan was going to require an accomplice ... but who? Then, almost as if the gods had answered her prayers, in walked her savior.

"Okay, bitches! The party can start now that I'm here!" *Allie was here? Oh thank God, Allie is here!* Gillian sighed in relief and felt her body sag a bit when she saw Allie walk through the door. She was so excited to see her that she didn't know what to do. So she stood there quietly and watched as her best friend walked into the throes of family to greet her. Allie was Logan's sister, and Gillian's best friend, even though she didn't live in San Diego anymore. This, of course, was something they all hoped would change sometime soon, but she knew that Allie had her reasons for moving away; she didn't have to agree with them, she just had to support her.

This rationale was exactly why Allie was going to be the perfect accomplice to help her escape for the evening. She just needed some space and time to break down. She needed to cry and be away from Logan to develop a plan. She could just tell Allie what she needed, and like Jake, she wouldn't ask questions now but would expect some answers later. Later she could handle, just not in front of everyone else.

Gillian was so grateful to see Allie, especially since they weren't expecting her to make it down here this weekend. She watched as

Allie stopped to greet her parents, stooped down to kiss Morgan on her pregnant belly and told her not to get up. She hugged Logan, Sean and Jason, too. Then Gillian's breath hitched when Allie stopped and introduced herself to Adam and HER. She felt like growling when they shook hands. *That is my best friend, not yours! You can't have her! Okay, calm the fuck down.*

Allie then continued her journey toward Gillian and greeted her with a smile. "Hey you!" she said to Gillian. But before she could respond, something in her face must have tipped Allie off because she immediately when on alert. "What's wrong, Gilly?"

Gillian just shook her head and smiled back at her best friend as tears started to fill her eyes. "I'm so glad you're here, Al. I really need you; I just didn't realize how badly until I saw you … thanks for being here." And with that, Allie stepped closer and threw her arms around Gillian. She hugged her … hard. As she pulled back, she looked to Allie and knew she would help her. "Allie, some stuff is going on, and I really don't want to stay here tonight. Problem is, I'm sure that Logan will do what he can to prevent me from leaving. Can you help me get out of here without causing a scene? Or telling your brother?"

"Gilly, he may be my brother, but you know you're my girl. Hoes before bros and all." She said it with a slightly gansta-like slang and winked at her. "Tell me what you need."

"All I know is that I need to get out of here. Maybe after the cake and presents are done, can you get your brother to pay attention to something other than me? Jason knows what's going on, and I'm sure he can help."

Allie nodded and looked toward where Jason stood near Logan. "Hmm, Gigantor knows the four-one-one? Must be juicy if he's the one who knows and not Jake … Interesting." Allie, of course, said this while raising one eyebrow in question and cupping her own chin and tapping it, like she was deep in thought. Gillian just rolled her eyes at the theatrical and jokester ways of her best friend. "You know I'll tell you everything, but it's just not something to do here and now," she said, silently pleading for her friend to not dig yet. "In fact, the only people who have any idea that something is going on other than Logan and me are Jason and Jake. But Jason knows it all."

Allie stared at Gillian, and her eyes softened. "Girl, he fucked up bad this time, didn't he?" All she could do was nod once as she fought to keep her emotions in check. The constant battle of anger, shame, humiliation, and shock were beginning to take their toll. Allie leaned in and hugged her again. "Have no fear, SuperBitch is here, and I got your back. Just tell me, though, is this a *Oh-no-he-didn't-moment*? Or is it a *Bitch-hold-my-hoops-and-get-me-the-Vaseline-moment*?"

Once again shaking her head, Gillian laughed at her friend's finger snapping and head-rolling while she said that. "Maybe both," she replied.

Allie understood that and said, "Go get the cake ready so we can get this show on the road." She nodded and headed toward the house, feeling slightly relieved that she was going to be able to avoid the confrontation with Logan tonight. She really didn't care if it made her a coward or not, she deserved some time and space.

Gillian made her way into the house to get what she needed for the cake and ice cream. Once inside, she overheard Jonathan telling his friends, "Go ahead guys, I'll meet you there." He turned to her as his friends were leaving. "Hey boys, heading out before the cake?"

"Sorry Mrs. B, we were gonna meet some friends at the movies," they said as they waved and headed out toward the front of the house. Gillian turned to Jonathan. "You heading out, too?"

He stood there and stared at her for a few moments, and then he leaned in and hugged her. "I love you, Mom," he said to her as he kissed her on the cheek and pulled away. "I love you too, kiddo. Are you okay?" He nodded a yes and gave her a weak smile that didn't reach his eyes. "Is it okay if I go to the movies and then stay over at Nick's?"

"Of course, but you need to make sure you say goodbye to your brother. He will be upset if you don't."

"Okay, Mom," he said as he hugged her one more time. As he let go and went to head out to say bye to Dylan, Gillian grabbed his arm and made him turn back toward her. "Baby, did something happen? Is there a girl causing you heartache or something."

"I guess you could say that, Mom," he said with another weak smile.

"Well, if you need to talk, you have plenty of people to choose from." Motioning to the backyard that was full of plenty adults that would offer any support Jonathan needed, she added, "Don't forget that."

"I won't." And then he turned and walked out the back door. She watched him out the kitchen window as he told his little brother goodbye. They did that half-handshake one-arm hug thing that all guys do. That made her smile. Then she watched as Jonathan made his way out the side gate without acknowledging Logan's call to him. Her poor boy was hurting over something. The desire to smack some teenage girl for doing that to her son gave her a temporary reprieve from her current issues. She made a mental note to mention this to Logan so he could try and talk to him, too.

Well, time to get this show on the road. Armed with her camera and a well-lit cake, she announced to the yard, "Time to sing to the birthday boy!" She could see Dylan's face light up as soon as he saw the cake shaped like a Lego Guy. *Yep! Perfect choice of cake!* Gillian gave herself yet another mental pat on the back for that. Apparently she was starving for some kind of appreciation since she repeatedly had to mentally pat herself on the back today. *Jeez!*

Walking over to Dylan, Gillian saw Logan head her way. He gently eased the camera from her shoulder and got into position to take the best shots of him. They always worked together as a team. No communication was needed for them—they just knew. This thought brought her pain up to the forefront again, and the tightness in her chest intensified. They were so great together, why would he need anyone else? Well, at least she thought they were great together. Fortunately, the sight of her son's smiling face, as she lowered herself in front of him with his cake, helped edge the pain back under control. They sang, Dylan made his wish and then blew out the candles.

"Mom! This cake is awesome!" Well her day just got a little better with that bit of appreciation. He jumped up from where he was sitting and moved around the cake toward her, throwing his arms around her neck. She fumbled to set the cake down so not to drop it. Someone took it from her, and she was able to wrap her arms around her youngest son. It gave her strength. Her kids always had that effect on her. She could battle any monster or demon as long as she had her kids.

"I'm so glad you like it, buddy. I couldn't think of anything better than a Lego Guy cake for you."

"Look this way you two," Logan said from behind the camera.

Both of them looked to the camera and smiled for Logan. He peeked out from behind the camera to smile at both of them and said, "Perfect." Their eyes locked, and she could see nothing but affection for them in his eyes. How could he have that look in his eyes for her when the proof of his indiscretions was somewhere around five feet in any given direction at this very moment?

"Your turn," she said to Logan as she stood up and went to retrieve the camera from him.

Morgan decided to speak up at that moment and say, "Both of you get in there with Dylan. Sean, go take a picture of the three of them. I would totally do it, but somebody went and knocked me up making it more of a challenge for me to get up right now." A few people chuckled at her, and Sean made his way over to them. For a second she wanted to smack her sister-in-law for making it possible for Logan to touch her, but how the heck would Morgan know what was going on. Gillian had kept all of the skeletons in her closet under control and away from everyone in her life. It wasn't Morgan's fault. Her inner desire to inflict pain on her sister-in-law was interrupted by her brother.

"What the hell do you mean *someone*? We know darn well who did that!" Sean grumbled at his adorable wife while he got up and did as he was instructed. He continued to grumble under his breath, "Don't make me give a damn demonstration as to who did that to you."

Her brother was yet another one of those alpha males who she was always surrounded by and absolutely loved the relationship he had with his wife. It made her smile at their antics.

Logan assumed his position next to Gillian and flung his arm around her shoulders while Dylan stood in front of them. It was almost like he'd caught what he had been after all afternoon and wasn't letting go. Logan's grip was strong as he held onto her and he didn't let go as soon as the picture was done being taken either. Once Dylan moved back toward the cake, Logan managed to pull Gillian into a full embrace and buried his face in her neck, holding her close. Of course, being surrounded by everyone, she couldn't just push away from him. That was a great excuse to hug him back. But it was a natural reflex anyway because she loved to hold her husband. It wasn't hard to do, by any means, even though he was a pain in the ass and was the source of her current heartache. He was one of her best friends.

She felt Logan's warm breath on her neck as he held her and then he kissed her cheek. "I love you," he said to her just as he leaned in and kissed her gently on the lips. "Thank you for giving me him," he whispered in a hoarse voice that she recognized as one full of emotion as he motioned his head toward Dylan. Gillian pulled back to look at him and saw all of the emotion in his eyes. He looked scared and sad. To others it probably looked like he was choked up over sentiment, but Gillian knew better. She understood he needed some comfort from her, and being the sap that she was, she was going to give it to him. Reaching up, she placed her hand on his cheek. "It was my pleasure." He visibly relaxed a bit, but didn't let her go, and therein lies the problem. She needed to get the hell out of his grip, or she wouldn't get her time and space to figure things out. He had terrible powers over her, and she always caved to him. It was irritating as hell.

"Who wants cake?" she announced and used it as a perfect reason to encourage him to let go, though he was obviously reluctant. Gillian moved to get the cake cut and her family moved in to help dish up the ice cream and serve the birthday desert to everyone. Now she just had to get through the presents, and she could get the fuck out of there. The mental reminder gave her a little more strength to continue.

~*~*~*~*~*~*~*~*~*~

Jake stood back and watched Gillian continue to put that fake smile on her face while watching her son open his presents. Even though there were some real smiles mixed in there while she enjoyed Dylan's enthusiasm, they were mostly forced. He felt like a stalker or some kind of creep for watching her all night, but he couldn't help it. It was almost as if she was a second away from completely falling to pieces over something. Or someone, that is. He glanced over at said 'someone' and saw that he, too, was watching Gillian, instead of his son. And Jason seemed to be hovering over Logan all night. He shook his head trying to piece together the mystery and figure out what the fuck was going on.

An arm coming up around his shoulders and a warm kiss on the cheek snapped him out of his musings. "Hey handsome, how goes it?"

He smiled and turned toward Allie while swinging his arm up and over her head to drape it across her shoulders. He pulled her into his side and hugged her back. "Hey yourself, I thought this weekend was a no go for you?"

"Yeah, I wasn't supposed to make it down but something just told me I needed to be here." She looked in Gillian's direction and sighed. "I'm really glad I did."

"I'm glad you did, too. She looked like a cat in room full of rocking chairs 'til you showed up. Do you have any idea what the hell is going on with them? I mean, we can assume, but I'm hoping that it isn't what I think it is."

"No, but whatever the hell it is, it sounds major so I'm sure you aren't too far off base. Your brother apparently knows it all though."

"Yeah, so it appears," he continued as they both looked over to where Jason was standing, which continued to be in close proximity of Logan. "I can't figure it out, it's almost like he's Logan's bodyguard."

Allie snorted. "Well I don't like it one little bit that your bro knows and we don't. Clearly whatever the hell my brother did was bad. It

60

looks as if Jason is trying to keep Logan away from Gillian, though."

Jake conceded the point. "That makes sense. When I went into their bedroom I found Jason standing next to Gillian with his arm around her while Logan was kneeling in front of her. He was holding her hands, almost like he was begging her for something."

"Forgiveness would be my guess." As they stood there musing over what they thought could be the problem, people started to get up to say good night. One by one the partygoers started to collect their kids and thank their hosts for inviting them. Gillian, of course, had pasted on her sweet, and totally fake, smile again. It wasn't as if she looked that way to others—Jake just happened to know what that fake one looked like. *You really need to knock off the creepy dissection of her smiles man ... It's cause to revoke your man card!*

"Hey who is that over there?" Allie asked, pulling him out of his creepy smile dissection, and nodded her head in the direction of a family that got there at the same time he did.

"I think their names are Jody and Adam, but I'm not sure. I do know the guy works with Gillian."

"Well why does the chick seem to be ogling my brother? She has barely taken her eyes off of him since I got here."

Interesting observation, he thought as he shrugged his shoulders. He hadn't noticed. But of course that was because he was watching Gillian.

"Well anyway, I need your help." And with that statement, Allie had his full attention.

"Shoot."

"Gillian says that she needs to get out of here tonight, that she doesn't want to stay, but that she doesn't think Logan will make it easy for her." Jake nodded and she continued, "I'm supposed to help her do just that. She made it sound like she was going to try and leave on her own, but that is *soooo* not happening. I'm going to take her to a hotel since she is clearly trying to avoid Logan. I've already got a room reserved, cause I got an app for that." She smiled and winked at Jake, making him laugh and shake his head at her. She was such a character, so much fun to be around. He was suddenly so glad that she was here for their friend. Gillian had his support, but he knew that Allie was the key to getting her to smile. Allie continued, "I need to go get her some necessities from the house ... got any ideas on how to get Logan's eyes off of his wife??"

Jake shook his head at Allie as he looked toward Gillian. "Think on it. I'm gonna go get her an overnight bag."

"Why can't she just go in to use the bathroom and not come back out?"

"If he screwed up as big I am assuming he did, then I'm sure he will follow her." Allie pushed off the wall they were standing against and made her way into the house. As Jake watched Allie disappear into the house, he realized that there were really only a few things that Logan could have done to hurt Gillian like that— the most common being that he cheated on her. Just thinking that he would do something like that to Gillian brought a sour taste to his mouth. He knew exactly what it felt like to be on the receiving end of that action. His need to seek out Gillian to offer comfort became overwhelming. But just then, he spied his son and Dylan making their way toward him, talking back and forth to each other as if they were working on a plan. Clearly, they wanted something. It amused him to watch them intensely plotting like it was something serious when all they probably wanted was to spend the night somewhere. He watched as they walked closer to him and then looked up at him in unison. "All right guys, out with it, what do you want?"

"How do you know we want something, Dad?" Ryan asked, trying to sound like he was insulted that his father assumed he wanted something. Jake just laughed.

"Because you do. I know you two and can tell you were devising some plan to get something out of me."

Dylan chimed in. "Can Ryan stay the night at my grandparents' house and then go to Sea World with me tomorrow? *Pleeeaassseee*, Uncle Jake?" He gave Ryan a look as if to say *told you that you wanted something*, then asked, "Have your grandparents agreed to this already?"

"Yes, they said they assumed that Ryan was coming, too, because we're always together," Dylan said with a big smile on his face. Well that was true, it was a good assumption. "That's fine with me but Ryan you need an overnight bag, and I will have to get some money for a ticket."

Dylan started shaking his head. "He doesn't need a ticket, Uncle Jake. My mom bought him an annual pass when we got ours. And I think he has some clothes here. My mom keeps his stuff in a basket in the laundry room after she cleans it."

Jake smiled at him and his proud stance for solving what he thought was going to be a problem. "Of course she does." He turned toward his son. "You know you can speak for yourself sometimes. Dylan doesn't have to be the only one to talk."

"I know Dad, but we figured that since it was his birthday you wouldn't say no to him."

"Hmm, good plan," he said as he laughed at the two boys. "You, young man, need to thank your Aunt Gillian for doing everything she does for you. Dude, you have a basket of laundry here, and she got you a pass to Sea World; she didn't have to do that."

Ryan nodded his head vigorously as if his assent was all that his dad required in order to let him go with Dylan. "All right, go ahead and get some stuff together." And with that, they both turned and ran toward the house as Allie was coming back out.

Allie put her hands up to both boys in a universal request for a high-five. Both boys of course obliged and simultaneously smacked hands and continued into the house. Jake just smiled and shook his head; it was certainly a move they had perfected with their Aunt Allie over the years. Even though she wasn't around as much as they would all like, he loved how close the kids still were with her. He hoped that she would be coming home to stay sometime soon, but in the interim, the kids saw their aunt via Facetime. She was a great aunt and would regularly call just to chat with them, which was something he absolutely loved about her.

CHAPTER FIVE

"All right, Little Bitch, let's do this!" she said with enthusiasm while she rubbing her palms together like she was ready to tackle some major task. It would've been funny, except it just dawned on him what she called him.

"What the hell did you just call me?"

Allie smirked at him. "Little Bitch ... It's your sidekick name." At his shocked and blank stare she continued, "Super Bitch is my superhero name, so I figured that my sidekick needed a name, too. So, Little Bitch seemed to fit."

She said it to him like he was dense for needing an explanation. "Wait, why are you the superhero and I'm just a sidekick? Why can't we both be superheroes?" he grumbled to her. *There is no way that I'm only a sidekick!*

"Well what would your superhero name be then?" she inquired. He thought for a few moments, and then it came to him. A big smile came across his face while he looked at her and unabashedly said, "Super Dick, of course!"

After a few moments of silence passed between them, while they just stood there staring at each other, Jake could see Allie trying to contain her amusement at what he said, but she didn't last long. Allie burst out laughing and grabbed onto his shoulder for support as she doubled over in front of him. *Was it really that funny?* She couldn't stop laughing. *Okay, guess so.*

"Okay, why is it that funny?" he basically growled at her, growing annoyed. Allie stood and looked him square in the eye with a big smile on her face. "It's funny because that name means one of three things." She had to pause to catch her breath a little before continuing. She put up one finger to count the three things she planned to point out to him. "One, you *are* a dick." Putting emphasis on the word *are,* she then paused another moment to take in another breath, because apparently she still hadn't recovered from her laughing fit. Putting up a second finger, she continued, "Two, you *have* a super dick." And finally, finger number three. "And then there's number three, the one that most people will assume is most likely the case. That *you think you have* a super dick, but really don't."

Oh hell! Clearly they were getting off track with what their mission was supposed to be right now. He rolled his eyes at her as she continued to laugh, but tried to keep it from bursting out. She failed miserably. At least she wasn't doubled over and holding her stomach anymore.

"Come on Al, it's not like anyone else is going to hear our superhero names, just humor me." He pleaded his case as he started to see the hilarity of the whole conversation. The look on her face straining to hold it in made it even funnier, making him laugh a little. Then she tipped the scales further by saying, "Actually, I was planning to have shirts made. I just can't decide if I want a black shirt with pink letters or a pink shirt with black letters."

Jake couldn't control it then, the vision of him wearing a pink shirt that said Super Dick or even Little Bitch was too much. He burst out laughing and threw his arm around her shoulders as they laughed at each other.

"Just for the record, I don't think it, I know it ..." he paused then continued, "I sure do miss having you around all the time, Al," he admitted as he kissed her on the top of her head as they slowly started to calm down. His statement sobered her up a bit causing her to look up at him, giving him a weak smile. "I know ... me too. I'm doing better, though, so anything's possible." He didn't mean to cause her any pain so he changed the subject back to the important issue of Gillian's escape.

"All right, how do we rescue our girl?" he asked and they both turned to search out Gillian.

~*~*~*~*~*~*~*~*~*~*~*~*~

With the party winding down and people taking their leave, Gillian could feel her restlessness and anxiety begin to climb. And it wasn't at a steady pace; no it was at a full sprint. Slowly, families that had come to celebrate Dylan's birthday were packing up their stuff, collecting their kids and saying goodnight. She should be feeling relieved that the evening was coming to a close, but she wasn't. She felt like a caged animal. Her need to pace back and forth was strong, but she held it back, mainly because she would look like an idiot doing so. She really needed to get the hell out of there. *Where is Allie?* Looking around she spotted Allie with Jake—they were laughing at something. She was jealous of that, not jealous of them laughing together, but jealous that they were not feeling pain like she was. Not that she wished this on anyone, but she wanted to laugh, too.

What she wouldn't give to go back to the day she invited Adam and his family to the party right now and not do it. Ignorance was certainly bliss in some cases. Of course, the fact that she even had that thought irritated her. Telling herself that line of shit was unacceptable. But let's face it: she was only human after all. And the fact that she would prefer to avoid knowing something rather than face the knowledge that her husband had once again brought her so much pain, only enforced that. She was stronger than this, and it pissed her the hell off that she was thinking that way. Of course, she would want to know that he was violating every promise he had made to her! But, damn it really hurt.

Feeling this course of thinking bringing down her ability to keep up a strong front, she looked up again to try and signal Allie, in hopes that she would understand her need to go. Instead though, she looked straight into the eyes of Jody Spencer.

Her knees threatened to buckle under the shock of realizing that she was once again within an arm's reach of this woman. She felt her breath catch in her throat and her lips began to tingle from the lack of oxygen. All that bravado she was boasting in her silent reverie took an immediate departure. *Backup … we need backup over here! Anyone … please don't make me do this alone!* She flung her silent plea out into the universe hoping someone would just come and give her strength, hoping it didn't boomerang its way around and nail her in the back of the head. She could really use a little extra support, because at this very moment, she felt like she was going to break.

As her strength continued to waver and the moments in front of this woman stretched, she felt the panic begin to rise to a fevered pitch. They just stood there, staring at each other. If she were an outside witness to this scene, she would think it was weird. But Gillian felt frozen in place, unable to move or talk, only stare. Jody's face was also a mask showing her struggle over her emotions. *Well good, I better not be the only one who feels strung this tight!* That annoying buzzing, hollow sound was beginning to set in again as the numbness threatened to envelope her. *Goddamn this feels pathetic. Just making eye contact with her can make me feel like this … so not cool!*

The sudden touch of a hand at her waist jolted her for a moment, and then she instantly leaned into the body at her side, pulling whatever energy she could from this person. The arm snaked its way around her waist and secured her against a body as she felt another arm move across her upper back from the other side and settle down to rest on her shoulders. She was surrounded, and God, it helped tremendously. The numbness paused in its pursuit to take over. Breaking eye contact with *The Whore*, Gillian looked to her right to see Jake, and then to her left to see Allie. Back up had arrived.

Allie smiled at her and then Gillian heard Jake, "Jody and Adam, right … heading out?" he said as he extended his hand out to Adam, who she hadn't even realized was standing there. Adam took Jake's hand and shook it with gusto. Apparently Adam was enjoying being around her friends, or didn't have too many of his own, because he sure seemed a bit excited from the attention. *Too bad he wasn't allowed back ever again. Not when he could have Slutty McWhore in tow! The little girl was sweet, though.*

"Yeah. Jake, is it? Nice to meet you, but yeah, we're ready to call it a night. Although I'm pretty sure my daughter is going to be mad at me for the rest of the night," Adam said with a chuckle as he motioned to the sulking child at his side.

He looked to Gillian. "Thanks so much for inviting us; we had a great time. I do hope we can return the invitation to you and your family sometime soon."

Gillian was silent. *Wait, I'm supposed to respond to something.* She felt Allie nudge her a bit on the left side. "It was our pleasure. We look forward to it." Okay, got it out, and it sounded semi-believable. *Good job!* At that point, Adam's daughter, Rachel, started whining. "Daaadddy ... do we have to go?" She stretched out the word, daddy, in a typical Daddy's Little Girl fashion. Gillian could totally relate because she had witnessed the same scene at least a million times between Maddie and Logan. "Sorry kiddo, it's been a long day, and I'm sure these nice people want to have some family time now." With that, Adam picked up his little girl and continued, "Now, be a good girl, and thank Mrs. Baxter for inviting you to play in her pool." He nodded in Gillian's direction, and the little girl took his cue and smiled at Gillian before she said, "Thank you for letting me play in your pool. I had fun ... could I come and swim again sometime?" There was such triumph in her voice as if she had just figured out the key to getting what she wanted. This made Gillian smile. Kids were just so enjoyable sometimes. Gillian was about to answer the little girl when Jody joined the conversation.

"Rachel," she scolded. "Don't be rude! It isn't polite to invite yourself places." As the woman's voice washed over Gillian, she felt her body tense up, and she barely held back the strong desire to wince away as though she had been slapped. Then, like a chain reaction, Jake stiffened slightly and pulled Gillian tighter to his side, while Allie squeezed her shoulder in a comforting manner. They gave her strength. Gillian cleared her throat to speak since it had dried out and filled with sand once again. "Don't worry about it—it comes with the territory of owning a pool."

Turning toward the little girl she said, "I'm sure we can figure something out to make that happen sometime real soon, sweetie. I'm glad you had a good time; thank you very much for coming."

The little girl smiled at Gillian and then leaned forward from her dad's arms and wrapped her arm around Gillian's neck, giving her a hug. It was sweet and innocent and totally took Gillian by surprise. She took one of her arms and reached around the little girl to hug her back. Even though she hated those stupid one-armed hugs, she wasn't about to let go of her life support next to her. How strange it was to think that she was accepting a hug from the daughter of the woman who was most likely sleeping with her husband, while at a birthday party surrounded by family and friends who had no idea that said woman even existed. *Oh my god! This is the shit that soap operas of are made of! Pardon me while I go answer the phone; I think Jerry Springer is calling.* She inwardly groaned at that. When they let go of each other, Gillian smiled and said, "Thank you for the hug." The innocent child just shrugged one shoulder and replied, "You looked like you needed one … Bye!"

And with that, Adam escorted his adorable and very intuitive daughter, along with his whore of a wife, out the side gate of the Baxter's backyard. Gillian was still staring at the gate moments after they left.

"What the hell was that all about?" Allie said under her breath so only they could hear. "The tension radiating off you was palpable. Who was that?"

Gillian knew it was still not the time, but she had to give Allie something. Especially since she had moved to stand in front of Gillian with her hands on her hips and everything. Clearly, Allie was losing patience with her silence. She closed her eyes and took a deep breath. "I work with Adam …" she paused, trying to figure out what else to say before opening her eyes and continuing, "And let's just say that his wife is not someone I expected."

"Do you know her?" Allie pushed on, knowing there was more. *Well here goes nothing.* Gillian looked her best friend in the eye, hoping she could convey the hidden message to her without having to say the words. For some reason, just the thought of speaking the actual words that would tell her who that woman was took Gillian's breath away. "No, I know *of* her. But she knows my husband … *very well*."

"Oh, okay …" Gillian watched Allie process what she said, and when her words trailed off and her eyes widened in shock, Gillian knew she had figured it out. It took about five seconds for Allie to go from being stunned into silence to one pissed off Super Bitch. If Gillian hadn't been staring directly at her, she wouldn't have been able to stop her from stomping directly over to where her brother stood and laying him out flat in one punch.

She grabbed Allie by both arms and held her in place. "Don't do it, Al. I'm barely keeping it together, and I really need you to get me the heck out of here … please." As the emotions were all brought to the surface, Gillian was having a hell of a time trying to keep the tears at bay. They continued to gather and started to trickle out the corners of her eyes as she looked at her best friend. Allie immediately softened, relaxed her need to kick her brother's ass and nodded at Gillian.

"Sorry, sweetie, the lid is back on the can of whoop ass, but I want you to know that I reserve the right to open it again." Gillian gave her a weak smile and nodded her assent. "I would expect nothing less from you. And thank you, but can we go now?"

Allie nodded at her just before pulling her into another hug. "Okay, so now that I know what the heck was going on, I could really give a flying fuck whether or not my brother likes it if you leave tonight … so we are going to march the hell out of here, and if he tries to follow, he's getting a nut-shot from me. And believe me, he knows I'm capable of it." She finished her statement with a slight growl, but with complete confidence. The two siblings were close in age and spent plenty of their childhood terrorizing each other. Gillian knew that Logan feared his little sister on a physical level because he always said that she fought dirty and used being a girl to her advantage. "Where are the kids going to be tonight?"

"Jonathan and Maddie are each staying at a friend's house, and Dylan is going to my parents' house. I believe Ryan is going too …" Her words froze at the mention of Ryan's name because she had forgotten that Jake was standing there still, and he had heard everything. She may not have said it directly, but he wasn't an idiot, so he probably figured it out. She turned to look up at Jake, who looked like an angry bear. He had a scowl on his face, his nostrils were flared, and his lips were pressed into a thin, tight line as he looked over at Logan. *Oh shit! Time to get the hell out of here.* "Jake … please calm down," she said to him as she turned to face him. She put both of her hands on his chest in an attempt to soothe him. He had no tolerance for people who cheated and even less when it happened to someone he cared about.

CHAPTER SIX

Jake stood there and listened to Allie and Gillian as they talked, but couldn't believe what he was hearing. "... but she knows my husband *very well*," Gillian had said. Is she flat out saying that the woman who just left here, with her husband and child, is cheating on him with Logan? *No fucking way!* Jake looked in Logan's direction and saw that he was also looking in their direction. He and Jake made eye contact and Logan's expression faltered and fell a bit, like he just realized that Jake knew his secret. He felt his pulse increase exponentially. Looking over at Jason, and his position next to Logan, it all made sense. Jason was either there to keep Logan away from his own wife, or to keep the other woman away from him? *Holy shit! This was so not cool!*

Jake was glad he was holding on to Gillian because if he didn't have the reminder that she needed his support, he, too, would've marched right over to Logan and laid him out like Allie wanted to do. How the hell does a man do something like that and then come home to his wife? No matter how many different ways Jake thought about something like that, he could never come up with an answer. The truth of the matter was that it would never be something Jake would understand, because it simply wasn't something he would do or tolerate. A promise is a promise, and if a man doesn't stand by his word, he really doesn't have much to offer.

Jake was still staring in the direction of Logan and Jason when he felt Gillian's hands on his chest. "Jake ... please, calm down," she said and then slowly started moving her hands in a circular

76

motion, drawing his attention to her. Jake looked down at her as he tried to rein in his temper. He closed his eyes and took a deep breath before reopening them and focusing on Gillian.

With his jaw still clenched and teeth grinding against each other, he said. "Gillian, are you saying that your husband is cheating on you with the woman that just left this party with her own husband?" He saw a look of shame cross her face just before she nodded and looked down at her hands, which still rested on his chest. Jake placed his hand under her chin to tilt her head up to look at him, but her eyes continued to evade his. He made sure he softened his tone before speaking to her. "Gillian, please look at me." She slowly brought her eyes up to meet his, and he felt a tightening in his chest at what he saw there. Her eyes were overflowing with tears, and she looked so tired, so sad, and so ashamed. Not embarrassed, but ashamed. That really didn't help his temper at all, that's for sure. *What the hell did she have to feel ashamed about? What did Logan say to make her feel that way?*

Once again making sure his voice was soft and not showing the exceeding level of hostility that was brewing within, he said, "Gilly, you know you have nothing to be ashamed of, right? You didn't do anything wrong here." She again averted her eyes from him, confirming that she did, in fact, feel shame. *God, that guy needs a good ass kicking!*

Jake's need to comfort her maxed out at that moment. He couldn't stand it any longer so he pulled her into his arms and held her firmly against his chest. "I am so sorry, Gilly. So sorry that this happened to you," he crooned to her while rubbing her back. Then he felt her relax against him. Support—that's what she needs right now; she needed his support. Jake looked up to see

Allie watching them with glossy eyes and one pissed off expression. "Let's get her out of here. The kids are all gone so it really doesn't matter whether she stays or not. You take her to the car, and I'll take care of Logan. I will text you in a bit to find out where you girls will be." Allie just nodded at him. He knew that Allie was just as pissed as him, but also conceded the fact that Gillian needed them now. Placing his hands on Gillian's shoulders, he gently moved her away from his chest and immediately noticed the absence of her warmth. Why did that bother him? *Focus.* Rubbing her shoulders and upper arms in a gesture meant to be nurturing, he looked her in the eyes and said, "Go with Allie. I'll catch up with you two later." He felt her tense up, and he needed to reassure her more. "Don't worry, I won't beat his ass for being a giant prick. I know you don't want a scene, so I'm not going to cause one. But I, too, reserve the right to do so later." He gave her a pointed look, and a slight smile came across her sad face.

It struck him that even with watery green eyes and tear streaks down her cheeks she was a beautiful sight. But he really wanted to put a happy smile on her face. Just then, she placed her hands on his shoulders, and using them as support, she rose up on her toes and placed a kiss on his cheek. He could feel the wetness from her tears as she pulled back and attempted another weak smile at him. She must have noticed the wetness on his cheek because a small giggle escaped as she reached up and wiped it away. "Sorry. I bet you're really hoping those were tears and not snot, aren't you?" He smiled down at her. *There's my girl.*

"Well, I didn't think about that until you brought it up." He reached up and swiped his hand across his cheek even though she had already wiped it clean. "But now that's all I can think about. Gross, Gillian, thanks a lot." Her smile grew bigger.

"Thanks, Jake." He leaned down and kissed her forehead, and as he pulled back said, "I really had to fight the urge to lick you as payback." She giggled, and his anger at the situation decreased because as long as he could get her to smile, things weren't as bad as they seemed.

"Go with Allie. I'll see you soon." She nodded, and he moved them toward the back door of the house. Allie gave him a look over her shoulder, and he nodded, understanding the unspoken information. She was clearly furious at her brother, and he could tell she barely had a grip on her feelings about that. It took a lot for Allie to hold things back; she was always very vocal and didn't take any crap from anyone. There was really only one subject that she was tight-lipped about and that was her late husband, Marc. Just the fact that she was controlling herself showed how much Gillian meant to her.

Once the ladies had disappeared into the house, Jake turned to where Logan and Jason had been standing. When he made eye contact with Logan, he saw the recognition dawn on his face. He wasn't sure if it was the realization that Jake knew what was going on or if Logan just realized that his wife was gone. *That's right, jackass, she's gone AND I know*. Jake crossed his arms over his chest and raised his eyebrows up at Logan, basically goading him, but who cares. If he got a punch in at Logan in defense, that would be fine, too. And with that thought, Logan was up and heading toward the back door of the house, Jason hot on his heels. Too bad Jake was between him and the house. Keeping up his stance, effectively blocking Logan, Jake decided that yes, he wanted to fuck with him.

"Hey man, you going somewhere?" he asked as he moved to prevent Logan from going around him.

"Out of my way, Jake. I need to get inside *my* house … to talk to *my* wife." Logan's emphasis on the word 'my' in his statement didn't escape Jake's notice. Well, if he really wanted to point out things that were *his*, Jake would just have to help him with that.

"Well, YOUR wife is not inside YOUR house." Of course, Jake's emphasis on the word 'your' didn't escape Logan's attention either. He paused in his attempts to get past Jake and stared at him, confusion and irritation very evident on his face.

"What the fuck are you talking about?" Logan asked through clenched teeth.

Jake got directly in Logan's face and growled back at him. "What I mean is that YOUR wife left YOUR house shortly after YOUR mistress left YOUR son's birthday party!" Jake stayed in his face, begging him to do something about it. Logan just glared back at him, so Jake continued, "Oh, and she probably left here in YOUR car with YOUR sister. Yep, I think that about covers it." And with that, Jake relaxed back in his stance, put some distance between them, and waited for Logan to respond. Jake once again raised his eyebrows in question at Logan, daring him to continue the conversation.

The distant sounds of mumbling and a chair being roughly slid across the patio surface caught Jake's attention. He leaned to the side to look behind Logan. Then Logan was in motion. He shoved

80

Jake aside so he could get through the door and started to run toward the front of the house after Gillian. As Jake tried to right himself, he noticed that Jason looked to be scuffling around with Sean. *Oh shit! Sean must have heard what I said to Logan. Way to broadcast it to everyone, you moron.* He hadn't paid attention to who was still in the backyard because his only concern had been for Gillian to get out of there, and then, of course, to provoke Logan. Now there was one pissed off looking big brother. Well, join the club, man. Jason was barely holding him back, especially since Logan had made it into the house.

~*~*~*~*~*~*~*~*~*~*~*~

Gillian and Allie had just made it out the front door when she heard Logan calling for her. "Gillian! Stop, Gillian, stop!" *Shit … I knew I shouldn't have gone back for my damn cell phone.* Allie grabbed her arm and propelled her forward even faster.

"You better move it girl unless you want this to go down right here, right now!" Gillian could feel her heart pounding against her ribcage as her adrenaline levels spiked. She didn't want to deal with Logan now. She wasn't afraid of Logan—she knew he would never hurt her, physically that is. But she was afraid that if she listened to him 'plead his case' she would forgive him just as she had before. And look where that got her. If there was one thing she knew about her husband, it was that when he was determined, and he wanted something, very little held him back. The man could sell ice to a freaking Eskimo he was so damn persuasive! It was a handy trait to have when what he wanted was mutually beneficial, but otherwise, not so much.

You're avoiding him based on the assumption that he even wants you still. Maybe he wants to tell you that he picks her. It may be a damn good point, but very mean, nonetheless, and it brought a deep ache to her chest. This wasn't cool at all considering her chest wall was already taking a beating from the inside.

"Gillian! Please stop!" He was out the front door now. Damn, this was going to happen, wasn't it … well, I guess it was best to get it over with. She had just finished her thought when she felt her husband's hand wrap firmly around her upper arm, halting her determined stride. He used her arm to turn her around and then wrapped his other arm firmly around her body and pulled her against him. Her hands remained at her side as Logan pressed his entire body against hers and buried his face in her neck and hair, while both of his arms held her tightly to him. She wasn't going anywhere … yet.

"Baby, please don't leave. Please … we need to talk. You can't leave, baby." His voice was soft and thick with emotion as he begged her to stay. God, how she loved to be held by him, it was her weakness. She knew it. He knew it. Even though he was the cause of her pain right now, his arms around her offered comfort. *You are bat-shit-crazy girl … do you know that?*

"Come back inside. We need to talk and fix this. I can't let you leave." Logan pulled his face from her neck and looked down at her as he smoothed her hair away from her face. Gently stroking her cheeks and wiping away the tears that she hadn't realized were streaming down her face, he wrapped his arm back around her, securing her against him once again. "Give me a chance to explain myself," he pleaded as he bent down and pressed a kiss against her lips and then pulled back to see her response. She couldn't speak, couldn't move. She felt physically numb—paralyzed.

"Let her go, Logan! She wants to get out of here. You are just gonna have to sit and stew over it," Allie yelled at her brother. This just made him hold on to Gillian tighter.

"Back off, Allie. She's my wife, and I'm not just going to let her walk away from me without letting me explain!" he barked back at her. "I deserve the right to explain myself."

He deserves? He thinks he deserves something? Why that arrogant bastard! That snapped her out of her inability to speak. How dare him! How he could think he was entitled to anything at all was beyond her comprehension. "You deserve?" she managed to croak at him, and he turned his attention from Allie back to her. She looked up into his eyes and said, "You think you deserve something from me?" Her voice sounded a little stronger that time, which was clearly the result of the anger that was beginning to boil up in her veins. Logan was about to speak when she interrupted him. "What exactly is it that you think you deserve from me Logan?" She was able to achieve full volume and yell at him this time.

The adrenaline that had been slowly rising in her system before was now flowing full force as she struggled to get her arms free from the grip he had around her. He loosened his hold on her, and she moved her arms, effectively pushing him off of her. She knew that she was only able to do that because he allowed it, but she needed the space. Distance was a must if she was going to stay strong.

"Answer me!" she demanded of him. "Tell me, what exactly it is that you think you deserve from me Logan Baxter? What more could I possibly give you that you haven't already been given?" He attempted to close the gap between them and take her in his arms again, but she halted him with a hand on his chest. "NO! You don't get to touch me!" She felt a small amount of relief when she saw his shoulders sag before he spoke, "Baby, please, let's go inside and talk about this. I know you must be in shock, and I understand that, but we can work this out." *He understands? Seriously, he thinks he knows what all this shit feels like?* Once again she felt a spike in her anger and adrenaline level. That whole fight-or-flight thing was really gonna kick her butt when she finally tried to calm herself down.

"How could you possibly understand this, Logan?" she growled at him. "How could you know what this feels like?" She continued to yell at him, completely unaware of the people that had made their way into the front yard. "You know what it feels like to stand face-to-face with your husband's mistress and her family … in your own backyard … at your son's birthday party?" It certainly wasn't a question because, of course, he had no idea what that felt like. Her voice picked up in volume as she continued, "You know what it feels like to find out that not only is your husband cheating on you, but probably has been for the past year, when he swore that he was not?" Logan just stood there silently as she continued her chastising. "You know what it feels like to find out that you are not the only woman in your husband's life?"

After a few moments, Logan shook his head and mouthed the word, "No."

She hadn't realized that she had stepped closer to Logan and was now poking him hard in the chest, emphasizing each word with a new jab. "You're right, Logan, you don't! Because your wife didn't put you in that position! But I can tell you how it feels if you'd like." The sarcasm and nastiness dripped off her words as she mentally prepared herself to open that well of emotions and let them spill out all over her driveway. Those damn skeletons were out in the open and dancing circles around everyone as Gillian finally noticed that this exchange had an audience of family and friends now. Oh well, she wasn't going to back down now, so it looked like everyone was in for a show.

"I will tell you how it feels, Logan. How about you imagine the feeling of a hand … plunging deep into your chest, locking your heart in its firm grip and squeezing it until it explodes. Or how about you imagine yourself underwater, and your lungs are almost completely spent and the burn from lack of oxygen is growing … and even though you can see the surface, you somehow know you won't be able to reach it as you slowly suffocate." Her voice was losing its steam, and those wretched tears were like a water faucet down her face. "Or try to imagine someone just took a bat and swung it full force into your gut, and no matter what you do, you can't catch your breath—you can't escape the pain."

She paused, took in a deep breath. "Can you imagine that Logan? Can you imagine what it feels like knowing that you have given everything you have to another, only to find out that it wasn't enough. Can you imagine what it feels like to find out that the person you have loved and have given your whole life to, loves someone else?" A small sob escaped her as her emotions just became too much to handle at that last thought. She immediately felt the support of a body when two arms hugged her from behind and a head rested on her shoulder. *Allie.* Allie knew she needed help, but didn't want to stop her. Her best friend once again infused her with a small surge of energy allowing her to continue.

"Tell me, Logan. Can you tell me what it feels like for you to close your eyes and visualize me in the arms of another man." He visually tensed. *A nerve, people, we have hit a nerve!* It was time to stop pulling the punches and go for the kill shot—to see if she could make him feel a fraction of what she felt with his betrayal. Lowering her voice, to an almost seductive whisper, she went for his balls, figuratively, of course. "Close your eyes, and imagine my naked body pressed up against another man. His naked body pressed against mine."

Clearly this was getting the desired affect because Logan's hands were clenching repeatedly, and he looked like he was reining in what control he currently had. Too bad she wasn't done with her visual for him. "Can you see it, Logan? His hands against my skin— my body responding to his touch. His body inside mine, claiming a part of me that has only ever been yours, Logan. Imagine me calling out his name as he brings me over the edge of ecstasy and then takes his own pleasure ... deep inside my body."

Well, if flames could come from a man's ears, they would certainly be shooting from Logan's at the moment. His face was red, his jaw was clenched, and his hands were fisted at his side. *Good! He should know how this feels!*

"I don't need to imagine that, Gillian, because it's never going to happen. You. Are. Mine," he practically growled. That was a shockingly bold statement coming from him. Funny, he was such a possessive man. It was always a turn on to her in the past, but now it just pissed her off. He knew what the stakes were, and he still risked what they had for that woman. He claimed that she was his, yet his actions clearly proved he was willing to risk it all.

Especially since the last time it was discovered that he was involved with *Slutty McWhore*, she had told him in no uncertain terms that this was it—he had used all of his chances. Three strikes, and he was out. There would be no forgiving him the next time, and their marriage would be over. It was overwhelming to think that this was probably it. Even though she had set the rules, and she knew she had to stick to them, she was expecting to have more time to come to terms with what was going to happen. She wanted more time to accept that even though Logan had been aware of the risk, he took it anyway.

Logan following her out into the driveway and declaring that he deserved a chance to defend himself was forcing her hand. That made it even more difficult for her to do. It made her want to waiver and postpone it, but she knew if she did, Logan would somehow prevail. But the bottom line was that she told him if he was involved with her again, she would end their marriage. And while he had yet to admit to being with her, he had avoided directly answering her questions about it. Well, if she was going to end her marriage, she had to be sure.

She had to ask; she had to find out whether or not Logan was involved with that woman again. Considering he hadn't denied anything yet, she knew he probably was, but there was a tiny sliver of hope deep inside of her that prayed it wasn't the case. Sure, it was possible that the woman lived here, in San Diego, and that Logan had no knowledge of it. It was do or die time, and she had to ask him specifics, and it looked as if she was going to be doing it front of their friends and family. She had to know if her marriage was over or not, because she certainly wasn't going back on what she said. Trusting Logan had been hard after she had found out about his infidelity, and she knew without a doubt that if he had broken it again, there would be no repairing that trust again.

Taking a deep breath, she leveled her tone and asked, "Tell me, Logan, did you ever stop sleeping with her? Or have you been screwing her this whole time?" Logan's eyes closed, and he looked as if he was trying to process something. She had her answer. There was no denying it with his response, but she really needed to hear it. "Tell me you didn't forget, Logan. Tell me you didn't forget that I told you, if you cheated on me again it was over!" With that, his eyes opened wide, and he reached for her.

Gripping her shoulders, eyes actually tearing, he pulled her close to him, and begged her, "Please Gillian, no, please don't do this. I'm begging you, don't do this."

"Don't do what, Logan? Don't remind you that because you couldn't control your dick, you effectively threw our marriage away."

"No, Gillian, we can work this out. We are strong enough to do this … I know it."

"No, Logan, we aren't. Because I'm not strong enough."

"You don't mean that, baby. Of course you are. We can fix this." He said the last of his statement with such determination; she almost wanted to believe him.

"There is nothing to fix anymore, Logan. You made your choice, and clearly, I'm not it. There is nothing to fix because you threw it away."

"No, Gillian! That's not true. I love you! It's not too late ..." he declared, and she saw a tear roll down his cheek as he continued to hold on to her.

"Do you love her?" she whispered to him. It broke her heart further to ask it, but she had to know.

"What?" He looked shocked by her question. But didn't they say that when you answer a question with a question it was the person's way of avoiding the answer? Maybe he really didn't hear her? *Well, fuck! Let's ask again, shall we?*

"Do. You. Love. Her." she said with a level tone, emphasizing each word with a pause for good measure. She had to make sure he wasn't gonna play coy with her.

"I love *you* Gillian." Once again Logan managed to avoid answering her question. That can't be a coincidence.

"It's not enough anymore, Logan. I needed you to stand by your word—I needed to know that I was the only woman in your world just as you were the only man in mine."

Logan took in a shocked breath before whispering to her, "Were?"

"Yes, Logan … were." She paused, delaying the end of this because as much as she loved her husband, she knew she had to walk away. Laying her hands over Allie's, which were still firmly around her mid-section, she looked over Logan's shoulder and saw Jake, Jason, Morgan and Sean. *Well, crap!* Her brother looked none too happy at the moment. His wife had her arms wrapped around his body and looked like she was hugging him, when in fact, Gillian knew that Morgan was holding Sean back. Her gaze made its way back to Jake, and he gave her a weak smile, which warmed her a bit.

Her tears continued to stream down her face when she brought her gaze back to Logan, who stood there looking expectant. He was waiting for something from her, but he wasn't going to get it. She knew she was a glutton for punishment because she needed to know one more thing, and honestly she needed another burst of anger to get her through this. One more thing was needed to prove she was strong enough to walk away. Unfortunately, he had yet to answer any of her questions so she was going to have to do this one with the help of the onlookers. This was where being a smartass came in handy.

"I'll tell you what, Logan, even though I said there were no more chances left, and that our marriage was over if you cheated on me again, I will talk with you and see if we can save our marriage—try to fix it for us—if you can tell me one thing." Now she was looking at him expectantly, waiting for his answer. She could tell that what she offered gave him some hope that she would actually do just that. She almost felt guilty about that because she was pretty sure she already knew the answer to her final question. But she just had to ask it. "Were you with her this week? When I was waiting for you at the store to get Dylan's birthday presents, and you didn't show up or call me—were you with her?"

That spark of hope she had seen in his eyes dimmed as he processed what she had asked. He knew there was nothing he could do or say to cover his tracks because she had figured it out. "I do believe you told me that you and Jason were in a meeting over some botched blueprints. Should I ask Jason about that?" she said with full confidence, because she knew Jason would tell her if she asked. But she wanted to actually hear something from his mouth that was the truth about what he had done. She heard Jason, behind Logan, grumble a few choice four-letter words confirming that there was no meeting. With Gillian's final statement, the glimmer of hope in Logan's eyes vanished completely as he realized that he had no choice but to answer truthfully.

~*~*~*~*~*~*~*~*~*~*~

Jake couldn't believe his own ears. This was crazy. Logan and Gillian appeared to have the perfect relationship, or was he so blinded by his own envy that it was an illusion? Okay, he wasn't seething with envy, but it did rest comfortably below the surface. He had always possessed deeper-than-friendship type feelings for Gillian, but felt that he had them completely under control. Or at least he did.

The anger coursing through Jake's system was at peak levels as he watched this horrible scene unfold in front of all of them. It truly broke his heart to think that Gillian had gone through all this with Logan already, and he had no idea. She was such a strong person, but everyone deserved a friend to help them through a shit-storm like that. His desire to protect her from any more harm was almost unbearable.

Jake looked around him at everyone watching what was happening. Sean was barely restrained by his wife. Thank God for tiny pregnant women who can control their giant husbands with only a touch of their hand. Jason stood next to him and held a similar posture as Jake did—hands were fisted at his sides, jaw was clenched, a deep scowl across his face, and he was rocking from foot to foot like a caged lion ready to pounce. He wasn't sure if his brother's ready-to-pounce-stature was aimed at Logan for being a total douche bag, or if it was aimed at Sean in case he needed to restrain him when he finally went for Logan's throat.

"... were you with her?" He heard Gillian ask Logan, and then he could hear Morgan trying to calm Sean some more.

"Relax tiger, she's a big girl, and she's doing just fine over there. Let her do this," she was saying to her husband as she continued to gently rub his chest. Apparently a woman could sooth a beast by rubbing their chest. Interestingly, he recalled that that was exactly what Gillian did to his own chest in the backyard. He hadn't realized that she had that kind of effect on him.

"Yes ... I was with her," Logan said in a shallow, emotionally spent voice of defeat, and hung his head forward. And then all hell broke loose.

Jake barely registered it when Gillian drew back her fisted arm and shot it forward into Logan's face. Morgan released Sean and said, "Now you can help her." He promptly lunged for Logan who was now trying to stand up straight from the hood of the car he fell back on when Gillian clocked him. Jason was following after Sean. Allie now had Gillian turned into her and was trying to console her loud sobs.

Jake turned to Morgan, "You doing okay with all this excitement?" he asked, while motioning toward her very pregnant belly with his hands.

"I'm great Jake; my husband didn't just cheat on me," she said with total sarcasm. "Help Allie get her out of here. She doesn't need to see this, and I'm not about to jump in and stop my husband. Jason might be able to, but I'm not."

Jake smiled at Morgan, then made his way around the three men who were arguing, not quite sure who was going after whom at the moment, but he could leave it up to them. He got to Allie and Gillian who were just off to the side and started to move them toward Gillian's SUV where Allie had already stored her stuff. "Let's get out of here girls," he said, catching Gillian's attention, causing her to turn around and throw her arms around his neck while she sobbed into his chest. Immediately wrapping his arms around her, he paused to try and soothe her. He felt about ten feet tall when she relaxed a bit. "Shh, I've got you Gillian. Shh," he said to her while holding her with one arm and stroking down the length of her hair with the other, soothing her.

When she pulled back and looked up at him, his heart actually constricted in pain at the look on her face. "Why wasn't I enough for him Jake? Why wasn't I good enough?" she managed to choke out and then put her face back into his chest to sob some more.

He looked to Allie who stood there with tears rolling down her face, gritting her teeth. She was furious with her brother for sure. He motioned his head toward Gillian's SUV and said, "You drive, Al. I'll get her in the back." With a nod of her head, she made her way to the driver's side door. Jake bent forward and slipped his arm under Gillian's knees and lifted, carrying her the rest of the way toward her car.

But when he tried to put her in the back of the car, she wouldn't let go of him. Allie noticed and said, "Just get in with her, and put her on your lap." So he did just that. He was slightly grateful that Allie suggested it because he didn't want to let go of her just yet. Aside from all the shit that was going on at the moment, he couldn't help but contain the feeling of rightness from having her in his arms.

He was struggling to put the seatbelt around the two of them as Allie put the vehicle in motion. As she backed it up and made the shift into drive, Jake looked out the window to the driveway and saw something that was one of the saddest things he had ever seen. There was Logan, on his knees in the middle of the driveway, with Sean and Jason standing just behind him, tears visible on his face as he watched the car drive away with his wife.

Jake looked down at Gillian in his arms and noticed that her sobbing had calmed down a bit. She may have actually passed out since her sobbing seemed awfully close to hyperventilating, but the noises she was making confirmed she was fine. He couldn't believe that she thought she wasn't enough. Logan was a moron, and a fool and any other stupid ass name he could come up with to describe a man who had something this perfect and didn't cherish it. *Stupid ass, that's a perfect description!*

As he stared down at her, he knew she was asleep because of her breathing pattern. He gently wiped the tears from her cheeks and then wiped them on his shirt, which was plenty wet with her tears, and he was pretty sure there was definitely snot this time. He smiled thinking of her comment about that earlier. The fact that she could make someone smile when she was experiencing such turmoil showed you what a great person she was to be around. She was a necessity in Jake's life, and he didn't know what he would do without her. He decided, then and there, that he was going to make sure that she never thought she wasn't enough ever again.

He leaned forward and kissed her on the forehead, whispering, "You would be much more than 'just enough' for me Gillian." When he pulled back to look down at her some more, he didn't notice Allie watching him in the rearview mirror.

CHAPTER SEVEN

She felt like she was floating. The music was playing as she felt herself gently swaying to it. His arms were resting comfortably around her waist while she had one of hers on his shoulder, and the other was playing with the hair at the base of his head. She knew he loved it when she played with his hair. She, too, loved playing with it—it was so soft and thick, and she was so glad when she convinced him that he didn't need to get it cut short just for the wedding. To her it was perfect. The day was fantastic, and their first dance was turning out to be perfect as they swayed to their song in the middle of the empty dance floor, while he softly sang it to her. He didn't sing it loud enough for everyone to hear, it was just for her. Suddenly the music stopped, and he stopped singing, too. She looked into his eyes, and he smiled. Then someone nudged her shoulder. "Mom … Mom … Mommy."

She turned her head to see who was interrupting her dance with her new husband and looked straight into the eyes of her youngest son, Dylan. "Your alarm was going off Mom, it's time to get up, and I have to be at school early today so I got dressed already," he said with a satisfied smile and way too much energy for this early in the day.

She looked him over and smiled back at him. "And what a fine job you did, buddy. Good thing you wear uniforms to school still, it kind of makes things easy, doesn't it?"

He gave her a little laugh then asked, "Can I have cereal for breakfast today, please?"

"Of course, you go feed yourself, and I'm going to jump in the shower. Are your brother and sister up yet?"

"Yes, I heard Jonathan yelling at Maddie, and that's why I woke up," he said as he left her bedroom.

She swung her legs over the side of the bed to sit up and glared at her alarm clock. *It was a damn dream … A wonderful memory. Stupid music playing alarm clock.* She was going to have to pick another radio station, or better yet, take a hammer to it. Hearing that song playing definitely threw her into that dream. She sighed. *It felt sooo damn real.* She really felt like she was back on her wedding day, in her dress, dancing with Logan to their song. Their life was still new and fresh and nothing like it was now. Oh sure, things were complicated for them considering they were already the proud parents of a bouncing baby boy by the time that day rolled around. 'Just Married' wasn't the only banner they flew. The judgmental attitudes of the adults around them were always fun and barely tolerated, but hey, they were kids and didn't know anything. Sometimes it bothered her that the focus was always on her getting pregnant, instead of focusing on the way they handled it and they were doing just fine.

The most commonly offered title for her and Logan was 'teenage parents.' 'Unwed parents was the one most often heard around the religious folks. And her personal favorite to hate was the 'Got-Married-Because-They-Had-a-Child' title, which was the one whispered behind their backs, so fortunately she didn't have to hear it that often, but she knew it was there. They were all wonderful titles to be listed under, and she battled to make sure that she didn't fall into any of those stupid stereotyped categories again. That was, until two months ago, when her world fell apart.

97

Welcome to a new statistic, Gillian Baxter. Sometimes she felt like she should wear a silk sash across her chest like beauty pageant contestants wore, only hers would say something like, 'Divorced Previous Teenage Mother … duh.' Because, of course, that was what everyone expected from girls who got pregnant in high school.

She stood up, stretched, and tried to shake off the dream and her apparent bad mood. She was about to head to the shower when she heard her daughter and all her attitude yelling for her, "MOOOOM! Jonathan says if I'm not in the car in five minutes he's leaving without me!"

Looking toward that damn traitorous alarm clock she saw that it was still plenty early enough and she wasn't sure why he was placing that demand on her, but no big deal, she had to drive Dylan anyways. "I can drive you to school today if your brother needs to go. Just tell him I will."

"Eww! No way, I can't have my mom drop me off at school." Madison was the epitome of female teenage drama and said that with complete and utter disgust in her voice. *You love your daughter … You love her, it's just a phase … You will be the best of friends someday.* She chanted this to herself so not to snap at her daughter because that just brought on a whole other set of problems.

"Well then, it looks like you now only have four minutes 'til you need to be in your brother's car, or you will be walking to school." Gillian's reply to Madison's complaint elicited a grunt and a foot stomp before she went back upstairs. Well, if she was here when she got out, then she would know what her wonderful, moody daughter's decision was.

Stepping into the shower, she let the hot water pound down onto her strained muscles. She had just finished four twelve-hour shifts in a row, and her body was certainly feeling the effects of it. Thankful that today was her day off, she finished her shower and reluctantly got out so she could get the kids to school. She had just finished wrapping the towel around her body when she heard his voice calling her.

"Gillian?" Logan said in a questioning tone. "You in here?" Gillian looked up as he rounded the corner into what *was* their bedroom and saw her. His eyes widened momentarily in surprise before he spoke, "Oops, sorry, babe." He didn't make a move to leave or cover his eyes. She watched as a gentle smile graced his face, and his eyes showed emotion she didn't want to have to handle today. So, since sarcasm was a good friend of hers, she would go with that instead.

"You know, this isn't yours to look at anymore, so stop staring," she said while gesturing to her towel-clad body, and then proceeded to bend forward and wrap her hair up in another towel.

He was still staring when she stood back up and shrugged one shoulder as he said, "Believe me when I say that I *do* know that, it's just that old habits die hard, Gillian." Didn't she know it? Sometimes it was a constant battle in her head that she and Logan weren't a couple anymore. They were still married, of course, but legalities were being worked on. It was exhausting sometimes, trying to remember things were different, but she knew that it would get easier. Just seeing him in their room felt so normal, as did her initial reaction to seeing him. She had to resist the urge to walk up to him, wrap her arms around him and just hold him. She really missed his hugs. They say it takes twenty-one days to form a new habit, or get over an old one, but she was past that and still struggling. *Maybe it was twenty-one days per year you were together? Who the hell knows.*

She resisted the cloud of funk threatening to take over whenever she dwelled on the status of her marriage, and realized that there was no reason for him to be here at this time of day … in her room … while she was wearing only a towel. Making sure the towel was secure around her body, she cocked her head to the side as she asked him, "What are you doing here? It's not your day to take them—I'm off today."

"Maddie called me. She said you were making her walk to school, and she didn't like walking to school in her cheer uniform," he said and finished with another shrug like it made perfect sense to him.

Oh no, she did not! Gillian felt her anger hit like a punch to the gut as she sucked in a startled breath of air. "She told you that?" Her voice was high and full of disbelief. Logan, who has known her for at least half her life, picked up on her tone and realized that something was amiss.

"Uh-oh … I knew that didn't sound like you, but hey, who am I to pass up a chance to see my girl?" Gillian wasn't sure if he was talking about her or their daughter. The look on his face made it seem like it was Gillian, but she wasn't going to touch that one with a ten-foot pole! Gillian grabbed her robe off the hook next to where she was standing and swung it over her shoulders, tying it tightly around her body, before she dropped the towel. Oh, she was fully aware of the fact that Logan most likely caught an eye full of something, or everything, but she couldn't resist. Not only did it feel normal to do that in front of him, but also it was just too damn tempting to remind him of what he couldn't have anymore. Plus, like he said, old habits die hard.

"Did you get a good look?" she asked as she strode past him and out of the bedroom to find their daughter.

"Oh, it was good. Definitely not long enough, though, so could you do that again, but in slow motion?" he asked as he followed after her.

"You wish," she shot back at him over her shoulder.

"You're right, I do." She heard him say before she yelled up the stairs.

"Madison Marie Baxter!" she yelled in her best Mom-means-business-voice. "Do you want to tell me why you told your father that I was making you walk to school today?"

Her beautiful daughter came trotting down the stairs in her cheer uniform with a big smile on her face, eyes only for her father. "Hi Daddy!" she said as she kissed him on his cheek and walked past both of them, ignoring Gillian and her question entirely. As soon as the teenage drama queen had passed, Logan looked to Gillian and raised his eyebrows in question.

She grumbled under her breath at her husband, "This is how she has been toward me for the past few months, and it's worse than she used to be with me."

"Madison!" Logan's stern use of her actual first name, and not her nickname, had her halting her stride and turning around to face them. "Your mother asked you a question; do you want tell me why you completely ignored her?"

"I didn't hear Mom say anything, Daddy," Madison said in a sickly sweet voice. Damn, that kid was a piece of work all right. She was actually trying to play her father right in front of her. If it wasn't her own daughter doing it, she might actually be impressed, or even amused by it.

"Now I find that hard to believe. I was standing right next to her when she called you, and there is no way you didn't hear her." Madison must not have had a response to that, so she remained silent and tried to look all sweet and delicate.

Undeterred, he continued, "Do you also want to tell me why you told me that your mother was making you walk to school today, because I get the feeling, based on your mother's response, that this information is incorrect?" Gillian could see her daughter's body stiffen when she realized that she had been caught trying to pull a fast one on her father.

She had obviously intended to leave before Gillian got out of shower, or figured that her father wouldn't come in the house to seek her mother out. Madison apparently assumed that because her parents were divorcing, they didn't speak to each other. It was clear that this was a play from the my-parents-are-getting-divorced-let's-pit-them-against-one-other playbook; thankfully, Logan wasn't an idiot and didn't fall for it.

Madison was clearly mad at Gillian because of the separation and took Logan's side in the matter—especially since they had decided that the information about Logan's infidelity was not something they needed to share with the kids. All that the kids knew was Mom and Dad were not going to live together anymore, and that they were going to share custody of the kids.

Even though it was slightly refreshing to see her daughter squirm under the glare of her father, Gillian said, "Are you going to tell him the whole story, or should I? If you want to play games, you should remember that you are no match for me."

Her daughter was once again silent. Gillian didn't like to tattle on the kids to Logan. She was not one of those moms that used the 'wait 'til your father gets home' line unless the situation seriously warranted it. To hell with that, they better be just as worried about what Mom thought as they were about what Dad would think. No way was she a weak person, and her children better fear her wrath. But the fact remained that her daughter was trying to make her look bad in front of Logan, and it needed to be handled. Separations and divorces are hard enough without the kids causing unnecessary drama and pitting parents against each other was not something she was going to sit back and watch, especially when everything seemed to be going smoothly between the grown-ups.

"Got nothing to say about that, huh? Okay." Gillian turned to Logan and continued, "As I was getting into the shower, without so much as a 'Good morning, Mom,' Madison yelled to me that

Jonathan told her she had to be in his truck within five minutes, or he was leaving without her. So I told her that was fine, to tell Jonathan that I would drive her to school. Madison's response was something to the effect of *'Eww, I can't be seen at school being dropped off by my mom.'* My response to that wonderful remark was, 'Well then, I guess you better be in your brother's car in four minutes, or you would have to walk." Gillian looked over to her daughter, smiled, barely restraining her desire to stick out her tongue, and said, "Your move, little girl."

Madison had the smarts to realize that she had been out-maneuvered, and that her father would be mad at her. Logan had a slightly amused expression on his face as he looked at Gillian and asked, "She actually said eww? What the hell is that all about?"

Gillian shrugged her shoulders at him and said, "I'm guessing it's because I either dress in an embarrassing manner," she continued, counting the options on her hands, "my car is not something a teenager wants to be seen in, my big hairy mole on the tip of my nose is showing again, or she just plain doesn't like me." Gillian watched Logan stifle a laugh at her smartass ways before addressing their daughter.

"Well, which is it, Madison?" Again, no response, but she clearly understood that it wasn't going in her favor. But seriously, what could she say? "So, you have nothing to say for yourself, and you *lied* to me." When Madison predictably tried to speak up, most likely to defend herself about being accused of lying to him, he stopped her and continued, "You omitted information about why your mother said that. I'm not sure what your deal is, young lady, but treating your mother like that is not going to be tolerated anymore. So since your brother is already gone, and you don't want your mother to drive you, I guess you better get to walking because you have twenty-five minutes 'til the bell rings."

Logan looked to Gillian and smiled like he was so proud of how he handled Madison. Gillian had to laugh at that just a little bit.

"Coffee?" she asked him.

"Would love some," he said, and they both walked away from a stunned teenager.

They made their way into the kitchen and found Dylan sitting at the table, eating his cereal, and deep in video game mode, complete with headphones. He looked up and saw his dad and smiled. "Hey Dad!" Logan hugged him when he leaned over and kissed him on top of the head.

"Hey yourself, little man." Gillian's heart ached a little at the smile on her son's face when he saw his dad, like it was a surprise to see him. She had never wanted to raise their kids this way, but she could only sacrifice so much of herself.

"What are you doing here, Dad?"

"Your sister tricked me into thinking your mother was making her walk to school."

Her son gave him a horrified look and said, "Mom would never do that."

"I knew that, but I couldn't turn down a chance to say good morning to you," Logan said to him, and again her heart ached. She had to remember that he did this to them. He was a great father—that had never been an issue, so she would do everything in her power to make sure it stayed that way. Regardless of what was going on between them, she would make sure that her children had their father in their lives completely. There'd be none of that every other weekend and three evenings during the week crap. They would figure something out so that the kids were not as affected by it, but until then, it would hurt.

"Hey Dad! Could you drive me to school today? I have to be there early for safety patrol duty!" Dylan spoke with such excitement about it that she couldn't help but smile at him.

Logan smiled back at their son and said with as much enthusiasm, "Sure, I can. I'm here already, that would make my morning perfect. Go get your stuff, and we will get going in just a few minutes, okay?"

With that, Dylan got up and ran from the room in search of his school bag. She gave Logan a pointed look and said, "You do know that Madison is only going to be mad at me for having to walk to school today, don't you?"

He looked confused by her statement and responded with, "Why? I'm the one who told her she had to walk."

Gillian just shook her head, wondering if he would ever understand the teenage girl psyche. In her best high-pitched, teenage girl voice she declared, "Because, not only did I tattle on her, I told you that she was mean to me, and then she got in trouble." Then she rolled her eyes at him, doing an exaggerated version of Madison's eye roll and turned toward the coffee maker. "I wouldn't be surprised if she didn't talk to me for a couple of days," she said as she got Logan a portable coffee cup ready to go. She was slightly excited about the fact that she would have the whole house to herself, and she didn't have to go anywhere.

Looking ever so stumped at what she told him he said, "I don't think I will ever understand her. You said she has been terrible to you lately ... like what?" She didn't think it necessary to point out specifics to him because she knew it would pass. Jonathan had been acting strange, too, lately, so clearly it was because of the separation. Dylan seemed to be the only one unaffected, which was odd since he was the youngest.

Gillian shook her head as she sipped her coffee and handed him his. "It's not worth going into specifics about it, but she and Jonathan are clearly having issues with everything. We need to come up with a permanent arrangement so we can work on their structure." He nodded in agreement as he took his coffee from her. "Madison gives me attitude. Jonathan is quiet, but seems angry and Dylan is well ... Dylan."

Logan thought about that for a moment, and then said, "Jonathan won't speak to me except to answer a direct question—with a one word answer. He is clearly mad at me, and Madison is clearly mad at you." He paused and then continued, "We could tell her, you know. Maybe that's why she's mad at you; she doesn't know why you are mad at me."

"No, there is no reason for us to burden our children with that kind of information. As far as they are concerned, their parents don't have sex—never have and never will. Why would we tell them that not only do their parents have sex, but that Dad has had it with someone else, too." Logan visibly flinched. "Sorry, but that's the truth of it. I will not be pitied by my children, and your sins against me will not affect how they feel about their father."

Visibly taking in a deep breath, he sighed before talking. "Thank you, Gillian. Any other woman would have been yelling from a rooftop how they were wronged ... but not you." He shook his head as he looked down at his coffee cup then back up at her. "We should talk about what we are going to do soon so you aren't tortured by our daughter for much longer."

Gillian nodded at him in agreement. "I'll text you with my schedule, and we can find time to sit and talk about it, okay?" He nodded, and then Dylan came bounding into the room, ready to go to school. She kissed her son goodbye and allowed Logan to kiss her on the cheek when he left. And then she stood in her kitchen—her house—alone. Suddenly, she wasn't as excited to have the time and space that she used to welcome. Being alone with her thoughts wasn't healthy these days.

Maybe she would go see Morgan and the baby. She and the baby had come home from the hospital just under two weeks ago, and both were doing great. But Gillian knew that the routine of newborn babies could be overwhelming, especially with two other little ones at home. She decided that would be just the therapy she needed for today. Shooting a text in her sister-in-law's direction, she made her way to the bedroom to make herself presentable to the world. And so it wouldn't be obvious that she was still broken on the inside. She was obviously doing much better than she had been those first days—well, those first weeks was more like it.

Allie and Jake had rallied and basically supported her through some serious ugliness in those first days. The hardcore sobbing and overwhelming sadness, coupled with the overdosing on Rocky Road ice cream, would've scared away lesser friends, but not hers. Nope, even Jake handled the crying jags and ice cream bingeing well. He just made sure he not only had her favorite, but had his too, that way he would sit and eat it with her. Of course he would make jokes about it and say stuff like, "I'm sure I'm going to grow a uterus any day now. What with all the crying and chick flicks I've endured. Then there's all the ice cream I'm taking in—my dick already fell off. I figure the spontaneous growth of a vagina and uterus has to be next."

This of course would make her laugh, and then Allie would chime in with her take on that with, "Cool! So if you grow a snatch, do you think you'd want chicks or dicks?" And then the whole conversation would spiral out of control from that point, the crying would've stopped, and we all would weigh in as to whether that made Jake gay or not. It was the perfect therapy, they were the best, and she didn't know what she would have done without them.

Allie had stayed with Gillian for the first two weeks after everything happened and basically kicked Gillian's ass back in gear. She let her wallow and grieve the death of her marriage and helped snap her out of her funk, but then had to get back up to her clients. She handed the reigns over to Jake, with everyone else as back up, but Jake made it his personal mission to look after her. At that point, she was able to go about her daily routines without appearing like a zombie. Fortunately, she loved her job, and it gave her some direction and allowed her to forget about what was going on at home. That, of course, was after taking four sick days to get to that point. She was embarrassed about appearing so weak that she needed to call into work sick, but her supervisor had reassured her that there was nothing wrong with it at all. Especially since that was not something she frequently did.

When she did go back to work, Jake always came by to check on her. He always said it was because he had a call and just brought a patient into the ER, but Gillian knew better than that. Jake would've found any reason to come see her. He had seen her at her worst, and she was sure that all that sobbing would haunt him for the rest of his life. She was so thankful to have him around. Especially after that scene she caused two weeks back when he had come by, and she was alone, feeling sorry for herself.

She had been standing in the game room, drinking a glass of wine, listening to music, just staring at the pool table, dwelling on the *whys* of her failed marriage, when Jake walked in. She looked up, and he gave her a great smile.

"Hey sexy, I knocked, but you didn't answer so I just followed the music," he said with a smile that must have been contagious because she smiled back. Which was funny because a minute before he came in, there was no smile to find anywhere in her. Jake seemed to have that power, though. It was never hard to smile around him.

She took a big gulp of her wine and said, "Yeah, I was just out here sulking and ignoring the world, trying to drown my sorrows just a little bit." It had been a rough day after speaking with an attorney about divorce advice. The whole thing seemed so nasty and clinical, and she felt the need to escape from it all. She drove her point home as she tilted her head back and polished off the rest of the wine in her glass. When her head came back down, she saw Jake glaring at her, so she just glared right back.

He shook his head at her and said, "The Gillian I know doesn't sulk." He continued to press her with his stare as he rounded the pool table toward her. Looks like he wanted to challenge her. Well, she could prove him wrong; this Gillian wanted to sulk. *Bring it on, Michaels!*

"Well, the Gillian you know is a pathetic chump!" she declared with a pouty huff as she made her way over to the counter to pour some more wine before turning around and continuing, not even bothering to offer him any, "The Gillian you know couldn't even keep her husband from seeking out another woman. That sounds pretty damn pathetic to me." Putting her wine glass to her lips, she downed a big gulp before coming back up to continue, "And that same Gillian is so tired of trying to be strong and protecting everyone else, when apparently she was the one that needed the protecting!" Then she polished off the rest of wine in the glass in an attempt to stop the tears she was holding at bay. *Further proof of how pathetic I am. God, cry much, Gillian?*

Those wretched tears that she thought had been all cried out started to gather and spill over. Jake was good, though, because he just stood there and let her rant and get it all out. He didn't hide from girls' tears like most men did. "The Gillian you know is spineless and weak. She is just a useless housewife, completely devoid of anything remotely attractive or sexy." *Ouch, that hurt to say out loud.* But it was how she felt lately—ugly and blah. She wanted her sexy back.

When she completed her little tirade, the emotions she was feeling, combined with the half bottle of wine she managed to consume in less than ten minutes started to overtake her. She dropped her head into her hands and let those damn sobs take over as she once again felt shame and embarrassment over her failed marriage. Once they fully took over, she dropped herself to her knees and sobbed some more. Jake bent down to the ground, too. He placed himself in front of her, with his knees spread open, surrounding hers as he pulled her to him, engulfing her in his embrace and just holding her against his body. He was so warm, and it was so comforting.

"Get it out, Gilly. Just get it out, so you can let it all go," he whispered to her in a soothing tone as he rubbed her back in a soft, circular motion. *Sigh …*

When the sobbing ceased a bit, she whispered against his chest, "How could I be such a fool, Jake? How could I let him do that to me?" She pulled her head back to look him in the eye and asked, "How come I wasn't enough for him?"

Jake then shook his head at her. He looked as if he was searching for the words to say as he lifted one of his hands and brushed the hair out of her face—the hair that just so happened to be stuck to her tear streaked cheekbones. Or at least she hoped it was only tears. *There is no way I have snot up by eye.*

Once he seemed to figure out what he wanted to say, he placed both of his hands on either side of her face, again reminding her of his warmth and comfort. He used the pads of his thumbs to swipe the tear streaks that ran down her face as she stared into his eyes and he softly said, "I've told you this before, and I will tell you again, Gillian. You are *so* wrong." Still shaking his head at her, he repeated himself putting emphasis on each word, "You. Are. So. Wrong." He mesmerized her, and when he swiped his thumbs across her cheeks again, she realized that the tears had slowed down as she just stared into his beautiful face.

"There is only one Gillian in my world. There is no person who fits the description you just gave me. There is only one Gillian and she is one of the strongest women I know, and I admire everything about her. She is vibrant, determined, and full of love. She is in no way *pathetic,* and she is definitely not a *chump,*" he said that as if the words alone put a sour taste in his mouth just repeating them. He then leaned in and pressed his lips to her forehead. She just closed her eyes and absorbed his touch, his warmth; it was so consoling and felt so good. So right. It felt so right, in fact, that when he pulled back, she immediately felt the loss and almost leaned toward him, seeking the warmth again. *Maybe I'm addicted to Jake? Nah, just missing a man's touch, probably.*

"Fighting for your family and the man you love does not make you spineless. It is the exact opposite. You are an amazing person and a phenomenal mom. The only person who is to blame for what happened is Logan. He is the pathetic one." He smiled at her and then continued, "I have no idea why any man would do to you what Logan did. He has been my friend for a long time, too, but all I see now is a selfish, undeserving man who took something so perfect and threw it away." He truly was mesmerizing—she felt like she was in a trance, and the more he talked, the more she felt her anxiety lessen.

Jake was always so good to her, and she couldn't help but wonder why Logan couldn't be more like Jake at times. She felt so lucky to have him in her life. Then a thought occurred to her, and a slight bit of concern and worry rose to the surface as a fist of panic gripped her. People who got divorced usually didn't get to keep the same friends, and that was one of the worst things she could think of. Before she could realize she was being irrational, she blurted out, "Who gets you, Jake?"

His confusion was apparent, so she repeated the question, "Who gets to keep you in the divorce? Logan and I aren't a couple anymore, so that must mean that our friends have to pick a side, doesn't it? I'm sure Jason will have to pick Logan since they are business partners. But what about you?"

Jake pondered her question, but then clearly decided to tease her a little. "If you get me, does that mean Logan will have to pay support for me, too?" She giggled at the absurdity of the whole thing, but it was a real worry for her, and she poked him in the gut for his stupid joke. He let go of her face and bent forward in an attempt to prevent her from doing it again.

Jake grabbed her hands in his, effectively stopping her from poking him again, then continued, "Logan, Jason, and I have been friends since high school, but you have been there just as long, Gilly-bean. There is absolutely no reason for any of us to have to make a choice of sides. I will say that I don't like Logan very much at the moment, but that is between him and me. That being said, you have to know you are one of my best friends, and if I had to choose, I would definitely pick you." The tears that came to her eyes this time were from the sweetness of Jake's words instead of the pain she had been feeling. Jake smiled at her and continued, "Besides, you cook better and are far better to look at. That husband of yours is really rough on the eyes," he said with a disgusted look on his face.

That certainly earned a laugh from her. She tugged at her hands to get them free, and he let them go, allowing her to cup his face and look directly into his eyes. "I don't know what I would do if I lost you, too." She leaned in to kiss him on the cheek, just to the side of his mouth, but somehow she missed and landed on his lips. It was a shock to her senses when she realized what had happened. She let herself linger there for a moment longer, to enjoy the feel of his soft lips surrounded by his stubble, before pulling back to look at him. The warmth and tingling of her lips where they'd met his was unsettling, as were the butterflies that suddenly appeared in her stomach.

After letting her hands linger a little too long on his face, she slowly let them slide down his face to his chest. They just stared at each other quietly for a few moments before Jake broke the silence, "Gillian ..."

"I'm sorry, Jake, I didn't mean to kiss you on the lips. I'm not sure what happened," she said quickly.

He lifted his finger to her lips and said, "Shh, it's okay. You have nothing to say you're sorry for." Of course she did. Here she was on the floor, marriage freshly in ruins, accidentally kissing her best friend, and trying to destroy something else. She was about to speak up when she heard her oldest son come in the house looking for her.

"Mom, Uncle Jake, are you here?" Jonathan called. Gillian quickly disengaged from Jake and got to her feet, feeling like a teenager who had almost been caught by her parents. She gave Jake one more apologetic look before responding to her son, "We're out here, sweetheart." She didn't understand the look on Jake's face. He almost looked disappointed, but he could easily be irritated. Damn, she sure hoped she hadn't screwed things up between them. *When did my aim get so bad?*

Gillian had worried for a day or two that she had made him uncomfortable. She should have known better than to think her friend would be affected by something like that. He was sitting in her chair at the nurses' station a day later, flirting with her coworkers while he was waiting for her. It was as if it never happened. Strangely, she wasn't sure if she was happy he felt that way or not.

CHAPTER EIGHT

"Damn, what a day," Jake said as he blew out an exasperated sigh and climbed back into his ambulance. He was especially glad that call was over; he hated responding to calls where it wasn't really an emergency, but they just wanted a ride to the hospital. It happened way too often. Now he just had to get through the paperwork for the day, which should only take about an hour, so he wasn't going to complain about it. *It could always be worse*!

His partner, Eddie, climbed up into the driver's seat and started the rig. "You can say that again," he said as he got himself situated and got them on the road back to the station house. "I heard some of the guys mention heading over to Hooley's after our shift. You up for grabbing a beer tonight, or do you have to get home to Ryan?"

Hooley's was a great Irish Pub chain here in San Diego and was a great spot to hang out and unwind from the day. He hadn't been out for a beer with the guys in a while and realized that his work friends all probably thought he was avoiding them. Surprisingly they hadn't given him shit about it. The reality of it was that he just always seemed to be checking in on Gillian. Not that she needed to be checked in on; he always found excuses to do it because *he* needed to see her. *Damn!* He knew he had it bad, and it's not that he wasn't aware of his attraction toward her, but he had always been able to keep it in check. Until recently that is. It was almost as if, at the exact moment in her driveway two months ago, when Gillian told Logan that they were over, his mind, and apparently his libido, knew she was on the market and wanted to claim her as his.

He was almost embarrassed as his body responded to her voice that night when she was telling Logan to imagine her naked body pressed against another man, while she called out his name in ecstasy. You better believe that Jake was visualizing such a scenario, but it wasn't just any man, it was him. It was his name that she called out, and it was him who took his pleasure deep inside of her body. *Well, shit man … calm yourself down.* Just remembering it had the same effect on him now, which was not cool because sporting wood with only your male partner in sight—well, there was really no defense for that.

He needed to get out, maybe even get laid. Too bad the only woman that came to mind when he thought about sex was Gillian. And didn't that just make him an asshole. She wasn't even divorced yet, and she was all he could think about. Knowing his friend was waiting for an answer, and knowing that Gillian wouldn't be home tonight because it was high school football night, and she never missed Madison cheering, he replied, "No, Ryan is over at my parents' house for the night. Drinks sound good." *Nope, not creepy at all that I know her schedule.* Of course, the fact that Gillian would be at the high school approximately one mile away from where Jake was going had nothing to do with his decision to go out. It was just lucky because if she needed him, he wasn't far away.

~*~*~*~*~*~*~*~*~*~*~*~*~

After spending a fabulous morning with her sister-in-law and her beautiful nieces, which turned out to be just what she needed,

118

Gillian felt refreshed and even relaxed. Who didn't feel great after being showered with toddler love while holding an infant? Plus it was nice to see the relief in Morgan's eyes when she was allowed a few moments to herself so she could shower in peace. All moms knew exactly what that moment felt like when you were completely exhausted, yet wide awake, because you were literally at the beck and call of a tiny human.

Then after hanging out with a less-frenzied looking Morgan and enjoying some lunch, she had picked Dylan and Ryan up from school, fed them and passed them over to Jake's parents for the night. Since those two were joined at the hip, they were a packaged deal. Even though they were Ryan's grandparents, they still expected Dylan to call them Gramps and Nana. Since Ryan was their only grandchild, they welcomed Dylan into the fold. It was always so sweet to watch them love on her son. Since they had known her since she was a teenager, they felt like another set of parents to her, so she had no problem with Dylan viewing them as surrogate grandparents, as well. Gillian's parents had relocated to Temecula, about an hour away, so it was nice that her kids had a backup set.

Now she had some time to kill with a little peace and quiet before embarking on the chaos of enduring high school football games. Coffee in hand, Gillian set it down as she searched for her phone, blindly reaching into her bag on the floor next to the chair she had luckily claimed from a group of kids who had just vacated the coffee shop. After digging around for a few moments, she finally came across it. She wanted to check how much time she had before she had to be back at the school. Parking always sucked for the football games, and she was determined to avoid the damn back lot again.

Of course, Madison's solution to this was for her not to come at all. *Oh, the joys of having a teenage daughter.* Gillian was sure that what she had to tolerate with her own daughter had to be some cosmic payback for what she had done to her own mom. Well, if she was being honest, and Madison did to her what she did to her mom, Gillian would be a grandmother within the next eighteen months. *Note: lock up daughter very soon.*

There was just over an hour before kickoff, which meant she had at least another thirty minutes of kid-free time to do some reading and enjoy some coffee. Too bad she somehow forgot to charge her eReader and had to use a more traditional format for reading—an actual book. It was comical how strange it felt to be holding a book instead of an electronic device, right down to the fact that she actually caught herself tapping the far right side of the page to get it to turn and looked to the top corner for the time. Anyway, lucky for her, she found a book in the back of the car. Considering how she spends an awful lot of time sitting and waiting at one practice or another, it came in handy. It didn't matter if she had read the book before, she always loved to revisit her favorite scenes.

Once again her thoughts ventured to her daughter, who would be mortified to see that her mother was reading *Twilight* out in public, where everyone could see. She barely contained her desire to stick her tongue out at Madison, for the second time today, even though she wasn't there. *Gotta love little victories.* Since the kid-free time was so infrequent, she eagerly dove back into the world of Forks High School.

While deep in the imaginary world of sparkling vampires, Gillian leaned forward to reach for her coffee and barely registered the fact that someone was talking to her. Except that the deep timber of his voice caught her attention and quickly distracted her from the book. Looking up, she found a striking set of blue eyes set within a very masculine face surrounded by thick black hair, staring down at her expectantly. Was he talking to her? *Only one way to find out.* "Excuse me?" she asked. He smiled down at her and holy shit, what a smile it was. It was hands down a jaw-dropping-panty-melting-excuse-me-while-I-wipe-the-drool-from-my-chin kind of smile. *Am I drooling? Oh, please don't let me be drooling.*

"I was just wondering what team you were on?" he asked in that very sexy voice again. It was intoxicating. Shaking herself out of her sudden case of swooning, she found her voice.

"Varsity, my daughter cheers."

He smiled at her again and motioned toward her book and said, "I was actually referring to your book. Isn't that the book where everyone is on a 'team.'" *Oh you are a spaz, Gillian!* She felt her cheeks blush with embarrassment at misunderstanding his question, but seriously what man asked that kind of question. *Aw dammit! He must be gay.* Well, that would be a big disappointment. *Just answer the man, and let him get out of here before you really do something stupid.*

"Oh, sorry, I thought you were asking because of my shirt," she said, motioning to her shirt that sported the name of the high school and mascot proudly on it, and just so happened to showcase a view of her cleavage very nicely. *Thank God for*

121

Victoria's Secret. "But to answer your question, Team Edward," she said with a smile because this was just a funny topic to have with a stranger. Hopefully she wasn't about to find herself in a conversation where she felt she was being judged for liking *Twilight*.

He looked like he was processing that bit of information before he said, "And what are the other options for teams? What's the other guy's name?"

She smiled bigger before responding, "Jacob."

"Yeah, Team Edward and Team Jacob. Now which guy is the one who never seems to be wearing a shirt?" She practically snorted at his question as he continued, "This is important information, you know. I think a single guy nowadays needs to be knowledgeable in this kind of stuff."

Gillian laughed out loud at that comment, but knew it was true. "You are absolutely correct about that. A guy must know the basic information about *Twilight*. The best advice I can offer you is that if you're dating a *Twilight* fan, never tell her you think she is weird for loving it. It's more than just a movie, you know," she said as she gave a little wave of her book. "And the shirtless one is Jacob." She dramatically sighed and fanned herself to be funny. His smile got bigger.

"Good to know. Not that I would ever *do* something like that. You know, make fun of someone for being a fan." Then he leaned toward her and lowered his voice like he was sharing a secret. "Closet *Star Wars* fan here," he said, while exaggerating a look over his shoulder to see if anyone heard his confession. Then when he looked back at her, he winked. As he stood back up straight, she noticed that he had to be a few inches over six feet tall, and his shoulders looked nice and broad under the jacket he was wearing, which was unzipped and his scarf was hanging down in front, denying her the God-given right of women everywhere to objectify his chest.

"If you would allow me to buy you another cup of coffee, you could provide me with any other *Twilight* no-no's for the single man. Either that, or we can chat over the fact that our children apparently go to the same school," he said as he gestured toward her shirt. Okay, so he must not be gay since that was the second time he mentioned that he was single. Was he flirting with her? It seemed very likely just by the fact that he winked and kept smiling at her. And that smile alone was lethal for crying out loud. Should she flirt back? She was feeling a bit tingly inside, and had a swarm of butterflies demanding attention in her abdomen. Could she do this? There was no reason *not* to flirt back, it wasn't like she was throwing herself at his feet, but if he gave her a little time she just might be. *Just do it, girl! What have you got to lose?*

"Sure, I would love another cup of coffee, but I've got to warn you, I like the most expensive drink on the menu. I'm a bit of a coffee snob. Not sure you will want to make that kind of investment just for some advice on *Twilight*," she said with what she hoped was a flirty tone.

"Oh, it's already proven to be a very good investment. I'm Mike Lawson, by the way," he said as he extended his hand toward her. Gillian reached up and placed her hand in his big strong hand.

"Gillian. Gillian Baxter."

"Very nice to meet you, Gillian." There was that smile again. "What's your vice? I want to get you that coffee before you change your mind and give that empty seat next to you away."

As she rattled off what her Starbucks beverage of choice was, she couldn't help but enjoy the cool feeling she was experiencing. Someone was flirting with her, and she was hopeful that what she was doing back was flirting. Definitely a cool feeling, she thought, as she watched him head to the counter for their drinks. He certainly looked good coming and going, and clearly he was way out of her league.

Oh well, he may be out of her league, but it'll be fun while it lasts. Worst-case scenario, she could have friendly conversation with a fellow parent since he said his kids go to the same school. She quickly pulled her phone back out and checked the time—she still had twenty minutes before she had to head to the school. She decided to send Allie a quick text.

> *Gillian: Wanna know what my coffee and the guy buying it for me have in common?? They are both HOT!! LOL*

She sent it off, and it only took a few seconds for her best friend to respond while she quickly peeked up to see where said guy was.

> *Allie: You slut! How hot is hot? No wait, I don't want description, I want a pic!*

> *Gillian: I can't take his picture! We just exchanged names you freak =)*

Allie: Just give me his name and I will stalk him on Facebook later….

Gillian: You scare me sometimes girl…I will give you his name so if something happens to me you have somewhere to start looking for my body…

Allie: Now why the hell didn't I think of that….gimme it!!

Gillian: It's Mike Lawson…I will text you later.

Allie: You better call me slut =)

Gillian: Slut!

Allie: Very cute…call me later, I want details.

Gillian: Love you too…xoxox

Allie: xoxoxoxo

She laughed and put her phone in her bag as Mike walked back over, coffees in hand, and that damn magnificent smile on his face. "Here you go. You didn't change your mind did you?" he asked as he carefully placed her cup in her hand. Cradling the cup in her hand, she closed her eyes and took a tedious sip of the coffee—filling her mouth with the melting whip cream on top—it was her favorite sip.

As she opened her eyes and looked up, she smiled at him and said, "Mmm … I'm sorry, did you say something? I was busy enjoying my yummy beverage." He smiled back at her as he sat down in the chair next to her.

"No, please, don't let me interrupt you. I would have no problem watching you drink that whole cup in silence if that was how you were going to do it."

"Sorry to disappoint you. The first taste is the best, and the only one worthy of such attention."

"Guess I'm going to have to get that drink next time then." She was still smiling at him like some fool, but she couldn't help it, this was fun. Flirting and being flirted with was not something she was familiar with in her recent years. Well, of course there were times when there was some form of harmless flirting during the course of her marriage. But this time, there was intent behind it for her ... and shockingly, it felt good. The anticipation of what could be, coupled with the fear of the unknown, was a heady feeling. She leaned back in her chair and got comfortable while still cradling her coffee in both hands.

"So, Mike Lawson, what is it you would like to know? I want to make sure you get your money's worth and all, and since I have to be on my way in about fifteen minutes, you might want to get to it."

"Well, what do you think I should know? I mean, if I were having dinner with a beautiful woman, like yourself," he paused and gave her a wink before continuing, "Is it inappropriate to bring up *Twilight* and assume that she's a fan?"

Gillian once again smiled and laughed at his questions. "You would really bring up *Twilight* in a conversation with a woman while on a date with her? Wouldn't you prefer to bring up a topic like work or your children? I believe it would be far more tolerable for you. You know, since you are a man and all."

He considered her question and responded, "True, I would prefer to talk about my children or my work because they are important to me. But I am currently sitting in a coffee shop, talking to a beautiful woman about *Twilight*. And I'm tolerating it just fine. In fact, I have a newfound respect for the franchise all because of you. Besides, how else would I get to know the woman I am dating if I don't listen to her talk about something that she might be passionate about? So hit me with the need-to-know stuff."

Taking another sip of her coffee, she watched Mike talk over the top of her cup. She couldn't even tell if he was intentionally flirting or if it was just honest comments. He could totally be working an angle, or he could be genuinely curious—she had no clue. This guy was good. Considering what to tell him, she realized that she didn't want to talk about *Twilight*; she would rather talk about his kids or his work.

"Well, as a woman, sitting in a coffee shop, with a handsome man," she winked at him, copying what he did earlier. "I would prefer to talk about your children or your work rather than *Twilight*. I have girlfriends and a teenage daughter for that. So let's conclude the *Twilight* lesson and say that it's good to use to get the date, but maybe not while on the date." Knowing full well that she just made it sound like she would go on a date with the man, she sat back and waited to see how he would proceed. Keeping his gaze on her, he waited a few moments before he replied.

"So, Gillian, what you're saying is that you will go on a date with me?" he asked with a triumphant smile, proving that he picked up exactly what she said.

Wanting to have a little more fun with him, she said, "I'm sorry, Mike, but I don't recall being asked out on a date." She smirked back at him as she leaned over to get her phone out of her bag. If he just so happened to get a glimpse of her cleavage while she did, so be it. *Allie would be so proud!* Sitting back up, she glanced at the screen on her phone for the time.

"That's because I didn't ask you out on a date, Gillian," he replied. And that took the wind out of her sails. For a split second, she wanted to crawl into a hole and hide, as she realized her maiden attempt at flirting backfired terribly. She was about to get up and thank him for the coffee when he said, "Yet."

Touché, Mike. Touché. And just like that, the anticipation of seeing where this would go built itself back up inside her belly. He looked down at his watch and said, "I believe my time with you is almost up. I, too, have somewhere to be, but I would really love to get to know you, Gillian. Could I take you out some time?"

If she had her wits about her she would've messed with him some more and played hard to get, but she didn't want to. She wanted to say yes and didn't want to delay it. Even though she hadn't realized she wanted to try and date. Besides, she didn't have much time before she needed to get to the field, so she couldn't string him along. Smiling at him once again, she said, "I would love to go out with you some time, Mike."

"Is it too late to ask if you are available tomorrow night?"

She felt her confidence start to climb again. "Well I do believe that is a trick question," she said as she slowly stood up and started to slip her jacket back on in preparation of leaving. "If I say yes to tomorrow, then you will know that I have no life and was going to be home on a Saturday night. But if I say no, that I'm not available, I will just be sitting home all alone wishing I had said yes."

If it was even possible, his smile got bigger when he said, "Well, when you think about it, since I asked if you wanted to go out with me, you clearly know that I didn't have any plans for tomorrow night either. So I couldn't judge you for that. And if you say that you are not available, then I, too, will be sitting at home all alone wishing you had said yes."

"Good point."

"So clearly you're the only one who could put us both out of our misery. The only option is to say yes, and allow me to take you out tomorrow night."

"*Clearly* I am the one with the power here ... decisions, decisions," she jokingly said while pretending to consider it. She bent over and picked up her bag and slung it up onto her shoulder. "Well since we would both be miserable if I say no—I guess you're right—I'm going to have to say yes."

"Glad to hear it, Gillian. How does six-thirty sound to you?"

"Sounds like a date," she said as she reached down into her bag and pulled out the first piece of paper she could find. She wrote her number and address on it, and handed it to him. "I look forward to it."

As she handed him the paper, he took her hand and gently pressed it against his lips. With a soft chaste kiss to her knuckles, he said, "Until tomorrow night, Gillian Baxter. Unless, of course, I get lucky enough to catch a glimpse of you before then." Giving her one more beautiful smile, he turned and walked out of the coffee house.

Feeling warm and tingly all over, coupled with a weak-kneed sensation, she dropped back down into the chair behind her to catch her breath. She clasped the hand that he kissed in her other hand and just enjoyed the sensation of firsts: her first time flirting with a man other than her husband; her first cup of coffee with another man; her first kiss to the back of the hand? *Oh who cares, I have a date tomorrow!* She had to text Allie. But first, she had to get her butt to the high school before all the parking was gone.

CHAPTER NINE

The atmosphere at Hooley's was always an inviting one. The dark wood was everywhere, from floor to ceiling. The high booths against the walls provided a perimeter, which allowed a person to sit back and enjoy the entertainment in the corner on weekend nights and whatever games might be on the screens above the bar, depending on what season it was. On the weekdays, the atmosphere was a bit tamer, but still a great hangout. They also had a restaurant for people to enjoy with their families during the day, when the craving for good fish 'n' chips should arise.

This was where the guys from the station house loved to come to unwind. It was in a great location. Not only was there a movie theater next door for date nights, but the YMCA that was just built butted right up against the parking lot. There were adult softball leagues and indoor soccer leagues that a lot of his friends participated in, so Hooley's was where they always seemed to end up. He had just sat down and ordered a beer when his partner Eddie came in and sat next to him. Signaling the bartender for one of what Jake was having, they both settled in to unwind from their day.

"So, what's going on with you?" Eddie asked as he finished taking his first sip of the cold beer in front of him.

Jake thought it was an odd question, considering they had just spent an entire shift together. "Um, nothing much…" Jake replied with an amused tone as the bartender came to see if they wanted to order food. Never one to turn down an opportunity to get his hands on some hot wings, they placed a double order. Lifting his beer to his lips for another drink, he heard his friend and partner sigh next to him, and he looked over in time to see him shake his head side to side before looking at Jake.

"No man, I wasn't asking how your day was. I was asking you why you've been moping around with your head up your ass for weeks?" Pausing to take a sip of his drink before he continued, "I've worked with you a long time, Jake, and it doesn't take a rocket scientist to figure out that something is clearly bothering you. That being said, I'm gonna try my hardest to not sound like a chick when I say, you can talk to me if you need to man." Eddie said this last part while giving a good manly pat to the back.

"I'm sure two guys talking about their feelings is less girly when there is beer and hot wings involved. Maybe we should scratch our junk and burp a few times afterward for good measure," Jake said, laughing at the inner visual he had of the scene.

"Works for me man. Although it would be a lot more masculine if there were strippers on this bar, but I'm secure enough to know I'm all man. So let's have it … what the hell has been going on with you?"

Jake looked at his friend and weighed his options in regards to spilling his inner turmoil. It wasn't really something he felt like he could discuss with the inner circle of friends that included Logan, Sean, and Jason. Specifically, because Gillian would be at the center of that discussion, and it might be awkward with all parties involved.

Eddie knew Gillian and all, but Jake didn't think it would be weird to discuss it with him. And damn would it be nice to get this off his chest. Taking a deep breath, he asked his friend, "You sure you want to hear me whine like a little bitch?" He smiled at the memory of Allie calling him that, which in turn reminded him of Gillian, which then reminded him of later that night and listening to her talk to Logan in the driveway. Every thought he had circled its way back to Gillian. *Damn! He needed to talk about this with his friend or hire a therapist … quickly!*

When Eddie nodded at him, he decided he had no choice but to spill it all. "All right, you asked for it … you know my friend, Gillian?"

Before he could continue, Eddie interrupted him, "Yeah, of course I know who Gillian is. She's your *friend* you've been hung up on for years." The shock at Eddie's statement must have been crystal clear on Jake's face because he continued, "Don't look so shocked, man. I've seen the two of you together and the way you look at her. Especially since she left her husband. You think I don't know the reason we have to stop at the Medical Center on a daily basis?"

Seriously? Was he that transparent? Eddie continued, "What I don't understand, though, is what your problem is? She's single now."

Jake could answer that one. "Dude, we've been friends since junior year in high school. She was married to one of my best friends for seventeen years. Our families are connected and intertwined in such a way that it is almost impossible for them to come apart. My obsession with her is a little inappropriate, don't you think?"

Eddie laughed at Jake's comment and was about to respond when the waiter showed up with their orders and placed a platter full of hot wings in between them. Eddie dug in and started eating, which only made Jake want to smack the chicken wing out of his hand and make him answer the question. He had been dying to talk to someone about this, and now that he had a listener, the guy thought it was more important to stuff his face? He was about three seconds away from actually doing it, and Eddie must have noticed, because he set the bone down and turned to face Jake.

"Guess you're waiting for an answer ... No, I don't think it's inappropriate at all. Did you break up their marriage?" he asked.

"Hell no!" flew out of his mouth with an irritated tone that was intended to clearly inform Eddie that he was *not* like that.

"Calm down, dude. Seriously, I know you wouldn't do that; I am only trying to make a point." When Jake visibly calmed, Eddie proceeded, "How long have you had a thing for Gillian?" he asked, stuffing another chicken wing in his mouth, while waiting for Jake to answer.

Resolved to spill it all, so he could get an honest opinion, Jake recalled the first time he saw her. "From the moment I saw her swinging a bat in PE our junior year." Eddie looked at him and raised his eyebrows in question, so Jake continued, "I saw her first period—we had to pick teams, and she was on mine. She swung a bat like she could play, and I thought to myself how cool she was. I watched her all period and even talked to her a little bit at the

134

end of class. At lunch, I pointed her out to my brother and Logan, which was the biggest mistake of my life. After school, I went to go find her and see if she needed a ride home from school or something, and I saw her getting into Logan's car. He had beat me to her; I didn't even get the chance to try."

He took a swallow of his beer in an attempt to wash out the nasty taste in his mouth he always seemed to acquire whenever he remembered or talked about that day. He had confronted Logan the next day, demanding to know why he did that. He gave him a shove into a locker, and was going for a second shove when his brother, Jason, jumped in and stopped him. Logan's defense was that Jake never said he liked her; he only pointed her out to them and said she could really play softball. Which, unfortunately, was true. At that point, all the fight had left Jake, and he quietly decided that he would wait until Gillian dumped Logan, and then he could have a shot. Little did he know, that it would take eighteen years.

"She was pregnant within six months, and then married to him a year after their son was born. She was happy with him, and I was sufficiently placed in the friend zone."

"And you've been pining away for her all these years?"

"No, it's not like that. More like carrying a torch for her? She seems to be the one I compare all women to. She's one of my best friends, if not the best, and I have been fine with that over the years. But man, the night all the shit went down with her and Logan …" He shook his head at himself just remembering his inappropriate reaction. "I got to hold her. I mean *really* hold her. And she looked to me for support—she needed me. I don't know what, but something just switched over in my head, and I haven't been able to turn it off since."

Feeling the same disgust at himself for his uncontrollable reaction to her that night, he picked up his beer and took a long drink to calm himself down before continuing, "She was literally breaking up with her husband, in her driveway, surrounded by friends and family, and I was standing their watching it happen with a freaking hard-on just listening to her."

"Dude, you got a hard-on listening to a chick yell at her husband?"

Jake laughed a little at that. "No, it wasn't that she was yelling, it was what she was saying. She was clearly trying to inflict pain on him, for sure. She was telling Logan to imagine her being naked with another man, to imagine another man touching her, being deep inside of her … I was imagining myself as that man." He groaned as he propped his elbows on the bar and dropped his head into his hands.

"And that makes you a bad guy in what way?" Jake looked up at Eddie, confused. "Man, of course you had that kind of reaction. Hell, I'm sure if I heard it coming from a woman, I would, too. It's not like you walked up to her in the middle of the break up and said, 'I can show you what that would look like, so you don't have to imagine it.' So give yourself a break."

He sat up straighter and asked his suddenly wise friend, "What the hell do I do about it?"

Eddie shrugged as he finished another wing and licked his fingers while he looked like he was thinking about it. "She left her husband because he cheated on her?" Jake nodded. "You have

136

provided emotional support for her since?" Jake nodded again. "Is she still crying about her husband? Is there a chance they are going to get back together?"

"Last I saw her cry was two weeks ago. She was drinking a bit and feeling down on herself. I told her she was wrong and being hard on herself ..." Jake trailed off as he remembered that night. How he had been so close to her, and once he had finally gotten her to smile, she leaned forward to kiss him on the cheek, but he turned his head so that his lips met hers.

He shook his head to dispel the memory and continued, "No, there is no chance they're getting back together. They have permanently separated and are living in different places. She made it pretty clear that there was no chance."

"Then I think you're in the clear, man. Once she is ready to date, feel her out—see if you can get yourself out of the friend zone. Can't you get some help from Allie ... I'm sure she would be able to tell you if Gillian was ready to date, and if she thought it was a bad idea. I do think it's worth a try ... it's been eighteen years, man, so you either need to light that fire or put out that torch you've been carrying." And with that last comment, Eddie proceeded to belch before he reached down and adjusted his package.

"All right, I feel more like a man now," he said as he looked over at Jake. "You better eat those wings. I just saw Brooks come in. Your food is as good as gone when he gets over here."

"Thanks man, I appreciate the advice." Jake patted Eddie on the back, then turned forward to tackle the rest of the wings on his

137

plate. A hand came from behind him and proceeded to grab his wings, piling them onto a small plate. He looked back to see Brooks, one of the guys from the station, loading the plate.

"What are you two girls talking about?" Brooks managed to mumble while gnawing on one of Jake's hot wings. Again filled with the desire to knock a wing out of another man's hand, Jake restrained himself. Brooks was a bit obnoxious at times, but he was still a good guy. Jake just knew he was on edge about Gillian and what he thought were his inappropriate feelings. But according to Eddie, he needed to do something about it. Taking a chance, he thought he should see what Brooks thought.

"Hey Brooks, since you are enjoying my wings, maybe you can answer a question for me."

With a mouth full of wings, Brooks said, "Shoot."

"Would you date a woman who was getting divorced, before her divorce was final?"

"Sure, why not? If she put herself back out there, she's fair game," he managed to finish his words before another wing found its way into his mouth.

He was about to follow up with asking Brooks if he would date someone who was an old friend, but stopped. What Brooks said had an effect on him. Jake didn't like the sound of Gillian being referred to as "game," but again, Brooks had no idea who he was referring to. But it gave him pause when he realized that if Gillian did decide to put herself out there, she could be exposed to guys like Brooks. And he really did not like the thought of that.

"Dude, why the hell do you look like you're gonna choke me out … I'll get you more wings, man," Brooks mumbled as he started to back away. Jake realized his reaction to what his friend said was a bit extreme, but he felt it nonetheless. His irrational emotions continued as he was suddenly swamped with the need to see her.

"Sorry, man, got a lot on my mind," he mumbled to Brooks as he downed the last of his beer and began to stand up. He reached for his wallet and tossed a twenty on the bar in front of his partner. "I gotta go, man."

"Tell her I said hi," Eddie said with a smirk on his face, which just made Jake shake his head. He had no idea he was so transparent.

"It's really that obvious?"

Eddie gave a gentle nod of his head and responded with an "Oh yeah," out of the side of his half-turned up smile.

Jake had no idea when he became such a pussy. Maybe it was all that time he spent with Gillian and Allie in those days after she left Logan. They had all joked about it, but maybe he was turning into a chick. With that final thought, Jake patted Eddie on the shoulder and said thanks one final time before saying goodnight to Brooks and heading out the door. Looking at his watch, he noticed that the game was about to start, and he knew just where he would find her.

CHAPTER TEN

Gillian was snuggled tightly in her jacket, her hat pulled far down on her head, and her legs securely wrapped with a blanket when she spotted him. She had wondered what Mike had meant when he said "unless I see you before then," but now she knew. Mike was scanning the crowd and slowly walking past the people in the stands who were watching the football game. For a split second, she wondered if he was looking for her ... she didn't think so, but wouldn't that be cool. To be sought out in a crowd was more than a little romantic. But knowing that he probably wouldn't recognize her wearing a hat, she openly watched him, feeling safely hidden.

So when his eyes roved past her in his sweep over the section she was sitting, she smiled to herself like she enjoyed the game of hide and seek. But then his eyes snapped back to her, and a smile spread across his face. Yes, there was that smile again; she couldn't help but smile back. He raised a hand, gave a little wave, and mouthed "hi" in her direction. It wasn't until the heads of quite a few peopled turned in her direction to see whom he was talking to that she blushed. She ducked her head a little in embarrassment before she was nudged from behind by one of the other moms she sat by. "Well if you aren't going to give a little wave back, I might be tempted to. Go on, don't leave the guy hanging."

Her hand flew up and she waved as if a string had pulled it from her lap and dangled it above her head like some fool. What the hell was wrong with her, and why did this giddy feeling make her act like a moron? Reigning herself in, she slowly pulled her hand closer and gave a tight wave. He just smiled at her and gave a little nod as he made his way toward another section of the bleachers. She felt like a schoolgirl with a crush. It had been a long time since she had felt this specific set of emotions, and strangely, she wasn't as reluctant to feel them as she thought she would be.

"Well, well … looks like you've decided to get over that husband of yours. Good for you," said the same mother behind her. *What was her name again?*

Another mother to her left interrupted her thoughts when she tapped on her shoulder. "I don't know about the guy you were just smiling at, but I would really like to see you with that one." The woman finished her statement with a nod in the opposite direction that Mike had walked, drawing Gillian's attention toward the people making their way into the stands.

Her eyes landed directly on Jake and she smiled. She hadn't seen him in two days, and it always bummed her out when that happened. She continued to smile as she watched him help an elderly woman up the steps, because that was just the kind of guy he was.

"Well, if the smile on her face doesn't speak a thousand words …" Julie, the woman who had pointed Jake out to her, said. Then she turned back to Mother Number One and said, "Oh yeah, Brenda she's gotten over that husband of hers. You should see the look on her face."

Brenda, that's her name! Wait, what did she say? A little taken aback by her statement, she shook her head at both women.

"What are you talking about, that's just Jake. He's one of my oldest and best friends, nothing more."

All three women looked in the direction of Jake and watched as he ascended the steps, still assisting the elderly woman. He helped her to the bench as she sat down, then Jake stood up and looked in their direction. As soon as his eyes met hers, his face lit up, and he graced her with his smile. She instantly felt that flutter in her chest that she had noticed a few times before and dismissed. Could Jake be more to her than just a friend?

Julie once again interrupted her thoughts, "You can keep telling yourself that, but I don't know why you would fight something like that." And with that, Julie got up from her place next to Gillian and moved behind her to sit next to Brenda, allowing room for Jake to sit. *Be with Jake? Something about that sounded so wrong, but so right at the same time. Be with Jake …*

~*~*~*~*~*~*~*~*~*~*~*~*

"Hey you, I knew this was where I would find you—far enough away so Madison will not see or hear you, but close enough for you to see her clearly," he said as he leaned down and kissed her on the cheek. She offered her cheek up to him as she always did. But just like he was accustomed to lately, he couldn't help the desire he had to be pressing his lips against her lips, instead of her cheek. He had only the privilege of a few seconds to feel her lips against his that day at her house. But he remembered exactly what they felt like. *Soft and perfect.*

He knew his train of thought must be redirected before they cycled back around and left him standing in the crowded football bleachers with another erection. Quickly sitting down, he turned slightly to the women he recognized sitting behind Gillian.

"Hi there, ladies ... good game tonight?"

They both smiled at him, and one of them replied, "Great game! Up by ten, and if they keep this up, CIF playoffs are in the bag."

"Cool. Glad I've got Fridays off. I can follow the team now."

"You should definitely come to all the games. We love having you around," the other woman said in a slightly odd tone. Clearly, she was insinuating something, but what, he didn't know. After giving one more polite smile, he turned his attention to the woman he came to see.

"How was your day? I heard you went for pizza with the boys after school before bringing them to my parents' house."

"You know I'm a sucker for anything with cheese on top," she said, smiling at him before loosening the blanket around her legs to include him in its warmth. This, of course, required him to scoot all the way against her 'til there was no space. No complaints from him in that department. He swiftly put his arm behind her, planted his hand on her hip to hold her in place and slid right up against her. And no, he didn't feel it was necessary to move his hand from where it was located. He was going to feel this situation out, and besides, he was helping her stay warm this way. *Man—so full of shit!*

Once he was snuggled in nice and tight against her body, he relaxed a bit when he felt her relax into him. He just wanted to absorb the feeling of her body touching his. The hat she was wearing bothered him because he couldn't stick his nose down into her hair and take a deep breath of her scent. *Bet that wouldn't look creepy at all*. Although he could smell it by being close to her, he wanted more. That was what it all came down to.

Jake wanted more from Gillian, and he had to make her realize what his intentions were. On the way over to the game, he came to terms with the fact that what he was feeling for her was never going to go away until he tried. He had to see if she could accept him as more than a friend, and even though it was possible that she wouldn't, it was time for some action. He needed to formulate a game plan … to figure out a way and find out if there was any possibility that she would want Jake the way he wanted her. A jolt of anxiety hit him as he wondered what would happen if she didn't. *No, she would; she had to.*

He was staring out at the football field, not really seeing anything—lost in thought and the feeling of her body against his—when a hand on his thigh caught his attention. His quick intake of breath must have given the impression that her touch was unwelcome, and she quickly withdrew it. Immediately, he regretted its loss. Truthfully, her hand being that close to another appendage that wanted her attention was not a good idea, so he would just deal with it. He gave her a little squeeze around her waist to make sure she didn't try and retreat too far.

"Sorry," he said. "You startled me a little."

She gave him a timid smile. "You were a million miles away. What were you worrying about in that head of yours?"

He so wished he could just profess his feelings, right here and now, so that everyone could stop seeing him look like an idiot in public. Apparently, thinking about Gillian made him look and act like an idiot ... Thank God there was a cure for it, though. "Nothing much, just a long day," he said, giving her a slight smile. And then her hand was on his knee again, giving it a slight squeeze under the blanket.

"Do you want to talk about it?"

With her hand on his leg, he could think of a few things he wanted to do, but talking was not one of them. He leaned in and kissed her on the side of her head and said, "Don't worry about me, Gilly-bean. I'm fine." He couldn't help but notice the two women behind them staring at him. One of them gave one of those half-smirks, very similar to the one he had seen on Eddie's smug face not but an hour ago. Damn, he really must be transparent. He turned himself back and settled against her again to finish out the game.

"Okay, just remember that I am here if you need me." He couldn't help but think to himself how that little statement could mean so many different things.

Oh, how I need you Gillian.

CHAPTER ELEVEN

Gillian could feel the sun penetrating the bedroom window, telling her it was time to get the day started. She refused to open her eyes. She was too comfortable and relaxed after a dreamless night of sleep. *Take that, stupid music-playing alarm clock!* She was about to peek open her eyes and give it a glare for yesterday's dream when she picked up the distinct scent of coffee. Knowing she slept in the house alone last night, that could only mean one thing: Allie was here. With her eyes still closed, she smiled and said, "I refuse to open my eyes 'til I know for sure that I'm not just smelling your coffee … that there is some for me, too?"

"Duh. I like the way my hair looks today, so why would I risk a cat fight with you over coffee?"

Rolling over in her bed, she knew she would find Allie perched beside her like she owned the place. And yep, there she was, sitting cross-legged on what used to be Logan's side of the bed, a coffee cup extended in Gillian's direction. Her head was down, looking through a magazine that was spread across her lap as she was cautiously sipping her own cup of coffee. Gillian took the graciously offered cup of her favorite coffee shop recipe and lifted it up to her lips for that first sip she loved. She sighed at how good it tasted when a laugh from Allie caught her attention.

"Oh my god, you did that when you met Mike at the coffee house last night, didn't you?"

Remembering last night's events, Gillian smiled as she opened her eyes, gave Allie a mischievous look and replied, "You would have been so proud of my flirting last night. It was like I channeled my inner Allie."

"Whoa now, you can't go channeling your inner Allie on the first run out the gate; you could hurt yourself. Did you at least stretch beforehand?"

Gillian leaned over to give her best friend and sister, in every sense of the word except blood, a kiss on the cheek. "Good morning, by the way. Not that I'm not happy to see you, but what are you doing here this weekend?"

Allie gave her a wounded look. "Did you really think you would be getting dressed for your first date after marriage without my help? There is much to prepare for today, so drink up and get your ass dressed. We have appointments at ten for facials and nails, and I brought my kit with me so I could do your roots."

"My roots were showing last night, and a hot guy still asked me out. You don't have to go to all the trouble," Gillian said while drinking down more of her coffee, still not wanting to get out of bed. "Besides, wouldn't I look desperate getting all this done for a first date?"

"Don't be ridiculous. Of course you have to go to the trouble … what kind of woman goes on her first *first* date in over eighteen years without fresh nails and hair? How's your wax job by the way? I wasn't sure if you needed to get that done or not, so I just included it. You haven't let that go have you? Gotta make sure the hardwood floors are shining."

Gillian almost spit out her coffee. Even after almost two decades as friends, Allie could still surprise her with her brashness. "No, I haven't 'let that go.' Jeez, I didn't wax just for my husband, although he reaped the benefits of it. Besides, I won't be showing Mike the 'hardwood floors' tonight."

"Why not?"

"Come on, Allie, my marriage *just* ended, and I don't think jumping on the first guy to show an interest in me is the smartest thing to do. Besides, I've only ever been with Logan—you know that. I'm going to need a bit more confidence before I take that step."

"But he's *oh so dreamy*," Allie said while mimicking a lovesick teenager, clutching her hands to her chest and heaving an exaggerated sigh. "I bet he kisses great, too, with those perfect lips of his."

His lips? Dreamy? Facebook stalking must have paid off. Smiling, Gillian said, "I take it you must have found him on Facebook?"

"Of course I did. Did you doubt my ninja stalking abilities? It was a piece of cake. Do you want the 4-1-1 on him?"

Did she? Isn't that what the first date was for—getting to know a new person? Gillian decided she wanted to go into this without the benefit of the electronic revolution. She knew that the guy must appear to be a stand-up citizen if Allie was allowing him to date her. "No, I don't want to know. I assume you approve, so I will just find out what I want to know by talking to him. Besides, he was really easy to talk with." She finished her remark with a smile on her face.

"Okay, well time is wasting, and we have a full day planned. Where are the kids ... all their beds are empty?"

"Dylan is with Ryan at Jake's parents' and both Madison and Jonathan stayed at their friends' houses. They will all be with Logan tonight."

"Great. No need to find someone to watch them. Get up and get in the shower. I want to stop and get some bagels on the way." With that, Allie promptly got up and bounced out of the room. Knowing it was best to do as she was told because there was no stopping Allie when she had a plan, Gillian climbed out of bed and started the process of getting ready. All the while the anticipation for an evening of firsts for her grew rapidly.

After her shower, Gillian came out to find Allie once again perched on the bed, tapping away at the keys on her phone with what could only be described as an evil grin.

"I know that look ... what are you up to over there?" Gillian asked.

"Not a darn thing. Quit worrying about me and get dressed. Just throw your hair up in a messy bun or something, cause I will be working on it later. No sense in over treating it today." She looked in the mirror and debated whether or not to listen to her friend. "Just put it up Gillian, not many people can rock the messy bun like you do."

Allie said all of this while still tapping away at her phone, but she knew Gillian well enough to know exactly what she was thinking. Well, Allie knew what was best when it came to hair, so she piled it all up on top of her head and did what she was told. She went into her closet, pulled on her jeans, and had just pulled a tank over her head when Allie appeared and started perusing the clothes.

"Any idea what you're wearing tonight?" Allie asked. Considering her friend already planned her day out, she knew what she was asking. So Gillian wasn't going to fight it.

"No not yet, but that's because we haven't gone shopping for you to tell me what I will be wearing."

Allie turned to her and smiled a big smile before leaning in to hug her. "I love it when you see things my way, Gillian! Let's get going." She grabbed her hand and dragged her from the closet. Yep, this was gonna be a busy day, because when Allie was excited like this, it was full steam ahead.

Allie tossed Gillian the keys to her SUV and said, "You drive, I've already driven close to two hours today, and I have some catching up to do on my phone."

"Just remember that when you're tired of making that drive, you can come back home to all of us."

Allie looked up with a sad expression and nodded. "I know that, Gilly, I know." Then she turned and made her way out the front door. Feeling that she said all that she should about the subject of Allie moving back down to San Diego, she followed her best friend out the door.

~*~*~*~*~*~*~*~*~*~*~*~

Jake was just finishing his workout when his phone vibrated. The notification that he'd received a text filled him with anticipation, hoping it was Gillian. Even though it was only nine in the morning, and he knew it was her day off and would probably be sleeping in … he hoped she was awake. He had decided to try and spend some time with her today, maybe put his plan in motion. But trying to wait 'til his self-imposed timeline of ten o'clock before calling her didn't mean he wasn't hopeful that she called first. The day was all planned out, and he was excited about it. He knew that her kids would be with Logan tonight and that Ryan was going to be with Dylan, so they were both without children for the next twenty-four hours.

He looked at his phone and saw that it was Allie who texted him. Although he loved talking to her, she was not the *her* he wanted to talk to.

> Allie: Hey you! I'm in town…meet at Gillian's house at 6:30 for dinner.
>
> Jake: You here already?
>
> Allie: Yep! Can't you feel my awesomeness from there??
>
> Jake: LOL, you with Gilly?
>
> Allie: Of course, on way to get girly stuff done…want to come?
>
> Jake: Will you make me get something waxed?
>
> Allie: Hell yeah! Price of admission to hang with us…you game?
>
> Jake: I'll pass…have great day…see you at 6:30.
>
> Allie: Later Little Bitch =)

Gotta love Allie. Well at the moment, he really didn't. He had plans for Gillian today, and Allie had to come into town and screw them up. "Dammit!" he grumbled as he threw his water bottle across the garage before storming back inside the house. Now what the hell was he supposed to do? Spend the entire day sitting on his ass stewing over this? The night was already long enough; he didn't know how he was going to do it all day, too. Standing there in the middle of his living room, he closed his eyes and took a deep breath in an attempt to calm down.

Working out was his usual vice when angry or frustrated, but since he already worked out, that was out. He could always go for a run … or have sex. Sex would take care of it for sure, which of course brings us back to the original problem. Wanting to be with Gillian. *And hello erection … this is ridiculous!* Just a quick thought of Gillian had his dick up and ready to play. Jake was set in his path; he didn't want any other woman, and he wasn't that kind of guy to begin with. He wanted Gillian. No … he needed Gillian. It was becoming more and more painful as the days went on. But he knew what he was going to do now—he just needed a little more patience.

"Well since sex is clearly off the table, running it is." Grabbing another water bottle from the fridge, Jake pulled his shirt off over his head, plugged his ear buds in, and out the door he went. Pounding the pavement a little harder than he needed to, since he had just worked out his legs, was probably going to make his legs feel like Jell-O when he was done. But he needed it. He needed to feel the physical exhaustion to help distract him from the ache he felt when he thought of Gillian. When he thought of taking that terrifying step and making her see that they could be together, the ache intensified. He knew it was a risk, but like Eddie said, it was time to take a chance or put out that torch.

Quickly modifying the plans he had spent last night coming up with in his attempt to making his intentions with Gillian known, he pushed through five miles and made it home before ten o'clock. Now he just had to find something to occupy his time for the rest of the day so he didn't go crazy. After a quick call to his son to say good morning, he decided to head over to his brother's to see what he was up to.

~*~*~*~*~*~*~*~*~*~

After Gillian spent the morning being waxed, buffed, and polished at the spa, she and Allie had lunch at the mall before hitting the stores to buy what Allie insisted was the perfect outfit. This was followed up with a root job, insisted upon by a more than determined Allie. Since Gillian loved the personal treatment she got from having a best friend who happened to be a beautician, she gave in.

Now, here she stood, in front of her mirror, staring at herself, trying to come to terms with the fact that she was about to go on a date with a man—a man that was not her husband—that she really didn't know. It was slightly surreal and a bit overwhelming to realize where she was in her life. A separated, soon-to-be divorced, thirty-something year old going out on her first *first* date in roughly eighteen years.

The chain of her necklace felt tight as she fought the panic that started to rise in her system as her mind started to play the reel of *what-ifs* through her head. *What if he doesn't like me? What if he only wants to get in my pants? What if I don't like him? What if, what if, what if.* She closed her eyes and tried to take in a deep, calming breath. This was just the next step in moving forward. She knew this was the natural evolution of her personal life. She wasn't someone who needed to be with someone, but it was very nice to have someone. *Calming breath my ass ... I need a drink!*

Just as she was about to turn and head out of her room to find one, Allie walked in. "Knock it off, Gillian. There is no reason why you shouldn't relax and have a good night out. You look fabulous ... thanks to me." The modest person that Allie was took a bow as she accepted her own compliment before continuing, "So stop doing that internal freak-out thing you do. I can see it in your eyes. Why are you panicking?"

Trying to force her voice out past her tight throat, Gillian managed to squeak out, "I don't think I can do this, Allie."

"Of course you can, so stop worrying about it. You said that you were able to flirt with this guy, so there has to be chemistry there." Gillian smiled a little as she recalled how she did enjoy flirting with Mike last night.

"I stalked him on Facebook and he appears to be an upstanding citizen." Allie paused and came up to Gillian, turned her to face the mirror and wrapped her arms around her from behind. Then she made eye contact with her in the mirror. "But most importantly, it's time to move on and be happy. You deserve to have someone who will treat you the way you should've been treated all along." As Gillian began to speak up and repeat the same defense for Logan she had already done with Allie countless times, she was cut off.

154

"Yeah, yeah I know, it was the only mistake he made in your marriage. He was always good to you other than that … blah, blah, blah. You may have forgiven him Gillian, but that doesn't mean I have. He's my big brother, and I hold him to a higher standard than others. He wronged my best friend in a way that he never should have. So you can keep your defense for Logan stashed away for someone else."

When she was sure that Allie had finished her little tirade, Gillian smiled at her. "You know you're more than my best friend. You're my sister … I love that you always have my back and would kick anyone's ass for me if I asked." She turned around and hugged her friend. "And I love that you knew just what I needed at that moment. Thanks Al, I am glad you came down for me today. I probably would've just cancelled it."

"And *that* is the exact reason I kept you busy all day. Here, stand back; I want a picture of you and all your hotness. You're totally a MILF."

Gillian laughed out loud at that comment. "Yeah right," she said while watching Allie once again tap out a message on her phone to someone.

"What, you don't believe me? I'd totally do you." That comment brought more of Gillian's laughter out, making her realize that Allie had worked her magic. She was more relaxed and was feeling like she could do this … and then the doorbell rang.

Allie smiled big, and in a slightly mischievous manner, before smacking Gillian on the ass. "Let's get this party started, shall we?" She tugged Gillian toward the front door where her "moving on" was waiting for her.

CHAPTER TWELVE

After finding every possible thing to do to kill time today, it was finally time for Jake to make his way over to Gillian's. Even though he knew Allie was there, too, and they wouldn't be alone, he just had this innate pull to be closer to her right now. It was almost like something was telling him to get over to her. *Very weird*. He was freshly showered and got dressed as quickly as he could. As he pulled a shirt over his head, he heard his phone chime in the bathroom where he had left it. Heading that way to finish doing his hair and other grooming, he saw he had a text from Allie.

Once again, he was slightly bummed it wasn't Gillian; he pressed the button to access the message. When he spoke to Gillian earlier today, she had said that they had 'done all the wonderfully female things that women liked to torture themselves with.' Jake could only imagine what that meant. Some could be good and some could be *very* good … but he wasn't gonna go there right now. Trying to maintain control of the southbound blood flow, he refocused on the message from Allie, instead of what Gillian could have had done at the spa today. A picture popped up on his screen and he felt his heart pick up its pace. On his phone was a picture of Gillian, completely done up to go out for the night. She was beautiful in a simple dress, which left her shoulders exposed, showed off her cleavage, and stopped a few inches above her knees. Her long brown hair flowed in waves over one of her shoulders, and she had a flower or clip just above her ear on the opposite side.

The shy smile on her face told him that she was not so sure about something, and it made him smile when he realized exactly how well he knew her facial expressions. And then he focused in on the boots she was wearing and how they accentuated her toned legs. Her perfectly toned legs, which he wanted to run his hands over. Her perfectly toned legs that he wanted to have wrapped around his waist. Her perfectly toned legs that he wanted to be buried deep between … *So much for maintaining control of the southbound blood flow.*

He needed to get to her. The purely predatory sensations that came over him lately when he thought about Gillian were becoming slightly uncontrollable. Saving the picture to his phone, he shot a text to Allie letting her know he was on his way as he rushed to grab his keys and hop in his jeep.

It only took him five minutes to get there, but it felt like longer. At least he had gained control of his body in that timeframe. He knew he couldn't step out of the jeep in front of Allie without her making some smartass comment about what he might be "packing," so he was damn grateful to have gotten himself under control. He could feel his pulse quicken again, and his physical excitement started to jump as he gained sight of his destination. The sight of an unfamiliar truck in the driveway made it falter a bit. But it damn near stopped completely at the vision of Gillian in the driveway … with some man … being helped up into the unfamiliar truck. Once she was inside the truck, she turned and smiled down at the man and all the air left Jake's body. *What the hell is going on? That smile is supposed to be for me!*

Jake swung his jeep into the opposite part of the semi-circular driveway and slammed it into park as the truck began to pull out of the driveway. Feeling everything begin to slip away as he watched it slowly back out, he started to panic. He threw his door open and jumped out. Feeling an eerie sense of déjà vu come over him as he recalled the last time he watched her climb into a car and drive away from him, his heart stuttered in his chest. Not knowing what to do, he momentarily thought to run toward the truck, to stop it. Then he realized how crazy or desperate that might look, gave that thought pause, and ultimately decided he really didn't care how crazy it made him look. Gillian was not going to slip through his hands again. He made that mistake once, and it cost him eighteen years. He was about to take off in the direction of the road when he felt a hand curl around his arm and form a firm grip around his tense muscles.

"Hold off Jake, don't do it," Allie said to him in a calm voice. But before he could turn and say anything or pull out of Allie's grip, he saw Gillian turn and look at him from the truck. She had a small look of surprise when she saw him, and then she gave him one of those smiles he loved so much. It was almost like that smile was all his. She gave him a small wave and he was paralyzed in place. He couldn't move, he couldn't smile, he couldn't even wave back as he watched the truck start to accelerate and make its way down the street—taking her away from him. His knees threatened to buckle and toss him on the ground. A small recollection of Logan in that position in this very driveway two months ago flashed through his head. He remembered what it felt like that first time he watched her drive away, but this felt worse. His head began to spin; his stomach felt sour and his chest physically hurt from the emotions that were swirling around in his body. *I have to stop her … I have to go after her!*

He shook off Allie's hand, which still gripped his arm and turned to jump back in his jeep, but fumbled with his keys. Dropping them from his shaky hands, he cursed as he bent down to pick them up when another hand snaked out in front of him and grabbed them. Momentarily surprised, he followed the hand with his in an attempt to snatch them back, but failed as Allie swiftly moved away from him. *He didn't have time for this—she was getting away.*

"What the hell are you doing, Allie?" Jake barked at her, not caring that he sounded like an asshole. His level of panic was starting to spike higher with every passing second that Gillian got farther away from him.

"Don't do it, Jake," she said again in a firm, but calm, voice. "You can't go after her. It will mess everything up."

Mess everything up? "I don't have time for this Allie. Give me my damn keys … now!"

Raising her voice, Allie implored, "Why Jake?"

"I have to stop her. I can't let her go this time." He knew he was mumbling as his fog of desperation started to choke him, but all he could think of was how he needed to get his keys and get to Gillian. "Not again."

His determination to get those keys from his friend faltered when she dodged his attempt once again and then slipped his keys inside her shirt. Taken aback by this maneuver, he stopped and just stared at her. "No Jake," she said again as she took another step back. Still holding his keys hostage. Still preventing him from getting to Gillian.

160

"Why do you have to go after her?" Allie asked him calmly. He just stood there staring at her, trying to figure out his next move. Knowing that if Gillian were here, she would just reach into Allie's shirt and grab his keys, but Allie knew Jake would never do that, so it was a great move on her part. But desperate times called for desperate measures. He was actually considering going in after them, but Allie must have figured that out from the look on his face because she put her hand out in front of her.

"If you so much as think of going anywhere near my bra, Jake Michaels, I will totally take your ass down!"

Considering that he was actually contemplating crossing an inappropriate line and doing just that, he immediately stepped back, away from his friend. *God, what the hell is wrong with me?* He jammed his hands into his hair and gave a tight squeeze of the strands between his fingers. The slight bit of pain helped calm him a little as he let out an anguished growl into the night air. He started to pace the small space in front of his jeep. Staying clear of his pacing, Allie made her way to the front of the jeep and perched herself on the bumper, watching him as he paced like a caged animal.

He fought the agitation he had at her for stopping him. He cursed the fact that history was repeating itself. Just the thought of that deflated his anger and allowed the other conflicting emotions of fear, desperation, and severe need to surface. He had no idea what to do. The fear of not getting a chance to let Gillian know how he felt again was becoming a suffocating feeling that threatened to take him down. He stopped his pacing, bent over and placed his hands on his knees for support as he began to feel the dizziness associated with hyperventilating. *I'm really losing it.*

"Relax, it's only a date, she'll be back before you know it ... it's not forever this time," Allie said to him in a comforting tone, extending her hand and placing it on his back, as he tried to slow down his breathing. The tingling of his lips started to dissipate, and he looked over at her.

A flash of embarrassment for behaving like this passed through him, but then he disregarded it when he processed what she said, "What?" he asked.

"I said that it's only a date. It's not forever this time," Allie replied with a knowing smile.

"How do you know that? And why didn't I know that she was ready to date?" he asked in an irritated tone that was completely ignored.

"First of all, I know everything, so don't question me. Secondly, she didn't even know she was ready to date 'til this guy asked her, so don't act like you have been kept in the dark or something."

"I thought I was coming over here to have dinner with the two of you?" he asked in a suspicious tone.

Again, with a knowing smile, she said, "No, my text said, meet at Gillian's for dinner ... I didn't say she was joining us."

Jake felt like he had been played. But being played would have implied that Allie knew what Jake's intentions were, and there was no way that she could have known anything. Then he remembered how Eddie seemed to be able to see right through him, which made him realize that if anyone else could see it, it would be Allie. Not surprised at the fact that she must know and suddenly curious at what her game was, he asked, "Why did you send me a picture of Gillian all dressed up to go out on a date with another man?"

Allie just shrugged and said, "Because I wanted you to see that she was ready to date. Try and shock you into figuring out that it was finally time for you to make your move."

Irritated, Jake stood to his full height and looked down at his tiny friend. "So let me get this straight, instead of telling me Gillian was ready to date … you thought it would be a good thing to send me a picture of how she was dressed up for another man?"

Allie stood toe-to-toe with Jake, smiled up at him, and said, "Well I knew she was ready to date, I just hadn't realized that *you* were ready to date, Jake."

"What the hell does that mean? I date … why wouldn't I be ready to date," he barked incredulously.

"It means, that I know you are capable of dating … I just didn't know if you were ready to date Gillian," she said as she stepped back, crossed her arms, and glared at him. "Why didn't *you* tell *me* that you were ready to date Gillian?"

Once again momentarily surprised by her turning the tables on him, he recovered quickly and asked, "How long have you known that I have feelings for Gillian, Allie?"

She smiled and said, "Well I knew you kind of had a thing for her in high school … but the night that she left Logan, I saw it in your eyes. I could see the way you were looking at her, and how you looked like you would do anything to take her pain away."

"I would do anything to take your pain away, too, Allie, but it doesn't mean that I have those kind of feelings for you. So how would you know that I felt that way about Gillian?"

She thought over his response and nodded as she replied, "True, but you never have that kind of lust in your eyes when you look at anyone else. I don't even recall you having that look in your eyes for your ex-wife."

Knowing there was no use denying what Allie was so sure she knew, he agreed, "That's because I have never had these *kind* of feelings for any other woman before." His admission left him feeling suddenly deflated and once again weak. He turned and sat next to Allie on the bumper of his jeep.

"If you know how I feel for her ..." he paused and looked at her, before continuing, "... then why did you let her leave with another guy?"

Allie once again shrugged. "Like I said, I didn't know you were ready ... and I didn't know what you were waiting for. I figured this was the perfect opportunity to shock you into action."

Jake just shook his head and looked away from her. She certainly provided a shock to his system, and he wasn't sure he liked the way she went about it. In fact, it was starting to piss him off the more he thought about it. Running his hands roughly through his hair once again, he let his anger and frustration take the forefront of the emotions he was experiencing. He stood abruptly and took several steps away from Allie. His anger was suddenly becoming a living, pulsating creature inside of him, demanding to be set free. He turned toward Allie and couldn't stop it from flying out.

"Well, I'm shocked, Allie! Is this what you wanted? To make me feel like complete shit! To be standing here, raging at you because I just had to witness the one woman who I have always wanted, drive off with another man … AGAIN!" He finished off his statement by turning his body to the side and driving his fist into the stucco wall of Gillian's house. The instant result of pain and numbness helped calm him down as he felt it spread from his knuckles up through his wrist and forearm. The throbbing would follow shortly, but he would welcome the distraction.

He turned to face his friend; fist still clenched, he just stared at her. Allie was clearly a little startled by Jake's actions. He had never yelled at her, and it had been a long time since anyone had seen him lose his temper like this. It bothered him that she was seeing it now, but he felt like a cornered bear, and he needed to get the hell out of there.

"Well congratulations …" Sarcasm heavy in his words, he continued, "… I am very aware of how it feels to let her slip through my fingers. So thanks for letting me experience it again! But now that she has gotten completely away from me, would you mind handing over my keys so I can go home and drown my sorrows … AGAIN!"

"You can't go, everyone is coming over … you know, like how we used to do in high school." She spoke with a slightly timid voice, which only made him feel like more of an ass, because although Allie was small in size, she made up for it in confidence and strength. "Why didn't you tell me you were ready?"

"I only figured it out last night, Al. I hadn't had a chance to tell you since you were with her all day—a day I had planned to try and get close to her and see if I could take it to the next level. Then you came and derailed it for me ..."

Clearly his brain was foggy since it took him a few seconds to catch up to what she was saying. ... *how we used to do in high school? Oh no, she couldn't mean what I think she means?* He shook his head at her when he realized what she was saying. Looking at her he asked, "No, Allie, you didn't?"

She quickly jumped up to defend her actions. "Of course I did! Gillian was the only one of us girls that didn't have to deal with this torture. I have wanted to do this to her forever!" Jake shook his head at the enthusiasm in her voice. He was thankful that she had recovered from his tirade already, but he was not about to endure what Allie had planned for the evening. He was agitated, irritated, annoyed, and a little heartbroken at the moment, which all combined to make for one wrung-out-guy-who-didn't-get-the-girl.

"I have to get out of here, Allie ... I can't do this. Give me my keys, or I'm just going to walk home." When Allie shook her head no, Jake took in a deep breath and let it out before saying, "Goodnight Allie." As he turned to walk away, she called out to him, but he didn't stop. He was not in the mood for pretending he didn't care anymore.

CHAPTER THIRTEEN

As Mike made the turn onto her street, the butterflies in her stomach that had been dormant for the latter part of the evening took flight. And boy-oh-boy did they make themselves known. *Don't puke. Don't puke. Good God, whatever you do—do not puke!* While chanting this mantra in her head, she hoped her nervousness didn't show on her face. She needed a distraction. *Oh, yeah right ... what could possibly provide a distraction?*

Mike let go of her hand that he had been holding for the drive home and reached to turn off the radio, which was on low, no more than background noise. She felt comfortable sitting without talking, which was a good sign, but didn't change the fact that she hadn't been on a first date in almost two full decades. Or the fact that she was sixteen at the time, and those dates were a little bit different than the full grown up date she just went on.

What was expected? Was she supposed to wait for him to open her door? Well, yes, she thought, because he had gotten her door at every stop during their evening, and he helped her climb out of the truck because it was so high, and she was in boots. That thought made her smile. He was certainly a gentleman, and he definitely did everything right so far.

They had had a great evening together. As far as first dates go, it was more than she would have expected. He had made reservations at a quaint French Bistro in the Hillcrest area of San Diego, which had a nice atmosphere, and her pork tenderloins were fantastic. The little fat girl inside her was ecstatic when they went to Extraordinary Desserts afterward. They then wrapped up the evening with a stroll over the bridge that led to Balboa Park. All in all, the company was great, the food divine, and the scenery was simple and perfect. She decided that if he asked to see her again, it was definitely a yes. Yes ... he was definitely worth getting to know.

But it wasn't until about five minutes ago when they got off the freeway that her nerves started to get the best of her as to what would happen next. *Oh God, was he expecting to come in? Should I invite him in? Would that imply that more was being offered than just a drink or conversation? Oh gosh, why didn't I do more research on this?* Those damn butterflies were multiplying and appeared to be dive-bombing in her stomach now, getting everything all churned up. *Ugh!*

She broke the silence when she suddenly thought of something. "Keys! Oh no, I hope I have my keys ... I am terrible at remembering them when I'm not the person driving." She dove into her purse with a vengeance, thankful for the distraction. If she didn't have her keys, he would have to leave her on her doorstep while she waited for someone to come with a spare, and then he couldn't come in. That was good ... it took that possibility off the table. She wasn't sure if that was a relief or a disappointment. But being the gentleman that he was, he most likely wouldn't just leave her sitting on her porch. Oh, she hoped her keys were just evading her in this bottomless pit of a purse.

She thought maybe Jonathan had come home tonight since he wasn't really speaking to Logan. But no, they had talked with him about staying with Logan whether he liked it or not because it helped provide a good front for Dylan with regards to the divorce;

168

even though Dylan seemed to be the only one of the three kids that was unaffected by it. Gillian just wished she could get Jonathan to talk to her … she knew that he would come around— she just had to be patient. *Wow, that was a second distraction.* Guess they weren't in as short a supply as she thought.

Mike smiled over at her, gave a small chuckle and brought her back to the moment. "Well that would make sense, but I don't think you have to worry about that. It looks like there might be a party going on at your place."

"What?" She looked up from her diligent digging in her purse, which she really needed to clean out by the way, certain that Mike was looking at the wrong house and didn't know what he was talking about. She quickly realized that he was right. *Oh no … they didn't! Of course they did!* Just great—this was more than a distraction—this was a clusterfuck!

Her driveway was full of trucks—at least eight—of varying sizes filled her driveway. With a quick glance on the street as they passed, she guessed there was at least six more vehicles that she recognized parked there, too. Looks like they called everyone for the event. *Oh, Allie is so gonna pay for this one.*

"Is it okay if I park in front of the driveway, blocking it? There doesn't appear to be anywhere else for me to park," Mike said, interrupting her thoughts of how exactly Allie was going to pay for it.

"Yes, of course," she answered quickly, and he started to maneuver the truck around to be parked. She looked at the house to see it was fully lit up with the lights on in the backyard and everything ... they were probably out in the game room just waiting for her to bring her date in.

Mike finished parking his truck, pulled the keys from the ignition and turned to get out of the truck. But Gillian wasn't ready yet, so she reached over and grabbed his arm, keeping him in his seat. "Mike wait ... not yet." He looked over at her, and then closed his door, the light in the cab slowly dimming 'til it turned off. He scooted a bit across the bench seat toward her and reached for her hand.

"Is everything okay, Gillian?" he asked as he took her hand in his.

She smiled at him as she turned her hand around in his palm so she could give it a gentle squeeze in return. He was just so sweet. She didn't want her friends to scare him off yet ... and that was exactly what they were trying to do. Well maybe not scare him off exactly, but it was certainly a test of theirs. She had forgotten all about said test and didn't expect to ever have to subject anyone to it. Well, nobody except dates her daughter brought home.

All the guys had given Maddie a heads up that they would be doing this to her when she had her first date. At the time, Gillian thought it was funny and was looking forward to subjecting her daughter to such an event, especially since she could point the finger of blame toward Logan, Sean, and all the rest of the guys. That's what she gets for laughing at her daughter's expense; this was certainly a dose of karma if ever there was one. Gillian took a deep breath and gave Mike's hand another squeeze ... hopefully he would be able to handle this crew of misfits she loved so much.

With a small smile she said, "I had a great time tonight. I'm so glad you asked me out."

"I'm happy to hear that, and hopefully it means we can see each other again. I really enjoyed your company, too," he said as he reached his other hand up and gently moved a strand of hair from her forehead. It was a tender and intimate gesture that made her pulse increase and her skin tingle. *How cool was that?*

She let out a deep breath and sighed.

"Well, I hope you still feel that way in about five minutes."

He raised an eyebrow and one side of his lips curved up in a smirk as he leaned a little closer and said, "And what's going to happen in the next five minutes that would change my mind? Are you really a man or something? 'Cause honestly, Gillian, that is about the only thing it would take to change my mind."

That made her laugh. "No, I can say with complete confidence that I only possess girly parts." He unleashed a full blown smile on her as he reached his hand back up to her face and caressed her cheek as he moved it into her hair at the back of her head ... and leaned in ...

"That is very good to hear, Gillian," he whispered against her lips, just before he pressed his lips against hers. He stayed there for a few seconds and then slowly pulled away from her, but he didn't go far. Oh, he smelled good ... a slight bit of cologne or maybe his soap. But it was all man and completely yum.

She opened her eyes and met his stare directly. She felt that tingly sensation erupt all over at the thought of more contact like that. Whatever he was looking for in her stare, he must have found.

"*Very* good to hear," he repeated and emphasized *very*, just before he pulled her closer and slanted his lips over hers for a deeper kiss.

She felt his tongue slowly make contact with her lips, seeking entrance. She placed her hand on his chest, felt the hardness of his body as she surrendered to him. Her lips parted on a sigh allowing him entrance, and she felt his tongue slip into her mouth. Her surrender didn't go unnoticed by him, if the groan she felt rumble in his chest and the simultaneous tightening of his grip meant anything.

His taste burst into her mouth. The sweetness of the chocolate dessert they shared earlier still present, coupled with another one that could only be described as all man. Definitely a good flavor … what woman wouldn't like a chocolate flavored man?

He let go of her hand and slid his arm around her waist, pulling her the rest of the way across the bench and tighter against him as he continued to kiss her.

Her breasts were now pressed up against his chest, and the sensation made her sigh again. He felt so good against her. It felt so nice to be touched by a man, to feel like a desired woman again. She felt the unwanted sorrow of what that meant creep into her mind, but shut the door on that quickly. There was no room in the cab of this truck for those kinds of emotions. She had moved on. Her inner confidence was empowering and invigorating.

Fully into the kiss now, she slowly slid her tongue against his and took her now free hand and brought it up to his jaw, feeling the slight roughness from the end of day stubble all men had. It was very sexy. She then slid it around his neck and up into the hair at the back of his head, dying to know what his hair felt like.

Running her hands through it—it was so soft and thick, just like she thought it would be. "Mmmmmm," she moaned into his mouth. Was that her? Maybe it was the high of being a first kiss, but wow! She was beginning to feel dizzy, even a little drunk, as he continued his gentle, yet commanding, assault on her mouth. He was literally making her breathless. They needed to come up for air.

As if he heard her thoughts, or maybe he was feeling low on oxygen as well, he slowly pulled away. Gently pressing one more soft kiss to her lips, he leaned his forehead to hers while they both waited for their breathing to return to normal. She slowly opened her eyes and let them focus on his as she pulled back to see his face, and smiled at him. The look of lust in his eyes was unmistakable and completely arousing.

"Thank God for having girly parts 'cause I wouldn't have wanted to miss a kiss like that." He chuckled at her comment.

"I think I'm going to avoid commenting on your girly parts for this evening. It would be ungentlemanly of me to do so." That earned a laugh from her. "Now, do you want to tell me what might change my mind about wanting to see you again?"

She had completely forgotten that she was sitting in a truck, parked in front of her driveway, while making out with her date … just like a teenager. Gillian couldn't contain her giggle at that thought. All she needed now was her father to flash the front porch light, signaling his awareness of her in the driveway. Or better yet, to glance at the front window and see the curtains drop back down to hide whoever was spying. Then she would really feel like a teenager.

Reflexively, she glanced over to the front of her house and saw her brother standing in the front window. Not secretly spying, no he was openly watching, showing them he had no qualms about being seen. Sean was standing tall with a scowl on his face and a beer in his hand. He was obviously trying to be intimidating. Well, at least he wasn't wearing his police uniform, the stupid bully. *Gotta love big brothers.* And next to him was Allie, the one most likely responsible for this, with a big shit-eating grin on her face. *Oh yeah, she was guilty as hell.*

She turned back to Mike. "Okay, so what I was referring to was all these trucks in my driveway. Apparently, my best friend has decided that we are still in high school and felt it necessary to call the whole gang over to check out my date for the night." She gave him a weak smile, hoping he wouldn't run for the hills. "This was something they did in high school to us girls … all the big brothers and their friends would make sure they were at the house when our dates brought us home. Whether or not the new guy was allowed to take us out again was based on how he handled this group of guys. It's not to say us girls listened to our brothers if they told us we couldn't date the guy, but they sure made it difficult for any guy they didn't approve of."

Mike glanced at the house and smirked, "So this is a test I take it ... to see if I am worthy to date you?"

She bit her lower lip and nodded at him, and he laughed out loud. Clearly, he had a sense of humor, which was certainly a point in his favor. He then moved closer to her, as if he was going to kiss her again, but leaned farther to whisper in her ear, "Do you want me to pass this test, Gillian?"

"Oh, yes, Mike, I do," she replied, breathless. "But, it's not my test ... you've already aced mine." She gave him what she hoped was a sultry smile and waited for his response.

"How 'bout we get in there then and see if I can get straight As tonight. You wanna tell me who the big guy in the window is first, though?" She chuckled a little, knowing what he was seeing ... all six-foot three-inches of her brother. He probably looked even bigger standing next to Allie, who came in somewhere around five-foot five-inches—in high heels.

"That would be my brother, Sean; he's married and just recently had his third kid. If you want to win him over, you just need to say nice things about his kids; he turns into a marshmallow. I'm sure you can handle him, though ... if not, just win over his wife, Morgan, and he will have no choice but to like you."

Yep, that's right, her brother, the big alpha male, would do anything for his adorable wife. He truly was a softy. She turned to get out of the truck, and he stilled her. "Now what would people think if they saw you getting out of the truck without my assistance? Don't go sinking my ship before I even get out of the port, little lady."

"My apologies, sir." She smiled and watched as he turned to get out on his side, then made his way over to her door. He opened the door, and as she went to get out, he reached up and put his hands around her waist, pulled her into his body and eased her from the high truck, down to the ground. Gillian slid down his body as he lowered her. They stood there, her hands on his shoulders, and his still around her waist—bodies pressed firmly against each other.

"I know you're fully capable of climbing down, but I'm sure that drop to the ground in boots could be slightly painful after doing it more than once tonight."

"You have no idea, but it's totally worth it." Whoa, was that her voice? It sure sounded hoarse and raspy to her. She cleared her throat before continuing, "You ready for this?"

"Bring it on," he said as he let a big smile spread across his face. Did he seriously just quote a cheer movie? She laughed out loud at that.

"You better contain your movie quotes in there to movies that aren't about cheerleaders … or they will eat you alive."

"What? I have a teenage daughter. I had to make sure those movies were appropriate for her to watch. I was just trying to be a good dad."

"Sure you were, and I'm sure you read *Playboy* for the articles."

She looked over at him as she said this, and his smile got impossibly larger and exclaimed. "Exactly! You have no idea how refreshing it is to meet a woman who understands that."

Mike then reached out and held her hand, just as he had done earlier, as they walked to the door, laughing at how they were able to banter back and forth that way. It was relaxing, almost like they had been friends for a while.

"I have a feeling you will be able to hold your own in there just fine, Mr. Smart Ass." And with that, she opened the front door.

~*~*~*~*~*~*~*~*~

About thirty minutes later, after subjecting her first adult date to her group of friends, she quietly stood on her porch in front of Mike, a little unsure of what to do. They had kissed in the truck, and it was a great kiss, but now they sort of had an audience. She looked up at him and gave him a shy look to convey her uncertainty. Being a complete gentleman, he leaned down and gave her a soft kiss on the cheek before standing back up and smiling at her. "I would like to see you again, Gillian. Can I call you?"

"Yes," she blurted out a little too enthusiastically, which only made him chuckle at her again. Apparently her inability to control her reactions was becoming a habit around him. Taking a second to compose herself, she said, "Yes, Mike, I would like that."

Mike reached down and gripped her hand gently as he lifted it to his lips. Placing a sweet and simple kiss on her knuckles, he whispered, "'Til next time, Gillian … goodnight." And then she watched as he slowly pulled away from her and backed down the steps of her porch. She was admiring the view as he climbed into his truck when she caught sight of Jake's jeep parked in the middle of the chaos of trucks in her large driveway. Realizing that she hadn't seen Jake inside, she wondered where he could be. She made her way back inside and found her brother waiting for her, with a diaper bag over one shoulder and an adorable baby cradled in the other. Walking over to him to retrieve her niece, she smiled at the mass of contradictions that was her brother at that moment.

"You know you don't look as imposing with eight pounds of baby in your arms and a pink and brown diaper bag on your shoulder," she chided him while taking the baby and cradling her like the pro she was. Of course, the slight longing that most women have when holding a new baby was there. Even though she knew she was done having babies, she couldn't help but sometimes wish she wasn't.

"It's all part of my disguise. I can still kick some guy's ass with one arm 'cause they wouldn't be expecting it while I was holding a baby. Besides, who would hit a guy if he was holding a baby?" her brother retorted. Gillian just snorted at her brother and shook her head.

"Tell me I did not just hear you say you'd punch some guy while holding our baby girl in your arms?" Morgan huffed at her husband as she came into the room with all her spunk and ire. Gillian loved to watch her brother around his wife. The big man visibly melted when she came near him, almost like he didn't realize he missed her until he was near her again. Sean adored Morgan, and it was written all over his face. Gillian watched as her brother followed his wife's path as she walked into the room; it made her smile as she watched him melt in front of her eyes.

"You know I would never do that, my love."

Shaking her head, she put her arm around Gillian's shoulders, she replied, "Yeah, you're all talk, Sean Cooper." Then she turned to look at her new daughter before she let out a big sigh and said, "What have we done Gillian … bringing daughters into this world, so that they have to put up with these big gorillas."

Gillian laughed at that, because it was true. She never had to endure the torture of this ritual of theirs, where all the friends gathered at the girl's house the night of her first date with a new guy, and she was thankful for it. She made a mental note not to let anyone know the next time she went on another first date again. "'Til tonight, I hadn't realized how nerve wracking it would be to introduce a newcomer to this crew. But I think Mike handled himself well … what do you think big brother?"

Sean just smiled at his sister as he said, "I trust your judgment Sis; I just want you to be happy." And with that she nodded her thanks, leaned down to kiss the beautiful bundle in her arms and then handed her back over to the big gorilla.

Morgan leaned in and kissed Gillian on the cheek and said, "I liked him. He seemed like he could fit in with this group."

"Thanks for coming over guys. I'm going to find Allie and give her crap for doing this to me. And here I thought she only came down to help me with the fun stuff like getting ready, when she obviously only came down for the torture." She hugged her brother and sister-in-law and made her way to the back of the house where she would find the guilty party planner.

As she walked into the poolroom, she noticed Allie and Jason talking in low tones off to one corner of the room, and a few other friends playing pool and just hanging out. "All right everyone, give me a show of hands … who got the order to be here tonight from Allie?" she questioned the room. Everyone's hand went in the air with the exception of Allie's. It was just as she had thought.

"You know you could've just asked me, and I would have taken full credit for it!" Allie yelled from across the room where she was still standing with Jason.

"Oh, I have no doubt that you would've. I just wanted to see that I wasn't the only one who gets bossed around by you," Gillian said with a smirk as she headed into the group of people to say goodnight, since the events of the evening were over. She was sure that a few of them had been here a while based on the empty pizza boxes piled up on the bar. "And just so you know, you're the one that's going to clean up the mess around here. Your gathering … your mess."

Allie walked away from Jason to start her clean up, and Gillian laughed as she saw her order a few of the guys to take stuff to the trash and pick up. They, of course, jumped at the order. She wasn't sure if it was because they were being gentlemanly, if it was because a few of them worked with Jason and Logan and didn't want to be seen *not* doing it, or because Allie was tiny, but fierce, and it was likely a few of them had crushes on her. Either way, Gillian didn't care; she just didn't want to be the one doing it.

She watched as Jason grabbed himself another beer and sat down on a stool to watch, throwing a few irritated glances at Allie in the process. Looking at Jason reminded her that Jake was missing. It kind of bummed her out that he wasn't here, and she wanted to know why, especially since his jeep was. A sudden thought that he might be sick had her worried. Making her way across the room to Jason, she leaned in and kissed him on the cheek before perching herself on the stool next to him.

"Hey handsome, where is the other Mr. Michaels? I see his car is in my driveway ... but I don't see him." She gave him a questioning look as she waited for an answer. She caught that he glanced over at Allie before he looked back at her. Gillian turned and looked in time to see Allie glare back at Jason. Gillian wasn't really sure what was going on, but was really curious now, and pressed Jason more. "Out with it, Jason, or I tell Allie over there that you told me everything."

He just huffed and shook his head, obviously irritated. "He and Allie didn't see eye to eye on something, so he left."

He finished his statement by lifting his beer bottle toward his lips, but Gillian put her hand up and stopped him as she asked, "Without his jeep? Is he okay?" Jason's shoulders, which had been bunched up with tension a few seconds ago, relaxed a bit, and his features softened as he gave her that big brother look.

"I'm sure he's fine Gilly; just give him some time to cool off, and you can call him tomorrow." Jason finished his beer and stood to leave, but not before looking down at Gillian with a pleading look and saying, "Please ... make sure you call him tomorrow."

A bit surprised by Jason's insistence, she nodded. "Of course, I would check on him right now if you hadn't just said to let him cool down." Accepting her at her word, he nodded and made his way out, taking a few of the guys with him along the way.

After saying good night to everyone else and taking one last look outside at Jake's jeep sitting in the driveway, she couldn't help but be a little concerned about whatever had happened between Allie and him tonight. She knew it took a lot to get him mad, but she also knew if anyone could push a person's buttons, it'd be Allie. Letting out a big sigh of exhaustion as her body started to come down off the rollercoaster of emotions she had been feeling all day long, she couldn't think of anywhere she'd rather be than tucked under her blankets for the night.

As she went about her nightly routine, she thought about what Jason had said. Even though he felt she should give Jake some space—for whatever reason—Gillian wanted Jake to know she was thinking of him. So, as she climbed into bed, she decided to send him a text. Picking up her phone from its place on her nightstand, she ignored the text from a number she didn't recognize and sent a quick one to Jake.

> Gillian: I missed you tonight, call me when you get up and I will get your jeep over to you...

She waited for a few minutes, hoping for a response from him, which would let her know he was okay, but nothing came. A slight bit of uneasiness came over her as she lay down and tried to relax. Sleep eluded her for a little while, all thoughts of her date had fled and only Jake remained on her mind. Finally, though, her body succumbed to the exhaustion.

CHAPTER FOURTEEN

Thud … thud … thud … Jake couldn't figure out who was pounding on his head. He tried to open his eyes and see, but the sharp, stabbing sensation that hit his poor eyeballs was too much to handle. Slamming his lids shut, he turned his head to the side in hopes of getting away from the source, but that only made his stomach pitch and roll. He broke out in a sweat and attempted to keep the need to vomit under control. Lying there, with his eyes closed, he took slow, steady breaths—in the nose and out the mouth. The less movement he made, the better he felt. He really did a number on himself last night. *Good ol' Jack Daniels … Ugh! Just throw up and get it over with, you'd feel better.*

"You're right … you would feel better once you throw up and get it over with."

Okay, so maybe I'm still a little drunk since I seem to be answering myself now. This time, though, the voice didn't respond to a comment, it gave instructions.

"There's a trash can next to your bed, and a sports drink and pain killers on the nightstand. Are you going to be able to get yourself up and in the shower, or are you going to need help?"

Great, the voice in my head was Gillian's … well isn't that just a kick in the balls? He attempted to roll toward the side of the bed again.

"Why the hell would my voice, in your head, be like a kick in the balls, Jake Michaels?"

What the ...

His eyes shot open and landed straight on the woman who possessed the voice, and who happened to look amused at his state of distress. His stomach did a complete nosedive before leaping into his throat. Of course, the mother and nurse in her recognized the signs, grabbed him by the nape of his neck and pushed him toward the trashcan she had lovingly placed next to his bed. As he emptied the contents of his stomach, it took him a split second of embarrassment to realize this was not how he wanted her to see him. But then, the convulsing of his stomach distracted him from everything else as he fought, once again, to gain some control.

Once the heaving started to calm down, a wet hand towel appeared in front of him and pressed against his face, and he felt the bed dip from the weight of someone gently sitting down. Fortunately, it didn't make his stomach revolt. He cautiously rolled to his back with the hand towel covering his face as his embarrassment set in. He groaned out loud at the thought that he just puked in front of the woman he wanted to be with.

"Now that your stomach is empty, take these and drink this. I'll be right back." He felt her hand place the pills in his, but he quickly grabbed on to it and gave it a squeeze.

"Thank you."

"You're welcome. I figured you would need them after Ryan told me you were sleeping in your clothes and shoes. Then I saw the half empty bottle on the counter." Jake pulled the towel half way down his face to look at her as he realized Gillian had just told him that his son witnessed him in this condition.

"Don't worry, I told him that you didn't feel very well last night so you must have fallen asleep with your shoes on. He didn't see the bottle, I put it away." She finished her sentence off with a smile, knowing exactly what he had been thinking. He settled back down, and she gave his hand another gentle squeeze before slowly standing up from the bed. As she leaned back down to remove the trashcan, Jake put his hand out to stay her.

"Oh dear God, please do not take that out ... this is already humiliating, I don't need to add you cleaning up after me to the list."

She just shook her head at him. "I seem to recall a really cool friend of mine holding my hair back a few months ago when I was puking. Was that you, or did I just repay the favor to the wrong guy? Because that would really suck. Besides, I do this for a living, and I'm a mom ... it means nothing to me."

But he truly thought that was totally different since she was only getting sick because she was so upset. She had managed to cry so much that she had made herself sick. All he did was hold her hair back and pick her back up off the floor when she was done. She had needed him. He was getting sick because he acted like an idiot and didn't handle something very well. Although he didn't agree that it was a favor she needed to pay him back for, he relented on the topic and just nodded his head at her.

She accepted his nod with one of her own, ending the conversation on that topic before she made her way toward the hall. Jake couldn't help but watch her as she walked. She turned and looked at him, gave him one of her smiles and said, "And when I get back, you can tell me what the hell happened to your hand." Then she walked out of the room, trashcan in hand.

His hand? At the mention of his hand he automatically flexed it, and the pain that shot through his knuckles gripped him. He lifted it up from where it had been holding the wet towel on his face and took a look at it. It was just as he had expected. There was some dried blood, a moderate amount of swelling and broken skin. Thankfully, though, he didn't think any bones were broken. He quickly popped the pain medication in his mouth before taking a cautious sip of the sports drink. When his stomach seemed to handle it well, he drank half the glass. His body was clearly dehydrated from his evening activities, which, unfortunately was not how he had planned to spend it.

He remembered the events from last night that led to him punching a wall in front of Allie, which was something he regretted doing, simply because he shouldn't have lost his temper like that. He tried to come up with a way to ask Gillian how her night went. He clearly needed to come up with a backup plan. Should he just tell her? Confess his love? He quickly decided that was a bad idea, especially in his current condition. It probably wasn't the best way to go about revealing things. He decided to get up and shower, to wash the night off of him, and maybe clear his head a bit. He slowly stood and assessed his ailments: headache... yes; stomach ache ... not so bad anymore; throbbing, swollen hand ... absolutely.

Shower and icing his hand were first and foremost on the to-do list, followed by something simple for breakfast. Gillian had brought Ryan home, and he wouldn't want his son to see him like this. That was unacceptable. He took a hesitant step toward his bathroom, fearing that his stomach might revolt again. Fortunately it didn't, so he pressed on and made it through his shower with minimal issues. Well, excluding his hand, because that made things a little difficult as far as washing his hair and everything else was concerned. Oh well, you usually pay hard when you make dumb ass decisions.

Coming out of the bathroom, he made his way over to the night table to finish off the sports drink and noticed his phone sitting there. There were a few notifications there when he opened the screen, but one that really jumped at him. There was a text from Gillian from last night telling him she was thinking about him. Once again, his heart picked up in pace a little at the giddy feeling that gave him. Even though she had just gone on a date with another guy, she was thinking of him. Hope bloomed inside him while he finished getting dressed so he could get his day started.

When he walked out of his bedroom, he could hear the sounds of Dylan, Ryan, and Gillian in the kitchen. It sounded like they were setting the table. Jake walked out to see all three of them doing just that while the boys debated over who was going to sit where. "Where do you want to sit, Aunt Gillian?" Ryan asked. Jake noticed that his son looked excited to have Gillian there. Of course, he saw her all the time, but on most occasions, it was Jake and Ryan going over to her place. It was rare that she was here to eat a meal; she always seemed to be feeding them.

"I can sit anywhere you want me to, buddy. You decide," Gillian replied as she busied herself, pulling some kind of takeout from a brown bag. She placed items on everybody's plates and turned to see Jake.

"Hey you, how are you feeling?" she asked him as she made her way toward the freezer where she reached in and grabbed an icepack for him. Motioning for him to sit down, he took his usual seat at the table and the boys took theirs, leaving the seat next to Jake available. He noticed that his son took the seat on the other side of Gillian, and he once again picked up on his enjoyment of having Gillian there. Other than Jake's mother, Gillian was the closest thing Ryan had to one. Although it made him a little sad to think his son may have been lacking something, he wouldn't have it any other way, considering his biological mother would never have paid him any attention. Once seated, Gillian reached over and grabbed Jake's injured hand and placed the icepack on top of it. He quickly winced from the tenderness and the cold as she expertly used an ace wrap to secure the pack in place, allowing him to still have some function of his hand.

"Serves you right. I'm pretty sure I know what you did to it, but what I don't know is why. And I expect the full story later," she said to him in a low tone with a pointed look.

A little embarrassed that he acted like a child, he just responded with a nod and said, "Thanks."

She smiled back at him and said, "I ran out while you were in the shower." Then she gestured to his plate. "I figured beans would be a bad idea this morning, but I got you the breakfast burrito and some rice instead." Then she handed him a stack of cups containing hot sauce, and he almost melted. He loved that she knew his preference of hangover food. He loved that she was taking care of him. He loved having her here in his house. He loved *her* ... bottom line. As he sat there and saw her interacting with the boys, treating them both the same, he knew that she loved Ryan as one of her own. It was perfect; they would be perfect together. He just needed to make her see it.

"Hey, you've got that faraway look in your eyes again... you okay?"

Jake snapped his attention back over to Gillian. The concern he saw on her face was heartwarming, and it only spurred him on. He was going to do this, and he was going to make this happen. The anticipation that overwhelmed him yesterday and then turned him into a crazy man when things fell apart was back. He reached over and gently laid his injured hand over hers, then gingerly wrapped his fingers around hers, as best as he could with the wrap on. He gave her hand a tiny reassuring squeeze before smiling at her and saying, "Couldn't be better."

When he probably should have let go and moved his hand back into his own personal space, he left it there. He hoped her perception of this move would be curiosity, and not awkward contact, as he glanced down at the sight of their hands. Aside from the bulging icepack and bandage, the sight of their joined hands thrilled him. He chanced a glance back up at her and found her watching him. Not being able to control his smile, he let her have it. The responding smile of hers was exactly what he had hoped for.

He kept his hand firmly in place, but he looked over at the boys. Ryan was looking at him inquisitively, and Dylan was busy stuffing his face. Jake gave his son a small nod to acknowledge he was aware he had questions, and that they would discuss it later. Ready to move on with the day, Jake asked, "So what's on the agenda today, boys?" He proceeded to take a big bite of his burrito.

Both boys, who apparently shared a brain, said in unison, "We want to go to the batting cages today." Jake and Gillian laughed at the boys. It was clear they had discussed this and planned a unified front to present to the adults.

Gillian spoke up first and said, "While I think that would a great thing to do today …" she motioned to Jake's hand for the boys to look at. "We have an injured player in our midst." She shrugged her shoulders in an "oh well" type gesture for the boys, but Jake knew he wanted to do it. He wanted to go to the batting cages with Gillian and the boys. What better way to start off his pursuit of her than in the same situation he first laid eyes on her … when she was swinging a bat? It was perfect.

"Nonsense, I don't recall getting placed on the disabled list. I'm not benched, Coach. A little tape, and I can do it just fine," he said with a smile before he continued to eat with one hand. Both boys erupted in victory cheers.

"Okay, tough guy, it's your hand. Batting cages, it is. We just need to stop by our house for Dylan's gear." She took her hand out from under Jake's and started to unwrap it. "All right boys, finish up your food, then you know the drill. Different house, same rules; I prepared, you clear." And with that, both boys jumped and got busy, knowing that if they didn't do what they were supposed to, their plans for the day would disappear.

190

As the boys made their way to the sink with the dishes from the table and began to load the dishwasher, Jake reveled in the domestic feeling this scenario gave him. Gillian continued to unwrap his hand and then cautiously removed the icepack. "It's okay … it's numb from the cold," he reassured her as she examined his hand.

She nodded and said, "That may be the case now, but it won't be in the batting cages in an hour. You sure you can do that? We can just promise to take them another time."

"No, I told Ryan we would do what he wanted today. And that is apparently what they both want to do."

"Okay, do you need help tying your shoes?" she asked with a smartass smile. Well, considering his humiliation of her seeing him vomit, help tying his shoes should be nothing. But he was still a guy and there was some serious pride involved. Then again, she would kind of be touching him, so he considered it, but realized he had to maintain some sense of dignity.

Letting out a small laugh, he said, "No thanks, I'm pretty sure you've done enough for me today. I'll be right back." He hurried to retrieve his shoes. His hangover was under control and practically forgotten at the thought of getting to spend the day with Gillian.

~*~*~*~*~*~*~*~*~

Gillian watched as Jake practically skipped down the hall toward his bedroom. Okay, maybe he didn't skip, but he sure looked giddy. Even though that was a little strange, she disregarded it, because that meant whatever he was upset with Allie about last night, must not be bothering him today. Well, the boys were excited, too, so it could just be the batting cages … the male species could be so weird. She laughed to herself as she stood and retrieved her purse and Jake's keys from where she left them. She went to check her phone for messages and send one to Allie letting her know Jake was fine, but when she reached into her purse and dug around, she couldn't find it. "I must have forgotten it at home," she mumbled to nobody in particular.

"Forgot what at home?" Jake asked, startling her a little.

"Where did you come from? I didn't even hear you come up."

He gave her a look that basically said, *duh*. "Apparently … What did you forget?"

"My cell phone must be at home. Help me remember to get it when we go there for Dylan's gear."

"Sure, I can do that." She handed Jake his keys and turned and called the boys. When she turned back around, Jake was much closer to her and once again startled her. She reflexively went to take a step back, but Jake halted her with a hand around her waist. He was very close, so she had to look up to see his face. The strong lines of his jaw, and the soft look of his lips, should be a contradiction, but they weren't. Jake was a very attractive man, and being this close to him was a new experience for her. Or maybe it was the feeling she got when she was this close to him. There was a feeling of anticipation and nervousness that had never been there before. And although foreign, she welcomed it.

Momentarily distracted by his soft lips—which she was staring at—he smiled at her and broke the spell. A little embarrassed for being caught staring at his lips, she could only imagine what she must have looked like doing that. It was almost like she didn't know how to act around him now. She realized it was because of those two moms at the football game. They had made her wonder about being with Jake … and now she was thinking about it. And she knew she shouldn't. Jake never gave her any indication that he wanted her … except now?

Since they were standing there in the front doorway of his house, a little too closely, she forced herself to look up into his eyes to see what he wanted. When her eyes met his, she felt herself now staring at those. *First the lips, now the eyes?* Mesmerizing. Jake was simply mesmerizing, and she couldn't help the fact that for some reason she was now seeing him in a different light. He cleared his throat, and she blinked a few times to focus again.

"I wanted to say thank you again. Not just for taking care of me this morning, but for looking out for Ryan. I love that you know me well enough to know that I wouldn't have wanted him to see me like that. I really appreciate that." She could smell the mint of his toothpaste—he must have just brushed his teeth. This reminded her that she just had a bunch of hot sauce and hadn't brushed hers.

Suddenly self-conscious, since he hadn't let her go, she brought her hand up to cover her mouth before speaking, "You're welcome. I always take care of the people that are important to me."

"You do more than most people, Gillian, and I am lucky to have you in my life," he said before he leaned in and placed his lips against her forehead. He kept them there for a few moments longer than a simple friendly gesture. No, this one was different, and not just for him. It felt different for her, too. She closed her eyes and felt her body sway toward his, seeking a little more contact than what they had. She felt his hand apply a bit more pressure on her waist as he confirmed with this gesture that he liked that she had done that. He wanted her body pressed against his. His lips lingered and remained pressed to her forehead a moment or two longer before he took in a deep breath just as he pulled them away.

Her hand that had been covering her mouth had moved its way to his chest. Their bodies were still pressed against each other, and she glanced up to see him looking down at her. She knew that she should move away, but he wasn't doing so either, which must have meant that he wanted to be pressed up against her. Once again making eye contact with him, something passed between them that she didn't recognize, but it was there nonetheless. She thought she felt his body tighten against hers as he began to lower his head again, but this time it was aiming for her lips. She started to close her eyes as she prepared for what was about to happen, when they were both startled by the boys running into the room.

When she pulled away from him this time, he let her. But he reached out and took her hand and squeezed it while positioning it out of view from the boys. She wasn't sure what he was trying to tell her with his eyes, but she knew that he felt something pass between them, too. She turned to face the boys as she tried to calm her racing heart. The feeling of almost getting caught by the boys, combined with the heady sensation of being pressed against

Jake's body was enough to make her a little breathless. Her voice sounded funny when she said, "You guys ready to go?"

They, of course, both looked at her because she sounded funny, so she cleared her throat. "What?" Jake helped by saying, "Batting order is decided by whoever gets to the car first." And just like that, they took off running out the door. She went to follow, but realized that Jake was still holding her hand. Turning her head back to look over her shoulder at him, he didn't let go of it—he just looked back at her.

"You coming, too? Or are you trying to cheat and prevent me from getting there before you?" she said in her cool, flirty voice she discovered the other night. This kind of surprised her since she hadn't intended it to come out that way, but it felt … okay.

Jake must have picked up on it because he used his grip on her hand to hold her in place as he moved in close to her again. He leaned down and placed another gentle kiss on her forehead, before whispering, "I would always put you before me, Gillian." When he pulled back and looked down at her, she could see the full meaning of the words he spoke. He wasn't talking about batting order anymore. A thrill of excitement tingled its way up her spine as she absorbed what he was saying. Or at least what she thought he was saying. She was fully aware of the fact that she could totally be seeing something that wasn't there … but for some reason, she really hoped it was. All she could do was give another little smile.

"We better get going."

"Yeah, we better," he agreed, and they both made their way out the door. Jake had to let go of her hand in order to lock his door, since his injured hand seemed to have a little trouble. She looked down at her now empty hand and didn't like how empty it felt. For about a second, she thought to wait for him and then hold his hand again, but figured that she might be out of line doing that, since she wasn't so sure what was going on. Instead, she made her way to the car.

As she climbed in, she asked, "So who made it first?"

"It was a tie! So we are going to have to get two cages … if we can," Dylan, the mastermind, said. She knew her son well enough to know that he came up with this approach so that both boys could bat at the same time. So either her son lost, or they wanted to bat at the same time to compete. Gillian was no fool, and her son knew it. Since Ryan wasn't speaking up, she knew it was true. Not that it mattered—getting two cages would only be a problem if the place was crowded; however, this was most likely the case since it was a Sunday morning.

"Odds on getting more than one cage on a Sunday are pretty slim boys. So how about the two of you quietly decide who gets to go first, and we will get the cage for an extended time."

Both boys slumped a little in their seats as they said, "Okay." She just smiled as she turned and put her seatbelt on.

Jake climbed into the driver's seat and it occurred to her that he might not be able to drive. "Can you drive okay?"

"I'm pretty sure I can. I'll just use the heel of my hand to push the shifter, but if I need help, you can do it." He looked over at her

196

and gave her a flirty smile. She had never been on the receiving end of that smile before, and it made her body tingle again. Jake started the car, and they were on their way. She was shocked at the fact that, for the second time in a twenty-four hour period, she was pressed up against a man and getting tingly all over because of the attention. Thinking that she was seriously out of control and must be horny or something, she tried to focus on other things. Things like trying to show a little self-control before she started to rub up against random strangers, simply because they said hello.

After a quick stop at her house to grab Dylan's stuff, and her cell phone, they arrived at the batting cages in no time. She loved going there with the kids and was really looking forward to doing it with Jake. It'd been way too long since they had done something like this, since the boys were usually together, it was either one parent or the other on these outings.

Her excitement began to climb even more when her body physically responded to his as he took off his sweatshirt. He was wearing a fitted shirt underneath that gave her the most decadent view of his strong upper body as he began to warm up and swing the bat. His body rotated at the waist as he swung the bat with one arm and gave his injured hand a few stretches, testing it to see if he could grip the bat well enough.

The tight short sleeves bunched up closer to his shoulders as his upper arms would flex and relax with each swing. Gillian had never noticed the definition in Jake's arms before now, which was a shame because they were amazing. But it wasn't until that moment, sitting there, watching him, that she realized how she had now moved Jake from the *just-friends* category to the *eye-*

candy category. She shook her head at this interesting development. She was still staring at him, maybe even lusting over him a little bit, when she was tapped on her shoulder by a small hand. Quickly swiveling around, she saw Ryan. "Aunt Gillian, Dylan wanted me to ask you to watch him swing."

Trying to pull herself out of the lust-induced fog she seemed to be swimming in, she reluctantly got up and made her way closer to the batting cage where the boys were hitting. After watching her son hit a few balls, she glanced over her shoulder to the where she had left Jake, and just watched him hit the ball for a few moments. It was such a beautiful thing to watch. *He* was beautiful. And as the tingles once again erupted all over her skin, the butterflies started to dance in her stomach, and the weird sensation in her chest returned. *Could she be more to Jake? More than just friends?* His time must have run out because he relaxed his batting stance and glanced back to where Gillian had been. The disappointment at her absence was evident on his face, and that ache in her chest constricted. He quickly shot his gaze toward where the she was, and when his eyes met hers, he visibly relaxed. She once again found herself smiling like a fool in response to his smile as he held the bat up in her direction letting her know it was her turn to bat. She was moving toward him, without even knowing it, and before she knew it, she was in front of him. He bent over, picked up her helmet, and placed it carefully on her head.

"Got to put your helmet on," he paused as he gave it his full attention to make sure it was secured. "Wouldn't want anything to hurt something so precious to me," he finished his statement with a delicate tap of his finger to her nose. This managed to snap her out of whatever hold he seemed to have on her, as she just stood and gazed at his face. Oh yeah, she knew was falling for her friend—she just didn't know if that was a good or a bad thing.

CHAPTER FIFTEEN

Before he knew it, their time in the cages had run out. Time sure did fly when having fun, he thought, because he could've stayed there all day watching her. Of course, it was even better now than it was when they were in high school. She was packing up the gear the boys brought with them when he heard her phone vibrate on the bench next to him. When he looked down, the screen showed she had a text.

"Hey, Gillian, you have a text," he said to her.

She looked up from what she was doing and responded, "Can you check it and see who it is?"

He opened the message folder on her phone screen, and saw that the most recent text had come from Allie, which only said '*call me.*' But the text in the line below hers was the one that grabbed his attention since it read, '*Just so you know … it isn't over.*' Jake thought that was a weird statement, especially since it came from a number that wasn't programmed into her phone. He thought it sounded kind of threatening, but knew that it could sound that way if you didn't know what exactly *was* over.

He was still staring at her phone when she placed a baseball bag at his feet and asked, "Who was it?"

"It was Allie, she just said to call her. But what is this other text here that came in late last night?" Mentioning last night reminded him of the guy she went out with, and he briefly wondered if it was possible to have come from him, but hoped not.

"A text from last night?" she questioned as she took her phone from him. He felt a little guilty for glancing at her texts, but for whatever reason, that one bothered him. She shrugged her shoulders as she examined her phone before looking up at him and saying, "I have no clue, it must be a wrong number. It doesn't make any sense to me. Should I reply to it?"

"No. If you think it's a wrong number, then just leave it alone."

"Okay," she agreed. She turned off her phone screen and shoved it into her pocket before looking at up at him. "The boys are hungry for burgers. They want to go to Brody's." The smile on her face was a dead giveaway that it was her that really wanted to go there.

He let out a small laugh and shook his head at her attempt to pin it on the boys. "Is that so?"

"Sure is, and you wouldn't want to disappoint them, now would you?" she asked, batting her eyes at him and giving him a pleading look. He couldn't help but notice that it appeared she was flirting with him. His heart accelerated slightly at the excitement of that, and he decided to flirt right back.

"Well that's true," he said as he stepped a little closer to her, forcing her to look up at him. "But honestly, it's you that I don't want to disappoint, Gillian." He finished this off by gently sweeping the back of his hand across her cheek. When he saw her shiver at the contact, he had to make sure he didn't pounce on her then and there. Seeing her physically respond to him was such a rush, it was hard to focus on anything else around them, which is why he didn't notice how they were standing in front of the entrance to the batting cage, blocking it. The sound of a man clearing his throat caught his attention, forcing his gaze from Gillian's to that of the random stranger next to them.

The stranger motioned toward the batting cage and said nicely, "Sorry to interrupt, but our cage time has already started. You mind stepping out of the way?"

Gillian jumped out of the way and immediately started apologizing for both of them. "I am so sorry. We were distracted because I was trying to persuade my friend here that we needed to go get burgers. You know how it is when there's a great burger involved, everything around you seems to pale in comparison. You could've been George Clooney, and I wouldn't have noticed." The way she smiled at the stranger and fanned herself dramatically as she mentioned George Clooney was cute, and *so* Gillian.

The man clearly agreed, judging by his answering smile and response, "That's quite all right, great burgers deserve that kind of attention."

Then the man paused and gave Gillian an appraising look before adding, "If your friend won't take you, I'd be willing to." Jake quickly thought about punching the guy square in the nose, but decided against it. Even though he knew Gillian wouldn't bite at a line like that, he realized that this was what would happen while Gillian was on the market. This was *that* guy ... the kind of guy that he didn't want her to have to deal with. He was about to say something to the jackass but Gillian didn't miss a beat. She slid right up next to Jake, put one arm behind him and the other planted itself on his chest as she stared up into his eyes. A little baffled by it, but loving the contact nonetheless, he wrapped his one arm around her and pulled her closer.

Gillian smiled at him and said, "Oh my friend is *always* willing to give me what I want. Aren't you?" The tone of her voice was playful and sexy, and it sucked Jake in. She may have been putting on a little bit of a show for the creep and his crappy pick up line, but he was not going to refuse the benefits of it. Or not take advantage of it.

So he leaned forward and as he gave her a sly grin and said, "You know I'm always willing for *you*, babe." And then he kissed her on the lips. Her quick intake of air, and her lips softening to his was exactly what he hoped for. When he pulled back and looked her in the eyes he couldn't help but smile again and say softly, with emphasis, "Always."

Creepy guy got the hint and made his way past the two of them, still staring at each other. Although he didn't want to break the spell weaving around them, he knew they were in public, and so Jake said, "Now how 'bout we go get you that burger."

Her stomach answered with a rumble loud enough for both of them to hear. Gillian's eyes got wide as she clutched her stomach with both hands and laughed, "I think we better!"

He bent over to get the bat bags that were sitting at his feet, when he heard a little voice ask him, "Did you just kiss my mom?"

Crap! He needed to realize this was about more than just him. Looking to see that Gillian and Ryan had already made their way toward the exit, Jake squatted down in front of Dylan and placed his hand on his shoulder before answering, "I did. Is that okay with you, buddy?"

Dylan gave the response a quick thought, and then answered honestly, "It's weird. You've never kissed her like that before. That is how my dad used to kiss her, before he moved out." He paused to think before Jake saw the light in his eyes as he finished with, "Are you going to move in now? Does that mean Dylan is moving in, too?" His excitement at the thought of that was funny, and Jake gave a little laugh at it.

"No, big guy, that doesn't mean that Dylan and me are moving in." The poor kid was clearly disappointed at this bit of information, but Jake pushed on, wanting to get this out there. "What it does mean is that I really like your mom. I like your mom a lot, and I want to spend more time with her. Maybe hold her hand or give her another kiss … would you be okay with that?" Jake wasn't sure if he was overstepping any boundaries here, feeling that he should include Gillian in this. But he didn't want to blow it off when Dylan asked, for fear that would give the kid the impression that it wasn't important, when it was.

Dylan was a calculating kid, usually had an agenda, but always thought stuff through completely. Jake could see the wheels spinning in his head as he processed all of the information. After a few moments, Dylan nodded his head and said, "I'm okay with that, Uncle Jake." With that, the eight year old turned and made his way to the exit, leaving Jake to follow in his wake. He knew that winning over the eight year old son over was going to be the easy one. Gillian's older son, Jonathan, was the one he was worried about.

~*~*~*~*~*~~*~*~*~*~

They arrived at Brody's for lunch, and Gillian was relieved that they were able to get a table. A definite bonus was they had a great view of one of the screens playing a soccer game. She always loved hanging out at Brody's—they had the best burgers and fries, not to mention the variety of brews they had on tap; though she usually ordered the chocolate shakes when she was there. She had sent the boys to the bathroom to wash their hands when her favorite waitress, Carrie, came over to take their orders. She ordered for herself and the boys while Jake ordered for himself. She was about to excuse herself to go wash her own hands when she noticed Jake staring at her with a weird expression she didn't understand. Pausing in her retreat to the ladies room she asked, "What's that look for?"

He smiled and said, "You know what everyone orders when they come here."

It was more of a statement than a question, but she nodded her head and replied, "Of course, I know what everyone orders, everywhere we go. I'm weird that way. I would have ordered for you, too, but I make it a point to let the adults handle themselves."

A big smile spread across Jake's face as he said, "I don't think it's weird at all. It shows how much you pay attention to everyone in your family." A flush worked its way across her cheeks, and she ducked her head at his compliment. It was so unlike her to react like this, but there was something new going on between them today. It was that school-girl-crush feeling she had the other night when she saw Mike at the game.

The thought of Mike, their date, their kiss, and her saying yes to him calling her again, slapped her across the face—effectively dousing the warm and fuzzies she was just enjoying from Jake's attention. The flush disappeared, and a feeling of discomfort took its place. Needing a moment, she quickly excused herself and retreated to the bathroom, leaving a worried Jake at the table.

Once safely behind the barrier of the ladies room door, she placed her hands on the counter and stared at herself in the mirror. She felt like she had done something wrong, like she was guilty of something. This was all new territory for her, but for some reason, it seemed wrong to enjoy the attention from Jake, when she similarly enjoyed it from another man just last night. Of course, she knew she was being ridiculous, but her conscience made her feel like she was being dishonest. Why hadn't she felt this way all day long? Why now? She realized that she hadn't even given Mike another thought since last night, which was just all sorts of screwed up … wasn't it? After a very nice evening with one man, all of her attention went to Jake. Her worry, her concern, even a dream or two, were about Jake … not Mike.

Mike was a great guy from what she could tell and last night when he asked if he could call her, she acted quickly and responded yes. But now, she believed that if she were to run into him, and he asked her out, it would probably be no. Trying to form a rational justification as to why she felt her answer would be different if he asked her now, the only answer she could find was sitting out at the table waiting for her. Jake made it different.

She still wasn't sure what exactly was going on between them at the moment, but she trusted it. She knew it was something worth giving a chance, and spending time with another man who was showing an interest in her, well, that just felt wrong. Nodding in the mirror, as if to acknowledge the conclusion she came to, she washed her hands and made her way back to the table.

The food hadn't arrived yet and Jake, Dylan, and Ryan were engaged in a conversation, or debate, of who could hold their breath longest underwater. Since these random conversation topics weren't unusual, she sat down and absorbed it. Jake looked over at her and asked, "You okay? All the color drained from your face before you left the table—I was worried you were sick."

She melted a little at the concern on his face and in his voice. Knowing for certain that she had come to the correct conclusion to see what was going on between them, she reached over and covered his hand with hers, gave it a little squeeze and said, "I'm fine, nothing to worry about."

Jake quickly covered her hand with his other one, trapping it between both of his. "Are you sure?"

"Of course I am."

When Dylan and Ryan's voices got louder, demanding her attention, she turned toward them, but left her hand comfortably between Jake's, enjoying the feel of his warmth. She peeked over at him for a second and saw that he was still watching her, and he gave her one of those big, satisfied smiles like he had just accomplished something. She wasn't really sure what that was about, but she answered with one of her own before turning back to the boys.

The food arrived to help put an end to the useless conversation the boys were having, but not before it was determined that the next event on their agenda that day was to go swimming at her place. This was fine with her, and since the weather stayed warm well into October, she could do some reading while lounging poolside. They all finished their meals, and she enjoyed more of the chatter that always seemed to surround Dylan and Ryan.

~*~*~*~*~~*~*~*~*~

Jake couldn't help but find complete enjoyment in all that he had done on his day of rest. That's what Sundays were for, after all— rest and spending time with family. This was what he wanted all the time. How funny that it was that just last night that he managed to lose his temper in front of Allie, punch a wall, storm off, and then go home to drink himself unconscious because he was so distraught. But now, he sat and enjoyed the company of the woman he thought he had *again*. He was more than glad that things had turned out better than he thought possible last night. He sat back and took it all in.

The waitress, Carrie, came by the table to drop of the bill, and Jake made sure to make a swipe for it when he saw Gillian reach for it. He gave her a look that said, *what the hell do you think you're doing*, so she backed off and continued to chat with the waitress. Jake sent the boys to the counter with the credit card to take care of the bill, and once the waitress left, he took the opportunity to tell Gillian about Dylan's questioning. He was a little worried that she would be upset with him for talking to him that way, but he hoped she was okay with it. After telling her how he asked if he had just kissed his mom, and that it was like the way she and Logan did, she seemed a little shocked.

"Did he really say that? Like me and Logan?" she questioned in a low tone, before she asked, "What did you say to that?"

"Well, before I could respond to that, your little mastermind asked if this meant that Ryan and me would be moving in?" he said with a little amusement. Gillian's hand flew to her mouth, surprised by her son's question. Jake could see that she found it amusing, too.

"No he didn't!" she said. Jake nodded. Then she asked, "And what did you say?"

"I told him no, it didn't mean that we were moving in," he paused as he thought about how that was his goal in the future. Reaching over, he grabbed her hand and said, "Then I told him it meant that I liked his mom a lot and that because of that, I might want to hold her hand." Glancing down at their hands together, he continued, "Or that I might want to kiss her again." He wanted to lean over and do it then, but knew it wasn't the place for it; although she looked like she had hoped he would. "Then I asked him if that was okay with him. He thought about it for a minute then said, 'yeah I'm okay with that Uncle Jake,' and he walked away from me."

Gillian let out a deep sigh, and said, "He said he was okay with it? Oh, thank God." She tensed up as if she realized she said something she didn't mean to.

He stood up from the table and helped pull her chair back, too. He gave her a smile and said, "Oh, thank God is exactly what I thought, too." She relaxed at his words, and it was then that he knew that up until that point, she wasn't certain what was going on, and that his agreement with her reaction put her at ease. Hand in hand, they made their way out of the restaurant and headed toward her house. Jake was more than a little excited at having pool time with Gillian—one of his favorite past times.

CHAPTER SIXTEEN

Jake's excitement at the thought of his favorite pastime came to a screeching halt when they pulled into Gillian's driveway and found Logan's truck there. As he put his Jeep in park, Logan strolled out the front door and stared, like he was the king of the castle staring down at them. Jake didn't like it at all.

"Damn, I forgot all about meeting Logan for dinner tonight," Gillian muttered in the seat next to him. He looked over at her as she stared back at her ex-husband. She turned toward Jake, nibbling her lower lip with a worried expression on her face. "Can I get a rain check on the swimming? Logan and I are getting together to go over details and arrangements for *everything*." Gesturing her head in the direction of her youngest in the backseat told him she didn't want to say more than that in front of him. Although he was completely disappointed, what could he do or say about it? He understood how these things worked, but that didn't mean he wanted her and Logan to spend time together, alone. Thinking quickly, he came up with an idea.

"Of course you can have a rain check, but don't expect me to forget it. How 'bout I take the boys back to my place, and you can let me know when you get home. I can bring Dylan back then."

A warm smile spread across her face, and the worried look disappeared as she considered his idea. "That would be great, Jake." Turning back to the boys she said, "We're going to have to swim later, boys. Dylan, go say hello to your dad before you leave with Jake and Ryan."

"Okay, Mom!" Dylan exclaimed before both he and Ryan exited the vehicle. Gillian turned and watched her son run up the steps to hug Logan. She sighed and then turned back to Jake with a sad expression on her face.

Taking her hand in his, he rubbed his thumb soothingly over the back of it as he said, "Hey, you okay?"

She nodded and looked back over at Logan and Dylan. "Yeah, I'll be fine. I feel bad sometimes when I see them together—like I'm the one keeping them apart." She paused and looked back at him, "Then I remember, he's the one that did this. It was beyond my control." Jake couldn't tell if the sadness he saw in her eyes was over *her* pain, or her kids' pain. But then again, her kids' pain *was* her pain, and he knew that.

"Do you need anything from me?" Jake asked, feeling a little lost himself at the moment. He wanted to console her, but couldn't with Logan twenty feet away.

She answered with a little smile as she cocked her head to the side and said, "What are my options?"

And just like that, the playful Gillian was back. Jake smiled at her, lifted her hand to his mouth for a kiss before responding, "Anything in my power to give, it's yours."

"I do believe that is one of the best things a girl can hear, Jake Michaels. I'll have to remember that. Can I call you when I get back?"

"Just let me know when, and all three of us will be back."

"Thanks," she said, as both boys jumped back into the Jeep, and Logan appeared at the passenger door to open it for Gillian.

Logan put his hand out to help Gillian from the Jeep and said, "Hey guys, heard you went to the batting cages this morning. Sounds like a great way to spend the morning."

Jake tried to control his irritation at the mere sight of Logan touching her, but wasn't successful with it. So, in a sarcastic voice, he said, "It sure was. I couldn't ask for anything more than spending time with Gillian and the boys. Cages first then Brody's for burgers—it was a *perfect* Sunday."

Jake was certain his sarcasm was picked up by Logan; the man may be a complete asshole, but he wasn't entirely stupid. Once again, Jake could care less what Logan's thoughts were about the day he just spent with Gillian. For Jake, it was a great day. He nodded in Logan's direction once the boys were settled back in, then looked at Gillian, gave her a wink and said, "Call me later, beautiful."

~*~*~*~*~~*~*~*~*~

Gillian giggled at how Jake winked at her, called her beautiful, and then backed from the driveway. Jake was obviously not pleased about Logan being there, and she liked that he was disappointed he had to leave. *She* was not pleased that her day with him had been temporarily cut short, but was looking forward to *later* and enjoyed the feeling of anticipation she felt about it. Her irritation set in as Logan's voice sounded next to her, and she felt his hand touch her lower back to lead her out of the driveway. "I would've taken you and the boys to the cages today if you had wanted. You

213

know I love going with you guys." The little bit of poutiness on his face used to be adorable, but now … not so much.

"Oh, stop it, Logan. I don't find that look attractive on you anymore. Something about you begging for forgiveness repeatedly kind of ruined it for me."

Logan huffed a laugh before nodding at her. "Touché, my dear. Touché."

"Do we need to go out, or did you want to talk here?" she asked him.

"I thought we could go grab a bite to eat. I haven't eaten since breakfast."

Gillian shook her head at him. "You know how I feel about that, Logan."

"I know, babe. Sorry, but the day just got away from me."

"Come inside then, I need to change. I had completely forgotten that you were coming by." Without seeing if he was following her, because she knew he would, she made her way inside. Once inside her bedroom, she closed the door and leaned against it. Taking in a deep breath, she smiled at the day she had. She marveled at the fact that she hadn't given anyone else a thought while she was with Jake. First came the realization that she had forgotten all about her date with Mike, who was a very nice man. But then she forgot all about her plans to meet up with her ex-husband to discuss custody and living arrangements.

It wasn't common practice for Gillian to forget things, or people, for that matter. It appeared she had lost her head, and it was over

Jake. Smiling like a fool once again, she decided a shower was in order. Not that she needed a shower to go somewhere with Logan, but because she was going to see Jake right after. No, her days of dressing up for Logan were over—she wanted someone else's attention now.

Dinner with Logan wasn't as uncomfortable as it was weird. There wasn't the usual hand holding or laughing. Logan seemed awkward around her, and it pissed her off. The least he could do was man up and act like a grown up. They'd been through plenty of things in life, and there was no reason why they shouldn't be able to get through dinner together. It was just as their dinner plates arrived that Gillian had had enough. Putting down her utensils, she dropped her hands in her lap and looked at Logan. "Are we going to be able to get past this, Logan? I don't understand why you're acting like we're complete strangers, and you're uncomfortable sitting across from me. Just because we ended the marriage part, doesn't mean all the other connections we had were severed." Maybe she was a little harsh in talking to him that way, but it was ridiculous to think two grown people who used to share everything couldn't talk to each other.

Logan looked at her, set his forearms down on either side of his plate, and took a deep breath before letting it out slowly. "That's one of the things I love most about you, Gillian. You never hesitate to call things how they are, and put me in my place. Truth is, I'm not sure how I'm supposed to act around you."

A little baffled by his response, she asked, "Why would you act any different around me? We're just having a meal, talking about our kids. We have done this plenty of times."

"True, but in each of those other times, those were dates between a husband and his wife, but not this time. I don't get to go home with you. I don't get to make love to you." He paused, and she wasn't sure what to say to that, so she waited 'til he continued, "I feel a little lost with all of it—not quite sure what to do."

Gillian couldn't help but soften a bit at the lost look in his eyes. Reaching over, she grabbed his hand and squeezed it. "I know how you feel. This could all be very confusing if you don't separate the parts of our relationship. There is no longer a husband/wife part for us to focus on, so you need to just look at us as two friends with kids. You have to, because I refuse to have an immature relationship with the man who fathered my children simply because he can't get over things. We no longer have a physical relationship; we have a parenting one and even a business one," she said the last part as an afterthought because they had yet to broach the subject that she was listed on the company papers for his business. He wasn't the only Baxter in the title of Baxter Michaels Construction Company. "So pull it together, Baxter, because we got shit to figure out," she punctuated her statement by squeezing his hand again before picking up her utensils to dig into her food before it got cold.

After she set Logan straight, their dinner was far more tolerable—almost normal. She and Logan had just come to an agreement on living arrangements, and who would be living where, when she felt her phone buzz against her hip. Leaving Logan to handle stuff with the waiter who just came to collect their plates, she dug into her purse, once again making a mental note that she really needed to clean it out. She pulled her phone out and was a little confused by what she was seeing. There was a text message, from the same unknown number as last night that read, *how could you be with him? I told you it isn't over!* And right below it was a picture of Logan's truck. It took her a few moments of staring at it to figure out what the picture was supposed to be showing her.

"Oh no," slipped out of her mouth just before she covered it. Looking up to Logan, she could see he was watching her with a look of concern. "I think we have a problem, Logan," she said in a weak voice as she handed him her phone. He was quicker at seeing the damage than she was.

"What the … son of a bitch!" flew out of Logan's mouth a few seconds before he leapt from the booth, taking her phone with him. She was about to follow him when the waiter appeared before her with the check, looking a little baffled about Logan's exit.

Gillian was quick to pull out her wallet and toss her card at the young man before saying, "Someone just vandalized our truck! I'll be back in to get the card!" With that, she fled the restaurant to find Logan and prayed that whoever sent the text was long gone. Otherwise, she and Logan would be making any further arrangements about their children through a glass divider.

~*~*~*~*~~*~*~*~*~

Jake couldn't help but watch the clock. It was after seven o'clock, and he still hadn't heard from Gillian. He had no idea how long she had planned to take with Logan, but he was thinking he had something to be worried about., He had an uneasy feeling in the pit of his stomach—not necessarily about Logan, although that was still a thought. He thought about texting her, but didn't want to interrupt, so he set his phone down on the coffee table and sat back on the couch. Ryan and Dylan were off playing in Ryan's room, thankfully, because he didn't want them to see his agitation. A knock on the door had him jumping to his feet, but at the same time he heard his phone ringing. He grabbed his phone and headed for the door, pausing when he saw it was Logan calling. This wasn't unusual, but since he was expecting Gillian, he cautiously answered, "Hello."

"Hey Jake, it's me," Gillian's voice came through the line, and he instantly felt better. The person at the door would have to wait as he gave Gillian his full attention.

"Hi there, beautiful, why are you calling me from Logan's phone?"

"The police still have my phone so I had to use Logan's." Immediately on alert, worry climbed to the forefront.

"Why do the police have your phone? Are you hurt? Do you need my help?" All three questions were fired in rapid succession as his attention was once again brought to the sound of knocking on his front door. He slowly walked in that direction while waiting for her response.

"I'm fine, Jake; everything is okay so please calm down. I promise, I'm fine."

Jake opened the front door to find Gillian's oldest son, Jonathan, standing there. Confused at why he was there, but wanting to find out more from Gillian, he motioned him in.

Jonathan asked, "Is that my mom?" Jake nodded, and the young man made his way into the house. He knew his way around, so Jake left him to it and moved into the other room to talk to her.

"Gillian, what's going on, and why is Jonathan here?"

"Oh, good, that was my next question. He's there to pick up Dylan. It's a school night so I want him to go home to get to bed on time. I'm not sure how much longer I'm going to be."

"You still haven't told me what's going on, Gillian. Are you trying to make me worry more?" He made sure to gentle his voice when what he felt like doing was demanding an answer. Thankfully, he knew to restrain that ogre inside him before speaking. He really was worried, and it was bothering him that she hadn't told him yet.

"I'm sorry Jake, I'm not trying to worry you—thank you for that though—worrying about me. It's sweet of you." She paused, and he heard her take in a deep breath before continuing, "Someone slashed the tires on Logan's truck, all four of them. Plus, they bashed in his headlights and tried to kick in one of his fenders."

"What the hell! Were you there when it happened?" he barked into the phone.

"No, Jake, I told you I'm fine so stop worrying like that. We were inside eating dinner when it happened …" Her long pause told him that he wasn't going like what she said next, but he waited.

Finally, he heard her take in another breath and let it out before continuing, "I got a text with a picture of the truck, outside, damaged. There was a message with it, too." It was his turn to suck in a deep breath as he felt his blood pressure begin to climb.

"What did the message say Gillian?"

"It said, and I quote, *'How could you be with him! I told you it isn't over'*." Her voice trailed off a bit as she said it.

He immediately recalled the text he had seen that morning and how it bothered him. Putting two and two together, he asked, "It was from the same number that texted you last night, wasn't it?"

"Yes," she said cautiously. He immediately went on alert. Not only did someone have her cell phone number, but also knew what Logan's truck looked like. Clearly there was a target. The question was whether the target was Gillian, or was it Logan? It didn't matter; all he knew was that she sounded scared, and he needed to comfort her.

"Gillian, baby, do you need me? I can leave Jonathan with the boys and be there right away." He didn't want to ask—he wanted to *tell* her he was coming, but didn't want to overstep any boundaries since things were obviously new.

"I know you would, Jake. I can always count on you." The smile he heard in her sweet voice, coupled with her acknowledging that she could count on him, filled him with satisfaction. It was a great thing for anyone to hear, but more so for a man to hear from the woman he wanted to count on him. "But don't worry, I'll be fine. Logan will drop me off at home when we're done here. You stay home, and please tell Ryan that I'm sorry I didn't make it back in time for swimming."

Jake huffed a laugh at that. He wasn't giving a second thought to the plans they had, was only thinking about her, and here she was thinking of his son. "I'm sure he'll be fine with it, but can I just tell you that I love how you love my son," he said, pouring all sincerity into his statement so she knew how much it meant to him.

He heard her say, "Oh, give me a break, Jake Michaels, that kid is the other half to my kid. He's mine, too, so you better never take him away from me."

Shaking his head, he said, "Never ... Please let me know when you get home. I won't be able to rest 'til I know, okay?"

"I will ... bye." Jake said his goodbye and went in search of Jonathan. He would make sure the young man double-checked the windows and everything at the house before they went to sleep tonight. Whoever vandalized Logan's truck clearly had some aggression issues, and Jake wasn't going to take a chance. Jonathan had made himself at home on the couch, watching television; Jake sat himself in the chair across from him.

"Did your mother tell you what was going on tonight?" Jake asked. Jonathan answered yes without even taking his attention from the screen. Not wanting to give away information that Gillian may have withheld from him, he probed further. "And what did she tell you?" The young man moved his attention from the television to Jake, and that's when Jake could see the anger on his face. His eyebrows were scrunched together, and his lips were pressed in a tight line as he leaned forward on his forearms and clenched his fists.

After glaring at Jake for a few moments, he spoke, "She told me that someone slashed my father's tires, bashed in his headlights and tried kicking in his fender. Then she told me that they found out it happened because somebody texted a picture of it to her." A sudden concern flashed through Jake's mind about who could possibly have done this, and he felt pretty shitty for wondering if the young man sitting in front of him could have. The thought of the semi-threatening message to Gillian cancelled out that concern. But still, the anger evident in the kid needed to be addressed.

Once again realizing he may be overstepping some boundaries regarding Gillian's kids, and for the second time in one day, he hesitated, but decided it was necessary to ask, "Hey Jonathan. You got something on your mind? Do you need to talk about it?"

"Talk about what Uncle Jake? The fact that my father deserved to have that done to his truck? How about how I wish I could've done that? Or how about the fact that whoever did that to his truck seems to be texting my mom about it?" Jonathan jumped up from his place on the couch and began to pace as he let his anger out. "Oh, I know what I can talk about! How about the fact that everything my father has taught me is a lie!" Jake was confused at the direction of Jonathan's rant. Clearly, he was mad at his father, but the why was not as obvious. *Unless, he knew why his parents were getting divorced.*

Wanting the kid to get it all out, Jake helped him along. "Come on man, what else?"

Jonathan paused in his pacing and gave Jake a look like he had sprouted a second nose or something, before saying, "Isn't this the part of the conversation where you jump in and tell me some crap about my father being a *hardworking, loving family man*? That I should respect him and be proud of him?"

Surprised at this, Jake went with nothing but the truth, "Hell no! Why the hell would I spout that shit at you?"

When what Jake said sank in, Jonathan slowly lowered himself onto the chair he was standing in front of. Jake must have been the only adult to answer him candidly like this, so the kid wasn't prepared for it. "Why wouldn't you, Uncle Jake?" the kid asked in a low tone.

Without hesitation, Jake said, "Because that's bullshit, I wouldn't lie to you like that. It's clear to me that you know things that have happened, and you've taken them upon yourself for some reason. Do you want to talk about it?"

"Why does she defend him, Uncle Jake? I heard what he did ... why she left him. If she knows what he did, why am I not allowed to be mad at him, too! He lied to me, told me that it was important to be good to women. Never be disrespectful, always treat them like you would treat your mother, like they were the most important person in the world." Tears shown in the young man's eyes as he looked at Jake. "He told me how I should treat a lady, and he didn't do any of that! And she defends him—all I want is to be angry at him!"

Jake could see the weight lift from Jonathan's shoulders as he sagged back against the couch. The poor kid was holding all that in for over two months? No wonder he was a moody little bastard. "So are you angry with her or with him?" Jake asked.

Jonathan paused to consider the question before answering, "I'm definitely mad at my father for being such a prick. But I'm upset that my mother is letting him get away with it—she defends him when she should be trying to destroy him. And now, there is apparently some crazy person doing some crazy shit around her, and it's probably his doing, too!"

He didn't like how the young man was upset with Gillian, so that was going to be Jake's first order of business. "So, you're upset with your mother for defending your father? Did you stop to consider why she does that? Have you considered that she has possibly handled the situation the way she did ... to protect you kids?"

Jonathan's silence allowed him to continue, "Did you know that your mother hid what happened between them for a long time? She didn't share it with me, your Aunt Allie ... no one. No, the strong woman that she is, she took it all on herself. Much like the anger you're carrying right now. Now, I'm not going to pretend that because your father has been a good father to you, that you should ignore his other behaviors. Truthfully, I feel much of the same feelings toward him right now and would have absolutely no problem telling him that. But I will damn sure set you straight with how you should see your mother." Jake cocked his head to the side in question to him.

When the young man nodded his head, Jake continued, "You mother didn't want you kids to know what happened because she didn't want what happened between them to cloud how you would feel about your father. You have to see the irony of this, don't you? She didn't want you to know, so that you wouldn't be angry with your father ... kind of like you are."

Jonathan rolled his eyes and said, "Okay, I get that. I do. But why does she let him get away with it? She talks to him like nothing has changed."

Jake shook his head at the seventeen year old—sad that he was so confused about this. This was a conversation he should be able to have with his mom or dad. "Think about it Jonathan. That's the kind of person your mother is. She doesn't feel the need to harp on something and dangle it out there for everyone to see. She made a decision, she owned it, and she's moved on from it. It's her strength that allows her to do that, because believe me, I was there that night, and I saw what it did to her. We both know she would never want you to see her fall apart like that, but she did, nonetheless. But now she has moved past it, and I think you need to, as well, for her."

"You're not asking me to forgive my dad, are you?"

"Again, my answer will have to be, hell no. But I want you to make sure that you're not upset with your mom. She's worried about you."

The young man hung his head in shame before saying, "I just don't know how he could do that do her. Why he would do that to her?"

"That's a question I think you deserve an answer to, but the only person you can get it from will be your father. So in the future, when you've calmed down, maybe you could ask him." Jonathan nodded before leaning his head back against the couch. It must have been a huge relief for him to get that out there. Jake wanted to make sure that he also knew Allie would be a good person to talk to about all of this. "Hey, just so you know, your Aunt Allie—she might be the person that's most upset at your father. You could always talk to her, too, you know."

For the first time that evening, Jonathan let a small smile creep across his face at Jake's words. "I'm actually surprised that Aunt Allie didn't have him hospitalized. Is it safe to assume that my mom also stopped her from doing that?" Jake nodded a laugh at the kid for picking up on that part of his Aunt's personality. Jake and Jonathan had moved past the heavy stuff and into a lighter mood when Dylan and Ryan came into the room. Both boys said hello to Jonathan as they sat on either side of him. Jake was about to comment on how the boys should give him a little space when Dylan dropped a bomb.

"Hey Jonathan, did you know that Uncle Jake likes Mom, and he kissed her, and wants to hold her hand, and maybe kiss her again?"

Jake almost choked on his own tongue when he heard all that roll out of Dylan's mouth. Jonathan's confused eyes met Jake's, and he raised his eyebrows in question. Of course, he wasn't going to lie, but he would've preferred to deliver it to the young man with a little more tact than that. But, oh well, it was out there now, so time to own it.

Jake smiled at him and said, "True story, man. I've loved your mother since I was seventeen years old, and I plan to make her a very happy woman."

CHAPTER SEVENTEEN

Gillian couldn't contain her yawn as she made her way back to the nurse's station. She was tired and hungry and ready for her lunch break. The chaos of last night took forever to end, and she was disappointed that her time with Jake had to be cancelled … again. She had sent him a message when she got home late last night, after eleven o'clock, not sure if he was still awake or not. It took all of ten seconds for him to respond.

> Gillian: I'm home now. You can call me if you want. Otherwise, sleep tight.

> Jake: I'm sorry, Mr. Police Officer, but I'm just not interested in you right now … I kinda like this girl. Her name is Gillian, and she is super-hot!

She was laughing at his text when her phone began to ring in her hands. Skipping a hello, she said, "What if it was a Ms. Police Officer?"

"I'd have to say that my response would be the same. Besides, I try to avoid women who sleep with guns and can totally kick my ass. In my book, that would be all female police officers, and of course, Allie."

"Oh yes, it's a good idea to include Allie on that list." She sighed then asked, "Why are you still up?"

"There was no way I could try and sleep 'til I knew you were home, safe and sound." Warmth filled her at that comment.

Giddy schoolgirl was becoming a good description of her lately; it was a bit embarrassing if she thought about it.

"Well, I'm home, so you can get some sleep now."

"Yeah, right, like that's going to happen anytime soon. How did everything go with the police? Do they have any suspects?"

"Well, first they asked me if it was possible that I had some disgruntled lover who had a problem with Logan." She snorted at her own comment before adding, "I made sure to set that detective straight by pointing at Logan and saying that I didn't, but he might."

"What about that number in your phone? That would be a dead giveaway as to who it was."

She responded, "You would think so, but apparently it's one of those throw-away phones." Yawning loudly in Jake's ear, she continued, "It's all very *Law & Order*, if you ask me."

"I don't like the thought that someone has your number and knows Logan's truck ... I told Jonathan to double check all the window locks and doors when he got home tonight. And I want you to make sure you set the alarm."

"Thanks for that. I did when I came in. Was Jonathan okay? He didn't seem too worried or anything?"

It was Jake's turn to sigh as he said, "You have one smart kid there, Gillian; he isn't an idiot. He knows that something is going on. Plus, you're not going to be happy to hear that he knows why you and Logan are getting divorced." Her sharp intake of air had Jake quickly trying to appease her. "Calm down, Gillian. It's fine.

He's very angry with Logan, but I set him straight on a few things. Apparently, he was outside your bedroom the day of the party and heard the details. He's seems to be upset with you because you are being too *nice* to Logan. And Jonathon feels you aren't allowing him to be angry.

Gillian hadn't thought of it that way. Unaware that Jonathan knew, had only led her to believe he was just moody about the divorce, not the actual actions leading to it. She knew she was going to have to talk with him about it.

"I'm sure if you talk to him, things will be better, but Gillian … from a male perspective, you have to let him be angry. Don't force his father on him if you don't have to."

She knew that Jake was probably right, and she wished that her son had come to her with this. Now even more drained, she and Jake said their goodnights, and she promptly crawled into bed before passing out.

Recalling last night's events, and the worry she had with her son, Gillian found herself yawning again as she sat at her station. A cup of coffee magically appeared before her, and she couldn't contain her smile when she saw the hand that was placing it there. Jake had brought her coffee.

"And how did you know that I was desperately in need of caffeine?" she asked as she accepted the cup and swiveled her chair around to face him. Since her seat was at bar height, she had a perfect view as he crossed his impressive arms across that equally impressive chest of his and leaned against the counter top.

"That's because I was up as late as you were last night, so call it a good assumption. Not to mention that yawn had you resembling a snake—unhinged jaw and all," he said while giving a little laugh under his breath.

Feeling a little guilty knowing he had stayed up for her last night, she quickly said, "I'm sorry about that. You didn't have to wait up for me, you know."

He shook his head at her, "I didn't *have* to, but I wanted to, Gillian. I was worried about you—still am. I really don't like the idea that this crazy person—whoever it is—has your number. You think maybe you should get a new one?"

"That's what my brother said last night, but I don't know. I like my number." She knew she was pouting a little, but it was true. It pissed her off to think that she had to change her number because of some crazy person. The truth was Gillian was pretty convinced that it was Jody Spencer. She always had this underlying concern about the woman making her presence known, and while it may not have been a rational concern before, it now seemed completely legit.

"Okay, I'll go to the wireless store as soon as I can. But I'm working twelve-hour shifts for the next four days, so I don't see it happening until after that." When it seemed like he was going to have something to say about that, she gave him a look that told him she wasn't going to argue about it. He put his hands up in surrender, and she changed the subject.

"Thank you for talking with Jonathan last night. I appreciate it."

Jake shrugged his shoulders and said, "It wasn't planned. He just sort of threw it all out there. He looked better once he got it all out, though. But you should be prepared—I told him that Allie also shares some of the animosity toward Logan that he does, so he'll be teaming up with her now."

"Oh great! Just what we need; Allie, the ring leader, with an angry following." She laughed at the mental picture that provided her with.

Jake stood up from his position against her station and placed his hands on both her shoulders, commanding her attention. The serious look on his face made her focus on only him as he said, "I want you to promise me that you'll pay attention to things around you, Gillian. Clearly somebody is angry, and we can assume that it's directed toward Logan, but the truth of the matter is that *you* are the one who got the messages. So I wouldn't like it if you disregarded your safety by ignoring it." He paused as he ran his hands down her arms 'til he could hold both of her hands in his, pulling them in his direction, forcing her to stand up.

It certainly was no hardship to stare at this beautiful man in front of her, but the fact that he could place her under this spell with just a look was mind-boggling. The only way she could answer him was to nod like a fool as she felt her body sway toward his. His swift smile as he lifted their hands up to kiss, had her stopping mid sway and remembering she was at work. She was at work and was trying to make out with Jake. She could feel the heat fill her cheeks when the embarrassment at her behavior set in. His knowing smile only escalated her embarrassment as she ducked her head a little to avoid his gaze.

His fingers at her chin forced her to tilt her head back up at him, and he tapped a finger to her nose playfully. "Promise me you'll be careful? Promise me you will not walk out of here alone tonight? If nobody can walk with you, I expect you to call any one of us—your brother, my brother ... me."

"I promise," she whispered.

Jake responded, "Good. Now I've gotta go. Eddie is down in the rig waiting for me."

She smiled at him. "Thanks for the coffee."

"Anytime, beautiful." He winked, and then he was gone. What the hell was it about Jake winking that made her swoon? She shook her head in an attempt to focus and snap out of her daze. Somewhat successfully, she managed to finish her patient charting in a timely manner, that is, once her caffeine kicked in. Before she headed down to the cafeteria for lunch, she quickly texted Jake to thank him again for the caffeine fix.

~*~*~*~*~~*~*~*~

The next three days were filled with busy work shifts, text conversations, missed phone calls, quick hellos at her work station when he had a patient to drop off, and enough pent up longing to choke an elephant. Jake was getting tired of missing Gillian and was determined to make sure he got to spend some time with her tonight. It was Thursday and the last of her four shifts in a row, so he knew she would be tired. He thought it would be a great idea to pick up some pizzas, his son, and head over to her place. Of course, he sent her a message first to make sure she was on board.

232

Jake: Hey beautiful! Pizza for dinner, your place, my treat?

Gillian: Yes please! I want pepperoni and mushroom on mine =)

Jake: You got it ... what time you off?

Gillian: I get off early at five today, but have to run by the police station to sign my statement about the other night. Shouldn't take more than an hour.

Jake: Okay, I'll try to time it for them.

Gillian: Perfect!

Glad they had set those plans in stone, he was able to push through the rest of his day.

After picking up both Dylan and Ryan from his parents' house, they all went and picked up the pizzas from Gillian's favorite place, Bronx Pizza. It was a little out of the way to go there, but the establishment was known around San Diego and was well worth the drive—especially if it put a smile on her face. Jake arrived at her house shortly after she said she would be home, and he smiled when he saw that her SUV was already there. He and the boys climbed out, carrying their assigned item:, a pizza for each boy while Jake had the drinks and ice cream. The first clue that his evening wasn't going to turn out as he had hoped was the sounds of feminine laughter coming from inside. Dylan opened the door for Ryan and Jake heard his excited son yell, "Aunt Allie!" before both boys took off in the direction of the laughter.

What the hell was Allie doing here ... and where the hell was her car? Jake looked behind him to see if he had somehow missed it, but no, it wasn't there. He decided that Allie was officially having her superhero name changed to Cockblocker, for her epic ability to show up and completely derail his plans with Gillian. Making his way into the house, he saw that Allie and Gillian were sitting on the couch together with a bottle of wine and two glasses on the table in front of them. When Gillian looked up at him, she smiled, and he almost forgot about his irritation with Allie.

"Hey you," she said, as she got up to help them with the pizza. She leaned up on her tip-toes to place a kiss on his cheek, but he wasn't having that anymore. He snaked his arm around her waist and held her against him, as he closed the space between them and kissed her on the lips. That was where her kisses belonged now—on his lips—not his cheek. Knowing they had an audience, he was mindful not to slip her tongue, but he sure thought about it. He could taste the wine she was drinking on her lips, and it made it even harder not to taste more of her.

Pulling back just a little, but still holding her against him, he smiled down at her and said, "Hey yourself. I've missed you."

She blushed at his comment and shyly whispered back, "I've missed you, too." Jake turned to see Allie watching them from the couch, completely awestruck.

"Allie, to what do we owe the honor of your presence today? Don't you have clients to take care of?"

A huge smile spread across her face as she said, "Well, I'll be damned. That was one of the coolest things I've ever seen." Gillian was still pressed against him, so when she giggled and buried her face in his neck, Jake couldn't help his reaction. His body hardened, and he knew he needed a moment alone with her.

Looking to Allie, he extended the bag in his hand toward her and asked, "Could you take this into the kitchen and give us a minute, please?"

Allie jumped right up, took the bag and said, "Absolutely." With a shit-eating grin, she went to the kitchen where Jake could hear the boys.

Now that his other arm was free, he wrapped it around Gillian and just held her against him. He pressed his face into her hair and smiled as her scent filled his nose, livening his senses. His body was on edge with need, especially since her hands were idly stroking a small area above his waistband. He just needed one more kiss—a real kiss. Sliding his hand up her back and burying it in her hair, he tilted her head back so she had no choice but to look at him. Her eyes met his gaze as he slowly leaned into her, and said softly, "I'm sorry, but I just can't wait any longer to do this." Pressing his lips against hers, he felt them soften and mold to his, before he let his tongue glide along the seam. Feeling her softness, tasting her, wanting more, he used his hand in her hair to position her for the perfect angle as he pressed his tongue through the barrier of her lips.

Jake felt her tongue slide out to meet his, and he couldn't control the rumble of satisfaction that escaped him as his body responded to hers. The hands that had been at his low back were now digging into his skin through his shirt, spurring him on further even as he felt her tongue slip into his mouth. He wanted to devour her, take all of her inside him and keep her all to himself.

It was like he couldn't get her close enough as the two of them stood in her living room, making out, with their sons in the next room. Jake wanted to care, but couldn't bring himself to do it. This kiss had been a long time coming, and he wasn't going to apologize for this inherent need to have her. Her lips on his, her tongue stroking his, her nails digging into his back, his body tightened further, and he pressed his hips forward so she knew exactly what she was doing to him. She moaned in response and pressed her hips back into his … *Oh yeah, he was a goner for sure.*

Not wanting to stop, but knowing he had to, Jake slowed down the kiss. He let his lips linger against hers for a moment before he gently sucked her lower lip into his mouth one more time before pulling back. When he looked down at her, he could actually see the lust hazing her eyes as she opened them, and a slow smile spread across her face. He rubbed a finger across her now swollen bottom lip, reveling in the softness and the fact that he could touch them—that they were his now. He sighed in contentment and said, "Sorry, but I couldn't wait another minute to do that. I hope I didn't embarrass you in front of Allie, but I really missed you."

Gillian let out one of those adorable snorts of hers before saying, "To feel embarrassed, I would have to be aware of people around me. I can only see you right now, Jake."

"Now isn't that the coolest fucking thing I've ever heard," he growled before pressing his lips against hers again for a quick, yet firm, kiss.

When he pulled back, she smiled at him again and said, "I seem to recall the promise of pizza. Are you going to feed me or what?"

Thinking of all sorts of crude comments to say in response to being *fed*, Jake amazingly held it all in and groaned at the thought of them. Giving her one more squeeze and getting one more smile from her, he reluctantly let her go. Well, let her go enough so she could walk to the kitchen with his arm still planted firmly on her waist.

When they got to the kitchen, Jake saw that Allie and the boys were elbow deep in pizza and talking about the whole who-could-stay-underwater-longer topic that they had talked about on Sunday. Gillian prepared a plate with a couple slices of pizza on it and handed it to him with a smile. He made his way to the table as Gillian went out to the living room for the wine that the girls had left out there. Taking the seat next to Allie, he leaned over and kissed her on the cheek before saying quietly, "Just so you know, I have revoked your superhero name. You are no longer Superbitch. You are now officially known as Cockblocker." Allie almost choked on her food as she laughed out loud.

The boys looked to see what was going on, and Jake just shrugged at them and said, "All I said was fart, butt-crack, and booger." Both boys started to giggle, which was exactly why he said it.

He huffed a laugh at them as he turned back to Allie, who was just recovering from her outburst, but managed to say between deep breaths, "Oh, I am *so* getting a shirt made with *that* on it!" Jake laughed before shoving a slice of pizza in his mouth.

Gillian had just made her way back into the kitchen and sat down next to him when she asked, "What's so funny in here?"

Ryan chimed in quickly with, "My dad said fart, butt-crack, and booger!" And then both boys were laughing like fools again. The adults were laughing at the fools who were laughing at stupid words, and Jake had finally gotten a taste of Gillian. Damn, it was going to be a good night—at least he thought it was. That is, until he heard the sound of Logan and Jason yelling hellos from the front of the house. Great, now the whole gang was there.

As irritation began to set in again, and the cloud of contentment he was residing in lifted, Allie leaned over and whispered in his ear, "Better make that Little Cockblocker because Super Cockblocker just got here."

~*~*~*~*~~*~*~*~*~

Gillian always knew her house was like Grand Central Station, but give a girl a break. Once again, the family had hosed her plans of a quiet evening with Jake. She always loved a surprise visit from Allie, but today, she was more than a little bummed, and she felt like complete shit for it, too. Her disappointment at seeing Allie at the door must have been evident on her face because her best friend said, "That sure isn't the look I usually get when I surprise you."

As she made her way into the house, Gillian composed her features and told her the truth, "I thought you were Jake."

Allie spun around and gave her a considering look, nodding her head when she seemed to be done with her assessment and said, "In that case, I understand. It's easier to tolerate disappointment when it's about me not being a certain person rather than just my presence in general." Setting her bag on the floor in front of the

238

couch, she bent over and picked up a bottle of their favorite wine and said, "Do we have time for girl talk before Jake gets here?"

Of course Gillian wasn't going to say no, but she was still a little bummed over the detour her evening had once again taken. That was until Allie dropped the best news Gillian had heard in a long time when she said, "So, I have decided to move back down here to San Diego." The wine in Gillian's mouth almost made the journey out her nose, but thankfully rerouted back into her wine glass.

"Jesus, Al, warn a girl before you throw that grenade," Gillian said as she wiped the wine dripping from her chin with the hem of her shirt. Looking at her friend, and the look of resolution on her face was comforting to Gillian. It had been a while since Allie had looked so peaceful. Allie had moved away after her husband Marc died in a car accident. She felt all sorts of guilty over it and had punished herself by moving away from her family. So her moving back was a very good thing.

Sliding across the couch, she pulled her best friend into a hug and said, "That's the best news I could've gotten. Especially after the week I've had." Allie hugged her back, and when Gillian leaned back, she could see that Allie was struggling with the attention to the matter. Knowing it was time to change focus, Gillian said, "I could really use some advice, or some ass-kicking lessons. After what happened Sunday, I'm hesitant to open the front door for fear Slutty McWhore will pull an Amy Fisher and Long Island Lolita my ass."

It was Allie's turn to spit out her wine. They were laughing over how they both successfully avoided shooting it out their noses when Dylan and Ryan arrived yelling, "Aunt Allie!" before they promptly lunged at her. Always one to enjoy the sight of them with Allie, Gillian was taking it in when she looked up to see Jake enter the room. She could see that he, too, was a little disappointed at the arrival of their friend, but also knew that he would be thrilled to hear that she was moving back down here since it was a source of worry for all them.

Smiling at him, she said, "Hey, you."

She got up to welcome him with a kiss to his cheek, like she always had, but Jake insistently pulled her body up against his hard body and kissed her perfectly on the lips. She was caught in a fog of surprise and arousal as she felt her body start to tingle with anticipation for more of his touch. When he pulled his lips away, she blinked up at him as he smiled and said, "Hey yourself. I've missed you."

As was becoming customary with Jake and his attention, she felt the warmth in her cheeks as she said, "I've missed you, too." When Jake turned to talk to Allie, Gillian noticed that he didn't relax his hold on her, so she stayed there. She enjoyed the feeling of being held against a warm, hard, male body. It was comforting, and exciting, and she couldn't help but notice that she fit perfectly against him.

Gillian was lost in the enjoyment that was Jake's body when she heard Allie say, "Well, I'll be damned. That was one of the coolest things I've ever seen."

Yeah, it was kinda cool, she thought as she giggled a little and buried her face in his chest, once again a little embarrassed at the attention, but not ready to pull away from Jake yet. His arms tightened around her, and she heard him ask Allie to give us a minute. Once Allie had retreated to the kitchen, Jake wrapped his now free arm around her and pulled her closer to him. She couldn't help but relax in his embrace. It was comfortable, like a place she belonged, made just for her to fit against. Her hands wanted to roam, to move his shirt out of the way and feel his skin spread over the expanse of his back. But she managed to control herself and settled for gently touching a small area … over his shirt … like a good girl. *No, there would be no stripping Jake in the front room*, she chastised herself and was about to laugh at it when she felt Jake's hand make its way up her back and into her hair.

When he buried his hand in her hair, she knew there was no resisting him. Her body lit up with need as she felt his hand tilt her head back, and her gaze met his. It was like everything was in slow motion as he leaned forward, but stopped just short of contact. His warm breath against her lips, his hard arms holding her against his firm body, she could barely take in all the sensations that were assaulting her as he said, "I'm sorry, but I just can't wait any longer to do this." And then his lips were on hers. A quick moment of surprise had her not responding to him instantly, but then she felt it—she felt his soft, full lips against hers—and melted into the kiss. His tongue swept across her lips, tasting her, and she was too overwhelmed to move, so she let him lead.

Positioning her head where he wanted her, she felt his tongue push through her lips and meet hers. Without thought, her tongue came out to greet his. When Jake's chest rumbled against hers and his body tightened, her desire for him jumped, and her hands curled into his back. She wanted to pull him closer, hold him there, and let him devour her, because that is *exactly* what he was doing to her. Jake was devouring her, and there wasn't a thing she could do about it. But to clarify, there was nothing she *wanted* to do about it. Except enjoy every single second. Longing wound its way through her body like a wildfire. He was everywhere without actually being everywhere; but she knew she wanted him more literally everywhere, and she wanted to give him everything. It was calming to come this conclusion, because until then, she hadn't understood how she was going to move on to have an intimate relationship with another man after her divorce. She understood now, and she knew without a doubt that she could give herself to Jake.

As if he heard her thoughts, Jake pressed his hips into hers, and she could feel his arousal for her. It was hard, and real, and very desirable since she had to fight her body's instinct to reach down and get better acquainted with him. Her body answered his by pressing her hips into his hardness. She moaned at the spark of awareness that came from that contact. It was an exquisite sensation that she wanted to repeat, but knew this wasn't the place for it. As Jake slowed the kiss down, because he was in complete control, he gently sucked her lip into his mouth. She wanted to follow it, as far as she could go, and as she felt his teeth graze the surface of her lip, her knees threaten to give out from the huge surge of heat that whipped through her body.

Jake had set her body on fire, brought it to life with need, and then slowly pulled away from her. She was in a cloud of drunken lust, and she couldn't contain the smile that crawled across her face. She was so drunk from that kiss, she barely registered that his finger was now touching the very lip he had just sucked into his mouth. Thankfully, he pulled it away before she thought to do something crazy, like nibble on it, or suck it into her mouth. She tried to focus on him as he sighed and said, "Sorry, but I couldn't wait another minute to do that. I hope I didn't embarrass you in front of Allie, but I really missed you."

Embarrass her … in front of Allie … who's Allie? She huffed out, "To feel embarrassed, I would have to be aware of people around me. I can only see you right now, Jake."

His growling words and quick hard kiss to her lips told her he loved what she said, but she knew that they shouldn't hide out in the living room all night. Even though she really wanted to do just that, she smiled at him and asked, "I seem to recall the promise of pizza. Are you going to feed me or what?"

Jake led her into the kitchen where Allie was hanging out with the boys. She quickly dished up a couple slices for Jake and herself and made a quick retreat to the living room to collect the wine she and Allie had started. She rejoined the group to the sounds of laughter. It was an infectious laugh, and she had no idea why. "What's so funny in here?"

She should have known that the stupid words, fart, butt-crack, and booger were responsible for the random bouts of laughter from the boys. Those usually did the trick. All of them were surrounded by laughter when she heard Logan and Jason calling out from the other room. "Seriously?" she groaned under her breath as the amount of people in her house—Grand Central Station—grew yet again.

CHAPTER EIGHTEEN

"TGIF," Allie said to Gillian as they made the turn out of the school parking lot. It was her day off and after dropping Dylan at school, the plan was to spend it with Allie—apartment hunting. Finding out yesterday that Allie had decided to move back home to San Diego had been great news, and Gillian was going to do whatever she could to encourage it and make it happen. Allie had taken the train down for the weekend because she planned on bringing Logan's truck back up to Los Angeles with her to load it up. Thankfully, his tires being slashed and headlights being smashed in didn't interfere, as it was back on four fully inflated tires and sported new lights in no time. The dent in the fender would be taken care of a bit later. The evil bitch inside her liked the thought of Logan having to stare at the dent for a while, letting it be a reminder to him of his mistakes. The little angel inside would remind her that Logan was already being punished because she was divorcing him. Then, of course, the evil bitch would again add her two cents, *or so you hope it feels like punishment*.

"I really wished you and Logan hadn't already rented out that house next door to yours," Allie added to the conversation that Gillian had yet to participate in.

"Yeah, actually, we decided the other night that we were going to give the tenant notice and then Logan was going to move in there. We have another property that the guy could move into and he said he'd be willing; he just had to see if he could get a roommate. He talked to a friend of his and got back to us yesterday that he would change properties." She glanced over at her friend to gauge

244

her reaction to that news. She and Logan hadn't mentioned it to anyone yet because they wanted to make sure the tenant was okay with it. Some people might have thought it weird that divorced parents would live as neighbors, too, but both Gillian and Logan felt that it was a great idea. They'd have their separate living spaces, yet the kids could see either parent whenever they wanted. They hoped it would be the solution to custody and visitation problems that other couples had. The plan was that they would give it a try for three months and then discuss whether or not it was going to work in the long term.

Allie broke into her thoughts when she asked, "And you're okay with that? More importantly, is Jake okay with that?" Gillian could the see the concern etched on Allie's face. Since she hadn't spoken with Jake about it, she didn't know how he felt. She didn't think she was keeping it a secret—it had only been confirmed last night—but that didn't stop her from feeling like she was being secretive. Bottom line, though, her kids were always going to come first and both she and Logan were going to try what they could to make things easier for them.

She confessed, "I don't know how Jake feels about it yet. You're the first person I've told because it was only confirmed last night." She added that at the end so Allie wouldn't give her any crap about it.

Allie shrugged. "Jake's a good guy. I'm sure if things between you continue, he'll make it okay." Gillian relaxed with Allie's statement. It was true; Jake was a great guy, and she didn't see him making a problem out of something like this, especially since it involved the kids. As she and Allie made their way to the coffee shop, Gillian couldn't help but feel glad that she had confessed that bit of information to someone. They planned to come up with some ideas for living spaces for Allie, and then Gillian was going to meet up with the other source of guilt this week. She had only been able to communicate with Mike via text throughout the week, and she really wanted to speak with him in person about not being able to see him anymore. Truthfully, she knew she didn't necessarily owe him that, but it was who she was as a person, and she really thought he was a great guy. He was going to meet her at around ten o'clock, so that would give her plenty of time to figure out what she was going to say to him.

It was about an hour and a half into the apartment hunting adventure when Gillian had to speak up, "Okay, Allie, I have to be honest with you. I'm really not a big fan of anything we have looked at in your price range. Maybe you should just move in with me, or with Logan, or any one of our friends. I want you here in San Diego, but not in a shady area."

Allie sighed, "I know. I didn't realize it was going to be this hard to find something. I already gave notice at my apartment, and at work. And since I wasn't under contract at either place, I told them my last day was the end of next week."

"Well, we can figure it out. It's not like you are moving anywhere you don't know people, and even if you found something, it might not have been available 'til after you came down anyway. So, you can just stay with me, or with Logan, unless you were considering your parents' place."

"God, no. Please tell me you wouldn't even think that?" Allie said in an offended voice. Of course she wasn't, but Gillian wanted to make sure. "Then take your pick—who do you want to stay with?"

A masculine voice to her left caught her attention when it said, "I know who I would pick, but whatever you do, don't pick the parents." Gillian turned to see Mike standing there, looking down at both of them.

Standing up, Gillian leaned in to hug him before quickly retreating, "Hello Mike."

"Hi there, Gillian," he said, and she was surprised because that sexy voice he had last week wasn't the same as today's. She knew it really was the same, but this time it didn't make her swoony or tingly inside. Lost in thought for a second, she realized that she hadn't introduced him to Allie.

Turning toward her friend, she gestured with her hand and said, "Mike, this is my best friend, Allie Baxter. Allie, this is Mike."

"Oh, so this is the best friend responsible for the meet and greet last week?" Mike said with a little humor in his voice, hinting that he knew who Allie was but that he hadn't actually met her

"Oh, wait. That's right, you two would've met last week ... but you didn't?" Confused by this, she looked down to see her friend staring up at Mike ... blushing? *Oh how very interesting this is*, she thought as she watched Mike extend his hand, while Allie stood up to accept it. Gillian was still watching Allie when Mike leaned over and pressed a kiss to the back of Allie's hand. Her eyes widened in surprise, and a giggle escaped as her cheeks reddened even more. Allie was acting like a schoolgirl in front of Mike ... *Allie liked Mike*?

"How did you two not meet last weekend?" Gillian asked Allie, effectively breaking the spell Mike had apparently cast over her.

Allie quickly pulled her hand from his, directed her attention toward Gillian and said, "What ... Oh, I was busy taking care of everybody so I seemed to miss him."

Even though Allie was speaking to Gillian, Mike responded, "I'm sorry I didn't have the pleasure of meeting you then." This successfully pulled Allie's attention back to him. The weight Gillian felt resting on her shoulders today over having to let him down lifted as she watched him interact with Allie, who smiled shyly at his comment.

"I could say the same about you," Allie came back. There was no witty humor, dry sarcasm, or crude attitude in her words—just plain sincerity. This was an unexpected turn of events for her, and she wasn't quite sure what to do about it.

Finally finding her voice hidden behind all of her surprise, Gillian offered Mike a seat, "Won't you sit down and join us?"

Mike looked at her, smiled, and sat down. "Thanks."

No time like the present, even though it was weird to address in front of Allie now, Gillian began, "Thanks for coming Mike, I wanted to talk to you in person ..." Mike put his hand up to halt her.

"Gillian, there is nothing you need to say to me. I get the picture. I understand. Although I do appreciate you wanting to tell me in person, really, there is nothing you need to say."

"Really?" she asked in a squeaky voice. Clearing her voice, she tried again, "Really?"

A big smile appeared on his face again as he answered, "Really. I've done the dating thing before; I can tell when someone has moved in another direction without me. The text messages that lacked a lot of conversation were a dead giveaway."

"I'm sorry," immediately came out of Gillian's mouth. She felt horrible for making it like she was stringing him along. "It's just that this old friend of mine and I … well we kind of started dating," she finished with a shrug of her shoulders.

"Gillian, it's fine. I understand, you have nothing to feel bad about. Now, would you both be okay if I still join you for a cup of coffee? Or do I have to leave now that I'm not potential dating material?"

Looking over at her friend to see her openly staring at Mike, she added, "Of course you can join us. Would you let me buy your cup of coffee?"

"Absolutely not. What kind of gentlemen would allow a nice lady to spend her money on him," he asked in a mocking tone, reminding her of his playful sense of humor she enjoyed last week. "Now would either of you like a refill?"

"No thanks," Gillian replied, but Allie just shook her head. She tried not to laugh at the cool irony of the situation. Her best friend accompanied her to let a guy down, and then goes ga-ga over him. Gillian had not seen Allie act like this since Marc was around, and it warmed her heart a little. Today, Allie looked a little more … alive.

After his first cup of coffee and a little advice on what areas he thought Allie should avoid living in, Allie opened up in front of

Mike, and Gillian loved that she got to see it happen. Gillian knew that regardless of the fact she and Mike would only ever be friends, he now had a spot on her list of favorite people.

Gillian and Allie spent another thirty minutes chatting with Mike before he had to excuse himself to return to work. He was definitely an easy man to talk to, and Gillian hoped that they could be friends. Once he had left the coffee shop, she turned to Allie to question her reaction to Mike. Allie had her hand up and shook her head saying, "No, Gillian, I'm not going to do this. Just let me handle my own emotions and stay out of it." Then Allie stood up and made her way to the bathroom. Since there was only one subject Allie was closed off about, and that was her late husband, Gillian knew to let her have her space. It was the only way to help Allie, and she didn't want to do anything to derail her progress. If she were to assume what was going on, she would venture to guess that Allie had some kind of attraction to Mike and was now feeling guilty about it.

Sitting there waiting for her friend to return, and feeling lighter now that she had gotten the conversation with Mike successfully out of her way, she focused on the person she'd been wanting to focus on. She took out her phone and was pleasantly surprised to see he had already texted her.

> Jake: In case you were wondering ... I'm thinking about you, and I miss you.
>
> Gillian: I think it's cool that when I pull my phone out to text you, I find a text from you already there.
>
> Jake: What were you going to text me?

Gillian: I was going to ask if you were going to the football game tonight? In case you were wondering.

Jake: If you're going to be there, then so will I. Will you share your blanket with me again?

Gillian: Of course, I don't want you to get cold.

Jake: So are you saying that you will warm me up?

Gillian: Yes, as long as you keep me warm, too.

Jake: I can promise that, beautiful.

Gillian: Oh, and I miss you too … In case you were wondering.

~*~*~*~*~~*~*~*~*~

Jake checked the time and smiled to himself before stuffing his phone back into his pocket. Recalling Gillian's text earlier today saying she would warm him up did just that. He was running late getting here, and even though she was fine with meeting him, he felt bad about it. Especially since he was supposed to be off on Fridays, but he got asked to cover a shift, and he was busy from call to call all day long.

Making his way up to the ticket counter, he put his money down for one ticket when the older woman said, "No charge, sweetie."

Jake looked up at the woman in confusion. "Why?"

She gestured to his uniform, which he didn't have a chance to change before coming. "Paramedics get in free on my watch." He felt a little bad with getting in and skipping the ticket cost. He knew how booster clubs worked and how every little bit helped the program, so he tried to give her the money anyway.

"No, that's okay. I'm off duty at the moment."

The money was shoved back at him as the old woman gave him a questioning look, "Are you saying that if one of those kids out there goes down with a bad injury, and they need help, you wouldn't offer any?"

Taken aback by her comment and a little offended, he said, "Of course not."

"Exactly my point, young man, so there is no need to pay because if you needed to work, I know you would. Now move along, you're holdin' up my line." Then she winked at him and shooed him away with her hands. He barely got a thank you out before she was helping the next customer. Shaking his head at the feisty old woman, Jake rounded the corner to find Dylan and Ryan coming out of the bathroom in a bee-line for the snack-bar.

He made his way over to join them. "Hey boys, what are we getting tonight?"

Hellos came from both boys simultaneously before Dylan said, "We're getting hot chocolate for all of us. Did you want one, too?"

"I sure do. Do you have enough money?"

"Yes, Mom gave me money. Told me to make sure I got the change before walking away, too."

"That's good advice, buddy, make sure you do. Can I go sit with your mom, or do you need my help?"

"We don't need any help. Mom is sitting with her friend. He's nice. He didn't kiss her on the lips like you do now," Dylan said in such a nonchalant tone that Jake almost missed what he said. Turning in the direction of the stands, Jake sought out Gillian and her *friend*. Since he knew where she liked to sit, it wasn't hard to do. Finding her, he could see that she was sitting next to a man and talking—she even laughed a little. The guy had her complete attention, and Jake didn't like it at all. The caveman in him was really getting a workout lately, and with that thought, he made his way toward Gillian, keeping his eyes on her as much as possible as he maneuvered through the crowd. He knew his reaction to seeing anyone near her needed to change, but this was still too new; he couldn't risk anything, he wouldn't. Climbing the steps, he made his way across the bleachers to where she was sitting. Her back was to him, so she couldn't see his approach, but the guy could. The guy looked up at Jake from where he was seated, causing Gillian to look behind her, too.

Before breaking eye contact with the guy to look at Gillian, a small knowing smile appeared on his face, and he gave Jake a slight nod. Slipping down onto the seat next to her, Jake's arm immediately found her waist, and he slid tightly up beside her.

"Hey beautiful," he said, and she gave him one of those smiles, relaxing him.

Turning toward him, she leaned in and gave him a sweet kiss on the lips before pulling back and saying, "Hey yourself." She kept her gaze on him, and he couldn't help but melt a little, so he gave her a smile back. "Jake, I would like you to meet Mike," she said and then turned toward the other guy and said, "Mike, this is Jake, the friend that I was telling you about."

Jake turned his attention to this Mike guy, who now had his hand extended in Jake's direction. For a moment he was thankful that he was sitting to Gillian's right, so that his right hand was free because he wasn't sure he would have let her go to shake the offered hand. Mike huffed a laugh before saying, "I figured that just by the look I got. Nice to meet you man, heard a lot about you."

Jake shook Mike's hand and asked, "How do you two know each other?"

Mike said, "I had the pleasure of meeting Gillian last Friday and was able to enjoy her company for dinner last weekend." The guy didn't say it in a nasty tone so Jake could only take it as sincere as he realized that this was her date last Saturday. He unconsciously stiffened a little, and Gillian leaned into Jake more, allowing him to hold her a little tighter.

"Mike's the nice guy who took me to dinner last week."

The soft tone of her voice had him calming down a little more; she was obviously worried about his reaction. He wasn't going to be an ass or anything, and clearly Mike wasn't, so Jake said the only thing he could say, "Well any friend of Gillian's, is a friend of mine."

"Thanks, I appreciate that," Mike said to Jake before turning his attention to Gillian again. "So you'll give that information to Allie? I think it would be a great opportunity for her. The complex is great, I know the condo has an alarm system, and it's ready immediately. When she calls, just have her tell him that I recommended her."

"That does sound like a great opportunity. I really want to make sure she isn't in some dump."

"Definitely not a dump," Mike said with a laugh.

Jake wasn't sure what was going on so he asked. Gillian responded with an excited little squirm as she turned and gave her full attention to him. "Allie didn't say it to everyone last night because you know how she is about attention, but guess what?" Her excitement was adorable and apparently contagious because he laughed at her.

With an excited, slightly mocking girl tone, he said, "Oh my god, what?"

She slapped his shoulder, before continuing, "Allie has decided to move back home! She is moving back to San Diego. Isn't that great?"

"Holy shit! Are you serious?" he asked.

"Yes! I'm so excited, can you tell? She told me last night just before you got there, but I didn't say anything because I figured she would. But today we tried looking for a place for her, and I didn't like any of the places we found. I suggested that she could live with any one of us, but she didn't seem too keen on that idea. So Mike just gave me some information on a neighbor of his who is subletting his condo for a year, since he moved in with his fiancé and can't get out of his lease. Isn't that great?"

Anyone could see that Gillian was super excited about this, but Jake knew what it really meant. He knew how much they all worried about Allie, and the fact that she was moving back to San

Diego meant that she had made some progress with the guilt she had over Marc's accident.

"That is great news, baby. I am glad to hear it," he said as she threw her arms around his neck for an unexpected hug. Jake couldn't contain his surprised laugh as he hugged her back. Once again, the sincere smile on this Mike guy's face as he watched Gillian get excited over this had Jake accepting him a little. Anyone who wasn't captured under Gillian's spell wasn't normal to him, and Mike was clearly under her spell.

The boys returned with the hot chocolates, including one for Mike. Gillian wrapped her blanket securely around their legs before making sure the boys had their blankets on. All snuggled up and warm with Gillian—it was a great night.

CHAPTER NINETEEN

Jake couldn't contain his excitement. Gillian was all his tonight and he couldn't wait. She had texted him while he was at work saying that the kids were all gone for the evening, and she would love to make him dinner. Well, there just weren't words to describe how he felt knowing that she wanted to feed him and spend time with him—only him. The speed of his shift today slowed to crawl once she texted him, and it didn't matter what he did, it wouldn't speed up. When there was a request for assistance on the radio about ten minutes before shift change he cringed at the thought it was going to prevent him from getting off on time. His partner, Eddie, knew Jake was eager to leave and gave him a knowing look—it sucked, but that they had to respond. He was just reaching for the radio when the voice of another rig came through claiming the call. He felt bad for not wanting to take the call, but was glad they didn't have to. Eddie just shook his head and gave a small laugh at Jake as he said, "You got it bad, man."

What could Jake say to that? He knew damn well he had it bad for Gillian, but he really couldn't give a shit about how that might look to others. He certainly wasn't going to deny it. It had taken almost two decades to get her, and he was going to embrace it tightly. "Sure do."

And being the great partner that Eddie was, he even offered to complete the shift paperwork for Jake so he could get to Gillian sooner. He made a mental note on his drive that he needed to send Eddie some steaks or something to thank him. After a quick run home to shower and wash off his workday, he was finally pulling up to her place. He made sure he didn't run to the door and make himself look like a fool. As he climbed the steps of the porch, he could hear music blaring from inside, which made him smile. Gillian loved to blare her music.

Knowing she wouldn't hear him if he knocked, not that he wasn't accustomed to walking right in anyway, he made his way inside. Following the sound to the kitchen, he found Gillian looking adorable in a pair of yoga pants and a tank top. Her long brown hair was piled on top of her head in a messy concoction of curls and swirled colors, exposing her bare neck to him. He could smell the scent of food baking in the oven, and it filled him with warmth knowing that she prepared it for him. Since her back was to him, she still hadn't noticed he was there as she worked at washing vegetables in the sink. He was about to make his presence known when she started moving her hips in time with the music she was blaring, and Jake's body jumped in awareness.

He stood there for moment and absorbed the sight of her dancing in the kitchen. It was sweet, and sexy, and a complete turn on. Hell, lately, just seeing her breathe was a turn on. He wanted to just press his body against hers and envelope her in his arms, but didn't want to scare her since she hadn't noticed his presence. Reaching over, he turned down the music, slowly, so as not to surprise her, but just enough to get her to notice and turn around. This had the desired effect because she glanced over her shoulder at the radio to see what was wrong. Her eyes landed on him, and she startled a bit before a big smile spread across her face at the sight of him. Seeing her reaction to him was like a drug to his system, and the warmth and heady sensation of her excitement spread. Oh, he knew she had always enjoyed his company, but now he could see the difference. He could see that he had moved past friends with her, and he was definitely okay with that.

He didn't want to wait another second, and he smiled back and made his way toward her. She was still busy in the sink as his hands found her waist, and his lips found her cheek. "Hey there sexy. I'm sorry if I startled you," he said while his hands ventured forward from her waist to gently pull her body against his. She went willingly and sighed as her body relaxed against him, like it was the only place in the world she wanted to be. Again that heady feeling of satisfaction spread through him. He knew for certain there was no other place in the world he wanted to be either.

"It's okay. I'm just wondering how long you were standing there and if you happened to bear witness to my horrible singing skills?" she said a little breathlessly as he pressed soft kisses to her bare shoulder and neck. His need was rising, and the desire to make her completely his was a living, breathing being inside of him. He was about to tell her that he unfortunately missed that part of the show when he suddenly felt his body pulled away from hers—flying backward. Jake felt his ass hit the ground with a thud as he tried to shake the confusion that surrounded him at what was going on. He saw Gillian spin around and surprise register on her face. Jake looked up only to see Logan standing over him, red faced and furious.

It took Jake a moment to gather what was going on as Logan proceeded to reach down and grab Jake's shirt to yank him back off the ground while growling at him, "Get your fucking hands off of my wife!" The adrenaline started to pump through Jake's body when he heard Logan say *my wife*, because that certainly wasn't the case anymore.

Jake's feet hit the ground, and his hands grabbed onto Logan's wrists to rip them from his shirt. He stood there for a moment just glaring at his longtime friend, knowing that this was the moment he knew was going to happen. Logan's chest was heaving from restrained anger that Jake could see playing across his features. Yet there they stood, just watching each other. He wasn't sure if it was the fact that they had been friends all this time, and Logan was trying to control his actions, but Jake knew it was time to test their friendship. This was when he stood up and staked his claim on Gillian, to Logan, instead of conceding to him as he did so many years ago.

"She's not your wife anymore, Logan," Jake said in a low, menacing tone. He needed to make it clear that he wasn't going to back down, but his words only seemed to fuel the anger that Logan was restraining.

"I should have known you would try and pull something like this, Jake! I should have known you would make a move for my girl!" Logan barked at him. Before Jake could say anything in response to that, Logan was lunging toward him with his fist in the air. He was preparing to defend himself when Gillian flung herself in their direction. She somehow managed to wrap her arms around Logan's arm and used all of her body weight to drop to the ground and pull him off balance. If Jake weren't so riled up from the whole situation, he would've found it funny to watch. Logan lost his balance and stumbled a bit then made a grab for Gillian to prevent her from hitting the ground as he grumbled, "What the fuck, Gillian!"

She immediately sprung to her feet in front of Logan, and Jake gritted his teeth as he watched his longtime friend put his hands on her waist, right where Jake's hands had been not two minutes ago. Jealousy, strong and abrupt, reared its ugly head as Jake readied himself to take out the threat. Logan had no business touching her there—she wasn't his anymore. Moving forward, Jake placed his hands on Gillian's sides, above Logan's, and started to pull her away from him, when she muttered words he wasn't expecting, "Get out of here, Jake."

Taken up short by that demand, it took him a moment to back off. He didn't want his hands to leave her body. It was almost like if he broke contact with her now, he wouldn't be able to get it back. When he didn't make the move to leave she repeated herself, and it stung a little bit more the second time he heard it. She hadn't made an attempt to break her eye contact with Logan, so she was still facing away from Jake. He didn't like it, but he knew that he should do what she asked him to do. He tried to convince himself that he wasn't conceding to Logan, but was doing as Gillian wished. He was unsure what this meant for him and her, and made moving one of the hardest things he'd done to date, but he did it anyway.

Jake took one step back, another step away from Gillian. It was difficult and painful to do. Still feeling the desire to beat the shit out of Logan for having his hands on her, he glared at him as he backed away. The smug look on Logan's face told Jake he thought he had won, and that didn't make leaving any easier. With all of his power, he took in a deep breath, turned around, and made his way out of the house. Away from Gillian … Gillian *and* Logan.

~*~*~*~*~~*~*~*~*~

Gillian knew the moment Jake had left, and she didn't like how it felt one little bit. She had to tell him to leave the room, because as much as Logan deserved humiliation, she wasn't one who dished that out. But she was going to put her *ex*-husband in his place, and she was going to make sure he knew that *his* place was not with her anymore. Reaching down, she placed both of her hands around each of Logan's wrists, and dug her nails into them, deep. Logan quickly retracted them in pain. "Ow, Gillian, what the hell?"

"You seem to be under some misconception that you have any right to touch my body, Logan Baxter! In fact, you seem to be delusional since you just called me *your wife* and *your girl*! Get it through your head, Logan … I am not yours anymore!" She finished off her statement by giving him a good shove into the counter behind him as she moved in the opposite direction. Knowing that the more space there was between them, the less likely she would be to inflict bodily harm. But Logan attempted to eliminate that space and advanced on her, so she quickly put her arm straight out in front of her, halting his progress. He looked as if he was taking a moment to process his thoughts and formulate a plan. She needed him the hell out of there, and she needed it now. She refused to let him take any of her time away with Jake. "Why are you here, Logan?"

Logan ignored her question and instead demanded answers from her. "What the hell is going on with you and Jake? How long has it been going on?" The tone of his voice was more than irritation or anger; there was clear implication in his question. He actually thought she was seeing Jake while she was still committed to him? She was certain that Logan having that impression was solely so he could feel better about himself, but that wasn't going to happen. He was the cheater here, not her.

Gillian stepped forward and got right in his face before growling at him, "I'm not sure I like what you are *implying*, Logan, but to answer your questions, one week! Whatever the hell is going on between Jake and me has only been going on for one week!" He visibly deflated, like the information was the exact opposite of what he had hoped for. It was clear he had developed some hope that she was as guilty as him. *Not in this lifetime!* She wanted to avoid discussing her and Jake with Logan, since she hadn't even spoken with Jake about it, so she asked in an exasperated tone, "Why are you even here, Logan? You're supposed to be with the kids."

"The kids went to dinner with my parents. I thought I would use the opportunity to come by and talk to you. Beg you even … to consider giving *us* another chance." The last part came out barely above a whisper. Her heart clenched at the sound of it because this man had been one of the main focuses in her life for so long. She knew she would always be connected to him, and she wanted him to be part of her life, but she knew he was no longer the man that her world revolved around. And for the first time in months, she was confident in that realization. Sure, she knew she was moving on, but now she knew with whom she wanted to move on. She had to make sure he understood that there were no more chances for them.

Feeling suddenly deflated herself, she leaned back against the counter next to the man who was supposed to be her forever and folded her arms over her chest. Glancing over at him, standing next to her with a resolved look on his face, he knew what was coming—she didn't have to voice it. He had finally let her words sink in. Logan let out a little huff and shook his head slightly before saying, "There really isn't ever going to be another chance for us, is there?"

Gillian gently shook her head before giving him a sad smile and confirming it for him, "No Logan, you already used up that chance. There is nothing left for us … it's time for you to accept that and move on, too."

The two of them stood there silently for a few minutes. The music was still playing, so Gillian moved away from her spot next to Logan to turn it off, before turning around and looking at him. She wasn't really sure what to do or say next, but she was anxious to get back to Jake. The timer on the stove went off and startled her a little bit before she quickly retrieved the contents from the oven. Once again, she turned and gave Logan a questioning look. He sighed and stood up straight, looked her directly in the eye and said, "I'm not sure I like the idea of you and Jake together."

Gillian snorted a laugh at him while saying, "Not that I care what you think about the topic of me being with any man … but you know that Jake would never do anything to hurt me." Raising her eyebrows at him, she dared him to refute that information. He didn't, because he couldn't. He knew what Jake was made of, and there was no argument he could make about her being with him.

Logan gave her a slight nod and started to make his way toward the front of the house. Gillian followed closely behind him, not wanting him distracted by anything that would give him an idea to stick around. She wasn't sure where Jake was at the moment, but she assumed that he wasn't anywhere in the path from the kitchen to the front door. When they made it to the front door, he turned around and faced her. He looked as though he was trying to find words to convey what he was feeling, so she figured she would help him along. "Go see our kids, Logan. Hang out with them … be with them. They always make me feel better." She gave him a smile and patted him on his arm. His answering smile was forced and pathetic, but it was still there. After another nod and no words, Logan turned and quietly left.

Thankful that was over, she made a hasty path through her house in search of Jake. She came up short when she found the poolroom empty. There wasn't even a light on, which meant he was never in there. Confused as to where he might be, she peeked out in the yard, her room, even the bathrooms. Jake wasn't anywhere. She began to get nervous and anxious. *Did he leave? Oh God, was he mad?* Thinking back at what she said to him, she realized it sounded bad, but she only meant for him to leave the room, not the house. She had to find him, hoping she didn't hurt him and ruin what was just starting between them. A pressure started to build in her chest as worry and panic took root. When she saw that his jeep was nowhere to be seen either, the pressure got stronger. "Oh no! Jake where are you?" she whispered desperately to herself.

Quickly retrieving her cell phone, she dialed him … no answer. Her panic began to rise as she tried to figure out what to do. She hoped she didn't hurt him and knew she needed to talk to him to set things straight. As her mind started whirling with fear and concern, she texted him.

Gillian: Where are you … why did you leave?

She stood there and stared at her phone, willing him to respond to her, waiting for it to vibrate in her hand. But nothing came. So she sent a second one ...

Gillian: Jake ... please come back.

She didn't know exactly how long she stood there staring at her phone, but when it finally vibrated and Jake's name appeared on her screen. Gillian let out a long sigh of relief as she parked herself in front of the window to wait for him.

~*~*~*~*~*~~*~*~*~*~

Pulling his Jeep out of Gillian's driveway was a very difficult task. He didn't want to leave, and he didn't like the anxiety that it caused him. While driving to his place, he fought his inner demons as they clawed their way to the surface and plagued him with horrible thoughts. *What if she picked Logan? What if he was able to plead his case successfully this time? She must not want to be with you since she told you to get out of there!*

They were cruel thoughts to have, and he knew he was torturing himself as panic started to bubble its way through his body. He pulled into his own driveway and sat there, trying to control the fear and panic he was experiencing. Pulling his keys from the ignition, he attempted to get out, but couldn't. This was not where he wanted to be—where he planned to be—tonight. He knew he wasn't going to be able to relax or calm down at home, so he started the car again and backed out of his driveway. Unsure where to go, but knowing he needed to drive, he turned toward the freeway. *A long drive up the coast would help,* he thought.

As he pulled up to the light for the freeway entrance, he felt his phone vibrating in the depths of his pocket, but couldn't take the time to pull it out since the light had turned green. Wanting and hoping it would be Gillian, he quickly pulled over so he could maneuver his body up to reach his phone. He felt it vibrate again as he finally got it out, but fumbled with it, causing it to fall to the floorboard. "Damn it."

Blindly reaching around under his legs he finally retrieved it and tried to focus on the screen, praying it was Gillian. Relief poured over him, and his tense body relaxed as he saw that it was her … Gillian was looking for him. He didn't want to take the time to process her question, so he just quickly pulled back into traffic to make his way back to her. His relief was strong and palpable, and his need to get to her was stronger than ever. He felt his phone vibrate again, and glanced at it, seeing a second text from her, making him realize he hadn't even responded to her first one in his haste. Once he pulled safely up to a light, he texted her back.

Jake: I'm on my way.

~*~*~*~*~~*~*~*~*~

Relieved that Jake was coming back but still anxious to see him, she paced a small path in her living room while she waited. He was coming back, but the need to comfort him—and even herself—by touching him was staggering. She couldn't help but wonder if she should be worried about this immense connection she now had with Jake. This was Jake, one of her best friends, there had always been a connection … it was just more intimate now. Jake had always been important, but she realized now that her need for him was physical—visceral. Gillian had to know that he was okay, and she knew that he would be able to ease her anxiety with his arrival. She shook her head and gave a little snort at the thought that this must be what an addict feels like.

She knew what it was like to be connected to another person, being married to Logan for so many years, but she had never felt this kind of need for anyone else, never felt the need like this hit her so strong in such a short period of time. Then again, Jake wasn't new in her life, just this role was. While lost in thought, headlights illuminated her front window, startling her. This filled her with more need. The need to get to him had her rushing out the front door, the need to touch him mounting in her system. She pushed open the screen door and practically jumped down the front steps to get there. She met him halfway, where she found him rushing to get to her, too. He opened his arms in time to catch her as she flung her body at him. When his arms clamped down tightly around her, she nestled her face and nose firmly at the base of his neck. She sighed a deep breath of relief as his scent enveloped her, calmed her … home. After feeling a little lost for months, she felt she was home again.

~*~*~*~*~*~~*~*~*~*~

Jake knew this was where she belonged, in his arms, safe, warm, and his. She had her face buried in his neck, and he could feel her rapid heartbeat against his chest, her breath on the skin of his neck, and his body reacted to her closeness. The need to make her completely his was so strong, and he didn't want to fight it anymore. He squeezed her a little tighter and turned to kiss her forehead, taking in a deep breath of her scent. "Why did you leave?" she asked in a timid voice buried against his neck.

268

"I thought you wanted me to leave. You told me to get out of there," he said while rubbing circles with his hands up and down her back, comforting her, and him.

She snorted adorably at his comment before saying, "I only meant out of the room, Jake. I wouldn't send you away like that."

Pulling her face away from his neck and looking up at him, she lifted a hand to his cheek and gently caressed it as she repeated herself, "I wouldn't send you away like that, Jake." The certainty in her eyes was trying to convey more than her words—he wasn't sure what just yet—but the relief that swamped him at that very moment was almost staggering as he fought his body's reaction. The look in her eyes, the worried expression on her face, she had to love him, he just knew it.

"I'm sorry if I worried you, but I thought you wanted me to go. I would never leave like that unless you told me to, and it was extremely difficult to do," he said as he leaned down to place a gentle kiss to her lips. Just the contact of their lips, however so slight it was, set Jake's body on fire—elevating his need, if that were even possible.

He felt her breath across his face, soft and husky, as she said, "I only wanted you to leave the room so I could put Logan in his place. I needed to remind him that the claim he thought he had on me didn't exist." She paused and tilted her head up to look him in the eye. "I didn't think it was appropriate to yell at him in front you." He should have known that, because she was always thinking of others. A feeling of calm settled over him as he looked at the beautiful, thoughtful person in his arms. Standing there in the driveway, he knew she was his. She was his, and it was about time he had her all to himself.

His hands around her waist tightened their grip allowing him to lift her up. Gillian wrapped her arms around his neck and her legs around his waist, just like he wanted her to. She looked down at him and must have seen the lust, and intent, in his eyes. She gave him a shy smile before burying her face in his neck again. He thought it was the most wonderful feeling in the world as he made his way into her house. Closing the door, and locking it behind him, he made a mental note to put a chain on her door to prevent being walked in on like that again.

Jake made his way to the couch where he sat down with her securely in his lap, both knees at his sides. Her face was still buried in his neck as he ran his hand up her back to the soft skin of her neck. His fingers buried themselves in the thick hair at the base of her neck and gently kneaded the area. When he felt her body relax to his hands ministrations, he moved her head so he could see her face. Placing his other hand on her cheek, enjoying the feel of her skin against his hand, he looked her in the eyes and gently asked, "Can I have you, Gillian?"

CHAPTER TWENTY

"Can I have you Gillian?" Jake whispered as he leaned in and gently placed a kiss on her neck, just below her ear. As if her body was answering for her, she tilted her head to the side, exposing more for him to taste. He groaned in response and slid his hand from her cheek into her hair, holding her in that position. She was open, submissive, and vulnerable to him. But this was Jake; he would never do anything to hurt her ... he never had. Her heart rate increased, and her breathing became more rapid as he continued to pepper tiny open-mouthed kisses to the side of her neck, using his grip on her hair to gently move her at his will. "Can I have you Gillian?" he repeated, and she realized she hadn't actually responded to his request. Her body was screaming *hell yes,* but she had yet to verbalize it to him. Could she do this? Could she take this step with one of her oldest and best friends?

"I have wanted you for so long, Gillian," he said as he moved up her neck and gently kissed her jaw line, making it almost impossible for her to form coherent speech, but she had to try.

"You have?" she whispered. She could feel his smile against her skin as he continued to feather kisses across her jaw and up her cheek. He then cupped both hands around the base of her head, tilting her face in his direction before answering her.

"I have wanted you since the first day of class, second semester of our junior year ..." He leaned in and placed a kiss over her right eyelid. "I have wanted you since the moment you swung that bat and caught my undivided attention." She felt another gentle kiss on the tip of her nose. "I have wanted you since that same day, when after class, you laughed at something I said to you. I have no idea what it was I said because the minute I heard your laugh, it was all I could think about." Then he placed another light kiss over her left eyelid. "I have wanted you since later that day when I pointed you out to my friends. I had told them how great you could swing a bat, but what I really should have said was that I had found the girl of my dreams." She could feel his warm breath feather across her forehead as he placed a lingering kiss there. But as soon as she processed what he had said, she startled a bit and opened her eyes. She pulled her head back slightly so she could see his eyes, but tightened her grip on his shoulders so he didn't think she was pulling away from him.

... *the girl of his dreams?* She wanted to question that statement, but the look in his eyes said it all. She could see nothing but love and adoration in his eyes. He must have sensed she was questioning his statement, so while still holding her face, his thumbs idly stroked her cheeks, he pushed on, "I have wanted you since we were seventeen years old, Gillian, and I fell in love with you shortly after that. I saw you get in Logan's car the same day I found you, and watched you drive away with him, taking a piece of my heart with you that you didn't even know you had." His eyes looked so sad, almost as if he was remembering the way he felt that day. Her heart clenched at the thought of causing him any pain, even if she had no idea. Breaking eye contact with her, he pulled her close to him once again and placed another lingering kiss to her forehead. "Then, the other night, when I pulled up to your house and watched you climb up into that truck, with some other guy ... I felt like history was repeating itself, and I was going to lose the chance I thought had finally arrived."

Oh my god! "Jake, I'm so ..." He placed a finger over her lips to silence her. He shook his head at her, and gave her a slight smile, looking embarrassed by what he had confessed.

"You didn't know ... I never told you, so you have nothing to apologize for. I'm not telling you this now because I want to make you feel bad. I'm telling you all of this because I need you to know that even though we have been best friends for seventeen years ... I want more. I want you." She could feel the passion in his next kiss. Jake wanted her ... Jake loved her. She felt that possibly, deep down, she may have known this, but knew nothing could ever happen because of circumstances. Of course she loved him already, but could there be passion ... could she be *in* love with him? It certainly felt like it because just a touch of his lips caused her skin to tingle in anticipation. *Fall in love with Jake? Yes, she could. She knew she was already more than halfway there.*

Jake ended the kiss and looked her in the eyes. There was questioning in his eyes ... waiting for an answer. "Can I have you Gillian?" She lifted one hand up and gently swept back the lock of hair that had fallen forward into his face. Her hand followed the hair back on his head as she ran her fingers through the thick locks, caressing him. Jake sighed and closed his eyes as he melted into her hand. Her hands met at the base of his neck, and she tilted his head so she could place her own soft kisses to his skin. First, her lips found his eyelids, then the tip of his nose, and finally his forehead, before returning to his lips.

After placing one more kiss on his lips, she pulled away ever so slightly so that she could whisper, "Will you catch me Jake?" She felt his hands tighten his hold on her. "I'm falling for you, Jake, but I need to know that you'll catch me."

Once again, his hands were in her hair, angling her face toward his, so he had her complete attention, before saying, "The only place you will fall, Gillian, is right where you are, in these arms, in my life. You are everything to me, and I will do whatever I have to do to prove that to you." He leaned in to her, and she could feel his trembling lips on hers. Leaning his forehead against hers, he whispered, "Fall, Gillian. Go ahead and fall, and I promise I'll catch you."

She knew he was holding himself back, and she wanted him to let go. His whispered reassurance sounded almost desperate—he was begging her to take a chance on him … so she took it. "Ask me again, Jake," she whispered back to him.

When he pulled his head away from hers, he looked her in the eyes and asked in a voice laced with passion and desperation, "Can I have you Gillian?"

She smiled at him, "Yes, Jake. You can have me … I'm yours." Before she could process his response, Jake's one hand tightened in her hair and the other wrapped firmly around her waist as he pulled their bodies tightly together. His lips descended on hers like he was afraid she might change her mind—or like he was expressing seventeen years of pent up need. It was a heady thought to think that this beautiful man had loved her all these years … wanted her all these years. She mentally tried to process that, but momentarily lost the ability to think when Jake's tongue swept across her lips seeking entrance, demanding. She opened to him and let the dance of their tongues begin. But the moment she felt Jake's hand smooth its way up her body and gently cup her breast on the outside of her shirt, she lost all coherent thought and gave into the sensations overtaking her body.

~*~*~*~*~*~~*~*~*~*~*~

Jake couldn't contain himself. The emotions and sensations that were surrounding him—them—were intense. But this was real. He was actually touching Gillian. She was going to be his in every possible way, starting here and now. It was an overwhelming realization to think that all of his dreams were about to come true. Maybe not all at the same time, but this was where it would all start. Having Gillian in his arms was what his dreams were made of, he thought, as he felt her place her lips gently over his. When he pulled away, she smiled at him, and he felt like he was standing on the edge of a cliff, waiting for someone to save him, waiting for her answer. Then she said the sweetest words he had ever heard, "Yes, Jake. You can have me ... I'm yours."

His body's response was instant as his hand dove into her hair so he could have her lips against his again. He could feel their softness as he slid his tongue across the bottom one, wanting in. A little sigh had her opening for him, allowing him to dive in. Never had he tasted anything so sweet, and he wanted more, needed more. It was as if his body had a mind of its own, as his hand left the small of her back and gently followed the curve of her waist, up over her ribs before curving around front to tenderly cup one breast through her shirt. It was a perfect fit for his hand, and he gave it a gentle squeeze. Gillian's body reacted, and she broke contact of their lips as she dropped her head back and sighed.

Leaning forward, he laved his tongue to the side of her neck as his hand continued its attention to her breast. Jake could feel her pulse beating rapidly at the base of her neck as his tongue passed over it. As if luring him in, his lips covered the area, and then

275

sucked it into his mouth. When he heard her quick intake of air and felt her hands tighten in his hair, he applied more pressure, taking more of her into his mouth. More, he wanted more. Making a path down her neck, he paused, only to take another nibble, first at the base of her soft neck, then the curve of her collarbone, across her shoulder, and finally to the freckles that peppered the skin there. He had to have more.

Wrapping his arms around her, he quickly moved her from his lap to lying beneath him on the couch. The momentary loss of her body against his was painful, but eased the moment he laid his body on top of hers, and her legs wrapped around his waist again. His arousal was evident to her now as his body nestled into her center, and he moaned at the firm contact of her warmth against his. He paused, taking a moment to absorb the contact, and sighed as he buried his face in her neck again. Gillian lifted her hips, applying pressure against him, and he couldn't help the groan that escaped him. "God, you feel so good against me, Gillian. It's like the most exquisite type of torture and the most satisfying addiction all at the same time."

She responded without words as he felt her hands grip his hair tightly and force his head to the side so she should feast on his neck. The warmth of her tongue against his skin sent a shock straight through his body, making his erection jump in his pants. Gillian felt it, too, and it spurred her on because her grip tightened as she sucked more of his skin into her mouth. It was Heaven and Hell all rolled into one. In an attempt to try and have more of her, he began to suck and lick a path down toward her breast. Cupping the soft flesh in his hand, he put his mouth over her nipple and gave it a little nibble through her shirt. She gasped and arched her body up into his as yet another groan escaped him. "More Gillian, I need more of you."

Sliding her shoulder straps off her shoulder and down her arm, he lifted his head and watched as her skin slowly revealed itself to him. All that beautiful soft skin made his mouth water. He knew Gillian was watching him as he gazed on the parts of her body he'd never had the privilege of seeing before, so he glanced up at her. Keeping his eyes locked with hers and his hand cupping her soft flesh, he leaned forward and laved his tongue across the top of her firm tip. The arousal in her eyes intensified as she broke eye contact and instead watched as he praised her breast with his mouth. Needing more, he maneuvered the other side of her shirt down to free her other breast, paying it the same attention. She began to squirm beneath him as he gently sucked and nibbled on her nipples. He felt her arch her hips against him, seeking more contact as her hands roamed across his shoulders, to his hair, down his back.

"Jake ..." she sighed to him. She was asking, pleading with him for something.

Wanting her to know he would take care of her, he said, "I've got you baby ... tell me what you need."

She pulled his head away from her skin, forcing him to look down at her. Her gaze captured his, and in a husky voice full of arousal, she said, "You, Jake. I need *you*." It was a growl that escaped him this time as he reached down to help her lift his shirt off. Levering his body allowed him to feel the torture of her body pressing against his straining erection. The feel of her hands against his bare skin shocked him momentarily, causing a shiver. Then she set out to drive him crazy while her hands roamed across his shoulders and chest. When her fingers gently swiped across a nipple, she looked up at him, as if asking permission. There was no question as to whether or not it was okay—it was one of the best things he had ever felt.

"I love the feel of your hands on me, Gillian. I have waited a long time to know this feeling … and I want more."

As if he had given her the permission she was waiting for, she leaned up and pressed her open mouth to his chest. He felt the soft warmth of her tongue, then the sharp nip of her teeth as she sucked the skin into her mouth. Arousal was sharp and fast, and whatever blood remained elsewhere dropped to the lower half of his body. He wasn't going to last, he wasn't going to make it; he had to have her … now. Lifting his body off hers was hard to do, but there were too many layers between them, and he was not doing this on the couch.

As he stood up, he pulled her shirt up and over her head. When her hands came back down, they went immediately to the waistband of his pants. He needed to get some control before everything ended before it even began. Pulling her hands away from his waist, she looked up and pouted at him as he held her hands in his. "I'm not denying you anything, beautiful, we just need to move this to a better location." Helping her up, he once again lifted her to carry into the bedroom. As her legs wrapped around his waist, he realized that it was possibly his new favorite position, and he would have her like this as often as possible.

~*~*~*~*~*~*~*~*~

278

Gillian was on fire, and the only person who could put it out was Jake. It was the only way she could describe it. Every cell in her body was on edge as Jake carried her to the bedroom, and it only magnified with each bounce his stride made. The friction of his jeans pressing against her core was enough to make her explode. If she weren't completely lost in the cloud of lust and need, she might fear being embarrassed about it. But she wouldn't be, because she couldn't recall the last time she had wanted something so bad. Her need for him was so great, she apparently couldn't even walk places on her own—he had to carry her.

Carrying her certainly had its benefits, though, because now she could kiss, and lick, and suck whatever skin she could get her lips on—his neck, his earlobe, his shoulder, back to his neck and earlobe. She couldn't get to all the places she wanted to be all at the same time. Vaguely hearing the bedroom door close and lock, she pulled her lips away from his neck and looked at him as they stood in front of her bed. He was staring back at her, and she couldn't tell for sure if he was asking her a silent question or not, but she felt the need to reassure him. So she pressed her lips against his, and then gently pressed with her tongue. Jake growled again, which was one of the hottest sounds she had ever heard, and then his tongue was on hers.

The lust that slowed down for a few moments was immediately amplified, and she was battling for as much of Jake as she could taste. Her body was slowly lowered to the bed, and then Jake was standing over her. "I have to get these out of the way, beautiful," he said as he undid the tie on her pants and slowly slid them down her legs. She was thankful she had prepared for this possible event as she felt Jake's hands travel back up the legs he had just stripped her pants from. Pausing in his venture up her body, he stopped and stared at her again. "God, Gillian ... you are one of the most breathtaking sites I have ever had the honor of seeing."

Now that her whole body was privy to him, she was certain he could see a flush blossom at his compliment. He didn't bother to acknowledge it, though, before he removed the last barrier that stood between her body perishing in this fire or experiencing the sweet satisfaction of release.

~*~*~*~*~~*~*~*~*~

Removing the last of Gillian's clothing had Jake almost losing it, once and for all. He had been waiting so long for this to happen and wanted to make sure it was perfect for her, for them. Finally seeing her body, laid out before him like this, was even more beautiful than he imagined. Standing over her, he removed what remained of his clothes as he stared down at her. It was comforting to see the completely lust induced fog in Gillian's eyes. There was no uncertainty there, and for that, he was thankful. He knew that for being best friends for so long, this was a huge leap. But he was more than ready to make that jump, with her.

As he crawled up her body, he made sure to taste as much as he could on the way. He tasted the soft skin of her belly as he laved his tongue across a few stretch marks that were there. She may not have considered herself perfect, but she was to him. She started to get impatient and began to squirm under him as he slowly made the trek up to her breasts, where he had to taste more. As she arched her body up toward his mouth, she begged, "Please Jake, I *need* you ... please."

Lifting himself up, he reached for a condom out of his pants pocket and met her hand instead. She gave a quick shake of her head saying, "You don't need that, Jake." He knew he would drown in the arousal visible in her eyes if he didn't do something about it. He didn't stop to question her statement, but instead lowered himself back on top of her. Positioning his hard body between her legs, he felt her warmth slide against his, and they both moaned at the contact. With his arms resting on either side of her head, he stroked her hair from her face and kissed her.

Pulling back to hold her gaze, he watched her face as he slowly rocked his body into hers. The sigh that escaped her lips as her heat now fully surrounded him almost made him come undone. Staying just like that for a moment, his body buried deep in hers, the woman he has loved for as long as he could remember, he felt complete.

"You're so beautiful. I've waited so long for this. It's perfect. *You're* perfect," he said, kissing her as he slowly slid back before pushing deeper, translating years of emotion into each movement.

~*~*~*~*~~*~*~*~*~

Gillian had had sex before. Obviously. She's had quite a bit of sex. Great sex, too. And with Logan—who she loved, deeply. This, though … this was different. As much as Gillian knew she loved Jake, and he loved her, she'd be lying if she said it didn't worry her a bit that this was happening. But Gillian could feel it, all the lust, all of the passion, all of the love that Jake had for her. It was there, in each movement he made and she couldn't imagine anything better for them and their relationship. The feeling of him inside of her actually took her breath away. She felt like she could only stare at him as he began moving inside her. There were no words. Nothing she could do. She was just lost in that moment. In that feeling.

"Oh, Jake ..." she breathed out as she dug her fingers into his back. It was instinctual as she felt her hips lift to meet his movements. Each of his thrusts filled her up, and yet her body was demanding more. Wrapping her legs around his waist, she tried to pull him deeper, she had to have all of him. She shifted her hips trying to achieve this and felt him moan as his lips found the side of her neck. Her answering moan had his control slip more when she felt his hand slip beneath her, holding her body up to his.

It was all so much—so intense—the connection she seemed to have with Jake was more than she ever expected. It was more than she could have ever dreamed of. She felt the familiar ache begin to build in her core as his movements picked up pace, becoming more rigid. Running her hands down his back she could feel the sheen of sweat building on his skin as he continued moving deeply inside of her. She could tell he was still holding himself back, and she wanted to beg him for more. He told her to fall, but *he* wasn't, and that just wouldn't do. "Jake, please. More. I need you."

"Gillian ... God ... you feel so amazing," Jake panted out between thrusts as he set a vigorous pace to achieve the release they were both seeking. She was so close, it was right there, and she wanted him there, too. Running her hands down the top of his firm backside, she could feel the flexing of his muscles as he continued to arch his body into hers. She dug her nails into his muscles demanding more of him, and it was all Jake needed. His thrusts became erratic as he pulled her body up against him again and slammed into her. The orgasm that rocked through her body had her gasping for air as his body went rigid, and his lips slammed on top of hers. He swallowed her cry as his lips took hers in a fevered kiss that consumed her.

Collapsing on top of her and staying connected in the most intimate way, she held onto him—afraid she would float away if she let go of him. She could hear his words play over in her mind as she recalled him telling her it was perfect, and whatever reservations she had had about this vanished. Of course it was perfect. *He* was perfect. *They* were perfect together. They'd known each other and been best friends for years. How could this be anything but perfect?

Lifting his head, Jake kissed her face, her neck, and across her shoulders as she softly ran her hands up and down his back. Trying to recover and catch their breath, Jake panted out, "Gillian … my God. That was … there are … no words."

Completely sated, she kissed him, then looked up into his eyes and said the only word she felt described what just happened between them, "Perfect."

CHAPTER TWENTY-ONE

The instant she woke up and felt the hard warmth of a male chest beneath her cheek, the flood of memories from the night before rushed in. Lying there quietly, she assessed whether he was awake or not. Steady deep breathing and a slight snore, along with the heavy weight of the arm that was holding her down against him confirmed that he was. *Wow, I really slept with Jake Michaels...*

Gently lifting her head, she peeked up at the strong lines of a distinctly masculine jaw slightly covered in beard stubble, the long eyelashes that lay on his cheek, covering up some of the most beautiful light brown eyes she had ever seen, the swoop of dark brown hair that laid across his forehead clearly tussled from their activities, and slightly parted lips that had been all over her body last night. She couldn't stop the dreamy sigh that escaped her lips as she continued to gaze at him and recall what they had done together.

Needing to extricate herself from his hold since Mother Nature was calling, but not wanting to wake him yet, she reached back and grabbed his hand on her back to hold it in place. Once secured, she rolled over on top of his arm. Careful not to hurt his hand once she had his arm flush with the bed, she rolled one more time, which had on her stomach at the edge of the bed looking back at the sleeping form next to her. *Yep, sure did,* she thought.

Another sigh escaped as she continued to take him in. Damn, he was a gorgeous specimen. It's no wonder she lost all semblance of control and practically climbed his body to get at him last night. She can't even blame it on the alcohol, considering she'd only had two glasses of wine when she came home. Gently shifting to roll onto her back, she groaned inwardly as she laid her arm across her eyes trying to block out the reality of what she had done— how she had seriously complicated her already complicated life.

Glancing over at his profile once more before deciding that she needed to get up and shower, and try to gather her thoughts while not laying a foot away from a man she shouldn't be trusted around. It was almost comical to think about how she couldn't trust herself around him when he was one of the people she trusted most in this world. Carefully rolling out of bed, she silently padded over to the bathroom and gently shut the door behind her.

Okay, it was time to get her shit together. So she slept with Jake ... big deal right? Well, yes, she knew it was a big deal; it's just that things seemed a whole lot scarier the morning after. Then she groaned out loud at the thought of doing the 'morning after thing' with one of her best friends. That was so not a cool thought.

She took care of her business, cringing slightly when she thought the noise she made could have woken Jake up. Well, he was bound to wake up sooner or later, and she would have to deal with it then. She knew she couldn't regret what happened last night; she just hoped that he didn't regret it either. Even though she had only been with Logan before last night, she would have to say it was very satisfying. It was great. Okay, who was she kidding? It was freaking fantastic! Perfect.

She sighed again as she turned the shower on. Completely lost in her recollection of last night's lovemaking, her body overheated at just the thought of what they did last night, she got in before it was warm enough and sucked in a breath at the shock of the cold water hitting her body. Standing back a bit to let it warm up, she took inventory of the aches and soreness her body was sporting this morning. Clearly Jake was a talented man and knew exactly what to do to a woman, which of course should serve as a reminder that Jake has had far more sexual partners than she did. Not that it was a stretch to have more partners than her, but it was slightly daunting to accept that she was probably not as satisfying for him as he was for her. The disappointment of that thought was more upsetting than she cared to admit.

Closing her eyes she let the soothing warmth of the water pound on her face and head, letting the pressure hit the tense muscles of her shoulders. Almost immediately, she felt some of her tension dissipate. That is, until she heard the distinct sound of someone relieving themselves in the toilet not three feet away from where she was. Instantly tensing, she kept her eyes closed as if she was the one intruding on someone when it was the other way around. It's not like she hadn't ever been in the bathroom when someone was using it; however, she was married to that man. This was Jake—someone she wasn't on that level of comfort with yet. But apparently he was. She smiled to herself, but kept her eyes closed and stayed quiet. Almost like she was hiding from him … in the shower … with the water running. A small giggle escaped her at the ridiculousness of her thoughts. She was still smiling when she heard the shower door open and a strong, distinctly aroused male body pressed up against her from behind.

Jake curled his arms around her waist and gently pulled her tighter against him as he leaned down to kiss her wet shoulder. "What's so funny in here?" he asked. She giggled more, which of course only made him harder for her. He continued to kiss and nibble on her shoulder as he moved up her neck while he waited for her to answer.

"Did you just pee in the same bathroom I was showering in?" she asked as her giggle turned into a small sigh while she tilted her head to the side, giving him more access to her neck.

God how hot was that, he thought. He couldn't help the slight growl that escaped him as he moved one of his hands up the front of her body to cup her breasts. The pure predatory feeling that overcame him with her was slightly overwhelming. He had never felt like that with any other woman. But then again, he knew that was because this was the one woman he had always wanted.

"Yes, I did. Does that bother you or something? I would've thought that after what we did to each other last night, something as simple as taking a leak would be nothing. Be thankful I remembered to do it out there. I was in such a hurry to get in here and touch your wet, naked body that I almost forgot."

"You're right, I am glad you remembered, because I draw the line at you peeing on me, Jake Michaels! That would be crossing a line … *every* line." She laughed a breathy laugh as she gave into what he was doing to her. He couldn't get enough of her—he had to touch her. When he rolled over this morning and reached for her, a moment of panic and disappointment hit him before he realized that she was in the shower. But then he couldn't get out of bed fast enough to get to her. Even though he had wanted to wake up with her in his arms, he would settle for an early morning shower with her.

"Exactly how I thought you would feel, my dear. Besides, I don't need to pee on you … I've already left my mark on you … in you. My essence was left deep inside your body last night. Several times I might add. You are mine, Gillian."

He felt her body tense slightly, and he knew that something was bothering her. He wasn't going to let anything ruin this, so he was going to address it now. He turned her around in his arms, but kept her tight against his body so she couldn't get away from him. Her head was down, and she wouldn't look at him. "Hey, what's wrong, baby?"

She took in a visibly deep breath before saying, "Nothing." He knew was a lie. Maybe she was upset that they didn't use protection. Shit, did he ruin this because he couldn't be patient enough to get inside her body? But she said he didn't need to use protection. Did she not feel as deeply for him as he did for her? Was she upset because he called her his? Before he could let panic engulf him, he took her chin in his hands and tilted her face up to look at his. "Tell me … please. I need to know what you're thinking because I could go crazy just fearing what you might be thinking. Do you regret what happened between us last night?"

"No! Oh god, Jake, no! Not in any way do I regret being with you. It was … wonderful." He relaxed slightly—that was good to know. Wonderful was a great description, he thought, as he mentally patted himself on the back for his performance. He could tell she was still tense, though, so he prodded further. "Then what is it? Is it because we didn't use protection ... because I promise you I am clean, and I know that you are, too."

She softened a little bit and gave him a slight smile. "No, Jake, I know you would never put me at risk. I know you're clean, and yes I am, too. And since I had my tubes tied when I had Dylan, there is no risk there for pregnancy." He couldn't help the slight bit of disappointment he felt at the thought of Gillian never being able to carry his child, but it was how things were. "It's just that ... I was worried about whether it was wonderful for you, too." The last part of her statement came out very low as she lowered her face to his chest to hide it in obvious embarrassment. *She didn't think she pleased him? Did she really think he didn't enjoy himself? Was she there?* Well he would squash that asinine thought out for sure.

Once again tilting her face back up to look him in the eye, he made sure she made eye contact with him before he spoke to her, "Do you really have to wonder that, baby? Did you really not know how I felt last night?"

"Well, obviously you were *satisfied* ... it's just that, I know I lack in the sexual experience department—as far as partners go. And I was worried that maybe it wasn't as good as it could've been for you because I know you have been with more people than me. And I don't want ..." He cut off her rambling statement when he slanted his mouth over hers. She didn't think he enjoyed it ... well, he would show her how fantastic it was between them.

With his mouth over hers, he felt her open to him, and his tongue plunged inside. She was his, and he was going to satisfy her and show her exactly how satisfied he was with her. He turned their bodies and pressed her up against the tiled wall. He felt her quick intake of breath as her heated body made contact with the cooler tiles. But it didn't give him pause. The caveman in him had one mission and one mission only: take his woman, and make sure she knew he didn't care how experienced she was because she was all he wanted. Almost breathless with his onslaught on her mouth, he moved to her cheek and jawline as he made his way down her neck. Her hands were on his neck, in his hair, almost guiding him where she wanted him.

Sliding his hands to her waist, he grabbed on and lifted her up the wall. On pure reflex, she held onto his shoulders and wrapped her legs around his waist as he lowered her body onto his. They both sighed at the feeling of her body wrapped tightly around his sex as he settled himself deep … deep inside her body. He tore his mouth away from her neck and looked at her. Her beautiful skin was flush, whether it was from the heat of the shower or the arousal he knew she was feeling, he didn't know. He allowed his body to withdraw part way and then slowly thrust back in. The sigh she made, coupled with her half lidded stare and the simultaneous clench her sex made around his, was one of the most erotic things he had ever witnessed.

Now that he had her total undivided attention, he would put her mind at ease. "I think last night with you was more than wonderful, baby." Pausing to kiss her softly on the lips, before he continued, "There is no word good enough to describe how it felt for me." This time he kissed her on the tip of her nose, maintaining eye contact as he slowly withdrew and thrust again. "I've waited for well over a decade to feel the passion that I knew we could have together ..." His kiss was on her forehead this time as he once again pulled himself from her body before slowly thrusting back in. He made sure she could feel every inch of his body entering hers. "It was more than I could have ever hoped for ... and it is all I will ever need in this lifetime." He punctuated his statement by claiming her mouth again and sliding his tongue against hers.

He felt her body respond once again when it tightened around him as her tongue dueled with his. The pure arousal he felt and the passion that ignited between them set him on the edge of losing all control. Again. She didn't say anything in response to his words. She didn't have to. He could see it in her eyes, feel it in her body's response to him. She knew enough about him to realize that this was it for him, there was no turning back ... she was his now. His always.

He pressed her hard into the wall and took up a steady pace of thrust and retreat that had them both climbing to the crescendo of bliss they wanted to reach. It just couldn't get any better than this, he thought, as he felt the signs of her body going over the edge. Gillian's head fell back against the wall and her body tightened around him as her orgasm began to take over. "Oh, God ... Jake ... Oh ..."

Jake bent forward and pressed his mouth to space on her neck, just below her ear, and gently suckled her skin as he kept up his rhythm. He felt the grip of her hands in his hair as she held his head to her neck. He growled as she spurred him on with her response to him. God, he loved the feel of her hands on him. And the moment he sank his teeth into the skin of her neck, he felt her come undone. Gillian gasped and cried out as her body once again came apart in his arms. The sheer ecstasy of the moment pulled Jake under, too, as he listened to her cry out his name in release. That was when he realized that it could get better, because there was nothing more satisfying than hearing Gillian call out his name while he was pulsing deep inside of her body … absolutely nothing.

~*~*~*~*~*~*~*~*~

Gillian couldn't get over how easy it was to be with Jake. Once she got past her concern that things would be too complicated, she was able to relax. They had known each other for so long and had always spent time together, that just *being* with him now felt like second nature to her. Only now, she was able to enjoy the benefits of his touch, and damn, that touch was fantastic. After Jake had her panting his name in the shower, they managed to untangle themselves and actually do what was necessary to get clean. He helped her wash her hair, which felt so great; she thought she could've fallen asleep on her feet. The way he caressed her body and tended to her was a little surreal, almost like she was being cherished … worshipped. The way he made her feel, and how comfortable she was with touching him, she realized how right all this felt. She knew this was definitely where she was supposed to be.

Standing in front of the mirror, in only a tank top and comfy shorts, she was brushing her teeth when Jake strolled in, looking delicious in only a pair of jeans. The mirror afforded her the ability to watch him as he pressed up against her, and his hands found her waist. She watched as he leaned down and reverently placed a kiss on the exposed skin of her shoulder and his hands snaked around her waist and just held her. He stayed like that for a few moments, inhaled deeply, and then lifted his head to meet her gaze in the mirror. Once again, she was surprised with how normal it felt to have him do that. None of it seemed awkward like she feared it would. It was as if the pieces just ... fit.

He smiled at her and said, "You smell so good." He buried his face in her hair that had just been dried and inhaled deeply again. "I just can't take in enough of you." She smiled at him as he looked back at her reflection, then she remembered she was brushing her teeth. She bent to spit in the sink and it pushed her bottom right into him, allowing her to feel his erection. After quickly rinsing and spitting again, she stood up and turned within the circle of his arms.

"You can't possibly want more," she said as her hands cupped his cheeks, and her hips pressed forward into his.

"Baby, I just told you, I can't get enough of you. Your smell." She felt his nose against her neck as he smelled her before he said, "Your taste." And then his tongue warmed the skin there, which tickled, making her laugh a little then squirm in his arms. He pulled back and smiled at her, "Your laugh."

"That's very sweet, Jake."

"It's true, Gillian. Yes, I want more, I *need* more. I can't get enough of your body, of your touch ... I want it all." He placed a kiss to her lips and slowly retreated, watching her as he did. He was waiting for her response.

There was only one thing to say to all of that, "I'm already yours, Jake."

His smile was electrifying as he proceeded to pick her up so she had no choice but to wrap her legs around his waist. She had to giggle again as he began to carry her out of the bathroom. "I can walk, you know."

"I like you better like this. I've decided this is my favorite position to have you in. Make sure you understand that means you will be in this position whenever I feel it appropriate or necessary," he declared as he carried her out of her bedroom toward the front of the house.

"Um, Jake, you missed the bed," she said in a playful tone that only had him grunting like a caveman in response.

"Must feed woman. Need food for energy. Jake have you again after."

Her laughter at his antics couldn't be contained at that point, and she leaned down to kiss him. As he placed her bottom on the cold kitchen counter, she squealed at the contact. "Oh my God, warn a girl before you do that."

"I'm sorry, baby. Should we do something to create some friction that will allow your ass to warm up the counter top. I've got an idea of what might work."

"I bet you do. But you're the one who said 'must feed woman,' and now I'm hungry."

Jake huffed a laugh then leaned in and kissed her again. "And what does my woman want?"

"What are you offering?" she asked.

He pressed up against her more firmly so she could feel his hardness again, "Oh you know what I'm offering babe."

She was really enjoying the sexual banter they had going on, since they had never done that before, so she played along. Reaching down, she cupped him through his jeans, gave him a sultry look and replied, "Oh, I know what you're offering."

"Fuck. It feels so good to have you touching me." He closed his eyes and groaned as he pressed into her hand more. "But if you keep doing that, I'm going to have you naked and bent over this counter in two seconds flat."

"You say that like it's a bad thing." She had barely finished her sentence before she was flung over the top of Jake's shoulder and presented with a perfect view of one very fine ass. Jake's stride as he hurried back toward the bedroom while carrying her wasn't slowed down a bit.

His hand gave her ass a smack, and she squeaked as he said, "You're damn right it's a bad thing, Gillian. People have a terrible habit of just showing up here and barging in. I'm not risking this sweet ass being seen by anybody else ever again. It's mine." Gillian wasn't giggling anymore as she once again found her system flooding with arousal when Jake tossed her down on the bed. And breakfast was all but forgotten as Jake proceeded to show her exactly how much he wanted and needed her.

CHAPTER TWENTY-TWO

Once Jake had Gillian again, he felt comfortable enough to let her out of bed without the risk of groping her in public. His need to touch her, though, was just as strong as ever so there was rarely a moment he wasn't holding her hand or wrapping his arm around her waist. He was very proud of the fact that he managed to control his desire to carry her around. After the morning had gotten away from them, he had to take her out for breakfast; otherwise he knew they would never eat.

Jake decided to head over to Coronado Island where they could get some good food and then take a walk. The scenery was great, the day was warm, and conditions were perfect to just enjoy the day. They were walking hand in hand along the sidewalk next to the Hotel del Coronado, one of the historic landmarks on the island that was well over one hundred years old, when Gillian stopped. Jake turned to see a hesitant look on her face so he asked, "What's the matter, beautiful?"

She was biting her lip, seeming to be thinking of how to answer. He didn't like that she felt nervous about whatever it was she was thinking about so he had to reassure her. He stopped and sat on a bench at the edge of the sidewalk and pulled her into his lap. Once she was there, and his arms were secured around her, he asked again, "Tell me what has you worried? You have to know you can tell me whatever you're thinking about."

There was a soft breeze, and it blew her hair forward so that it surrounded the two of them. There was so much of it that almost blocked out the beach around them, which he had no problem with. She smiled as she tried to gather all of it and then proceeded to twist and braid it over her shoulder in an attempt to control it. He watched the expression on her face as she pondered what she was going to say. She took in a deep breath and let it out slowly, then said, "I wanted to talk to you about Logan." Immediately on guard, for no reason other than remembering what happened between him and Logan the night before—which he had almost forgotten about completely—he rubbed his hand up her back, gently trying to encourage her to go on.

"I'm sorry about what happened last night. He apparently felt he should try to make one more attempt to beg me to reconsider our divorce." She wasn't looking at him as she played with the thick braid of hair she had just created. Jake wasn't going to push her since she was talking, so he just continued to stroke her back. He was fine with it so long as he was touching her. After a long pause, she said, "I, of course, made sure he knew that was a firm no— that there was no chance for reconciling, and that I was not his anymore."

She lifted her head to make eye contact with him, and smiled shyly. "But I realized something last night. I realized that for the first time in months, I didn't feel lost. I felt comfortable with the fact that I was no longer married to Logan, that I was moving on." After another pause, she placed her hand on his cheek, and he couldn't help but lean into her touch. "I realized that I was moving on, and that I wanted to do that with you."

Jake felt warmth immediately infuse his chest as he listened to Gillian's sweet confession. She didn't declare her love for him, but she would, he was sure of it. He smiled up at her and stroked her

297

cheek just as she did to him. "You have no idea how wonderful it is to hear words like that from you." Pulling her lips down to meet his, he whispered, "Thank you." Then he kissed her. He kissed her with all the passion he felt between them; it was the only thing to do. It was what the moment required. Sitting there in his lap, on a public beach where people were mulling about, Jake fell even more in love with Gillian, and he knew that no matter what, she needed to know that he was her future now.

Slowly breaking off the kiss, he held her forehead against his as they caught their breath. He hugged her tighter to him as he said, "Gillian, baby, you're mine. I need you to know that this is it. I'm not going anywhere. I'm so glad that you realized you wanted to move on with me," he pulled back and gave her a mischievous smile and said, "But I already knew that."

She did that adorable snort thing and said, "Is that so?"

"Oh yes, it is … and it's about time you caught up with the plan." Because he knew her so well, it was very easy for the two of them to have their conversation go from deep and emotional to light and fun.

So when she retorted in a playful snarky voice, "And what exactly is this plan you speak of, Jake Michaels? Or is it more of a *need to know* kind of plan?"

"Of course not. It's a simple plan, and it will be very easy to carry out. You see there is only one thing that needs to be done." He gave her a pointed look and said, "All you have to do is love me, because I already love you. Everything else, it's just fluff, it can be dealt with. Logan, the kids, our friends, all of it can be handled, so long as we get to love each other." She was quietly watching him, absorbing his words. He knew it was too much to expect she would actually say the words I love you, but he couldn't help but feel hopeful. And while hope was a dangerously evil emotion to have at times, he didn't think this was one of those times. He was confident that he would get it sometime very soon.

Still looking at him, she smiled sweetly, leaned in, and pressed her lips against his forehead before pulling back and saying, "So long as we get to love each other, huh?" Jake just gave a quick nod at her question. Then she said words that were as close to an *I love you* as he could hope for, "You know what? You're right. That seems like a very easy plan to carry out."

~*~*~*~*~~*~*~*~*~

Gillian knew that if their relationship was any older, she would have said the words I love you to Jake then. But for some reason, it just felt like a response. He deserved more than a response to his declaration. He deserved it to be delivered to him with all the emotion that she was feeling then. It deserved its own declaration, and he would get it that way. His answering smile to her response was big, and beautiful, and so full of happiness that she couldn't help but smile at him indulgently. He was definitely like a drug to her—she fed off his happiness. Knowing that there was still plenty to discuss about complications they could face, she knew the biggest was going to be Logan.

Jake leaned his head against her chest and sighed, holding her tightly to him. She wrapped her hands around his back and just let him rest there. They sat quietly for a little while just absorbing each other and the resolution they had come to. Jake loved her, and everything else would be fine as long as they had that. It wasn't long before life started to intrude on their solace, and Jake's phone started to vibrate in his pocket, which she happened to be sitting on. Startling a little, she unsuccessfully tried to extricate herself from his hold. He simply shifted her a little, pulled out the phone, and settled her back where she was. He glanced at the screen and said, "It's Allie, or as I like to call her now, Little Cockblocker."

Gillian laughed out loud at that as Jake answered the call. Listening to the one side of the conversation, she could tell that it was time to head home. So as Jake ended the call, he allowed her to stand from his lap, but she didn't get too far. He draped his long arm across her shoulders and pulled her against him, allowing her to wrap hers behind his waist as they walked back to his car. Figuring now was as good a time as any, she brought up one of those potential complications.

"You know, last week when I went to dinner with Logan, we came to a solution on custody."

"Great. I didn't think the two of you would have an issue with it. What did you decide?"

Thinking, *here goes nothing*, she said, "I am going to stay in the house, and then Logan is going to move into the property next door. We already spoke with the tenant, and he's going to move into the larger property we own with a roommate since the rent is more expensive."

"Why doesn't Logan just move into the larger one?" Jake asked her. She didn't detect any irritation at it, just a plain and simple question.

"Because we want the kids to be able to come and go as they please—to have access to each parent as they need, not just when the custody schedule says. We figure that this way, he and I have separation, but the kids don't have as much." She glanced up to see his expression, fearing he would be upset.

He looked down and said, "I can see that as being a good thing. I'm sure there will still be some issues, but I understand why the two of you should try doing something like that. Especially since you have the ability to with two properties next to each other like that."

Gillian stopped dead in her tracks. He was okay with it; he agreed that it was a good idea? Standing there looking at him, he huffed a laugh at her and asked, "What? You didn't think I would be fine with that?"

"I'm just surprised that you seem completely okay with it."

He moved to stand in front of her, and once again pulled her body up against his. Her hands were on his chest and his arms wrapped around her—probably her new favorite position to be in since it gave her the perfect view of his strong jaw and soft lips as he smiled down at her.

"Did you not hear what I said to you back there? I love you, and everything else is just fluff, which can be dealt with. There's no need to get bothered by something that might not be a problem at all. Regardless of where Logan is, I know that I'm going to be with you. I need you to understand that whatever preparations or plans you have made for your future should include me. I'm not saying you have to discuss decisions with me, but please keep in mind that they will affect me, too. But know that we have the same goal Gillian, you, me, some of the kids, all of the kids, together. I've waited for this a long time now, and I just ask that when you and Logan make decisions about the kids, make sure you fit me in the picture, because I'm going to be right there, baby."

Taking in all that he said, she couldn't find any words that would express how grateful she was to have his support. Her kids were everything to her, and he knew it. So she kissed him. She threw her arms around his neck and kissed him hard. Oh yeah, she loved him, and since she didn't want to say it yet, she had to show him somehow.

~*~*~*~*~~*~*~*~*~

Jake reluctantly pulled Gillian off of him and they finished the walk back to his jeep, hand in hand, silent. He didn't feel the need to fill the air with words—they just walked. It was comfortable. After helping her into her seat and buckling her in, she just smiled down at him and shook her head at his actions.

"Must keep woman safe," he grunted at her. She laughed, grabbed him by the cheeks and kissed him. Smiling at her, he removed himself and climbed in his side. The drive home was a content one as he made sure to have his hand on her leg every second he could, in between shifting gears. As they pulled onto her street, she asked, "Are you going to stay for dinner tonight?"

He turned and gave her a look that implied she was crazy for asking such a thing, then said, "Woman, I plan to stay for dinner every night. So get used to it." The pleased look on her face was very satisfying for him, and he wanted to reproduce that look over and over again. Turning back to road, he caught sight of Gillian's driveway and swore out loud.

"Oh, for fuck's sake, Gillian. I don't know how you put up with all of us. Why is it that there is always somebody at your house?" Jake heard her burst out with laughter as he turned to park his jeep in the only available spot, and then he realized what was going on. Gillian was still laughing in the seat next to him when he pulled the keys out of the ignition. He saw Allie standing in the window ... next to Sean. "Seriously, someone needs to get a handle on that girl. She has far too much control over the rest of us. Did she really call everyone over here to check me out as your date?"

Gillian's laughter was being muffled now as she tried to stifle it with her hands. A few snorts and a couple of deep breaths later, she was a little more composed and answered, "It sure looks that way." Jake just shook his head and got out. He noticed Sean stood there trying to look imposing with his hands crossed over his chest, and Little Cockblocker was standing next to him, waving like a fool. Jake couldn't control his smile as he opened Gillian's door for her and helped her out. She jokingly asked, "Now do I have to prepare you for what's inside that house? Or do you want to turn and run from my crazy group of friends?"

Jake quickly wrapped his arm around her and slammed his lips down on hers. His tongue demanded entrance, and she allowed it. He possessed her with his lips and tongue as he felt her body soften against his. Her hands wound their way up into his hair, and her nails scratched his scalp as she let herself fall into the kiss. Once he felt like she was good and ravaged there in the driveway, while her brother and Allie watched, he pulled his lips off hers. Breathlessly, he said, "How many times do I have to tell you, you're mine woman, and I'm not going anywhere."

"And do you think kissing me like that is the answer to help me remember? If you kiss me like that when I forget something, I will have to play dumb all the time," she said in a husky voice.

He kissed her one more time before letting her go, then turned to look at the window again. Allie was applauding their performance, and Sean just rolled his eyes and walked away. Jake laughed under his breath as he threw his arm around his woman and strolled into the house.

~*~*~*~*~~*~*~*~*~

Gillian should've known that Allie would do this again, simply because Allie was … well, Allie. As they walked into the house, Allie was standing near the front window still applauding them. Gillian walked over and hugged her before saying, "Do you like to torture everyone, or is it just me?"

"Pfft, I'm an equal opportunity torturer. This was a double whammy 'cause it was both of you. Everyone is in the back." And with that, she made her way to the back of the house.

Jake turned and looked at Gillian and said, "Maybe you should make a mental note to change the locks on your doors because, clearly, everyone has too much access."

"You have a key, too, you know. Are you saying you have too much access?"

"Not at all. I just think that maybe you should limit everyone else's access to you just in case I am accessing you at the time." He waggled his eyebrows at her before reaching back and smacking her ass. She was giggling again and was about to say something about his accessing her when someone cleared their throat. Both of them looked up to see Jason standing in the doorway to the kitchen, smiling at them. She smiled back.

"I thought I should interrupt before I saw something that I really didn't want to see," Jason said, and Gillian could've sworn she heard Jake mumble *cockblocker* under his breath before he let go of her. She laughed and walked over to Jason, who leaned down to allow her to kiss his cheek. "Hey there Mr. Michaels, how goes it?"

"It looks to be a good day, sweetheart, how goes it with you?"

She looked over her shoulder at Jake, then back up at Jason and smiled. "Perfect."

Jason's smile was a lot like Jake's, even though it wasn't seen as often. It was no less magnificent. "Glad to hear that. Do you mind if I have word with my little brother?"

"Of course not. I'll head to the back with the others."

"I won't keep him long. I just wanted to ask him something. And just so you know, Logan is back there, too. Allie threatened to staple him to the chair by his balls if he tried to get up and leave." Jason huffed a small laugh at that, while Gillian just shook her head. Leave it to Allie to force Logan to be a part of this. It was comical and uncomfortable at the same time.

"Great, this should be fun," she grumbled as she gave Jake a small wave before leaving him with his brother.

Gillian found everyone in the yard; the kids were in the pool since it was late afternoon. Her brother and his wife were watching the kids and chatting with a few other friends. Logan was sitting over on the other side of the pool, away from everyone else. Sunglasses on, his view was hidden, but she assumed he was glaring at Allie. Making her way over to him, she took up the chair next to him and sighed as she sat down. Logan spoke up immediately.

"Jake that tough to be around already?" he asked, sarcasm heavy in his voice.

She huffed at him and said, "That sigh was for you so don't be an ass. I know you are being held against your will."

"One of these days I'm going to challenge her and find out if she really is bluffing," he said with a bit of admiration. His little sister could always make him do anything.

"Just make sure whatever you choose to stand up to her about doesn't involve stapling your nuts to a chair."

Logan flinched and nodded. "Exactly why today wasn't the day. Even if I thought she wouldn't touch my junk, I'm afraid she could get some guy to do it for her."

"Oh yes, that's a good point," she replied as she watched Allie heading her way. "Speak of the devil herself. Did you really tell your brother you would staple his nuts to the chair if he tried to leave?"

Allie glared at her brother. "Had to go and tattle on me, I see." Logan's hand immediately went up in defense. "Whoa there, little sis. She got her information from another source, not me."

Gillian called Logan a wuss before telling Allie she heard it from Jason. The subject then changed to Allie moving home and getting her stuff moved down from Los Angeles. When the topic of her driving Logan's truck up to load smaller stuff in it arose, Gillian brought up her concerns.

"Logan, do you think it's safe for Allie to drive your truck, you know, with the vandalizing and everything?"

"I think it should be fine. She's taking the truck out of the area so I wouldn't worry. Besides, I'm going to take the train up there to drive it back down for her. I don't want her doing it with a full bed." Logan tried to reassure her, but Gillian wasn't convinced.

"It makes me nervous, Logan. I'm sorry if it bothers you, but I think Jodi is responsible for what happened. And I sure as hell don't like the thought of something else happening to your truck while Allie has it."

Logan sat up, took his glasses off, and looked at her, while Allie remained silent. "Gillian, the police say that she has solid alibi for the night my truck was trashed. I know you want to blame her, but it doesn't make sense. I haven't seen her in months, so why would it come up now?"

"It's just a feeling I have. It's obvious the woman is a liar, who knows what else she is capable of?"

Allie chimed in, "Seriously, Logan, we've all seen the movie *Fatal Attraction*."

That was as much as Logan could tolerate. He stood up and dropped his glasses back down over his eyes. He looked at his sister and said, "I assume I can go now, Al? Or would either of you like to rub my nose in my mistakes a little bit more? Maybe bring up how my son won't speak to me? Want to pour a little salt on that wound before I leave?"

Gillian just shook her head in irritation as she snapped at him, "Logan Baxter, why the hell did you have to turn that into something about you? You know damn well that it's a legitimate concern to have. But if you want to act like a baby about it, go ahead, it's not my problem anymore." Standing up, she glared at his glasses since he was hiding behind them, then she walked away. Her new niece was over on the other side of the pool, and that was just what she needed at the moment. Nothing was more calming than holding a baby.

~*~*~*~*~~*~*~*~*~

Jake and Jason just finished talking and had just made it to the back door when Logan came in. He stopped when he saw them, and the three men stood there in silence. There really was nothing anyone could say to clear the air. It's not like he could tell him what a fantastic day he had—that would just be fucked up. Jake decided that if he was going to be around his friend anymore in the future, he was going to have to treat him like he always had. So Jake nodded and said, "Logan."

Logan didn't respond, just stood there a moment, mumbled something toward Jason and then left. Jake didn't blame the guy; he wouldn't want to be here if the tables were reversed. Jake shrugged his shoulders at Jason and went looking for Gillian. Finding her with Sean and Morgan, he pulled up a seat next to her and watched as she held one of her nieces and talked with another. Sure, he felt bad for Logan, but he was right where he belonged, and he wasn't going to feel bad about that.

CHAPTER TWENTY-THREE

Jake had just handed his credit card to the salesman when his brother Jason said, "Are you sure man? This is a big step."

Annoyed, Jake turned, "Dude, what the hell? Of course I'm sure. Why would I be buying the ring if I wasn't sure?"

His brother chuckled and slapped him on the shoulder, "I know man; I just thought that was what guys were supposed to do when their friend was buying an engagement ring. I figured that was why you brought me." Jake just shook his head at his brother as the salesman brought back his card and little blue bag. *This was that famous blue bag he had heard people talk about?* Didn't look like much to him, but if it was supposed to make the ring more special, he was all for it.

As the two men made their way out of the store, he couldn't help but notice how good he felt. It was a great day when a man picked out a ring to give to a woman—to pledge his love forever. He knew he sounded like a total sap, but he would gladly forfeit his 'man card' if it meant he could be feel like this. Jake and his brother had made plans to grab some beer and hot wings at Hooleys tonight since the ladies were all busy at some kind of chick party that involved candles. And the fact that Gillian plans that were considered no-boys-allowed was the only reason he wasn't with her tonight. Well, not with her right now—he would be going to her place later, after all the women left.

It had been almost six weeks since they had first slept together, and since then, he spent every night he could at her place. Since

Gillian wasn't comfortable flaunting the sexual side of their relationship in front of the kids, the two teens especially, they kept it on the down low. He understood that, but really wanted to remedy the problem. Even though he wasn't above sneaking in and out the back door of her bedroom, he didn't want their relationship cheapened by being secretive. Jake thought Gillian was being a little too protective of Madison, when he thought the girl needed a dose of reality. The attitude that Gillian got from her was extreme at times, and she didn't want to rock the boat by flaunting a relationship with Jake in front of her. He was relieved that Gillian didn't allow her to get away with the attitude, and made sure to put the kid in her place, but he knew she wanted to avoid whatever confrontation she could. So he went along with the sneaking around at night, at least for now. His son had no problems with this, simply because he was spending a lot more time with Dylan, and he was allowed to sleep over on school nights now.

The two men made it over to Hooleys in no time and were just sitting down at a table when his brother asked, "So ... when are you going to ask her?" Jake wasn't sure about that yet. He wanted to make sure it was perfect.

"Not sure yet. I haven't decided how or when—I just know that I have to."

They placed their order, and Jason turned to him. "I'm happy for you. I'm glad you finally got the girl."

"You make it sound like I've been stalking her for the last eighteen years or something." He paused to take a sip of the beer that was just placed in front him, then continued, "I was a good person and put away those extra feelings I had for her a long time ago. They hadn't even resurfaced until that night when Gillian left him." He shook his head as he remembered that night.

"I'm not trying to make it sound creepy or anything. It's just ... I'm glad that you got her. Gillian has been like a little sister to me for a long time now. And I really like the fact that she could really be my little sister now." Jake smiled at his brother's comment. He was pretty much only thinking about the immediate people the relationship involved, which was the kids, and of course themselves. So for Jason to be remarking on the new connection between him and Gillian—it touched him. Then Jason said, "I just hope she says yes to you, man."

All the affection he had toward his brother for acknowledging him and Gillian as a good thing disappeared when he said that last part. He smacked his brother on the arm, and then he felt a little anxiety seep into his belly. *What if she didn't say yes?* She had to. He had never been an insecure man, but apparently there was one thing that he was insecure about, and that was Gillian. His concerns must have shown on his face because his brother tried to reassure him. "Jake, come on, you have to know I'm only joking. Of course she's going to say yes."

Jake gave his brother a sheepish grin and said, "I sure hope so. Not really sure where to go from here if she said no."

"You've got time. There's no rush, and you don't even know when and how you're going to do it. But you've got the ring, and you'll be ready when the time is right. And if she wasn't ready, it wouldn't feel right for you, man, so don't worry about it."

"Thanks, man," Jake replied as he took a drink. His brother brought up some good points, but the anxiety about it most likely wouldn't disappear until he knew she was his.

"How are things working out with Logan around? Being next door has to be a little weird for you two?"

"Hell, being with Gillian is surreal and all I seem to be able to focus on. I really don't pay attention to Logan. I could care less where he is, but Gillian thinks it's a good thing for the kids. It helps a little because Madison and her moods can go over there and not torture Gillian all the time. Jonathan is still angry with Logan, so he avoids him most of the time. At least Logan isn't just walking in the house unannounced when I'm there anymore. I would seriously have a problem with that."

"He's been tough to handle at work lately. Thinking I'm gonna have to kick his ass soon. I almost feel sorry for the guy," Jason finished off his statement with a huff and a half smile before reiterating, "Almost."

Jake lifted his glass in a toast to that comment. He felt bad talking this way about a long time friend, but things were different now, and they needed to figure out how to be friends again someday. Jason turned the conversation toward football, and the bartender jumped in with his opinions on the playoff season ahead of them. They were just a couple of guys, hanging out, drinking beer, and talking football … and Jake was counting down the time 'til he got to see her again. Oh yeah, he was definitely a goner.

~*~*~*~*~~*~*~*~

313

Gillian pulled into the parking spot and put the car into park before glancing over at Allie in the passenger seat. She wasn't in the mood to go to the mall, but Allie insisted she go with her. It had been over a month since Allie had moved back down to San Diego, and she was finally starting to get everything at her new place in order. Gillian usually couldn't contain her excitement over the fact that her best friend was moving on in grieving over her late husband, and that she was allowing herself to grow roots back with her family.

But today, Gillian couldn't get excited about anything—she just didn't feel well. She was tired, her stomach felt funny, and she had had a headache since yesterday. Not to mention they were having a get together over at Morgan's house tonight, so she was already reserving her fake smile for then. Allie convinced her to come to the mall with her to help her pick out some curtains, and her methods were definitely underhanded. She said that she needed another person's opinion; otherwise it would be a big, fat reminder that she lived alone. It was a low blow for Allie to pull out a comment like that, and if Gillian had felt a little more like herself, she would've called her out for it. But since she wasn't, she pushed on and went to the mall with Allie before they headed over to Morgan's. Her plan was to agree with whatever Allie picked out so they could get the hell out of there. She just hoped that whatever Allie picked out first wasn't something horrible, or else her plan would backfire.

"What's wrong with you anyway?" Allie asked as they walked into the mall.

"I have no idea. I must be coming down with something, which is the last thing I need with Thanksgiving this week. It's my year to cook for everyone." Gillian sighed as she made a mental checklist of all that she needed to pick up to make that happen. Feeding a small army usually wasn't something she minded doing, so hopefully she would feel better soon.

"Oh, come on, it's not like you won't have help doing it. You'll be fine."

"I hope so."

The two of them made their way into the department store and started their browsing in the home section. As they made their way past a section that permeated a strong floral scent, Gillian barely managed to control the urge to vomit as nausea hit her—swift and strong. She had to get out of there; the smell was getting to her. With her hand over her mouth and nose, she grabbed Allie by the arm to get her attention. Allie looked back at her. "Hey, what's wrong with you?"

All Gillian could do was shake her head and get the hell out of there. She didn't head for the mall exit; she went for the outer door that would get her out into some fresh air. Since it was mid November, the normally sunny California sky was overcast, and there was a crisp coldness to the air. Once she made it out the doors, she found a spot to sit down, and she took in a deep breath of clean air to chase away the smell that nauseated her. She had just gotten her stomach to calm down when Allie joined her.

"Jeez, Gillian, you turned a few shades of green back there. Are you pregnant or something?"

Gillian quickly snapped her head up to look at Allie as her words rang through her head. *Are you pregnant or something? Oh, God.*

Could she be? Just cataloging her symptoms had them returning, and she couldn't stop it from happening this time. Gillian quickly turned and disposed of her lunch in the planter she was sitting on. Once done, she turned to Allie again, put her hand to her mouth and said, "Shit, Allie, I can't be pregnant. I've had my tubes tied!"

Allie laughed as she sat beside her friend, then she scrunched up her nose in distaste. "On second thought, let's move somewhere else." Cautiously, she got up, and the two of them walked to a bench and sat down. "Okay, that's better. Now, when you had those tubes of yours tied, did it come with a hundred percent money back guarantee?"

Gillian just scowled. "Didn't think so. So why is it impossible to think that *maybe* you could be pregnant? Except, I would like to go on the record by saying that you are *so* pregnant. I remember what you looked like when you were pregnant with Madison, and I just saw the replay."

"Oh my God … Allie I can't be pregnant," she whispered and dropped her head in her hands. "I can't be pregnant."

Gillian felt Allie hug her from the side and say, "And why exactly would this be a bad thing?"

"Because …"

"Because, why? You love Jake, Jake loves you, couples in love make babies—it's the normal process, Gillian."

Shaking her head, Gillian lifted her gaze up and gave Allie a pleading look. "Allie, forgetting the fact that I might be pregnant with Jake's baby after being with him for less than two months,

316

let's focus on the part where I just got divorced from the first guy who knocked me up. The same guy who asked me to marry him repeatedly, but I wouldn't because I was afraid that people would think that was the only reason he asked!" Gillian's hysteria begin to set in as she felt her breathing accelerate while she continued to think about the situation.

"What will Jake think about this Allie? Apparently, I'm the kind of girl who has to go and get pregnant to lock a guy in for a decade or two. I can't seem to get a guy to commit to me without having a physical tie to him! Oh fuck, what am I going to do, Allie?"

"Well, I can tell you that the first thing you're going to do is snap the fuck out of this little panic attack you got going on. Jeez, woman, if I had a glass of water on me, I'd be throwing it in your face." Gillian laughed as a visual of that scenario played out in her head—Allie would definitely do that. "Good, there's a small smile. The second thing we're going to do is get you a test to confirm it, although I would bet some serious money on it."

"Not helping, Al," Gillian said in a voice meant to convey her annoyance.

"Oh, right, okay. The third thing you are going to do is tell that awesome man, who loves you desperately, that you are going to have his baby. This isn't a bad thing, Gilly … it's great news." Allie said it with such sincerity and enthusiasm Gillian almost got sucked in. A baby was a great thing; she had no problem with having another baby. Leaning her head on her best friend's shoulder, she tried battling the fear that if she and Jake ever got married, would it have only been because of the baby?

Unfortunately, that was something she'd never have an answer to now.

"You still want to go to Morgan's tonight? I can say I'm in a mood and need you to take care of me."

Gillian appreciated Allie's offer so she smiled as she shook her head. "We can't back out on Morgan. She needs girl time since she is so busy with the baby."

"Okay, only if you can handle it, though." Gillian nodded, and they got up. They walked to the car, without getting curtains. "Hey Al, I'm sorry we didn't get your curtains. Are you going to use that against me later?"

"No worries, this is cooler. And *hell yeah* I'm using it against you later." Feeling a little better, Gillian laughed at her as they climbed in the car. Then Allie announced, "I call dibbs on the baby when we get there since we didn't get my curtains today."

"Wow, that didn't take long for you to use against me."

Allie being the total smartass she was said, "I know right. I'm a little impressed myself."

"Hey Al, you know I love you more than my luggage, right?"

Allie looked at Gillian with a big smile on her face, all signs of the smartass gone and said, "Aww, you just used a *Steel Magnolias* line on me! I don't even have a good come back for it. I love you, too, sweetie."

It wasn't often that Allie didn't have a comeback, so Gillian silently congratulated herself and hugged her friend. After a few moments, she pulled back with tears in her eyes. "Thanks, Allie. Pretty sure you're gonna need to talk me off that ledge a few more times really soon."

"I know, right. I was going to ask if I could be there when you tell Jake because I think he will act like a total sap. But then I decided I would rather you just take a video and send it to me. That would be better for me."

Laughing again and no longer stressing about the possibilities, she pulled the car out and headed to her brother's house where a whole lot of different smells were awaiting her. She debated whether or not they should take a minute to pick up a pregnancy test but decided against it. She could just get one at work tomorrow. Until then, it would be business as usual.

~*~*~*~*~~*~*~*~*~

Jake smiled when he got the text from Gillian saying she was on her way home and asked if he was coming over. She said she missed him. Jason saw this and said, "I take it from that smile that it's time to go?"

Jake smiled big at his brother. "It sure as fuck is. My woman misses me." They promptly paid the bill and Jason dropped him off at her house. He decided for now he'd leave the ring with his brother. Hopping out of the truck and making his way inside, he was greeted by the sight of her sitting on the couch doing something on her phone. She looked up at him and smiled before coming over to hug him. "Hey beautiful, how was your night?" he asked as he hugged her back and pressed his lips against the top of her head.

He heard her snort against his chest and then she grumbled, "Allie needs a new superhero name. You need to change it to Babyblocker or something along those lines. That pain in the ass hogged the baby all night long. She's my niece, and I barely got to hold her because Allie wouldn't share."

He thought her pouting was adorable, but honestly, he was so under her spell, everything she did captivated him. "You know I would totally try and kick her ass for you, but I'm man enough to admit I wouldn't win. Did you tell on her? Maybe that would've been helpful." She was giggling against his chest now, and damn did it feel good. He reached down and tilted her head up to capture her lips before asking, "Where are all the kids?"

She pressed upward and met his lips for another kiss before answering, "Cockblocker, AKA Babyblocker, took Dylan and Ryan. Said she needed some big strong men to help her do stuff around the house. Of course both boys were all over that." Again, she pressed another kiss to his lips. "Madison is over at Logan's, and Jonathan is at his friend's house tonight since there is no school tomorrow. I think he was worried he might get stuck with babysitting duties in the morning."

No kids? They were alone … all night. He let a slow, knowing smile spread across his face as he said, "Are you saying that I actually have you all to myself tonight?"

"Why yes, it appears that I am."

He proceeded to pick her up so she could wrap her legs around his waist. Once she was in his favorite position he asked, "Did you eat dinner tonight? Because you are going to need your energy, my love."

A slightly hesitant looked crossed her face before she replaced it with a playful smile and said, "Energy levels are high and ready to be depleted, handsome." What better invitation did a man need? He answered with a growl as he took her lips and started walking toward her room. It wasn't often he had her all to himself, and he was going to take full advantage of the fact that he could make her scream tonight and not worry about the kids hearing it. Just thinking about that had his arousal spiking even higher than usual.

~*~*~*~*~~*~*~*~*~

Once they made it into the bedroom, Jake was quick to divest her of her clothes. Not like she made it difficult for him or anything. Lying there naked on the bed, she felt her desire and need for Jake climb as she watched him pull his shirt over his head. The firm, tan skin of his chest, which had a thin patch of hair across the center called out to her, and she wanted to touch him, taste him. She started to get up and do just that when Jake stopped her with a shake of his head and said, "Nuh uh, beautiful. Where do you think you're going?"

"I want to touch you," she said to him as he slowly revealed the rest of his glorious body to her, his erection standing long and proud in front of her. Just the sight of it had her licking her lips as he made his way toward her.

"Oh, you're going to be touching me, that's for sure. But first, I have to taste you."

Any words she was prepared to say died on her lips as she felt Jake's tongue sweep across her hot, wet skin. There was no way she could speak; he made it so her only option was to feel, and she felt everything. It wasn't long before he had her squirming and calling out his name … twice. She couldn't handle any more; she had to have him inside her. Pulling on the hair she had wrapped tightly around her fingers, she gave him no choice but to lift his head. Once she had his eyes on her, she demanded, "I need you inside me right now, Jake Michaels! Don't you make me wait another minute."

His one-sided smirk was ignored. Yeah, he knew what he did to her, and she loved every minute of it. Her grip in his hair prevented him from making a slow trail up her body. She wanted his lips on hers and to feel him inside of her. Just before his lips made contact, she felt him position himself, poised to enter as he said, "I love it when you want me so bad, baby. It tells me I'm not alone, because I need to be inside your body more than I need to take my next breath."

Then he slammed his lips down on hers at the same time he lunged forward. *Breathe … who needed to breathe?* She thought this as she felt him fill her and stretch her. He stayed still for a moment, allowing her body to adjust as he buried his face in her neck. She felt him nibble on the sensitive spot he knew she loved as he started to slowly thrust in and out of her body. It was exquisite, it was consuming, it was everything she needed and wanted.

Gillian felt those wonderful sensations begin to build in her center again; she loved how Jake always took care of her. He always made sure she had more than him, his attention and need to please her was overwhelming at times and only heightened her arousal. She could feel his warm breath against her neck as he growled, "Give me another, Gillian. I want one more." It was so hot how he talked to her and it spurred her on, causing her muscles to tighten around him.

Jake reached his arms down and wrapped them behind her knees, opening her up to him as he picked up his pace. His thrusts were harder as he lifted his head and gazed down at her. "I want it, Gillian, give me what I want." Once again his words heightened her arousal, and she amazed herself by finding the ability to speak.

"Take it, Jake, it's all yours," he growled again and slammed into her as her body came to pieces beneath his. His body dropped back down to hers as his thrusts became erratic, and she dug her nails into his skin, trying to hold on as she came apart.

"Jake!" She heard her voice call out his name as a roar rumbled in her ear. Jake's body tensed as he reached for his release deep inside of her. She briefly thought about sharing what happened earlier today with him, but decided it would be better if she waited 'til she knew for sure. Lying there in his arms, she was content to just absorb the feel of his body against hers and how safe and cherished he made her feel.

Once their breathing calmed down, she could feel his lips softly kiss her neck and then make their way up to her cheek and then her lips. He pulled back slightly, smiled down at her, and said, "I love you, baby."

Gillian smiled back at him and whispered against his lips, "I love you, too."

She felt his body slowly begin to harden inside of her as he said, "Say it again."

"I love you," she said, and her body responded to his hardening erection with a little squeeze. He answered her body's request by taking what he wanted ... again.

CHAPTER TWENTY-FOUR

After sitting at her station completely spaced out while she waited for her lab results to post in the system, she realized she needed to stop obsessing about them. She was pretty confident she knew what the results would say, but seeing them confirmed would just cement it all in place. Part of her anxiety was that it had been two days since she suspected it was possible, and she hadn't yet mentioned it to Jake. She felt a little bad about keeping that from him, but justified it by saying it wasn't confirmed yet ... so why say anything?

Shaking her head at her own internal debate, she had just finished updating her last patient chart for the morning when she heard one of her coworkers say something about 'two good-looking young men heading her way.' Of course her reflex reaction was to look up in anticipation of what the older nurse had spied. A giant smile spread across her face when she realized the two *good-looking young men* were hers.

Two of her favorite little people were strolling toward her like they owned the world with a gleam in their eyes. They were certainly on a mission and had some sort of agenda. This was just what she needed today—two doses of her favorite tranquilizers—Dylan and Ryan. Her kids just calmed her down and relieved her anxiety. And it didn't matter what anyone said—Ryan was as much hers as her own were, and he had the same effect that the other three did. A visit from her boys would help take her mind of the blood test results she was waiting for.

"Hey Mom Dylan called, followed by Ryan saying, "Hi Aunt Gilly!" Both of their smiles got bigger, only confirming her suspicions that there was some sort of plan-in-action going on here. She bent forward to hug each one and got a kiss on each cheek from them.

"Well hey there, you two. To what do I owe this honor? And why don't I see an adult with you?" she asked while she cocked one hip to the side and placed her hands on both hips. She attempted a serious questioning-mom-glare but must have failed because both boys giggled.

Dylan turned to Ryan and said, "See I told you that she would say something like that. Now you have to let me borrow your new Nintendo game for one whole day."

Ryan turned to Gillian and whined, "Aw man! Come on Aunt Gillian, you made me lose the bet."

Laughing slightly, she bent over and whispered in Ryan's ear, so Dylan couldn't hear her, "Well, next time you have to let me in on the bet, so we can beat Dylan at his own game." She winked at him before kissing his cheek and standing back up.

"Okay, so back to my question … spill it. What and *who* brings you here?"

Dylan, always the spokesman between the two boys, spoke up and said, "We are here to take you to lunch. We wanna go have some pizza, and I know you can't say no to pizza, Mom."

Ryan chimed in, "My dad is downstairs and said that we need to take our favorite lady out to lunch because we need to make sure we keep you happy."

"Oh, he did, did he? And you both think pizza is the way to do it?" she asked.

Ryan smiled and said, "Plus we want to play at the arcade. I've been saving up so I can get tons of tokens."

Laughing out loud at Ryan's blatant honesty she said, "There it is! I knew there was some motive there."

Standing up she took a look at her patient board, which appeared to be under control, then gave a questioning glance at her co-worker, Marsha. She was the shift leader and honorary grandmother figure around there, and she was apparently enjoying the scene in front of her. Marsha obviously knew what her question was before Gillian even had to ask because she smiled down at the boys then looked up to Gillian and said, "Go ahead girl, I've got the board. Besides, you *gotta* eat sometime. Take a few extra minutes if you want."

Marsha's emphasis on the word *gotta* reminded her that Marsha was going to be watching over her. If her test confirmed she was in a delicate condition, she was sure the woman would be all over her in the coming months. She was both equally worried and thankful for the older woman's motherly qualities. Gillian smiled at her as she stood up and walked over to her desk to grab her things. "Thanks Marsha."

While picking up her stuff, she saw the message light blinking on her screen. Thinking it was possibly her test results, she took a deep breath and clicked on the icon. She let it out slowly when she saw that it wasn't what she was hoping for, but then groaned when she saw it was a message from Adam. She had managed to safely avoid him since the infamous pool party at her house, but she knew it was bound to happen sooner or later.

The message stated that he needed her sign off on a verbal x-ray order for one of her patients from yesterday. She could've sworn she had already done that and sent it down to him via interoffice envelope. Even though medical records were electronic, there was the occasional piece of paper that needed to be submitted. She decided now would be the perfect time to pop in there and do it because she could use the boys as an excuse to avoid conversation with him, so she responded to his message saying she was on her way down.

She made her way back over to the boys, who were happily regaling the other nurses with the details of their most recent trip to Disneyland, even though it was almost two months ago. She was sure her co-workers knew all there was to know about the place, but the smiles on their faces as they enjoyed the animated details from Dylan about how they rode Space Mountain four times was great to see. Just like her boys made her feel better, they did it for others. She thought to herself that this was just further confirmation that her son had actual magical powers.

"Okay boys, we just have to make a stop on the second floor, and then we can go spend as much of Ryan's money as possible in one hour." Ryan turned to say something in protest at her declaration, but then she winked at him, and he realized that she was only joking. As they headed toward the elevator, the boys were engaged in a debate over who got to hit the button. It probably could have gone on forever if she hadn't jumped in with a suggestion. "How about one of you hits the button to go down, and the other hits the button inside the elevator?"

Seemingly satisfied with her solution, Dylan took it upon himself to hit the down button, and the doors promptly opened. Scooting inside with them she said, "Go ahead and hit the button for the second floor Ryan. I need to stop in x-ray to sign something."

When they got to the second floor, she didn't want to get sucked into having to talk with Adam. Thinking that she could hold the elevator to further her cause, she said, "Hey boys, I will only be a second, so how 'bout you wait here, and hold the doors for me? I would prefer that you weren't around the x-ray equipment." Since they would be in her direct sight for those few seconds, it didn't bother her that she was asking them to wait there. "But I need both of you to hold the button for me."

Both boys enthusiastically agreed to her plan, so she took each of their fingers and pressed them against the button to hold the doors. She smiled at them and said, "Hold it tight, I'll be right back." You would have thought that they were performing a mission that was a matter of life or death the way they held that button—almost like holding the clip of a grenade, and if they let go it would explode. It was definitely comical to see. Walking backward toward the entrance to the radiology control room so she could see them, a laugh bubbled up, and she smiled at those boys she loved so much. She was still smiling as she turned to the door of the radiology department and stopped dead in her tracks at the sight before her.

She was standing there, just outside the door in the hallway, in sight of Dylan and Ryan, face to face with the barrel of a gun. *Ohmygod! Ohmygod! There was a gun … pointed directly at her! Was this a joke? Who was holding it?* She could barely tear her eyes off of the giant hole at the end of the gun to see the person who was pointing it at her. It looked like a fucking cannon! Forcing herself to attempt moving her eyes from the cannon, she saw Adam. Was Adam really pointing a gun at her? This had to be a joke, because seriously this kind of shit only happens in the movies. She hoped.

Trying to actually get her tongue to move in order to allow the words to come out was one of the hardest things she had ever done. She mentally coached herself, *Come on Gillian, that's it, bring in the oxygen, and let the sound come out.* "Hey Adam," she managed to squeak out before needing to swallow again, "W-what's going on? Is this some kind of prank? 'Cause you got me, I think I peed my pants." She gave him a weak smile while trying to sound like she had a sense of humor in a situation that she could only hope was a joke. A fucking sick joke at that.

She glanced to her left to see that the boys were still standing there in the elevator waiting for her. They didn't look scared in any way, just devoted to holding that damn button down. Okay, so they must not be able to see the gun. Good. That was a good thing ... a very good thing.

Adam's growling response brought her back to face him when he said, "I have to make him suffer. Make him feel the pain." Just the sound of his voice confirmed her fear that this was in fact happening. *Holy shit, this was really happening! Wait, what? Him who? What the hell was he talking about*? In the span of a few seconds she tried to process all that was going on.

"Logan is going to feel what it's like to be alone, to feel pain." Recognition sparked in her head. Okay, so mental stability and strong morals did not run in that family. First, she had to deal with

331

his wife, now him? Panic started to rise, but was quickly overpowered when her motherly instincts kicked in. She needed to get the boys the hell out of there, and figure out where the hell everyone else was because the corridor was strangely empty.

This really is the kind of shit that happens in movies. What do they do in the damn movies? Oh yeah, the guy comes in and rescues the damsel in distress, takes out the bad guy, and they all live happily ever after. Well, that doesn't seem likely at the moment. Think, Gillian, think. Irritation and anger started to well up as she tried absorbing what was going on. She swore to herself as she once again damned Logan and his affair. She had refused to let his affair take one more thing away from her. This was not happening to her. Just the fact that she was in this position pissed her off more.

Trying to focus on what she needed to do, she knew she needed to talk to him. That's something they do in the movies—distract him by talking while you figure a way out of this. Or at least 'til you get the kids out of there. Kids. Well, she may not be able to protect all of them, considering the newest one wasn't going anywhere since she was the intended victim here. Trying to stop her thoughts from drifting to her unborn child she was possibly carrying, she had to make sure her boys were safe, so she steeled her spine and started talking to him.

"Adam, what's this all about?" she asked while cautiously looking from side to side, hoping not to draw too much attention to what she was doing. Her eyes landed on the fire alarm perched on the wall next to the doorway she was standing in front of. Fire alarms brought the cavalry in, lights and sirens blazing. It was a direct link to 911. She desperately tried remembering the procedure of what happens in the building when the fire alarm goes off. It was a state of the art system and was designed to prevent fire from spreading. The doors were secured by giant magnets that released their hold when the system was activated.

These doors and giant magnets were at the entrance to every corridor and every waiting room. As impressive as the system was, it could be annoying as hell sometimes because when there were false alarms, the magnets would release the heavy doors, and all you could do is hope you weren't standing in the doorway when it did release. The flashing lights and those damn heavy doors had made some days frustrating, but she was grateful for them now since it gave her the hope to get out of this.

If she could pull the fire alarm, the fire doors would then seal off this area in order to prevent the spread of a supposed fire and also call the fire department. It was the only way she could think of to get help. With another quick glance to her left she realized that there was a set of fire doors between her and the elevator—between the crazy man with the gun and her two favorite little boys. If she pulled the alarm, the doors would close off the boys from this scene playing out right now, but would the elevators work?

She once again tried her hardest to recall what happens to the elevators when the fire alarm goes off. They always say that if there was a fire, you should never take the elevator. But what happened to the elevators? Did they just stay there? She was having trouble focusing. Not like the gun pointed directly at her was going to help her figure it out any faster.

She was pretty sure that the elevators closed off and then got automatically called back down to the bottom floor to prevent people from using during a fire and risk being trapped. Perfect. If that's what they did, then that would be perfect. That would be enough to get the boys to safety. Besides, it's not like there really was a fire that could harm the boys. No, just a psychotic disgruntled husband seeking revenge. All of this sounded easy enough to make happen if she could just pull the damn alarm. She wanted to cross her fingers and hope there wasn't a delay once the alarm was triggered; she needed it to happen immediately.

Adam interrupted her thoughts with his response to her question. She had to try and remember what her question was. "I don't have a wife or a family anymore, and it's all your husband's fault! So it's only fair that he loses his wife, too!" Wait, didn't he know that she left Logan months ago? And did he just say that Jody left him? She needed to play into that, which could distract him.

"I'm so sorry Jody left you, Adam. I didn't know. But I'm not married to Logan anymore. I left him, and we've filed for divorce. He's already alone." Trying to inch a tiny bit closer to the doorframe to reach the alarm, she continued, actually feeling sorry for the bastard, "But I know how you feel. How betrayed you must feel right now." And the truth of the matter was that she did. She knew exactly what it felt like for your whole world to be pulled out from underneath you—like a rug being yanked away—leaving you with only one place to go and that was crashing downward. But she also knew what it felt like to stand back up again. To find that solid footing and recover from the pain. She knew what it felt like to move on and live again.

334

She took another step closer, which put her in arms reach of the alarm as she said, "But I also know what it feels like to get past that pain. I know what it feels like to realize that it's not the end of the world …"

He interrupted her, "I'm sure I'll get over this as soon as I know he's suffering, too!" That's when she realized that there was no way to get through to him; he was too full of hurt and vengeance. The crazed look in his eyes solidified it for her. Adam was going to do what he set out to do. And based on the gun he held aimed at her chest, it was going to be very effective at doing damage.

This was real, and this was happening. Strangely, the tears were only just now threatening to breach the wells of her eyes. She felt them start to fall when she squared her shoulders and realized there was nothing she could do except get the boys out of there. She turned her gaze to them and saw that they were watching her. She mouthed the words 'I love you' to them, then turned and practically lunged for the alarm.

Her only thoughts were to make sure the boys were safe and send them down to Jake. He would find them. She only wished that she could protect the baby. Their baby. Jake's baby. Her unexpected miracle. The miracle that she would have never anticipated and nobody even knew about yet. Well, Allie did, but Jake was the important one. She wasn't going to be able to tell him about their baby. Regret was a like a punch to her gut when she remembered how she could have told him in the last two days. There was nothing she could do about it now.

As she felt her hand latch onto the alarm handle, she yanked it down, hard. While she knew it took only a second or two to do so, everything seemed to happen in slow motion. She saw the elevator doors close, and the boys disappeared just before the fire doors released and started to swing shut. She vaguely heard Adam curse as he jumped out of the path the door to his x-ray room was swinging in. This also happened to be in the direction of his fully-extended-gun-holding-arm. At the same time, she had to jump out of the way of the door that separated the main corridor from the hallway that contained the elevators and stairway exits. She apparently didn't move quickly enough because she felt the door slam into her shoulder just as she heard the sound of a gunshot echoing loudly in the confined area. She quickly threw herself to floor and covered her head with her hands just like people tell you to do, but thinking to herself how ridiculous it was to do, since it was highly unlikely that her hands were going to deter a bullet. She could hear the sounds of all the other large doors positioned throughout the facility slamming shut beyond where she was. Everything started to sound a little hollow—almost like she was underwater—and there was a ringing in her ears, most likely from the proximity of the gun going off.

"Fuck!" she heard Adam yell over the ringing in her ears. "Fuck!" he yelled again as she felt his feet connect with her side while she was lying on the ground. It wasn't an intentional kick to her side, more like he slipped on something. Then, a few seconds later, she heard the sound of the stairwell door close behind her. And then she was alone. A quick swell of relief washed over her as she realized her plan kind of worked. She smiled to herself as she lay there on the ground, face to the floor. She cursed inwardly as her shoulder began to hurt like hell. She knew those doors were heavy and since one of them nailed her hard, she figured the pain was going to increase.

Deciding that she needed to make sure that Adam was really gone, she slowly removed her hands from over her head and glanced to her right. Nothing. Then to the left. Again nothing. Assessing it was all clear, she started to push off the ground when she felt the wetness on the floor beneath her left hand, causing her hand to slip forward and a sharp pain to make itself known in her left shoulder. Then she saw it—the deep crimson puddle on the floor that had a distinct impression of her hand in it. She turned her hand over to see it covered from wrist to fingertip in blood. Her blood. Well fuck! So much for thinking her plan worked.

It hadn't been the damn door that hit her shoulder; it was the gunshot that got her. All of her strength and courage that built up in her seconds before quickly evaporated when she realized that she was bleeding here on the floor, and there was nobody around to help her. Then the pain seized her, sharp and fierce as it took her breath away. She didn't really feel the severity of the pain 'til she realized what had happened. This changed things, and she had to do something fast.

She wondered how quickly the firemen swept the floors to clear it for fire? She was on the second floor, so they only had to methodically sweep the first floor, and then they would get to her. Thinking that wouldn't take too long was comforting, but how much blood could she lose before it affected the baby.

"Shit!" she declared as she rolled to her right side, putting her left shoulder higher and above her heart in an attempt to stop, or at least slow, the bleeding. The movement caused pain to shoot through her shoulder and down her left arm, once again taking her breath away with its severity. *Come on Gillian, you need to get*

337

up, and sit your ass up against the wall! You need to get the wound above your heart to slow the bleeding.

Her mental pep talk had her moving. Using her right hand, she pushed on the floor. This allowed her to get herself up onto her hands and knees, which only helped her see how much blood she had lost. Just the site of the amount of blood she had lost zapped a little more of her energy.

"This isn't good," she said out loud to herself as if hearing herself talk was going to help. But strangely it did. She began to talk out loud to herself, encouraging herself to move, to get up, to survive. "Just get your ass against that wall, Gillian!" she growled to herself as she plopped her butt down on the ground. She couldn't risk trying to stand up because if she moved too quickly, with her blood pressure likely being very low, she would be at risk for passing out completely, and then she would definitely bleed out.

In this upward position, she felt a bit lightheaded and knew she needed to get to the wall for support. The only way to accomplish this was to push herself with her feet toward the wall, scooting on her bottom. The first push had her sliding across the puddle of her own blood. The wetness was still warm and gave her a disturbing feeling as she accepted the fact that there was a lot of blood on the floor.

"Good, this will work." Once again cheering herself along, she repeated the movement with her feet over and over, which brought her closer and closer to the wall. All the while she tried to assess what she needed to do next. As she continued to push herself across the floor, she noticed the warm wetness of blood trailing down her back from the exertion. There was blood on both her front and her back. She had expected this on the front, but hadn't expected it on the back. "The bullet must have gone straight through then," she mused out loud as she paused for a moment before pushing again. This was good because there was no bullet just hanging out inside her body causing trouble. And it was bad because that meant she had to try and apply pressure to both wounds. "Fuck!"

The wall. She really needed to get to that wall. If she could lean against it, and apply pressure from the front, that should be sufficient to stop the bleeding. She pushed with her feet one last time when she felt her back hit the wall. She made a straining and painful attempt to move her left shoulder against the wall, which in turn, took her breath away. Trying to slow her breathing down because she was getting even more lightheaded, she made an attempt to apply pressure to the front of her shoulder and push it back into the wall. "Fuck!" she yelled again into the empty corridor.

She could feel the wetness of her scrubs and the sting of the wound itself as she pressed her shoulder completely back. Raising her right hand again to the wound in the front of her shoulder, she pushed it back in to the wall as hard as she possibly could. It was certainly becoming more of a challenge since her limbs were starting to get heavy and take on a resemblance to gelatin.

"Now what do I do?" she again asked herself out loud. Maybe the firemen weren't too far from where she was. "Help! Is anyone there?" she called out in hopes that maybe someone would be nearby. Could tell which fire alarm was pulled? If they knew which one was pulled, they could just go directly to it. Logic would tell you that if an alarm was pulled, the fire had to be in sight of that particular alarm, didn't it? All she could do now was wait. With her right hand applying pressure to her left shoulder, she made the painful attempt to get her left hand into her lap. Crying out loud as the pain once again shot through her shoulder and down her arm, she got her left hand up and cradled it around her stomach. This helped take some of the strain off of her shoulder.

Gillian looked down at her left arm across her lap and noticed how it was cradling her abdomen from one side to the other. It looked like the position an arm would be in to hold a baby. As the tears began to well up in her eyes, she thought to herself that she *was* holding a baby. She was holding her and Jake's baby. The tears started to overflow from her eyes, and she whispered, "I'm sorry, little one... I'm so sorry." She closed her eyes and leaned her head back against the wall to wait, holding her abdomen as tightly as she possibly could with her weak useless arm.

CHAPTER TWENTY-FIVE

Jake was sitting on the bench outside the entrance to the hospital waiting for the boys to come down with Gillian. He hated that she seemed upset or distracted by something last night. He couldn't be one hundred percent sure what was the cause of it, but he only hoped that it wasn't him. Being around a woman like Gillian could be equal parts funny and frustrating as he tried to figure out what was wrong with his girl and attempt to not be the cause of it. Clearly, Gillian was upset about something and while he didn't know what it was, he was going to do whatever he could to make her happy until he could figure it out. He had thought about asking Allie about it since he knew she was over yesterday, but he felt that was almost like cheating. It was his job to make her happy, and he wasn't about to take a short cut. Not yet at least.

The thought of that little blue bag, which contained that infamous little blue box with the ribbon around it that was stuffed inside his sock drawer made him smile. Maybe he should just propose sooner rather than later. No, he wanted to plan it out, and he wanted to wait and do it in a memorable way. It would mean more to the both of them that way. He wanted to propose, was going to propose, and he wasn't going to take no for an answer, but he wanted the memory of it to be a powerful one. A big smile spread across his face as he thought about Gillian as his wife.

His thoughts were suddenly interrupted by the sound of the fire alarm going off. He reflexively jumped to his feet and was met by the crowds of people making their way out of the building to escape whatever it was that set the alarm off. Jake knew for a fact that these alarms go off frequently, but a sinking feeling overtook him, sending him on high alert. He could hear the sirens of the trucks coming and was slightly relieved they were close by. He started to move, trying to make his way in through the doors that everyone was filing out of to see if he could help. Fortunately, the crowds of people appeared to be well controlled, and the scene didn't present itself as one of chaos like you might think— probably because this was routine for them. Hospital personnel, medical professionals, and patients who were mobile made their way out of the building, guided by those who were instructed on evacuation procedures.

The boys crossed his mind, but he was comforted by the fact that they were with Gillian, and she would make sure they got out safe if there really was a fire. He heard the fire truck pull up, but then he heard the police cruisers pull up, as well. He turned to see Gillian's brother Sean get out of a car with a radio to his mouth talking as he took in the scene around him. Well, that many officers showing up for a fire alarm wasn't normal procedure. He was turning to go talk to Sean when he heard Ryan call out to him, "Dad! Dad!" Both boys suddenly accosted him, looking a little on edge by what was going on around them. Of course they were freaked out. They may think it cool later, but at the moment, it was a lot to take in.

Right about that time he heard Sean call out to him, "Jake! Get the boys out of there now!"

Jake immediately concluded that there was more going on in there. He ushered the boys over to where Sean was standing and asked, "What the hell is going on, Sean?" The boys were trying to talk to him, but he was looking at Sean when he heard him say,

"We got a report of shots fired in the building just when the fire alarm went off! Now get the boys out of here!"

Then it hit him—the boys were here, but Gillian was not. He looked at the boys and demanded, "Where is your mom, Dylan? Did you see her?"

Dylan nodded and said, "Yes! We were on the second floor, holding the elevator doors for her, and waiting." He had to come up for air because he was breathing so fast. He continued, "She said I love you, and then she pulled the fire alarm thing on the wall. Then the elevator doors closed and brought us down here."

Sean, who was next to them, dropped to his knees in front of his nephew and asked, "Did you say your mom pulled the alarm?" Dylan nodded. Sean pressed on, "Did you see a fire? Or any smoke?" Dylan shook his head. "Was your mommy alone?"

Dylan shook his head no and said, "She said she had to see Adam before we went to lunch. She was standing there talking, but then pulled on the red box on the wall."

The child pulled in a deep breath and looked at his uncle Sean and asked, "Is Mommy gonna get in trouble for setting off that alarm if there is no fire?"

Sean smiled at his nephew, who looked a lot like his sister and said, "Don't you worry about Mommy getting in trouble. I'll take care of it." He then stood and looked to Jake and said, "Get the boys out of here, Jake." As he started talking into his radio, motioning to another police officer near him, his hand perched on the gun holstered at his side. Sean was on high alert, and Jake didn't like that Gillian had pulled that alarm. He had to get in there to her.

Just then Jake saw one of Gillian's coworkers stroll past him, and he reached out to her. "Marsha?"

She turned and looked at Jake, then at the boys next to him, and smiled. "Hey there boys, where's Gillian?"

Jake was relieved when the woman recognized him and asked her, "Could you please watch the boys for me? I need to find her." The desperation on his face was enough for the older woman to instantly see, so she grabbed each of the boys' hands as she continued with the crowd heading out of the building. Jake knew that Gilly spoke highly of the woman and would trust the boys with her. Right now, he needed to find Gillian because that sinking feeling in his gut was now like a ten-ton weight pulling him down.

Jake caught up with Sean near the elevators as he saw some familiar faces pass him by, but none of them were Gillian. "Sean, I have to get up to the second floor!"

Sean turned to Jake and barked at him, "Get your ass out of here, Jake!"

"Bullshit! I'm not going anywhere! The boys said Gillian pulled the alarm, and you said there was a report of shots fired! We have to get to where she was on the second floor. I know my way around the building! She had to be near x-ray because that is right where the elevators are." Sean just stared at Jake, obviously trying to figure out if getting Jake to leave was a battle worth fighting.

He saw the resolve spread across Sean's face when he decided he didn't care about procedure. Finding his sister was top priority. Sean nodded at Jake and then motioned for another officer to follow them. They made their way through the door to the stairwell that came out near the elevators. Jake stayed behind them and let them do their thing, making sure everything was safe and secure—not moving in a new direction without making sure all was clear. They got up the stairwell and looked through the window, but the fire doors were still closed so they couldn't see anything. They were going to have to go open them. As Sean opened the door from the stairwell, they could immediately detect the lingering scent of gunpowder. This is where the gun was fired. Shit! This is where the boys had last seen Gillian. Only years of working as a paramedic helped Jake control the panic that was starting to rise at the thought of anything happening to Gillian.

As Sean and the other officer made their way toward the fire door, Jake heard something. Was that someone crying? He rushed forward, touched Sean on the shoulder, and put his finger up to his mouth. He then pointed to his ear, gesturing for him to be quiet and listen. That was when they heard it—there was someone on the other side of that fire door, and they were crying. Placing his hand on the fire door to feel for heat, Sean then shoved the door slowly forward. As he pushed forward, the blood was the first thing that jumped up and grabbed Jake's attention. The puddle was in front of the door and the movement of the door just moved the blood with it. Until the door hit something, and they all froze. Was the gunman behind the door? This wasn't good.

Sean motioned for Jake to step back, which he did. He motioned for the other officer to cover him as he counted backward from three with his fingers in the air. Three … Two … One, and swung himself behind the door with his gun drawn and pointing at whatever it was that was there. Jake didn't realize he was holding his breath until he suddenly released it when he heard Sean curse and drop to his knees while holstering his weapon. "Get a damn medic up here! A doctor! Someone!" Sean yelled at the officer as if Jake wasn't even standing there. Jake was a medic—why was Sean asking for one when Jake was capable of helping. Unless … Jake sprinted forward around the officer calling for help to see Sean hovering over Gillian. His first thought was *thank God they found her*. Then he really took in the scene before him as he noticed all of the blood. All of the blood covering the floor and covering Gillian.

Her eyes were open, and she was trying to tell Sean something, but Jake couldn't hear it. Sean's jaw clenched as he reached for his radio. "The suspect's name is Adam Wallace! He is an employee of the hospital! He was last seen exiting the second floor approximately five minutes ago. He is armed and dangerous! I repeat, he is armed and dangerous!" Jake blinked and thought to himself, *Adam? Adam did this?* He saw that bastard walk right out of here like he was part of the crowd. Damn! He was responsible for all of this blood? Gillian's blood?

Jake dropped to Gillian's side, and he knew the minute she realized it was him next to her. She sat there against the wall, with her left hand over her stomach and her right hand covering her bullet wound. Jake hollered for the officer standing behind him to grab a cart he saw down the hall, which he knew would have

346

supplies. He then placed his hand over her hand, applying more pressure to the wound and said, "I got you now, Gilly. I'm here for you, baby." Her skin was pale and clammy, which were signs of shock, but her breathing looked good. When the officer came back with the cart, Jake let his training kick in.

He immediately had gauze in his hand and pressed it to the wound on her shoulder and told Sean to apply pressure to it. Gillian was clearly weakened by the blood loss, which was spread out over a few feet. He realized that she must have scooted herself against the wall to help apply pressure to the wound. "Gillian, look at me." He waited while her eyes tracked toward his and focused. She was in pain, and he knew it, which really pissed him off, but he had to concentrate.

"Is the wound a through-and-through?" She nodded once while breathing through the oxygen mask he had strapped to her head. "That's my girl; good job getting up against the wall to apply pressure." She gave him a weak smile, and a tear rolled down her face. "I know you're in pain, baby, but I need you to focus for a few more seconds ... can you do that for me?" She once again gave him a weak nod. "Are you hurt anywhere else? There is a lot of blood, so I can't tell for sure."

She tried talking, but he couldn't hear her through the mask. He pulled it away from her face slightly, but kept the flow of oxygen flowing toward her airways. "No ... only ... one ... shot ... shoulder ... arm hurts, too."

He nodded at her. "Good, that's probably all related. I guess the positive way to look at this is that you won't need to ride in the ambulance to get the help ... you're already here. And since you work here, I'm sure they have all of your information on file. No paperwork for you." He was talking to her as he was routinely placing an IV line in her right arm and going about his normal actions for this kind of trauma.

She blinked, and her eyes took a little longer to open back up and look at him. She attempted to say something to him, but her voice was weak. The lump in his throat was enormous, and he was afraid that he was going to lose his cool any second. "… boys … baby … sorry."

He couldn't make out all she was saying, but he assumed it was about the boys. "Shh, it's okay, baby, the boys made it down, found me, and told us you pulled the alarm. They're the reason we knew where to find you." Jake looked over to Sean who looked like he was ready to kill someone with his bare hands. "Remind me to buy those boys anything they want for telling us where she was." Sean gave Jake a tight nod and then looked back at Gillian.

Gillian again attempted to speak, but he could barely hear her. The only word he could make out was baby. All he could do was comfort her and wait for help to arrive. It took a few minutes to get help up to where they were since they had to reset the fire alarm and get the elevators working. Somewhere in that period of time, Gillian closed her eyes, but her breathing remained steady. While they were riding down in the elevator to take her to the emergency department, Jake called his brother and gave him the brief version of what happened, and most specifically, who was responsible for what happened. Jake heard his brother swear up a blue streak over the phone and gave him instructions to let everyone know and get over to the hospital.

They had to take Gillian down into the ER to get the doctors to work on her and figure out how bad things were. Of course, they wouldn't let Jake in with her, but he put up a fight because, let's face it, Gillian was worth fighting for. He didn't want her to be alone.

"Procedure, Jake! You know how it works—family waits out here. Give them the space to work on her," the head ER nurse told him. He did know it was procedure, but he also knew it sucked! He was usually on the other end of it. Not the receiving end of that line.

While standing there, feeling like he had his thumb up his ass, Sean marched in and headed straight for Jake. "We got him!" he said in low growl through his clenched jaw to Jake. All he could do was nod at Sean. Jake recognized the look in Sean's eyes, and he could totally relate. It was the look of pure anger, the look of pure menace that warned everyone around them of a man who needed to inflict pain on the person who was responsible.

"Have they come out yet?" he asked Jake. As he shook his head no, they both turned when the door opened again. Logan came running in, with Jonathan and Maddie at his sides, the look of panic on all their faces. Jake wanted to punch Logan for this. His hands fisted at his sides, and he glared at Logan. He knew it wasn't Logan who did this, but he really wanted to punch him anyway since he was the catalyst for what happened today. Sean talked to Logan through gritted teeth, obviously reciprocating Jake's feelings.

While Maddie stayed close to Logan for support, Jonathan walked up to Jake with a look of questioning in his eyes—almost as if he was afraid to talk 'cause he might lose it. Jake placed his hands on

349

Jonathan's shoulders and said, "She was shot in the shoulder; looks to be a through and through injury, which is good. She did lose a lot of blood, and the doctors are checking to see if there is any severe damage inside. We are just waiting to hear from them now." He pulled Jonathan into a hug to let him know he was there for him and felt the kid release a big sigh. He knew that Jonathan was not as close to his dad lately because of everything that had happened, and was already closer to Gillian before the family was thrown into turmoil. Jonathan was certainly a mama's boy, by definition, but really, who could blame him? All that being said, he knew this was definitely hard for him.

They all sat down and offered each other silent support while they waited for the news. It felt like forever. Sean paced the floor, while his wife, Morgan, sat in the corner with Dylan and Ryan. Then Allie walked in the room and paused just inside the doorway. She looked around and stopped when her eyes landed on her brother. Logan stood in a corner, leaning against the wall. He had his arms around his daughter, who was leaning against her dad, actually looking concerned for her mom. This was a shock in itself since Madison usually only delivered an attitude toward her mom lately. And if he were being honest, he felt she was quite selfish.

She had taken Logan's side in the divorce and really made a job out of being a bitch to Gillian. This was, of course, because Madison had no idea why her parents were getting divorced—she just blamed her mom. Jake tried to convince Gillian to tell Madison the reasons, but her only response was, "If she needs to be mad at me, then she can go right ahead. Her father may have done wrong by me, but he has, and will always make her a priority. I will not be the person who changes him in her eyes." Jake could understand where she was coming from, but it really pissed him off because Logan didn't deserve protecting. But he also knew it was about Gillian protecting her daughter, even if it was at her own expense. It was just another reason to admire Gillian.

Allie stood still for a few moments, her face hard, as she stared her brother down. Jake noticed when Logan looked up at Allie, his usually hard face was submissive and full of shame. Clearly, he realized that his soon to be ex-wife was lying in the other room with a bullet hole in her shoulder because of him. Well, it's about time he showed some shame or responsibility for his actions. Jake was aware of how hypocritical he probably sounded since it was Logan's actions that brought Gillian into Jake's arms.

He was still watching the two siblings stare at each other and then Allie was in motion. She stomped right over to her brother, who continued to look pathetic, and smacked him hard across the face. Logan's head whipped to the side and made contact with the wall he leaned against. Madison, who still stood in front of him must have had her eyes closed because she startled and looked up at her aunt in shock. Logan slowly let go of his daughter and moved her to the side as Sean went over to retrieve her from what was going down. All the grown-ups knew, but the kids didn't. Well, Jonathan knew, but that was only because he overheard his father pleading his case.

As Madison was unwillingly pulled away from her father's comfort, Logan's head came back to face his sister, and she slapped it again, hard.

"This is all your fucking fault, you selfish bastard!" she growled at him through gritted teeth with eyes full of tears. "You did this to her! She told us she feared something like this would happen, but you just thought she was overreacting. You said she was just trying to find a way to rub your nose in your mistakes! Well, guess what you ASS ... this was about your mistakes! My best friend was shot because her husband couldn't keep his dick out of another woman!" And then she slapped him again. His left cheek was a bright pink color now, and Jake saw the tears that were previously welling in his eyes finally slip down, but he didn't say anything to defend himself.

Allie started to cry as she began to pound her fists on Logan's chest saying, "It's all your fault. Why did you do this to her?" But Logan continued to let her beat on him and not say a damn thing. It was like watching a train wreck—you couldn't *not* look at it. As Allie began to cry harder, her body began to lose steam, and she slumped against her big brother. He instantly embraced her and cried with her.

"I'm so sorry, Allie ... so sorry." The siblings continued to comfort each other, and suddenly it felt as if watching was an intrusion. Jake looked over to Sean, who had an arm around a shocked Madison, standing there staring at her father and aunt, while tears streamed down her face. She certainly knew now that her father had wronged her mother, and that was the reason for the divorce. She looked up at her uncle with a pleading look on her face, almost as if she was hoping he would tell her otherwise. All Sean could do was give her a sympathetic look. She'd clearly heard it all.

Madison then looked to Jake with the same look. It was Jonathan, who had been sitting next to Jake, that finally got up and went over to his younger sister. She looked up to him with so much pain in her eyes before she burst into tears and threw herself into his arms. Jonathan didn't miss a beat and wrapped his arms around her and began comforting her.

"It's going to be okay, Maddie. Shh, Mom is strong, and she'll be fine."

Madison looked up into her brother's eyes and said, "She has to be, Jonathan ... she just has to be! I have been so awful to her. I need to tell her I'm sorry." And then she sobbed into her brother's shirt some more. Jonathan looked over at Jake and then over to where his father was watching over Allie's head, still hugging her. Logan gave his son a nod of acknowledgment and approval.

When the doctor finally walked in the room, they all stood quickly and just stared at him, waiting for him to speak. Waiting. And waiting. Then the doctor gave a slight smile and nodded. It was only then that everyone let out a collective breath they were holding.

Jake approached the doctor quickly and pleaded, "Please doc, can I see her?"

The doctor smiled as he replied, "Yes, Jake. You can. She's been asking for you. But I must warn you that she is not very comfortable at the moment. Of course, she has plenty of energy to boss us around, but is still quite weak. She lost a lot of blood so she was given a couple transfusions, and the bullet wound is closed up, but since we couldn't put her to sleep to fix it, she went through more pain than I would like my patients to go through."

Jake was slightly confused as to why they wouldn't put her under for that. "Why wouldn't you put her to sleep for that? She had to be in agony." The doctor looked at Jake as if he sprouted a second head. He wondered what the hell that was about as his irritation at the doctor rose.

The doctor just shrugged and said, "Because she wouldn't let us. She didn't want to risk the baby."

Baby? Did he say baby? "Excuse me doctor, but did you just say ... baby?" Jake heard himself ask the question, but didn't remember giving himself the order to speak it.

Again, the doctor looked at him like he was an idiot and nodded. "Yes, Gillian's approximately six weeks pregnant. Did you not know?"

The look of shock on Jake's face had to be enough to answer the doctor's question, as he muttered, "Well, I'm sure she'll chew me out for saying it, but she should've warned me. But, if she is well enough to chew me out, I'll be happy. I'll have the nurse come for you when she is settled in a room. We'll be keeping her overnight for one or two days to follow both her and the fetus, but things look good." Jake barely got out his *thank you* for the doctor before he was gone.

Baby. Gillian was pregnant—very newly pregnant. Was it his? Of course it was, it had to be his. Jake turned to see everyone looking at him expectantly. What was he supposed to say? *Hey Logan, I knocked up your wife. Or—hey Maddie and Jonathan, you're*

354

gonna be older siblings again. Hey Sean, I did the nasty with your sister and now she's having my baby? No words. There were literally no words to say to any of them.

The nurse came in and called Jake's name, but everyone rushed toward her. She calmly directed everyone to have a seat and that Jake was going back first. He glanced over at Sean then to Logan, feeling like he needed them to acknowledge that it was okay for him to go back first—that he was more than just a friend to Gillian. Not that they could've stopped him. Jake knew for a fact that he was now listed as her emergency contact, along with Allie, in her personnel files.

Jake numbly followed the nurse towards Gillian's room, lost in thought. Why didn't she tell him she was pregnant? She had to have a good reason … but whatever the reason, he was happy Gillian was carrying his child. He couldn't stop his smile.

CHAPTER TWENTY-SIX

Jake was overwhelmed by all of the thoughts and emotions that were bombarding him. Some of them were so intense they made his chest tighten, and his throat felt like it was going to close up at any moment. Breathing was becoming a chore, as it seemed to require more effort with each inhalation. He knew that he was panicking, and he knew that the only thing that could fix this was Gillian. So he had to pull himself together … for her.

The only thing preventing him from sprinting through the hospital halls screaming her name was the fact that the doctor said she was going to be fine … and they didn't tell him what room she was in. Jake also heard the doctor tell him that the baby appeared to be fine. That bit of information was hard for him to swallow because it was difficult to be worried about something that he didn't know existed thirty minutes ago. Was it even considered a baby yet … was he even supposed to refer to it as that? He wasn't discounting the pregnancy, it was just that none of it mattered if Gillian wasn't okay, so that was his first priority.

The need to see her with his own eyes, to touch her and feel her, was mounting with each step they took down the hall. It was becoming a painful need, a need for reassurance that would only dissipate when he felt her in his arms.

Lost in thought as he blindly followed the nurse leading him to Gillian, he almost tripped over her when she stopped abruptly and turned to face him. She was blocking a door that he could only assume had Gillian behind it, and she was in his way. He was seriously considering lifting her out of his way, and was assessing exactly how to do so, when she put her hand out to poke a finger in his chest. Shocked at the contact, he looked down at her hand and then back up to her face.

The older nurse, who he had never met, had a stern expression plastered on her face as she glared at him. What the hell? Finally, Nurse Ratchet spoke, "Don't upset her," she snapped at Jake. "We all love Gillian around here, so don't think I won't hesitate to throw your ass out if necessary. She needs to rest and stay calm … for both her and the sake of the pregnancy." Jake's first thought was to be annoyed at this woman he didn't know, and who didn't know him. He wondered who she thought she was to talk to him like that. All of his annoyance quickly vanished when he realized that the woman was only looking out for Gillian, and that was perfectly fine with him.

He nodded and smiled at her to show his understanding and said, "I love her. My only intention when I get in that room is to comfort her and make her feel safe. I would never hurt her." She continued her stern look at him as she absorbed what he said. Appearing satisfied with his answer, she nodded before turning to open the door.

~*~*~*~*~*~~*~*~*~*~*~

The door to her room slowly opened, catching Gillian's immediate and undivided attention. When she saw her friend and fellow co-worker, Jan, pop her head in, she didn't know if she was temporarily relieved or completely disappointed. She resolved that it was a strong tie on both counts. Through the door that still remained mostly closed, Jan smiled at her and said, "Hey sweetie, you up for a visitor yet?" Jan was a staple to her nursing profession and was pushing three decades here at the hospital. She was like a mother figure to some of the younger staff, and Gillian could tell that she was blocking the potential visitor from entering. It was heartwarming and appreciated. But the fact was that Gillian really wanted to see Jake, regardless of her cowardly thoughts a few moments ago. So she nodded her head at her protector before she could chicken out.

Gillian knew that seeing Jake would instantly resolve some of her anxiety and lessen her discomfort. Just his touch would ease her, although she was concerned about what he thought about her being pregnant. But honestly, she wasn't even sure if it was Jake standing there or not; she hoped it was, though. She assumed he was there, in the hospital, but maybe her brother or parents were coming back first. He technically wasn't family, per hospital standards, but everyone here knew him so that shouldn't be a problem.

Since she wasn't sure who it was coming in, she made her best attempt at looking like nothing was wrong. She didn't want to compound the worry her family was probably already feeling over what happened. Jan pushed the door all the way open, and Jake walked in looking like he was on a mission. He paused just at the end of her bed, took in a deep breath, and then he visibly relaxed. He looked as if he was struggling to do it, but Jake gave her one of his heart melting smiles and said, "Hey beautiful. How's my girl doing?"

Just hearing his voice dissolved whatever façade she had put in place to look strong. She felt instant relief, both physically and mentally. The tears that began welling up in her eyes started to fall full force down her face as she gave a slight smile and reached out for him. She could only touch him with her right arm, since her left was secured down against her body still, and that really bothered her. She wanted to fully embrace him so she could hold on and not let go—he would make her feel better.

There was no hesitation as he quickly responded to her request for him. Rushing toward her, he took her hand in his, pulled it against his chest, and held it there. The warmth from his contact made her hand tingle, and she couldn't help her smile at him. She was certain she looked like a train wreck, but she didn't care because she needed him. Standing at the side of her bed, he leaned down and cupped her cheek with one hand and stroked at the tears streaming down her face. They didn't say anything; they just looked into each other's eyes, before he leaned in closer and pressed his lips against her forehead.

Still holding her hand against his chest, she could feel the hard pounding of his heart, and the trembling of his lips. She knew that she needed him to make her feel better, but she had almost forgotten that he needed reassurance, too. Giving his hand a squeeze, she whispered, "I'm okay, Jake. I'm okay."

Jake took in a deep breath and then pulled back to look at her. The anguish on his face was unmistakable, and she once again cursed the fact that she couldn't crush him against her and hold him. His eyes were glistening as he looked away from her, took in another deep breath, and let it out slowly. When he turned back toward her, he gave her a shaky smile and said, "I can see that now, beautiful. But you've got to do me a favor ..." She gave him an answering nod, but his long pause was a little unsettling. "Never leave my sight again."

She snorted a little laugh at his comment and said, "Okay, sweetheart, never."

"You think I'm joking with you darling, but I'm not. You will never leave my sight again," he said with righteous determination as he brought his lips down to hers and kissed her sweetly. "And maybe I'll just have to carry you around all the time—satisfy all of my weird needs. My need to see and hold you constantly will be nullified if we can do both things at the same time." He paused again to consider something then added, "I can see how it might get awkward when I have to drive or go to work, but I'm almost certain you will adjust to it."

A small laughed bubbled up and out of her, jostling her immobilized shoulder. She winced a little and laid her head back against the elevated bed. Jake's calm face got tight with anxiety again as he tried to sooth her by stroking down her good arm and smoothing her hair back from her face. When she felt the pain subside, she composed her face again and looked at him. "I'm okay, just probably shouldn't laugh for a little while. Please change my order to giggles only."

Jake relaxed again and smiled. "You got it, beautiful, giggles only." Then his face got serious again as he asked, "Tell me how bad is your pain? On a scale of one to ten, give me a number."

"Don't you pull a pain scale out on me, Jake Michaels. I'm not your patient."

"Technically you are, beautiful. I was the first person to treat you, so tell me. And I want to know what they are giving you for the pain, and if you need more, you better ask for it."

Bringing up her pain and the medication she was taking reminded her of what she couldn't take and why. She was surprised that she had forgotten her anxiety over the pregnancy, but then again, Jake always calmed her so well that it shouldn't surprise her. She gave him another smile and said, "I'm sorry."

He was taken aback by her apology and asked in a voice laced with confusion, "What on Earth do you have to apologize for?"

"That I didn't tell you that I thought I was pregnant." Her voice came out low, but he heard it.

Letting go of her hand, he took two steps away from her and grabbed a chair. Pulling it toward the side of her bed, he sat down and then picked her hand up again, holding it between both of his before leveling his gaze at her. "And why is that, beautiful? Did you think I would be upset? Because you have to know that I wouldn't be ... I'm not."

Feeling a little foolish at her apprehension to tell him, she confessed, "No, I didn't think that. It's just that I didn't want to say something until I knew for sure. I mean, it's not even supposed to be possible. Yet, it is." She paused for a second as she absorbed the fact that she was, regardless of the trauma she just experienced, pregnant ... for now.

"Yet, it is." He repeated her words with a kiss to her hand and a smile that radiated his happiness at the fact that she was pregnant.

"You're not upset with me?" she asked because it was a legitimate concern for her. Not only had she told him that she couldn't get pregnant, but then she didn't tell him when she did, in fact, get pregnant. She felt he had a right to be upset at her, regardless of the fact that she had been shot by a crazy man. She wasn't trying to gain sympathy votes here.

~*~*~*~*~*~~*~*~*~*~

Jake didn't like that she thought he was upset with her. For what? Getting shot? She had lowered her eyes to stare at his hands holding hers so he lifted her chin back up. When he captured her gaze and saw the concern in her eyes, which was partnered with a little bit of fear, he was even more bothered. Still processing what she was asking him, he realized he needed to answer her before she got the wrong idea. So, with just a hint of agitation and a lot of incredulity, he asked, "For getting shot? Why on Earth would I be upset at you for that?" If he hadn't heard it from the doctor already that she was on minimal meds he would've dismissed it as being doped up, but this didn't make sense.

Then it dawned on him that she was referring to the fact that she was pregnant. The caveman in him puffed up his chest, and wanted to pound on it like an animal over his excitement for his baby in her body. It was primal, it was all male, and it so wasn't the time for it. Well, if she felt bad for not telling him, he was just going to have to let her off the hook for that one.

She shook her head at him, and when she attempted to speak further, he placed his finger over her lips. "Shh, baby. Let me start by saying that I have a lot of emotions flowing through my body at this very moment. I've been so scared for the past few hours over the thought of losing you." He paused, not wanting her to see exactly how afraid he was, and tried to control the emotions that were surfacing because of that fear "I am angry, but it's not at you, baby, it's at myself for not being there to protect you from that bastard." She once again tried to speak up, but he stopped her so he could get it all out.

"I feel relieved. I know what you did to protect the boys, and I'm so proud that you were able to figure out how to do that given the situation you were in." Gillian's body instantly went rigid when he mentioned the boys, so he quickly reassured her, "The boys are fine, Gillian. They are one hundred percent safe and sound with the family. Everyone was here when I left the waiting room, and they were safely cuddled up next to Morgan."

Jake shook his head as he remembered Dylan's concerns for his mother. "Although Dylan was worried about whether or not you were going to get in trouble for pulling the fire alarm when there wasn't actually a fire. Of course he asked this before we concluded that you were in serious trouble." Pausing, he clenched and unclenched his jaw for just a few seconds before he shook it off.

"Now, where was I? Oh yeah. I'm also feeling very anxious about my need to make sure you're okay," he said this as he stood up, leaned forward, and kissed her forehead. "I was so scared when we found you behind that door," he said against her forehead before kissing her on one eye and then the other, ever so gently. Then he pulled back and looked her straight in the eyes and said, "But most of all, I feel an overwhelming sense of love for you, Gillian. I love you so much, and I completely adore the fact that you are carrying my child. *Our* child." Tentatively he placed his hand on her still flat stomach, marveling at the thought that she was pregnant.

~*~*~*~*~*~*~*~*~

And there they were, the very words she wanted to hear. The words that she longed to hear since Allie muttered, "Are you pregnant or something?" Her eyes that had paused in their attempt to drain her of ever body fluid she possessed began to fill and overflow again. She placed her hand over his, which remained on her stomach and smiled up at him and repeated his words back to him. "Our child." Then Jake melted her heart even more when he moved their hands out of the way as he leaned over and pressed a kiss against her stomach. She wasn't sure how she managed to get pregnant when she had her tubes tied, but she wasn't going to question it. Her focus now was going to be on praying that the events from the last few hours didn't take that little miracle from her.

When Jake lifted his head, his gaze met hers, and she couldn't help but fall under the spell he was weaving. He cupped both of her cheeks and held her there as he pressed his lips against hers. Tenderly kissing her, once, twice, before pulling back and meeting her gaze again and whispering the same words again. "Our child."

She couldn't help but smile at the warmth she heard in his words and the sincerity so clear on his face. "Gillian, I need to hold you. Can I try and sit next to you, or would that cause you pain?"

Gillian couldn't think of anything she wanted more at that very moment than to be held by this man, so she nodded. Jake carefully helped her scoot over, which didn't cause her any pain since they had her shoulder and arm strapped to her body. Once there was enough room, he cautiously set his big body in the space next to her. When he moved a pillow behind her injured shoulder, she leaned forward allowing his arm to slip behind her, which not only provided support, but gave her the ability to lean into him. She sighed and relaxed into his embrace as he rested his other hand across her stomach, kissed her on top of the head, and said, "Rest, beautiful. You need to rest."

And rest she did. Gillian wasn't sure how long she lay there in Jake's embrace, but she knew she must have nodded off for a little while. It could've been five minutes or even five hours later, she had no clue. All she knew was that she was safe and sound, and secure in his arms … exactly where she belonged. She figured it must be a slightly uncomfortable position he was in, perched on the side of a bed like that, but she didn't want to move. She took in a deep breath of his scent, to replace that of the hospital type smells that were all around her, before lifting her head to look at him. He smiled down at her, "Do you know how much I love that you were able to relax against me and rest? Especially since you needed it so badly."

She answered his smile with one of her own, saying, "Do you know how much I love resting against you? It's my home; it's like my drug. Who needs Valium when I have Jake?"

"I feel the same way about you, beautiful. I love you so much."

"I love you, too." He kissed her lips again before he let out a sigh and said, "And as much as I would like to keep you all to myself, I fear the rest of the family will be barging down that door anytime now to see you. It's really all your fault, though. If you would just be mean or nasty to them every once in a while, maybe you wouldn't have to put up with them all the time."

She snorted a small laugh at that and was about to deliver her own snarky comment when a knock sounded on the door. Jake gave her a knowing look and said, "Told you so. Any bets on who's coming through that door first? My money's on Allie."

Gillian smiled because Jake was probably correct. If it was anyone other than Allie she would be shocked. "I don't take bets I know I'm going to lose, Jake Michaels. What kind of fool do you take me for?" she said to him as another knock sounded against the door. She laughed and said, "Oh yeah, it's definitely Allie. Better go let her in before she gets really worked up."

Jake laughed and said, "She can open the door with her own two hands. I'm not getting up from this position 'til you're strong enough to push me out of this bed." He smiled and then told whoever was behind the door to come in. Sure enough, it swung open with determination, and in came Allie saying, "Jeez, Jake. Hog Gillian much? I have a new superhero name for you now, but I'm just going to get the shirt made instead of telling you."

Jake huffed out a laugh next to Gillian at Allie, "Bring it on, Al."

Gillian smiled at the banter between the two of them, but she was surprised to see Madison had followed Allie in. The smile fell from her lips when she could see that her daughter had been crying. Not that her daughter wasn't a sensitive person—it had just been a while since her daughter showed her any emotion other than a nasty attitude. Once again cursing the fact that she couldn't rush to the person she loved, she took her good arm and nudged Jake off the bed.

Jake didn't question her; she knew he figured it out. He gently got up, and Gillian raised her hand to beckon her daughter closer. After a moment of hesitation, Madison started crying and moved toward her. Gillian felt like she was coaxing a scared animal, afraid it would run off and disappear when all she wanted to do was touch it. When Madison was standing next to the bed, Gillian was dying inside at the sight of her tears, so she just patted the open space next to her. Madison, still quiet, carefully sat down and laid her head in her mother's lap. All Gillian could do was console her daughter by stroking her hands through the long, dark, wavy strands so similar to her own and say, "I'm okay, sweetie. I'm fine, I promise."

Madison just stayed there and wrapped her arms around Gillian's legs and relaxed. It was almost surreal to her to see her daughter like this, and she knew this was probably as close to an apology as she going to get. Well, it was good enough for her. She looked up to Allie and Jake, as they watched the exchange with a look of awe on their faces. Apparently, Gillian wasn't the only one who was aware of her daughter's animosity toward her.

She smiled at them and said, "Well, this one isn't going anywhere, so see if you can sneak in another one for me to see." With a nod, Allie went to retrieve another, and Jake took up the seat next to her bed. The rest of her family came through and left, all while Madison stayed curled up with her head in Gillian's lap. It was the most wonderful feeling in the world.

CHAPTER TWENTY-SEVEN

After three long days in the hospital, Jake was finally able to take Gillian home. He knew she was way past ready to get out of there, but he assumed that the doctor was keeping her longer than necessary. The doctor and the rest of his staff clearly had cared a little more for Gillian than their average patient, and even though she wanted out of there, he was glad they kept such a close eye on her. Her shoulder was feeling better every day, but she still had lots of recovery time ahead of her. Jake was thankful that her body wasn't showing any signs of aborting the pregnancy, which the doctor said was a normal risk for any woman, let alone a woman who had experienced the trauma that she did.

He recalled the long conversation he had with Gillian about making sure she didn't disregard any possible symptom, as far as her pain or healing process. Jake wasn't an idiot, and his training told him that if she were to start cramping, there was nothing that could be done to save the pregnancy. And damn, did he want to make sure nothing happened to it. It was hard not to get excited about the pregnancy; just the fact that she conceived when she wasn't supposed to be able to told Jake that it was meant to be. But he knew the risks, so for now, he would take it one day at a time.

Jake had everything prepared for her homecoming and was just getting back to the hospital with a change of clothes that Allie had packed for her. He still had a little anxiety over being away from her, but felt she was in good hands since the nursing staff barely took their eyes off her. If she hadn't specifically requested the items he carried with him now, he wouldn't have left her at all. Fortunately, that special treatment Gillian was getting as a patient here rolled over to him as well. Since he wouldn't leave her at night, they brought in a bed for him to sleep on—not that he wouldn't have just slept on the floor, or even standing in the corner, if he had to. He wasn't joking with her when he said that he didn't want to let her out of his sight.

When he closed his eyes, he could still see what she looked like covered in blood as she sat propped up against that wall. A cold shiver worked its way up his spine as he threw himself back to that moment, but he quickly shook it off. Yeah, he knew that image would stay with him for a while to come, but it had only happened three days ago—it was still too fresh. Until he got over that, he would just have to stay as close to her as possible.

Once arriving on her floor, his anticipation increased as he stepped off the elevator. Turning the corner toward her room, he found Logan sitting in a chair outside her door—in the same position he had been in each and every time he came to the hospital with the kids. He was hunched to the side, somber expression on his face, his chin resting in one hand. Jake hadn't heard him speak since the shooting, not that Jake was seeking him out for full conversations or anything.

No, as much as Jake wanted to inflict pain on the guy for everything that had happened, he knew he didn't have to. Logan was punishing himself enough. He knew that his actions set what happened to Gillian in motion. Why attack a man when he was already at rock bottom? As Jake approached, Logan looked up and made eye contact with him, then immediately looked down. Jake didn't like seeing his friend look like this, but there really wasn't anything he could do about it; he would have to work that out on his own. However, he did need to address the issue that Logan had yet to see Gillian, and she was asking about him. She was worried about Logan, therefore, Jake was going to try and do something to help alleviate her worry.

Pulling up the chair next to Logan, Jake set her bag down on the floor beside it before taking a seat. Logan didn't say anything to him—just kept his head down. It was the first time that Jake noticed the man hadn't shaved in days and pretty much looked like shit. Shaking his head at that he asked, "You go in and see her yet?"

Logan sighed and shook his head in response. Jake didn't like the fact that Logan would worry Gillian even more if she saw him like this, so he decided it was time to try and snap Logan out this mood. "Good, 'cause you look like shit man. When was the last time you showered and shaved? You can't go in and see her like this, looking like that."

Turning his attention toward Jake, Logan finally spoke, "I'm not going in to see her, so don't worry about it."

"Why did you come here if you weren't going in to see her?"

"The kids. I brought Madison here to be with her."

"Okay, good. Now go home, clean yourself up, and get back over to her place so she can see that you're okay," Jake demanded of him.

Logan looked surprised by Jake's order and asked, "What? Why?"

The desire to smack the man he had known since high school was hard to control as Jake realized he had to spell it out for the guy. Once again shaking his head at the man, "You know for someone who was married to her for as long as you were, you sure don't know her, do you?"

Jake could see the heat and anger rise in Logan's eyes as he absorbed what Jake said. He was glad that he had another expression other than pathetic—this version of him was easier to tolerate. So it didn't bother Jake when Logan growled at him, "What the fuck is that supposed to mean, Jake?"

"It means that if you knew Gillian at all, you would know that she's been worried about you, and if she saw you like this, it would only upset her more. Now quit being a selfish asshole and snap the fuck out of it! Go home, clean up, and come over to see her. Your front door is now fifty yards from her front door, so the effort is minimal."

Logan slumped down in his chair, but Jake wasn't sure why. After a few moments of silence, Logan said in a low, pained voice as he hung his head again, "I don't deserve to see her, Jake. I know that. So I'm not going to pretend that I belong anywhere within ten feet of her."

"I'm not going to argue with you there, man; you don't deserve to be within ten feet of Gillian. You're lucky that my desire to physically harm you has lessened over the past three days. Partially because I can see that you are well aware of how at fault you are, but that's just about us. This needs to be about Gillian. She wants to see you; she wants to know you're all right. You know that she worries about her family, and just because you aren't her husband anymore, doesn't change the fact that you were. So pull your head out of your ass for a minute and see that this is about *her,* not you."

Jake couldn't see Logan's face, but he assumed he was processing what Jake said. It was irritating to think he had to convince him that he needed to suck it up for Gillian, so he brought out the big guns. "You owe me this, man."

Once again, Logan turned to Jake with a look of surprise and confusion. Jake had no qualms with throwing this out at him. "I'm sure you know by now that I love that woman in there. A woman who happens to be pregnant with my child ..." Jake paused and lowered his voice to express more of the anger he was feeling about the subject, "... and that pregnancy is now in jeopardy because of your indiscretions. She was fucking shot because of you, and now I risk losing a child that I never even thought was possible. So ... you fucking owe me."

He could see in Logan's eyes the moment realization dawned on him. With a complete shift in his expression, Logan nodded his head and stood up. Jake picked up the bag from the floor and faced his old friend; one he hoped could be his friend again in the future. They stood there silently staring at each other before Jake said, "We'll take Madison home with us. You go get cleaned up and come over. I'm pretty sure Sean, Morgan, and Allie will already be there with the kids."

Logan just nodded his head again and turned to head toward the elevators. Just to make sure the guy came over later, Jake added, "I'll be sure to tell her that you'll be there."

Logan threw a one-sided smile over his shoulder and said, "I'm sure you will." And then he disappeared around the corner.

Not wanting to waste another second, Jake made his way into Gillian's room. He laughed at the sight of Madison standing on top of the hospital bed, above her mother. She was apparently trying to do her mother's hair. When they heard him, Madison turned and explained herself. "It's the only way I felt I could work with all this hair without hurting her shoulder."

"Please tell me she isn't doing something to my hair that will make people laugh and point."

Laughing again, he reassured her, "Not at all. Besides, they will be too busy staring at that bandage to notice your hair."

Madison giggled from her perch on top of the bed, "Good one, Uncle Jake."

Gillian just snorted and said, "Don't encourage him, Maddie. We don't want him to get out of control like your aunt."

"I don't think anyone can get *that* out of control, Mom."

Jake circled his way around the bed to see Gillian's face. She was smiling up at him from her perch on the side of the bed, and he couldn't help but see how genuine that smile was. Whether it was for him, or the fact that her daughter was bonding with her, he didn't know, but he loved it. Leaning down to meet her lips, he pressed a simple kiss to them, "How are you feeling, beautiful?"

"I'm perfect," she said with a sweetness that he would never get enough of.

"Glad to hear it, 'cause I've come to spring you from this joint. Has the doctor signed you out yet?"

Gillian nodded as Madison spoke for her, "Yes, she signed her discharge papers, and the doctor said she isn't supposed to take her arm out of that sling for four more days—whether she begged us or not. And she needs her bandages changed every day." The young one smiled at him like she was proud of being able to provide the information.

"Hey, just whose side are you on?" Gillian whined at her daughter. Jake laughed at them again. It was great seeing them like this; it wasn't cool that it took Gillian getting shot for it to happen, but then again, it might just have been because Allie let the cat out of the bag about why her parents were getting divorced.

"She is on your side, of course. Why else would she provide important information that you would have otherwise ignored? But it doesn't matter. I would've asked the doctor myself, since he gave me the number to his cell." Jake smirked at her as he said the last part.

She groaned at him and said, "Okay, fine, you guys win. But I really want to take it off, it's rubbing me in all the wrong places."

"How about once we get you all settled in at home, I will change it and see if I can make it more comfortable for you," he suggested.

She managed to give him look that was somewhere between pouty and manipulative as she said, "Are you sure I can't talk you out of it? How 'bout I promise to not move my arm at all?"

Shaking his head, he replied, "Nice try, beautiful, but I'm not falling for it. I will make sure you are comfortable, but you will have that arm of yours secured to your body for four more days." Then he bent forward and playfully said, "And what kind of example are you setting for your daughter here. Trying to ignore the doctor's orders like that. Would you let her get away with that?"

"She most certainly would not!" exclaimed Madison as she got down from the bed. "Besides, Mom, you will be in bed the whole time resting, so you won't even notice your bandages."

Realizing that she couldn't win, she smiled at her daughter and said, "Fine, but just so you know, I plan on making you all watch whatever chick flick I feel like watching 'til you cave, and let me have my way. I'm thinking I will start with season one of *Sex In The City* as soon as we get home."

Jake and Madison groaned and looked at each other. He said to her, "I can do it if you can do it."

"Oh, please, I stand at the fifty yard line, behind a bunch of boys and pretend to be excited about the fact that they are playing a stupid game. I'm sure I can handle pretending to enjoy a show my mom likes to watch while sitting on my butt. Besides, that's what my phone is for."

Jake really liked this Madison; she was far more fun to be around than the other one. Laughing inwardly he said, "Well then, Madison, how about you go down to the nurses' station to see about a wheelchair for your mother here. I'll help her get dressed."

"I can help her get dressed," Madison offered, and even though Jake could probably let her do it, he wanted to.

He was about to tell her that was fine when Gillian spoke up, "Thanks anyway, kiddo, but Jake should probably help me. His training will be helpful with my arm strapped to my body. Is that okay with you?"

The girl offered them a smile, said okay, and left the room. Gillian turned to Jake and said, "You clammed up on her there, afraid to tell my daughter that you just wanted to cop a feel."

Laughing at that, he said, "Oh, does that mean I can? 'Cause I wouldn't mind a little bit of play time with my woman." Sliding his arms carefully around her body, she nestled against his chest as best she could with her arm. When he heard her take a deep breath against his neck, he smiled.

"Did you just smell me?"

"I sure did. It's one of the best smells *ever*," she said in a breathy voice, which only caused his body to react.

But he understood what she was saying, and replied, "I know exactly what you mean, beautiful."

After a few moments, she pulled her head away and said, "Can you please get me out of here? I'm dying to lay in my own bed."

"Of course, let's get you changed so I can do just that."

"Are you staying with me?" she asked in a tentative voice, which made him give her a questioning look.

"Again, I will ask, what part of *you are mine* did you not understand? You're kind of stuck with me lady, so deal with it." Placing a quick peck to her nose he continued, "Hopefully the fact that I come with an adorable eight year old should sweeten the deal enough for you."

"And how many times do I have to tell *you*, that boy is already mine."

"I'm kind of glad you feel that way, 'cause he is quite fond of you, too, beautiful."

"Like I said, he is already mine. Now help me get dressed so I can get home and see my boys."

With that final request, Jake helped Gillian from her hospital clothes and into something comfortable and easy to get on over her arm. They finished when Madison returned and asked where her father was. Jake responded to the questioning look from both of them, "He went home to get cleaned up, and said he will meet us at the house when we get there."

Madison smiled and went to help retrieve her mother's belongings. There were flowers and balloons and various other things sent to her by others, so it took her a few moments to get things gathered. As Jake directed Gillian to the wheelchair, she asked him quietly, "Is he really coming by the house?"

He nodded at her and said, "If he doesn't come on his own, I will drag him over."

That earned him another one of his favorite smiles, so he bent over to steal a kiss. When he stood up she said, "Thank you."

His only response could be, "Anything for you, beautiful."

~*~*~*~*~~*~*~*~*~

Gillian couldn't be happier than she was now. She was home. Out of that damn hospital and surrounded by her things. Even though she worked there, it was a completely different feeling being a patient stuck there versus being an employee stuck there. She prayed that when it came time to go back to work, it didn't bother her to be there. There was certainly some anxiety when she thought about being there, in that corridor, outside the x-ray department, but again she hoped it would lessen and not be a problem for her. She loved her job, and she certainly didn't want the fucked up shit that happened all because of an affair affect her ability to keep that part of her life. A little bit of anger rose to the surface as she recalled all the circumstances involved. Clearly, Logan needed to make sure his future mistresses didn't have crazy husbands. Laughing to herself at that thought, she shook her head and tried to dispel all thoughts of Slutty McWhore and her husband, Batshit Crazy.

She had been home for a little while now, and she had yet to see Logan. Gillian was sure that Logan was avoiding her because he felt guilty, and while he should feel guilty, she also refused to let that affair take away the friendship she had with him. It was crucial to their future as parents, and she knew he needed to get past it. If Jake wasn't hovering nearby, she would march herself next door and demand his attention. She was considering sending her daughter over there to get him so that they could get it out of the way before the rest of their group of friends showed up. There was talk of a turkey that was already cooked, and all the fixings were on their way over since Thanksgiving was yesterday, and they hadn't had a big family gathering. As she was about to call for Madison, she heard a knock on the door and then it opened. There was Logan, standing in what was his front door, looking at her with an expression she would always remember. The pain and shame that was evident told her exactly why he hadn't come around while she was in the hospital. She knew he was lurking nearby in the hall, but wouldn't come in to see her. His hair was still wet, and Gillian could smell his soap and aftershave, telling her he had just showered. The look of discomfort he had told her he wasn't sure if he was allowed to enter, so she told him so. In an attempt to lighten the mood she said, "You can come in, you know, I still don't bite."

Logan gave her a sheepish smile and moved farther into the living room. All her years as his wife told her that he was having a lot of trouble with being there. All those years also taught her how she needed to handle the situation. While she was sure that most women would probably demand an apology, just the look and demeanor of the man she loved for so many years told her how sorry he felt. She didn't need the words—she had what she needed.

Standing up, even though Jake tried to stop her, she made her way over to Logan and stood right in front of him. Looking up at him, she tried to make eye contact, but he avoided it. Just wanting to get this over with, she said, "I don't blame you for what happened."

That immediately had his attention, and his eyes snapped up to meet hers. The look of outrage on his face was kind of funny, and she attempted to stifle her laugh, but was only partially successful. Her tight-lipped smile probably fueled his irritation, which was just a bonus for her, but she managed to restrain the rest of the laugh from coming out. Logan took in a deep breath and attempted to say something, but then let all the air out in one big huff. Stuttering a few times as he tried to speak only made her want to giggle more because it was the best way to diffuse a situation.

When Logan finally found the ability to speak, it came out in a low exasperated tone, "I blame myself." All the outrage she saw a few moments earlier left his body as his shoulders slumped in defeat. "I'm so sorry, Gillian ... for *everything*."

She smiled at him. "I know you are, so let's move on from all of it." Logan just looked at her in astonishment, which made her uncomfortable, so sarcasm rose to the surface and she said, "But don't get me wrong, I am so going to bring up the fact that I have a bullet hole in my shoulder. It will be a cooler scar than any of you guys have."

Logan's eyebrows scrunched together. "That's not cool, Gillian. I really don't think we should joke about this."

Refusing to be persuaded she said, "You're just saying that because you know it's true, and you don't get to take that away from me. I will win that competition every time. Well, until someone else gets shot, which better not happen!"

He just shook his head at her and asked, "And we just move on from this ... just like that?"

She nodded and said, "Just like that. I refuse to focus on shitty events in my life."

He gave her that one-sided grin that she always loved and said, "Glass half full, right?"

She snorted a laugh, "Exactly! It's about time you see things my ways—only took you eighteen years."

"Thanks Gilly." Then he carefully pulled her into a hug. It was nice, but it wasn't the same as it used to be, which only reminded her of what she now had. Pulling back, she smiled at Logan, then turned to look at Jake who had been watching the exchange. She removed herself from Logan's embrace and walked into Jake's. It was easy to melt right into him as she wound her right arm around his back and nestled her nose into the crook of his neck. Feeling him kiss the top of her head, she sighed and asked, "Not that I'm complaining or anything, but didn't I hear something about turkey and all the fixings? I assumed you all meant that someone made it and that you all didn't expect me to prepare it. Hello, bullet wound over here. I'm pretty sure I have a free pass for a little while."

Both men laughed out loud, and she looked up at Jake as he said, "You can use that pass for anything you want, and for as long as you want, beautiful." Leaning down, Jake pressed a kiss to her lips.

She heard Logan huff an exasperated breath as he said, "That is really going to take some getting used to." Making his way out of the room he said, "I assume my sons are around here somewhere?" And with that, he left the room.

Gillian smiled up at Jake again, perfectly content with how things just played out. She was fully aware that many would have handled it differently, but it was how she wanted things to be. She was about to ask when everyone else was coming over when the doorbell rang. Madison sprinted into the room saying, "I got it!" Still holding onto Jake, Gillian waited for the rest of her family to come in when Madison said, "Mom, there's someone at the door for you."

CHAPTER TWENTY-EIGHT

Gillian looked up at Jake and shrugged her one shoulder. She had no idea who could be there, but left the comfort of Jake's embrace to see. As she came up beside her daughter, she smiled at her and took a moment to notice how they were close to the same height. Trying not to get distracted by her thoughts of how old her kids were getting, she turned her attention to whoever the visitor was. It took her moment to realize who was standing there, but when she did, she sucked in a sharp breath at the sight of Jody Spencer standing on her doorstep.

She quickly shifted so that she was positioned in front of her daughter and shoved her behind her with her one good arm. Once she felt her daughter was protected from whatever immediate danger there was, she lowered her voice and demanded, "What the hell are *you* doing here?"

The woman hadn't spoken and looked a little worried. Flashing back to the last time this woman was this close to her, Gillian couldn't help but notice how different things were. She almost felt bad for the woman last time, but this time the woman knew where she was and willingly came. If it hadn't been for the fact that Gillian had a bullet hole in her shoulder from this woman's husband, she might admire the woman. She certainly had balls to show up here, but she didn't deserve Gillian's respect, so she wasn't going to get it.

~*~*~*~*~~*~*~*~*~

Jake heard Gillian's sharp intake of air, and he was immediately up and moving. He didn't know if she was in pain or if something else was wrong, but then he heard her say, "What the hell are you doing here?" *This wasn't good*, he thought as he took up the position next to her. When his eyes landed on the petite blonde standing outside the door, he knew immediately who it was. He had no idea what this woman's intentions were, but she needed to get the hell away from Gillian.

Before she could answer Gillian's question, Jake stepped in front of Gillian and barked at the woman, "I think you better get out of here … now, or I'll call the cops." The woman flinched as if she'd been slapped. Jake didn't mind that one little bit, though, 'cause he wanted her gone. The possible stress she could put Gillian under wouldn't be good for her or the pregnancy.

The woman had yet to move or say anything, so Jake pulled out his phone to dial when she spoke, "I just wanted to apologize … I know what Adam did, and I'm sorry."

Jake wanted to pick the woman up and physically remove her from Gillian's property. He didn't care if she was sorry; she threatened to cause more damage now with just her presence. He began to dial when he heard Gillian speak from behind him, "Do you really think I want your apology? Do you really think it means anything to me?" Coming out from behind him, she tried to get in between him and her, but Jake wasn't about to allow that. He needed to keep control of this situation before it became a real problem and her health was affected. He needed to keep her blood pressure down.

Fortunately, Gillian didn't push the issue and let Jake hold her at his left side, leaving her right arm wrapped around him, and allowing full exposure of her restrained injured shoulder. When the woman still hadn't responded, Gillian continued, "You, and any words you feel you need to say, mean shit to me! Your husband tried to kill me because of your actions! I can only believe that you came here in an attempt to make yourself feel better for what happened." Gillian paused, then Jake saw her composed face turn to one of disgust with her next words. "You mean nothing to me, and I will not give you my forgiveness for what you've done to my family and me. I hope you live with those regrets for a very long time. Now get the hell off of my property."

Gillian's voice was cool, calm, and calculating as she delivered those words. The thought that this woman, whose husband shot Gillian, sought some form of absolution with an apology was mind boggling to him. Jake was proud of Gillian, because he thought for a moment that she would accept the apology and let the woman off the hook. He stuffed his phone in his pocket and reached for the door to close it because it really didn't matter what the woman had to say.

Suddenly, Logan's voice boomed from behind them. "What the fuck is going on? Get the hell away from my family!"

Jake prepared his body for Logan trying to move him out of the way when he heard Madison yell, "Daddy, No!" Jake turned to see that Madison had leapt in front of her father and wrapped herself around him, effectively stopping him from moving. It was quite similar to a move he remembered seeing Gillian do once before. Madison held on tightly to him as he looked down at her, a little shell shocked, and she said, "She isn't worth it, Daddy. She was just leaving, and we don't want Mom to get upset … please."

The pleading tone in her voice must have been the man's undoing as he wrapped his arms around his only daughter. "You're right, sweetie. I'm sorry." Then Jake got to see the emergence of his old friend when he looked to Jody outside the door and said, "I'm having a restraining order placed to protect every member of my family. If you or any part of your family comes within fifty yards, I will press charges. I'll make sure to tell the District Attorney handling your husband's case that you showed up here today." Then Logan turned to Jake and said, "Could you please shut the door now, Jake."

Smiling at his old friend, Jake did just that. Then he turned and gently pulled Gillian against him, asking, "How are you feeling? Do you think your blood pressure is okay? Maybe you should sit down and put your feet up." It all came out quickly and far more high pitched than he thought it should have.

A huge smile spread across her face as she placed her hand on his cheek. "Why Jake, I do believe you look like you're about to panic … maybe *you're* the one who needs to take a seat."

Her good demeanor calmed him instantly. His shoulders relaxed, and he lifted his hand to her hair to pull her into a kiss. He held her there, trying to absorb her into him, calming him completely. When he pulled back, she smiled again and said, "I feel fine, baby. Don't worry."

Pressing his forehead against hers, since he didn't want to get too far from her, he whispered, "I love you, beautiful."

"I love you, too, Jake." The two of them were enjoying their moment when the front door opened, interrupting it, and Allie came strolling in. She took one look at them and said, "Ugh! Seriously, you two. Jake, can't you leave her alone for one minute? And Gillian, shouldn't you at least be pretending that you're injured? You know … whine and say stuff like, 'Ouch, my bullet hole hurts.'" She and Jake just laughed at Allie as she kept walking through the room with an arm full of food, followed by Jason, Sean, Morgan, and their kids. All adults had an arm full of something.

Gillian called out to her, "I would totally help you with all of that, but I have this bullet hole in my shoulder." This made Jake laugh even more.

When Gillian turned and looked to Logan and Madison, she smiled at her daughter and said, "I wonder where you learned that move from?"

Madison gave her a smartass grin and said, "From this really cool mom I've got. She is so cool, she even has a bullet hole in her shoulder to prove it."

Logan jumped in and said, "Could everyone please just stop saying bullet hole, it's kind of morbid."

Jake laughed when all the women in earshot—Gillian, Allie, Madison, and Morgan—all yelled at the same time, "Bullet hole." He heard Logan groan as he dropped himself on the couch.

Following Gillian into the kitchen, Jake escorted her to a seat at the table so that she wouldn't attempt to help. He watched the banter between her and Allie as she called out, "Gillian, could you get some dishes out for kids to set the table?"

Gillian responded, "Sorry, can't help you with that. Bullet hole in my shoulder, remember?"

Logan yelled from the other room, "Oh, come on, I'm begging you, please stop saying that."

This of course just egged Allie on, as she proceeded to pretend she was put out by Gillian not helping get things ready. "Hi, I'm Gillian, I'm lazy and can't do anything because I have a bullet hole in my shoulder. Blah, blah, blah."

Once again laughing, Jake just absorbed it all. Looking into the family room, he could see Jonathan playing video games with Dylan and Ryan, while Jason gave his input as to what they should be doing differently. Sean and Morgan's two and four year olds were playing on the floor, while he sat with their infant in his arms, watching. Madison had made her way into the kitchen to help Allie and Morgan, and Logan took up a seat at the table across from where Gillian was sitting.

Taking it all in, Jake couldn't help but smile as he leaned into Gillian and placed his hand on her good shoulder. She reached up and gave his hand a squeeze as she watched everything that was going on around them. It was traditionally a time to give thanks, and Jake didn't think he could ever be thankful enough.

He was thankful that Gillian was okay. He was thankful that, for now, the pregnancy was okay. He was thankful that it appeared he and Logan could possibly move forward as friends. He was thankful that they could all be together. But he was most thankful for the fact that he was able to make Gillian realize that for him, it had always been her.

EPILOGUE

Gillian rolled over and groaned as she felt the stiffness in her neck from lying in the same position for too long. Reaching up to rub the stiffness out, her hand was immediately replaced by a warm, strong one, and she felt herself begin to melt into his touch. Jake knew exactly how to rub out her stiff muscles, which was good, because she couldn't seem to escape the stiffness. Even though her shoulder healed up as it was supposed to, it still got very stiff and achy at times. Knowing that today was going to be a long day anyway, since it was Jonathan's graduation day, his skilled working of her muscles was a good thing.

She groaned again, but this time it was because of the sheer ecstasy that was Jake Michaels's fingers. Feeling his body press up against her from behind, she melted a little more and pressed her bottom back into him. His hardness was always a welcome good morning for her, so without hesitation she reached back to slide her hand between them and show him her appreciation. Jake halted her hand's progression with his, as he groaned and moved her hand away. "Don't worry, beautiful, I'm not denying you anything. I just have to get you in a better position." He finished that off by kissing her shoulder.

She felt him shift away from her a little, and then he was back, pressing up against her entire body with his. Confused, she attempted to look back at him, but his arm stretched forward and rested on the space of her pillow in front of her. When he moved his hand, there was a little blue box, complete with white ribbon, sitting there in its place. Her hand flew to her mouth as she gasped at the sight of what could only be a ring. There had been times over the past six months where she was actually surprised that Jake hadn't asked her to marry him. It wasn't like she could ask him why, but she wondered. Allie told her that it was probably because she was a giant pain in the ass, and he was waiting to see if he really wanted to. This, of course, was Allie's way of deflecting Gillian's concerns, and she was grateful for it.

Jake made a nervous sounding laugh behind her, making her realize that she hadn't said or done anything yet. Cautiously reaching out, she tentatively touched the silky white bow. She rolled it between her fingers and verified it was really there. Still worried about it disappearing, she picked it up and gave the box a little shake. Yes, it felt real. Another nervous laugh came from Jake as he said, "I can't tell if you're afraid of it, or if you just don't know what it is. You do know that there is something *inside* the box, right?"

It was her turn to giggle nervously as she attempted to untie the bow. She was having trouble doing it in the position she was in, so she maneuvered her body so she was lying on her back and Jake was on his side, looking down at her. She now had the box in both hands as she held it out in front of her, and stared at it some more. *This was it*, she thought. Jake was going to ask her to marry him. Slipping the bow off, she stared at the box for another few seconds before she lifted the lid. Blinking a few times to make sure she was seeing correctly, Gillian couldn't help but be disappointed at what she found inside the box.

Looking over at Jake, who was smiling like a fool, then back to the box that didn't contain a ring, Gillian felt the tears well up in her eyes. One rolled, unchecked, down the side of her face as she pulled out the folded piece of paper from where she thought a ring would be. She couldn't tell what the paper was, or said, since it was folded up tightly. Looking over at Jake again, she couldn't help but get annoyed at the fact that he looked to be enjoying her obvious disappointment. He huffed a laugh as he removed the empty box from her hand and said, "Open it, beautiful."

Well, what else was she going to do? The anti-climactic discovery of a shitty piece of paper in a blue box from Tiffany's wasn't enough of a disappointment, so she needed to see what the hell could be on the stupid paper. Carefully unfolding it, since it appeared to have been folded for quite awhile, she didn't want to rip it. Once she got it unfolded, she squinted her sleepy eyes to try and make out what the markings on it. A receipt?

Pulling it closer to her eyes, she could see that it was, in fact, a receipt. Some of the markings were worn off, and she could see that there was a few that were deliberately covered. Then her eyes landed on one that was highlighted and circled in red ink. It was a date. Looking closely, she could make out that the date was November 15, 2012. Unsure what this was supposed to mean, she look to Jake to ask when he answered before she could, "It's the date I bought it."

Still confused, she waited for him to continue. When she felt the receipt removed from her hands, and the box being placed into them, she gasped again. This time, it was because nestled inside the box, where the receipt had originally been, was a beautiful diamond ring. It was simple, and elegant, and everything about it screamed her style. It was perfect. Looking over at Jake again, he smiled back and in a voice full of nervousness said, "I've waited so long to do this, that I was worried you might say no, so I had to come up with something that would give you all that you would need to know. That way, when I asked, you wouldn't be able to say no." He paused and took in a deep breath, then said, "Gillian, will you marry me?"

Gillian couldn't help the smile and giggle that bubbled up. Jake had just asked her to marry him, and he looked nervous as hell doing it. She was glad that she wasn't the only emotional one as more tears leaked from the corners of her eyes. He was still staring down at her expectantly, waiting for her to answer. Her head started nodding before her mouth was able to get the words out. But finally she managed a breathy, "Yes."

And then his lips were on hers, taking and taking more. She gave all that she could give and wanted to give more. Setting the ring box to the side, her hands dove into his hair to hold him against her. Their tongues battled for more of the other, and she moaned in disappointment when he pulled away too soon. Looking down her, he stroked her hair from her face as the two of them stared each other. He whispered, "Can I have you forever, Gillian?"

The sweet husky sound of his voice was enough to make her arousal spike. As her body heat rose, and her need to feel him inside her became insistent she said, "Yes, Jake. Take me, I'm yours ... forever."

Jake took her lips again, and his body began to make her body sing. The passion she felt when they were together could almost be described as overwhelming at times, but there was nothing in the world she would rather be overwhelmed by. As he claimed her body as his over and over, she fell into an abyss of pleasure that had her gasping for air, a place that only Jake could take her.

Sometime later, the two of them were still lying in bed when Jake found the ring box. Removing the ring, he smiled at her as he took her left hand in his and slowly pushed the ring up her finger. Once it was secured in its place, he leaned down and placed a lingering kiss over it. Lifting his head from her hand, he smirked and said, "I'm glad you finally listened to me when I said that you are mine, woman."

She laughed at his words, and then without thought, blurted, "Why the receipt?"

Again with the smirk, he replied, "I tried coming up with all sorts of ways to propose to you. Romantic, sweet, all that stuff that would make it memorable. But every time I came up with something, it came back to my concern that you would only think that I was asking because you had found out you were pregnant." Pausing, he took a breath. "I didn't want to ever hear you say the word no to that question, so I figured, if I *showed* you before I asked … you would have no need to say no. I bought that ring for you … before."

It was strange to her that she hadn't even thought of her concerns lately that if he had asked, it would have only been because of her finding out she was pregnant. She immediately felt bad that she had placed that kind of stress on him when she would have said yes no matter what. "I'm sorry, Jake."

He shook his head at her, shrugged, and said, "I also wanted to wait until your divorce was final, so since that was yesterday, I didn't want to wait another day. I had to make you mine."

"Oh, Jake. I'm already yours," she said as she pressed her lips up and met his.

Pulling back, she was met by his smile as he said, "Yeah, you are, beautiful."

Once again, her eyes filled with tears and started to immediately overflow. Embarrassed at her girlish ability to cry at everything, she wiped them away and said, "I thought it would take a miracle for me not to cry all day because of Jonathan graduating. We haven't even made it out of bed, and I've already been crying."

Jake gave her a knowing smile as he slowly slid his body down the bed. Both of his hands cupped her oversized belly as he placed a reverent kiss on the top. Gently rubbing the overstretched skin with his hands, she felt the baby shift and move around as if she knew Daddy was there. Placing another kiss to her belly, Jake lifted his gaze to hers and said, "Well, then I guess it's a good thing we believe in miracles around here, isn't it?"

About the Author

Melanie is an amazing mother of four, an awesome and tolerant wife to one, and nurse to many. If you don't believe her, just ask anyone in her family, they know what to say. She is also a devoted chauffeur, the keeper of missing socks, a genius according to a six year old, the coolest soccer uniform coordinator according to a twelve year old, and the best damn 'mac-n-cheese-with-cut-up-hot-dog maker in the whole world. Well that last title isn't really official, but it's still pretty cool to be called it.

When not being ordered around by any of the kids, you can find her with her nose in a book or on the sideline of a soccer game cheering on one team or another. But that's mostly because she has a thing for the coach. When she is not doing all of the above, you can find her obsessed with a group of fictional characters all vying for a spot on the page of whatever she's working on. It's a fun and crazy life to lead, but wouldn't have it any other way.

If you liked my book you can keep up with upcoming books, sneak peeks, and more at:

Twitter: @MelanieCodina

Good Reads: http://tinyurl.com/d8bz7mw

Facebook: https://www.facebook.com/MelanieCodinaAuthor

Website: www.MelanieCodina.com

89029509R20217

Made in the USA
Columbia, SC
08 February 2018